**FERN MICHAELS is
"THE NORMAN ROCKWELL OF
ROMANCE WRITING."**
—*Winter Haven News Chief*

**Praise for
*THE REAL DEAL***

"Exciting contemporary romantic suspense. . . . The exhilarating suspense plot is filled with twists. . . . Will appeal to fans of Nora Roberts and Jayne Ann Krentz."
—*The Best Reviews*

"If you are seeking a story of passion, suspense, and intrigue . . . *The Real Deal* is the perfect choice."
—*Romance Reviews Today*

**Acclaim for her other dazzling
USA Today and *New York Times* bestselling novels**

THE MARRIAGE GAME
"Side-splittingly funny."
—*RT Book Reviews*

HEY, GOOD LOOKING
"A fun, page-turning tale of familial feud and forgiveness in Louisiana."
—*Publishers Weekly*

"Once again, productive and imaginative Michaels creates a heartwarming saga. . . . Michaels's talent for crafting quirky characters and gratifying narratives makes every page shine."
—*Booklist*

CROWN JEWEL

"A wonderfully heartwarming, compelling story about families and the lock the past can have on the future, *Crown Jewel* is a grand drama of discovery and love."
—*Romantic Times*

"Long-buried secrets cause tension and emotion to run high."
—*Old Book Barn Gazette*

"A story of forgiveness and personal redemption . . . [from] the prolific Michaels."
—*Booklist*

LATE BLOOMER

"Entertaining, action-packed . . . fun to read . . . engaging romantic suspense."
—*Midwest Book Review*

"An action-packed plot . . . Michaels's fans will be satisfied."
—*Publishers Weekly*

"Michaels's snazzy tale reveals the ups and downs of friendship and small-town life."
—*Booklist*

"Heartwarming . . . *Late Bloomer* is nothing short of wonderful. You won't want to put it down."
—*Winter Haven News Chief*

NO PLACE LIKE HOME

"Uniquely charming . . . bursting with humor . . . this warmhearted confection is as soothing as a cup of hot cocoa."
—*Publishers Weekly*

Books by Fern Michaels

The Real Deal

FERN MICHAELS

Pocket Books

New York   London   Toronto   Sydney   New Delhi

Pocket Books
An Imprint of Simon & Schuster, Inc.
1230 Avenue of the Americas
New York, NY 10020

This book is a work of fiction. Any references to historical events, real people, or real places are used fictitiously. Other names, characters, places, and events are products of the author's imagination, and any resemblance to actual events or places or persons, living or dead, is entirely coincidental.

Copyright © 2004 by MRK Productions, Inc.

This Pocket Books paperback edition February 2020

POCKET and colophon are registered trademarks of Simon & Schuster, Inc.

For information about special discounts for bulk purchases, please contact Simon & Schuster Special Sales at 1-866-506-1949 or business@simonandschuster.com.

The Simon & Schuster Speakers Bureau can bring authors to your live event. For more information or to book an event, contact the Simon & Schuster Speakers Bureau at 1-866-248-3049 or visit our website at www.simonspeakers.com.

Manufactured in the United States of America

10   9   8   7   6   5   4   3   2   1

ISBN 978-1-9821-2345-1
ISBN 978-0-7434-9397-0 (ebook)

Prologue

Washington, DC
November 1999

Quinn Star had known she was special the day she was born. No plastic baby bottles with a hard rubber nipple for her. No sirree, she wanted the real thing, much to her tattooed, hippie mother's dismay. The hippie mother who stayed around just long enough to wean her from her breast at six months, then went off to climb the Himalayas in search of Enlightenment, Quinn's tattooed, hippie father in tow. First, though, they dumped her on her aunt Birdie, who was a real flake but nice and *almost* normal. *If* you could count writing flowery, sometimes humorous, obituaries and hanging out in funeral parlors normal.

All in all, though, Quinn had no complaints about her upbringing. Birdie had taken care of her. She made sure she did her homework, brushed her teeth, and ate her vegetables. She attended PTA meetings, saw to her social life, and made sure she got into a good Ivy League college, where she'd graduated magna cum laude. But most of all, Birdie had loved her. That love said it all as far as she was concerned.

It was Birdie who insisted she follow her dream of being a Secret Service Agent after she graduated law school. Unfortunately, it hadn't worked out that way. She'd done her stint in Treasury and moved into the FBI when she finally realized the Secret Service and a White House detail were never going to become a reality.

Quinn looked down at the black-and-white photo of her parents standing on a mountaintop in some third-world country. She winced at their flowing garb and turbaned heads. It was the only picture she had of her parents. She always brought the picture to work with her in the morning. At night she put it in her briefcase to take back home. She didn't know why. Maybe it had something to do with the fact that during her almost thirty-two years she'd only seen her parents twice. Once when she was nine, and she'd been so frightened of them she'd hidden out in her room. The second time she almost missed them. They had arrived when she was seventeen and about to board the bus that would take her to Camp Wicheguma, where she was to be a camp counselor for the summer. They'd stood away from the camp bus on the tarmac in the parking lot and waved. She wasn't proud of the fact that she'd pretended not to know them. Birdie herself had stood apart from them and said she understood.

Her parents had never sent her letters or postcards over the years. They'd never sent her any gifts either, not even a trinket she could hold close and wish on for something more.

Sometimes life was a bitch. Like now.

Quinn clenched her teeth as she finished packing her belongings into a cardboard Xerox box. There wasn't much. A photo of Birdie, the photo of her parents, a trashy paperback novel riddled with impossible sex scenes, a spare toothbrush and toothpaste, a comb, some nail polish, a small change purse full of quarters for the vending machines, a box of tissues, and a bottle of Visine. Her duffel bag, with her gym clothes and sneakers, rested at the bottom, making the box lopsided. Like she cared. All she wanted to do was to get out of there so she could go home and cry.

She looked around the small office she had called home when she wasn't out in the field. Once she had literally lived out of the office for three straight days when she was working a case the other agents had given up on. All she'd gotten for her efforts when she'd solved it were surly looks from her colleagues and a "good job, Star," from her section chief, Ezra Lapufsky.

She'd played the game for six long years. The only problem was, she went into the game not knowing there were two sets of rules, one for male agents and one for female agents. Being female, she'd lost out before she'd even gotten started. Angry with the garbage detail, the good old boy mentality, she'd hunkered down. And before long, she knew in her gut she was the best agent in the section. She could run rings around her fellow agents, both mentally and physically. She'd graduated first in her class at the Academy. Her best friend and fellow agent, Sadie Wilson, had come in second. Did that count for anything? No, it did not, she realized one week into the job. At best, she'd hoped for civility from the male agents, but she hadn't gotten that either. What she had gotten, even with all the sensitivity classes the agents attended, were snide comments, crude sex jokes, and blistering commentaries on her performance ratings. And, worst of all, weak backup when the action in the field got down and dirty. And yet, she'd saved their asses numerous times, covered for them at other times, and on more than one occasion kept quiet about some of their escapades. The Air Force's Tailhook scandal paled in comparison to some of their hijinks.

"Your loss, you bastards," Quinn seethed as she put the lid on her box of belongings. She poked her head out the door to make sure the coast was clear before she put on her coat. At that point in time, she didn't care enough about anyone in her section to want to say good-bye. She didn't even care about Puff.

And then he was there. Suddenly they were eyeball-to-eyeball because she was tall, and Puff was exactly the same height. He was a heartbreaking blot on her vision, one she would carry away with her forever. How could she banish those incredible dark brown eyes that crinkled at the corners, the cleft in his chin, his broken nose, which had never been set right. Not to mention the wry smile that always made her think he knew a secret she didn't. He wasn't handsome, but he was devilishly attractive. What her friends called a heart-stopper. Ezra

Lapufsky was the first one to look away when Quinn refused to let her gaze waver.

He moved forward a step, forcing her back into her cubbyhole. "The guys elected me to be their spokesperson. They all wanted to say good-bye, but you know duty, it calls, and we, as the nation's protectors, have to obey that call. They took up a collection for this plant," Lapufsky said, holding it out as though it were the Holy Grail.

Quinn looked down at the sorry-looking potted plant with yellow leaves. She reached for it and dumped it in the wastebasket, the dry soil and the little white beads of vermiculite scattering in a thousand different directions. "Kiss my ass and get the hell out of my way, Puff. I saw that plant in the cafeteria this morning when I had my coffee. I can tell you exactly how many yellow leaves it has because I counted them. What are you doing here anyway?"

"I came to say good-bye."

"Well, you said it, so move out of the way so I can be on my way."

"Quinn, wait."

Once, she would have fallen for the contrition in his voice. Once, she would have whirled around, her whole being breathless with what was going to come next. Now she just gritted her teeth and kept moving.

"That was an order, Agent Star."

Quinn looked down at her watch. "I ceased being a federal agent at twelve noon. I'm a civilian now because my watch says it's twelve-thirty. Save your breath."

She felt herself being jerked backward, her feet literally leaving the floor. She dropped the box and brought her elbow straight back at the same time she brought up the heel of her right foot smack in the center of Ezra Lapufsky's groin. "I could chop you right in the neck for a stunt like that. Tsk, tsk, all those sensitivity training sessions, and you still put your hands on me. I'll just add that to my harassment and discrimination suit when I file it."

He groaned, falling to his knees.

She smiled.

"You miserable witch! Why'd you do that?" Lapufsky managed to gasp.

"Because I hate your guts, that's why. I wanted to leave here in a dignified manner, the same way I came in the first day on the job. I still can't believe I allowed myself to have an affair with you. That was stupid of me, but it's the only stupid thing I did while I was here. I plan to mention that in my harassment and discrimination suit, too. I'm outta here, so it won't matter to me, but it will matter to you since you plan to live out your days in this job. They'll never make you director of the FBI. Never! If it takes me the rest of my life, I'm going to get every female agent on the payroll and drag them into court so they can testify about how those sensitivity sessions don't work. Sadie Wilson is going to be my star witness. You'll be famous, Puff. I'm not going to tell you again, get the hell out of my way."

The color was starting to return to Lapufsky's face. He reached for the arm of the chair to pull himself upright. Quinn kicked the chair out of reach and watched it sail into the hall on its well-oiled wheels.

He flopped back down to his knees, the expression on his face murderous.

Quinn leaned against the doorjamb. "I documented everything. I have reams and reams of tape. I just might go up to Capitol Hill and drop this off on some congresswoman's desk. You know how those guys and *women* up there hate you *guys* down here. Yeah, yeah, that's what I'm going to do. Start getting your résumé in order, Puff."

"Why are you doing this?" he snarled.

She wasn't going to sue anybody, but Puff didn't need to know that. Let him sweat and wonder when the subpoenas would roll in. "You have the balls to sit there—excuse me, kneel there—and ask me a question like that? You're dumber than I thought. You sidetracked my application to the Secret Service and the White House detail—a job I've coveted for years, that's why. After you snookered me into your bed. You said you would do everything in your power to get me assigned to the White House. You damn well single-handedly prevented me from getting what I dreamed of since I was a little kid. You, Puff. You called in all your markers and made sure it didn't happen. I should be the one asking you why, not the other way around. So, that's my question to you. Why?"

Puff was on his feet now, his face an unhealthy shade of red. He winced as he tried to straighten up. "Because you were the best agent ever to come out of this office; Sadie was the second best. I didn't want to lose you after she packed it in. Hell, the director was calling me once a month to congratulate me on picking such a fine agent as you. I had to be tough on you because of the others. If you're so damn smart, how come you didn't figure that out? I didn't snooker you into my bed either; you came willingly."

Quinn stood rooted to the floor, stunned at her section chief's revelation. She needed to say something, and she needed to say it immediately. "You'll say anything so I don't file this suit, won't you? I suppose you're going to tell me you loved me, too, but in a back-alley kind of way. Screw you, Puff. I wouldn't believe anything you said even if you swallowed the Bible whole." She jerked her head backward. "Tell your *manly* buddies back there to update *their* résumés, too."

Outside, in the crisp, cold November air, Quinn looked around. Her original intention had been to go home to her narrow little town house in Georgetown. Now she realized she didn't want to go home and be alone.

She stared up at the lettering on the cream-colored building. J. Edgar Hoover. He was a male chauvinist pig, too. She shrugged as she struggled to get a firmer grip on the cardboard carton. As far as she was concerned, this was just another building in Washington.

Since she didn't want to go home, she headed for her aunt Birdie's house on Connecticut Avenue. Birdie and her dog Winifred were what she needed. Birdie would hug her and say all the things she needed to hear. Winnie would lather her with kisses and crawl into her lap.

Quinn turned for one last look at the building

where she'd spent so many years. Tears glistened in her eyes as she stared at it. This part of her life was over. Not just the professional part of her life but her personal life as well. She had to get out of here before she started to blubber. She did her best to choke back a sob threatening to escape her lips. She needed to get angry, down and dirty angry at what she considered Ezra Lapufsky's betrayal. She shifted the box under her arm again so she could remove her bright red glove. She flexed her cold fingers before she offered up Birdie's favorite good-bye when someone made her angry. Her single-digit salute did not go unnoticed by the crowds of people rushing by.

Quinn pulled on the bright red glove as she turned away. The sob in her throat escaped as tears rolled down her cheeks.

1

Washington, DC
November 2007

The sun was barely over the horizon when Quinn Star exited her narrow four-story house in Georgetown. She locked the door, jiggling the knob to be certain it was locked before she pocketed the key in her baggy sweatpants. She ran in place, her mind whirling with what was on her agenda for the day. She took a moment to savor the cold, crisp November air, taking deep breaths and watching the little puffs of steam when she exhaled.

She loved this time of the day in the nation's capital. The day was new and fresh, not yet tarnished with smog, corruption, and deal making in the most famous city in the world. Not that she was a part of the corruption and horse trading, but she did read the papers. There was corruption everywhere, even in the heartland, and the real deal making, as everyone in Washington knew, went on in the cloakrooms on the Hill and behind closed doors. Sometimes on the golf course or tennis court. She thanked God the way she did every morning at this time that she was no longer a part of the federal government.

On those rare times when she couldn't fall asleep, she thought about Ezra Lapufsky and their time together, her face burning with her thoughts. Their relationship certainly hadn't been perfect, neither had her job. In fact, both had been riddled with problems. Both she and Puff should have known better than to get involved with a coworker, but they'd gone ahead and forged a relationship anyway. For almost three long years. Puff had been everything she'd wanted in a man. He was kind, gentle, had a wicked sense of humor, and he'd said he loved her. The only problem was, he loved his job more. An eerie feeling settled between her shoulder blades as she looked over her shoulder, not once, but twice. She didn't see anyone lurking about, but the feeling stayed with her as she started off at a slow trot. Her feet didn't pick up speed until she hit O Street, where she ran at full throttle till she came to the crossroads of Wisconsin and M. She waved to other runners, people whose faces were familiar but whose names she didn't know. There was Super Stud and his chocolate Lab. He waved. She waved back. Directly behind him was a woman she called Gypsy Rose Lee, in skimpy shorts and something that looked like a bustier. "I hope your tits freeze," Quinn muttered to herself.

She turned to look behind her again because of the hard, clomping footfalls she heard. The donut man, puffing along at an uneven gait, so bundled up he could barely move. Quinn concentrated on the pavement in front of her. Time to turn around and head home. She was a block ahead of herself today. On M, she was just in time to see a figure dart behind a tall, bare sycamore tree. A chill raced up her spine as the donut man chugged past her.

Is someone watching me? Who? Why? Some lunatic with a penchant for a woman who looks like a bag lady at a quarter to six in the morning? If it's a stalker, why isn't he stalking the hot-looking chick in the bustier?

Quinn lengthened her strides and flew down the street. She careened around the corner ten minutes later and galloped up the steps to her tall, skinny Federal house. Safe inside, she turned the dead bolt. Her breathing was ragged as she leaned back against the door, her body trembling. She didn't know why.

Federal Circuit Court Judge Alexander Duval, Quinn's significant other and newly nominated by the president to be the next director of the FBI, came through the dining room, fully dressed, a cup of coffee in his outstretched hand. Quinn smiled at the handsome man as she accepted the cup of strong, dark coffee. Quinn eyed Alex over the rim of her coffee cup. He always looked so put together, with his custom suits that fit him to perfection. His dark hair was always in place, and she knew he shaved several times a day. He had a year-round tan thanks to a tanning bed in his own personal gym at home. His eyes were slate gray, and at times she thought them hard as glass. She tried not to compare those gray eyes to Puff's melting brown ones.

"What's wrong? Did something happen on your run?" he asked, his face and voice reflecting concern.

"Yes. No. Oh, I don't know. It's just a feeling I have that someone is following me, watching me. It's not just when I run in the morning, Alex. I felt it yesterday when I went out to lunch, and the day before that when I got in my car to drive home. Don't look at me like that. I'm always careful, and I keep my wits about me. Hmmm, good coffee. Breakfast would have been nice," she said lightly.

Alex twinkled. "My thoughts exactly, but unfortunately, I can't wait for you to make it. I'll be late tonight, and I might not even make it at all. I'll give you a call. Be sure to turn on the alarm when you leave and don't forget to lock the door."

"You sound like Birdie. Don't worry about tonight. I think I'm having dinner with her unless someone died last night and she has to attend a wake. Call me."

Alex kissed her good-bye, not one of those peck-on-the-cheek kisses either. This kiss almost made her toes curl and her blood sing. Almost. He favored her with a wide grin and a hard pinch to her bottom. "That's so you don't forget me today," he said as he headed for the door. "I'm tired of being engaged. When are you going to marry me?" he called over his shoulder.

"One of these days," Quinn retorted as she sashayed her way to the bathroom.

Alex's parting shot before he walked out the door was, "Your biological clock is ticking."

It's true, Quinn thought as she gulped the coffee in her cup. She was fast approaching forty. Who was she kidding? In two months she would *be* forty. Birdie was on her back all the time about settling down and raising a family. A bride needed her parents in the church when she walked down the aisle. What kind of wedding would it be without her mother and father in attendance? Hell, she didn't even know where the happy wanderers were these days. It wasn't that she didn't love Alex. She did, but sometimes she compared what she felt for him to what she'd felt for Ezra Lapufsky, and it always came up short. Lately, though, she'd started to wonder if it was the sex she loved or the man himself. She just wasn't ready to make that final commitment. For all she knew she might never be ready.

Stark naked, Quinn padded over to the shower and turned it on. While she waited for the water to warm up, she looked out the window and immediately stepped back when she thought she recognized Ezra Lapufsky. Her heart pounded against her breastbone.

Quinn opened the shower door and stepped inside just as the doorbell rang. She debated a moment before she lathered up. She never had visitors this early in the morning. Alex had a key and would have let himself in. Birdie also had a key. Puff? Not in a million years. She grimaced as she shampooed her honey blond hair.

Puff?

Why now, eight long years after she'd broken up with him, was she thinking about Ezra Lapufsky? Because she felt like someone was stalking her, following her, spying on her. It was what Puff did for a living. It had to be her imagination. Or was it because Puff had been her first real love, and she'd never really gotten over him? Was that why she was dragging her feet about marrying Alex? Or . . . did it have something to do with Alex's nomination?

"I hate you, Ezra Lapufsky," she seethed as she let the steaming water cascade over her head.

Forty-five minutes later, dressed in a charcoal gray Armani suit, she walked into the kitchen to make toast for herself. The minute the slice of dark bread popped out of the toaster she spread it with the butter and jam that Alex had left on the counter. She gobbled it, finishing her coffee at the same time. It only took a minute to turn off the coffee machine, return the butter and jam to the refrigerator, and head out the back door. She was almost to her car when she heard the kitchen phone ringing. Shrugging, she ignored it. It was probably Birdie either confirming or canceling dinner that night. She'd call her aunt later.

She headed for Georgetown University, where she taught law classes three days a week. When she wasn't teaching, she practiced law from her own offices on M Street. When she had spare time during the day, she sat in Alex's courtroom and watched him. All in all, she had a rewarding, satisfying life.

More or less.

It was totally dark when Quinn parked her car at the side of her aunt's yellow house on Connecticut Avenue. She loved Birdie's old house, loved the old pine floors, with the knotholes so big you could stick your finger through them, and the sweeping spiral staircase. As a child she had slid down the banister thousands of times to land on the well-cushioned floor. Birdie still kept a pile of harem pillows clustered around the newel post at the foot of the stairs.

The sensor lights came alive as she walked from her car up the path that led to the three-story house she'd grown up in. It was always at Birdie's that she found the most comfort and the most love. In that big, old, yellow house, was her past and sometimes even her present. One day in the future, hopefully, a very distant day, she would take up residence there again when Birdie went to what she called the big BO in the sky. Birdie always referred to heaven as the Big Obituary.

At the age of sixty-seven, Birdie was full of what she called piss and vinegar. She still wrote obituaries for three different newspapers, still visited the homeless three times a week, taking them food and clothing, and she still faithfully walked Winnie, her fourth-generation basset hound, morning, noon, and night. She also did her own gardening, cooked on occasion, and kept scrapbooks of all the deceased whose lives she had doctored up and improved upon in her obituaries. When she wasn't tending to her normal activities, she managed to visit all nine funeral homes within a five-mile radius to pay her final respects. On a daily basis. If business at the funeral parlors was slow, which was sometimes the case, especially in late summer, according to Birdie, she worked on updating her scrapbooks. Birdie was quirky but lovable. Sometimes she was downright surly, like when she was really ticked off about something, at which point she could swear like a trooper and never bat an eye, and she didn't care who heard her.

Grinning from ear to ear, Quinn let herself into the house and whistled for Winnie, who trotted over. She immediately lay down and rolled over for Quinn to scratch her belly.

"Lordy, Winnie, you're getting fat. You need more exercise," Quinn said, rubbing the dog's belly.

"She is not getting fat. She hardly eats anything. She's just a little broad, but it's from neutering. I called you earlier, but there was no answer. Are you okay, baby?"

Quinn looked up at her aunt. She was as round as an orange, only five feet tall. She was dressed in her normal attire, a flowered dress that was a field of brilliant purple and white violets, and her Birkenstocks. Granny glasses perched on the tip of her nose. She peered through them, for a closer look at her niece. Her gray topknot jiggled when she huffed and puffed her way over to the staircase, where she sat down.

"Yeah, I'm fine. Alex asked me to marry him again this morning. I don't know why I can't say yes. I love him. I'm almost sure I do. We have a *spectacular* sex life. He's a wonderful man. He's kind, considerate, and generous. I don't much care for his parents, but I wouldn't be marrying them. He almost makes my blood sing sometimes. He doesn't care about my screwball parents either. I can't imagine my life without him in it. My God, the man was just nominated to be FBI director. What's my problem, Birdie?" Quinn challenged her aunt.

Birdie propped her elbows on her plump knees. "Your problem is you're crazy. You should have married that man years ago if you love him so much. I don't understand how he puts up with you. What I really think is you still have a soft spot in your heart for that FBI agent, Ezra. What exactly does *spectacular* mean?" she asked slyly.

Quinn stood up. Winnie howled and proceeded to do her one and only trick—she rolled over onto her back, then rolled back onto her stomach. For that feat, which was almost impossible considering her girth, she was entitled to an Oreo cookie. When one didn't materialize in Quinn's hand, she howled her outrage. Quinn ran to the kitchen for the cookie and tossed it to the basset, who stretched and caught it in midair, her long ears flapping in her own breeze.

"Good girl, Winnie." Birdie chuckled.

"You said she was on a diet and didn't eat much. Oreo cookies aren't for dogs; they're for people," Quinn said, her voice accusing.

"She doesn't eat the cookie; she just licks the middle like I do. You're trying to evade my question. What does spectacular mean?"

"None of your business, Birdie. Okay, okay, don't get a puss on. It means Alex likes sex. I like sex. Together we have good sex. *Really* good sex. Are you happy now that you know your niece has great sex?"

"There's more to life than sex," Birdie sniffed as she struggled to her feet. She puffed out her cheeks as she plopped a bright blue bowler hat on her head. "Where are we going for dinner?"

"I thought we could go to Chow Li's. He has the

best egg rolls and spareribs in the city. If you want to go somewhere else, it's fine with me."

"It doesn't matter where we go as long as I get back here by seven-thirty," Birdie said. "I have two viewings this evening. I just have to get my coat so hold your horses."

Quinn looked over at Winnie, who was sitting on her haunches. The two halves of the Oreo cookie lay on the floor. There wasn't a speck of the white cream left on either half. "I'd like to know what she *really* gives you for dinner," Quinn said.

"I heard that! She gets dry dog food, and she hates it. She's starving herself to death."

Quinn turned away so Birdie couldn't see the smile on her face. Birdie cooked specially for Winnie: chicken livers, ground sirloin, roast beef, and other human foods. She said it was okay because she made sure Winnie ate her vegetables, too. Maybe she was right, since Winnie's predecessors had all been on the same diet and lived to ripe old ages.

"So, who died today?" Quinn asked.

"Six people. Do you believe that? I said good-bye to Mabel Harrington this afternoon. I was disappointed in the job they did on her. I told Malcolm, too. She didn't look like herself at all. I had him deepen the shade of lip gloss and add a little more rouge. They didn't do those spit curls she favored by her ears right either. I made them fix the curls, too. You can't go wrong with Estée Lauder products. Mabel's daughters thanked me when Malcolm closed off the room and finished the job. She didn't look waxy at all. I felt satisfied when I left. God only knows what they're going to do to John Raleigh tonight. He was so grisly, with that long hair and even longer beard, if you know what I mean. Poor thing. He wanted to be laid out, but his son wanted cremation. It's cheaper."

"So you paid for his wake, right? I'm keeping score, Birdie. You must think you're independently wealthy."

"I am independently wealthy. I bought AOL when it was twenty-five cents and Intel when it was five dollars, and don't forget Mr. Softy when it first came on the market. You really don't want me to mention those dot com companies I got in and out of in the nick of time, do you?" Birdie smirked.

Quinn sighed. She could never win with Birdie. Every funeral home, every nursing home, every indigent in the city loved Birdie Langley. Other people took in stray dogs or became Big Brothers or Big Sisters to underprivileged youngsters, while Birdie Langley took it upon herself to give the dear departed royal send-offs.

Birdie's Obituary Column had often been likened to Erma Bombeck's humorous columns on life and family. Birdie professed to be flattered by the comparison. She said the first thing people her age looked at in the morning paper was the Obituary Column to see who had died the day before. She always summed it up by saying, "They're so glad they woke up alive they can't wait to see who wasn't as lucky."

Twenty minutes later, Quinn parked the car on the street across from Chow Li's. She climbed out of the

BMW, walked around to the passenger side, and opened the door for Birdie. She sensed rather than saw movement to her right. Peering into the darkness, she wasn't able to make out a form. Maybe it was a stray dog. She shivered inside her warm jacket as she hustled Birdie across the street to the restaurant, with its orange neon lighting.

Ninety minutes later, both aunt and niece professed to be stuffed when Quinn parked her car behind Birdie's sporty Lexus sedan.

Birdie hopped out and walked around to the driver's side of the car. Quinn rolled down the window to kiss her aunt. "Drive carefully, baby. All we did was talk about me tonight. Let's do this again next week and talk about you. Is it a deal?"

"Sure. Call me. I know, I know, if someone bites the dust and your services are needed, we can reschedule."

"That's good. Now I have to get John's jacket and slacks and my bag and I'm off. I enjoyed dinner, baby. Next week, I pay."

"You bought the guy clothes, too!"

"I couldn't let him be laid out in bib overalls. He liked those funny jackets. He said he had one once. You know, they called them Nehru or something like that, with a funny little stand-up collar. I had to chase all over town to used clothing stores to find one that looked decent. They're made out of *polyester*. You can't hardly find polyester anymore."

"But you found it! That's my aunt Birdie!" Quinn laughed.

"Yes, I did. Night, baby. Oh, I almost forgot to tell

you, there's a luncheon at the White House tomorrow. They want to give me some kind of humanitarian award. Would you like to attend? I wish Lettie," Birdie said, referring to the first lady, "would forget she knows me."

Quinn looked at her aunt. She knew there was no way in hell Birdie would ever attend any kind of awards ceremony, even if the award was being given to her by her former college roommate, the first lady, the wife of the president of the United States.

"I'm in court tomorrow, Birdie. I thought you hated the pomp and circumstance of the presidency, not to mention politics." Birdie knew everything there was to know about what went on in town. She had friends who had friends who had other friends. Plus she was on a first-name basis with first lady, Lettie Jaye. Thanks to those friends, and Lettie Jaye, she knew what was going to happen before it hit the front pages of the newspapers.

"I don't like any of those weasels in the White House but we're stuck with them. As for the president, he's starting to make me wonder if he's playing with a full deck. I wish he'd get his hair color right. It seems wrong to have a president of this fine country who's named Jimmy Jaye. Now, I ask you, how does that name play out with foreign dignitaries? Maybe I'll just tell them to mail the award to me. The food at these banquets always stinks, the speeches are boring, and everyone just wants them to be over so they can go home. Those awards ceremonies are always so *frivolous*. I have more important things to do. I'm glad you brought that up, baby. I'm not going. Night."

Quinn wasn't about to tell her aunt *she* was the one who brought it up. As always, Birdie would be a no-show tomorrow, and her award would be mailed to her. She laughed all the way back to Georgetown.

As luck would have it, with her second drive around the block she found a parking space. Parking was one of the things she hated about living in Georgetown, but as Birdie said, if you wanted a designer address, you had to put up with the inconveniences. As far as Quinn was concerned, the advantages far outweighed the disadvantages. She was just minutes away from her law offices and Georgetown University. She didn't have to worry about taking the metro or hiking over the Key Bridge to Foggy Bottom for the Blue and Orange line.

She loved the look of the residential neighborhood, with its tree-lined streets, as well as the cozy Federal, Georgian, and Victorian town houses.

The shopping was wonderful, and, when she had the time, she loved to peruse the stores on a lazy Saturday, stopping for lunch at Mr. Smith's of Georgetown.

Knowing it was unlikely Alex would be joining her that evening, she sighed and got out of the car. She pressed the remote control on her key chain to activate her car's security system. Seeing that the red security light glowed brightly to the right of the steering wheel, Quinn was satisfied that her car was locked down, so she started to walk the three blocks to her house on O Street.

The same eerie feeling she'd felt when she was jogging that morning settled between her shoulder blades when she was less than a block from her house. She turned to look over her shoulder. Across the street, Kevin Laker was walking his golden Lab. Farther up the street she could see a young girl walking three Yorkshire terriers on a triple leash. Other than the two dog walkers, the street appeared to be deserted.

She quickened her pace and literally ran the last hundred yards, bolting up the steps to her house two at a time. Her breathing was shallow as she fitted the key into the lock and turned it. A second later she was inside, disarming the alarm. She waited thirty seconds before she rearmed the security system. The side-by-side red lights allowed her to take a deep, relaxing breath.

She wished she had a dog. Alex had offered to get her one, but she had refused, claiming it wouldn't be fair to subject the animal to her crazy schedule. But the real reason she'd declined his offer was because Alex wasn't an animal person. Better to let sleeping dogs lie. No pun intended. One of these days, though, she was going to get a German shepherd or a golden retriever. Alex would just have to put up with the dog hairs. One of these days.

Quinn kicked off her shoes, the right one landing on Alex's favorite chair. The sight pleased her. The left one landed on the cherrywood secretary. Her coat and purse went on top of the foyer settee.

It was time for a nice glass of wine and the five mini Hershey bars she indulged in every night. But not until she shed her business suit and put on her old, fuzzy robe and fleece-lined slippers.

Ten minutes later, Quinn returned to the long, narrow living room, where she turned on the gas starter in the fireplace and watched the logs Alex had arranged the previous day burst into flame. She did love a good fire. It was always nicer, though, when Alex was sitting on the sofa next to her. Wineglass in hand, Quinn turned on the big-screen TV and sat down. She eyed the ornate Pier 1 chest on her coffee table that was full of mini Hershey bars, a gift from Birdie, who somehow, some way, always managed to replenish the contents. Quinn thought her aunt did it secretly in the middle of the night when Quinn was sleeping.

Knowing she had absolutely no willpower when it came to sweets, Quinn didn't bother trying to talk herself out of the candy. Instead she unwrapped five of the little candy bars and lined them up on the end table next to where she was sitting.

Life was good.

Will it be even better when I marry Alex? Would I be doing anything different than I'm doing now if I was married to Alex? Probably not, she thought as she stuffed her mouth with chocolate.

Would an impending marriage to Alex help his nomination? They were engaged. Wasn't that enough of a commitment for the men and women doing the background check on him? Would they make an issue of their relationship? Alex said he didn't care. But was that the truth? Would a commitment from her make his professional life easier? Would her background come into question? She had nothing to fear from her stint at the FBI. But her affair with Ezra Lapufsky might raise red flags.

One of the cherrywood logs in the fireplace split open with a loud, crackling sound. Quinn jumped as a shower of sparks roared up the chimney. Was that an omen of some kind? Birdie, who believed in the supernatural, would say, yes, it was an omen. Birdie would also say it was way past time to stop thinking about Puff. She would be right, too. Easier said than done.

Puff had been her first real relationship, her first love, her first sexual encounter. It hadn't been easy to stop thinking of him after they'd broken up. Especially when she constantly dreamed about him. Her thoughts drifted from one memory to the next. Her favorite one was a particular picnic in the brutal heat of the summer in Rock Creek Park. They'd spent the entire day, from sunup to sundown, lying on a blanket talking about their hopes and dreams. They'd kissed often, hugged, and kissed some more, knowing when they returned to the skinny house in Georgetown they would make love.

That day Puff had held her hand, touched her hair, caressed her cheek, nibbled on her lips as he professed his love for her. At one point he'd held her so tight she almost squealed, but she didn't when she heard him whisper, "Don't ever stop loving me, Quinn." And she'd promised to love him forever.

Birdie's advice to get angry at the situation, at Puff, had helped. "Just keep thinking 'used and abused,' and you'll get angry, then you'll be able to get him out of your mind," had been Birdie's mantra during the whole time Quinn was trying to get over the FBI agent.

Damn, why am I thinking about Puff after all these years? Because of Alex's pressing you to marry him, that's why, she told herself.

The phone on the sofa table behind her rang. She squirmed around and reached for the portable, clicked the ON button. Thinking it was Alex, she said, "Hi, honey, how's it going?" The heavy breathing on the other end of the phone told her it wasn't Alex. She immediately broke the connection, her gaze going to the windows and the drapes she'd forgotten to draw earlier. She ran over and yanked the long-handled drapery rods across the front windows; then she felt safe, as if she were inside a cozy cocoon. Then she remembered the kitchen and headed back there. First she checked the sliding vertical lock at the top of the kitchen door, the dead bolt, and the vertical slider at the bottom. The front door held the same three locks.

As she yanked at the venetian blinds covering the double-hung windows over the kitchen sink, she wondered if she was being stalked.

Back in the living room, she threw two more logs on the fire and poured a second glass of wine. It occurred to her then that she hadn't checked her voice mail after returning from dinner. She pressed in her code, listened, pressed more numbers, and finally clicked the phone off. Three hang-ups and a message from Alex saying he would see her tomorrow evening for dinner.

She rarely, if ever, got hang-ups because she had an unlisted number. On a rare occasion, she got a wrong number, but that was it.

Quinn looked at her watch. It wasn't even nine o'clock. Too early to go to bed. She could call Birdie or maybe her friend Sadie Wilson. She scratched the idea of calling Birdie because she was always the last one to leave the funeral home after viewing hours, so she wouldn't be home yet. But Sadie might be home. Sadie owned a small high-tech security firm that specialized in state-of-the-art security systems and had three very prestigious clients who touted her wizardry. Insisting on having a personal life even though she said she was married to her business, she somehow managed to work a nine-to-six day. She also lived in the Watergate complex, two doors down from Alex's apartment.

The sound of Sadie's voice when she brusquely said, "Hello," was music to Quinn's ears.

"Sadie, it's Quinn. Whatcha doing? No date this evening?"

"Honey, the man hasn't been born yet who is worthy of dating this intelligent, beautiful, kind, compassionate, caring woman."

"Guess you had another fight with John, huh? Did you boot him out?"

"Yes, and then I threw his bowling ball after him. He doesn't deserve me, and he knows it."

"I'm sure he does since you remind him every day. You know you two are meant for each other. No one else would put up with either one of you. Where did he go this time?"

"Where he always goes, to Alex's apartment, probably. I think he has a key. His being a homicide cop makes for easy conversation between the two of them. When Alex gets tired of cleaning up after him, he sends him back here. So, what's up, girl?"

"I'm thinking of getting married. I want you to be my maid of honor."

"You mean you're finally going to take the plunge? What color gown do I get to wear?"

"It's not definite. Whatever color you want. I'm in the thinking stages. Do you think it's a good idea?"

"Well, yes, Quinn, I do. Alex worships the ground you walk on. You love him, too. You do, don't you? He's a hottie, and he's got a great career ahead of him. I say snatch that sucker right up and go for it. When?"

"When?"

"Yes, when? Like soon, next year, next month, what?"

"Maybe in the spring, when the lilacs bloom. I don't know. I just said I was *thinking* about it. Listen, Sadie, I think I'm being stalked."

"Whoa, whoa, whoa. Back up and start from the beginning."

Quinn did. When she finished her tale, she felt better.

"I'm coming over right now. I'll ring the doorbell twice so you know it's me. Do not open the door to anyone else. We'll talk about this and jog together in the morning. Two heads are better than one. Do you have any beer, or do I have to bring my own?"

"There's plenty of beer. It's going to be like old times, isn't it? Remember all those nights we used to hang out together when we worked for Puff. I should have quit when you did. Why didn't I, Sadie?"

"Because you were young, dumb, and stupid, and you thought you were in love with that jerk Lapufsky. You kept saying it would get better."

"I did love him, Sadie. The only problem was, he didn't love me. Sometimes you have to get your nose rubbed in it before you can see what's right in front of your face. I thought I saw him this morning when I looked out the bathroom window, and then someone rang my doorbell when I was getting ready to take a shower. Yes, I had the alarm on."

"Just stay put and I'll be there in nothing flat. Turn down my bed and don't forget to put a few of those mini Hershey bars on my pillow."

Quinn laughed. She felt better already.

2

The moment Quinn Star opened her eyes the next morning, three things happened. The phone rang, Sadie poked her head in the door, and a vicious roll of thunder shook the entire house. Sadie hopped into bed next to Quinn, who was all smiles as she answered the phone, and said, "Oh, Alex, how nice to wake up and hear your voice. No, I'm not going to go running if it's raining. Sadie spent the night. No, no, nothing happened except for a few hang-ups on my voice mail. Is everything all right? Listen, Alex, I decided to accept your marriage proposal. Let's do it . . ." She looked at Sadie and grinned. "Valentine's Day. What do you think? Sooner? Alex, darling, I have to find just the right dress, and so does Sadie. That's going to take *months*. I'm so glad I made your day," Quinn purred before she hung up the phone. She looked at her friend, who beamed at her, even as Quinn tried to ignore the sick feeling in the pit of her stomach.

Sadie threw one of the fluffy pillows in her direction. "Last night you said you didn't know when or even if you were going to set the date. Did something come to you in the middle of the night to change your mind? *Oofff!*" she cried, when Quinn tossed the pillow back at her. They tussled with the covers and pillows until both of them were breathless from laughing so hard.

Quinn took a deep breath, the queasy feeling in her stomach lessening. "I don't know, Sadie. My biological clock is ticking, even I know that. Before I fell asleep last night I started to think about my life and what it would be like if Alex wasn't in it. I do love him, and I want to grow old with him."

Suddenly she felt sick again. "The other thing is, I don't want the media to make an issue of his staying over at my place occasionally. If our getting married will help, then I'm for it. Alex says he doesn't care, but I know he does. I don't want to be the one to drag him down professionally. It could still happen, Sadie. You know what this town is like."

"You need Birdie to put a good word in for him with the first lady." Sadie stretched her arms up over her head. "Now let's get this show on the road. I have to be at the shop early today."

"Why? You own the damn company. How many times do I have to tell you, when you own a company, you delegate."

Sadie swung her long legs over the side of the bed. "That would be great, but I don't have the kind of employees I'd trust to act in my name. My brother is off at one of those high-tech conventions, so I have to cover for him. Until I can find more people like him, I have to suck it up myself. Come on, shake it."

Quinn eyed her best friend. Sadie was neither

beautiful nor cute. She was a plain Jane with a fireball of red kinky hair and millions of freckles. Her deep blue eyes were her best feature and always seemed to sparkle with laughter. She was tall, almost gangly, with large breasts and a narrow waist. She laughed a lot and had crinkly lines around her eyes and mouth and the most beautiful smile in the world. She was fiercely loyal and dependable, traits Quinn admired. She couldn't imagine her life without Sadie in it.

Quinn hopped out of bed and pulled on her sweats. "Do you want a sweatshirt with a hood? Your hair is going to stand out like a firethorn bush if it gets wet. It is raining, isn't it?"

"It's drizzling. Hard rain is predicted for later in the day. Here's the deal. You start out first; do what you do every morning. Don't change a thing. I'll give you a ten-minute start, then follow you. When I return to the house, I'll come in through the back, so be waiting to open the kitchen door for me. You okay with this, Quinn?"

"Yeah. I think it's my imagination working overtime." She looked down at her watch. "Good, I'm on schedule. See you back here in forty minutes."

It was more than a drizzle, Quinn thought as she jogged in place on her front stoop. She yanked up the hood on her sweatshirt and looked to the right, then the left, before jogging down the street. She felt a hundred percent better knowing that Sadie would be somewhere behind her as backup. It was almost like old times.

She paid attention to the traffic. When you lived

in Washington, DC, you always had to be aware of traffic, especially when it rained. The truth was, you had to pay attention to what went on around you at all times, period. There were a lot of cars on O Street.

Normally, rain didn't affect the early-morning joggers. She was surprised not to see the donut man or the chick with cleavage. She picked up the pace, running at full throttle.

At the corner of Dumbarton and Twenty-seventh Street she stopped and jogged in place as she looked around. Behind her, and slightly to the left, was the donut man, who suddenly had puffed and chuffed across the street, dodging traffic. She thought she could see Sadie moving forward. Soaked through to her skin, she turned around and headed back down Dumbarton. A break in the sloshing traffic allowed her to hear a muffled sneeze coming from her right. She ignored it as she slowed her pace. As her feet took her closer to Sadie, she shouted, "Someone sneezed back there on the corner of Twenty-seventh Street."

"Gotcha," Sadie said as she whizzed past her.

He came out of nowhere and jogged down the street. Sadie doubled back and followed him. Runners did not run in wing tips. So her friend was right. Someone was either following or stalking Quinn. She quickened her pace and within minutes overtook the runner ahead of her. Then she slowed and let him overtake her. She stayed several lengths behind the runner all the way to O Street, where he collapsed against a dark green Honda Prelude. She heard the car door open and close as she rounded the corner of O Street to trot down N Street, where she cut through backyards and hopped fences till she was back on O Street, two doors up from Quinn's house. Squinting, she stared at the government license plate on the green Honda and memorized the number. She then backtracked and made her way to Quinn's kitchen door. It opened the moment she stepped near it."

"There was someone, Quinn. You're right. And, get this, he was running in wing tips and his car is a dark green Honda Prelude with a government tag. Boy, do I need a cup of coffee."

"It's almost ready," Quinn said, pointing to the coffeepot. She was busy shucking her clothes, which she threw into the dryer. She pulled out two flannel shirts and handed one to Sadie.

"That makes me feel better, Sadie. I'm sure it's just someone staking me out because of Alex and his nomination. That's what it is, I'm sure of it. Thanks, Sadie, I owe you one."

"You really think that it was someone checking you out because of Alex, Quinn?"

"Yes, I do. He's going to be under intense scrutiny. We both knew it as soon as the president nominated him. We talked about it. Look, the Oval Office knows we're engaged, and that means we're sleeping together. He has his own apartment in the Watergate, and I have this house. We are not cohabiting, as they say. He's here maybe three nights a week. I might be at his place one night a week. If they're going to tar and feather him for playing house, let them. I told you, Alex is okay with it."

"Okay, then I'm going to shower and head off," Sadie said. "Can you call me a cab to arrive in fifteen minutes? I wish to God you'd move someplace where you can park a car. By the way, when you get married, where are you going to live?"

Quinn looked blank. *Live? As in together.* The sick feeling in her stomach returned with a vengeance. "I don't have the foggiest idea. For now that's the least of my worries. Go ahead and take your shower. I'll wait for mine. Go, go," she said, making shooing motions with her hands. "Don't worry. I won't forget to call the cab."

Twenty minutes later, Quinn said good-bye to Sadie as she sprinted for the cab double-parked in front of Quinn's house.

She was almost to the top of the staircase when the doorbell rang. Her gaze immediately went to the keypad by the front door. The two red lights glowed comfortingly. Who would be ringing her doorbell at six-forty-five in the morning? One of the agents assigned to dig up all of Alex's secrets? She shrugged as she made her way to the bathroom. Let them come back at a decent hour to ask their questions.

The doorbell continued to ring as she stripped down and turned on the shower.

It was still ringing when she stepped out of the shower ten minutes later. With each ring it sounded more ominous. "My home is my castle, and if I don't want to answer the door, I don't have to," Quinn muttered over the foam in her mouth as she brushed her teeth.

By the time she put on her underwear and the

slacks to her pantsuit, her nerves were jangled. *Maybe I should answer the door.* She yanked a powder blue sweater out of the drawer and pulled it over her wet head.

She stomped her way downstairs and marched over to the door, where she looked through the peephole. She reared back when she stared into another eyeball. "Damn!" She ran around to the living room and peeped through the drapes. Her eyes widened.

Puff.

She padded back to the front door. "What do you want, Puff?" she called through the door.

"I knew you were in there. Open the damn door, Quinn."

"I will not open this door. Get off my steps, or I'll call the police. I mean it, Puff. I don't have anything to say to you." She was so angry she could hardly breathe.

"I have something to say to you. Now, open the door! I'll stand here and ring this bell till hell freezes over. I mean it."

"Go away, you poor excuse for an FBI agent, and stop bothering me."

"I need to talk to you. Please."

"No. How did you find me? You aren't that good."

Quinn leaned against the door, her head buzzing as she looked into her cozy, comfortable living room. She'd chosen each piece of furniture with care, trying to blend everything together. It had taken her well over a year to get it right. If she let her old lover into the house, it would be tainted. The deep beige couch she liked to snuggle in with Alex wouldn't be the

same. The plants she tended so lovingly would probably die if he breathed on them. If she let him in, he
might want to sit in Alex's chocolate brown chair.
He'd make fun of the watercolors hanging on the wall.

"I'm in the FBI, for Christ's sake. Do you think
having an unlisted number is going to stop me from
finding you? Will you please open the door?"

"Tell me what you want." Her voice was blistering cold.

"Do you really want me to stand out here and
shout about why I'm here? I'm cold, and I'm getting
more pissed off by the minute. I'm also soaking-wet.
I can break down this door if I want to and haul your
ass downtown to the office. I can do that, and you
know I can. Now, what's it gonna be?"

He would do it, too. Quinn undid the vertical locks
and opened the door. She smiled when she saw how
cold and wet he was. He looked miserable, but he still
looked like the same old Puff. He looked a few pounds
heavier, but it was not unattractive. He was still just as
tall, standing there in his dripping wet coat. The gray
at his temples was rather becoming, if anything it
made him more attractive. It gave him more character,
she thought. The eyes were the same, warm and dark,
and they seemed to be drinking her in. *Don't ever stop
loving me, Quinn.* And she had responded, I promise to
love you forever. She'd actually said those words a
lifetime ago. Her smile grew wider. "You're dripping.
Stand right there on that little carpet, and don't come
one step farther into my house. If you even think
about taking a step, I'll . . ."

"You'll what?"

"Let's just say you'll be one of Birdie's projects. Make it quick. I have an early class. You gained a little weight, didn't you, Agent Lapufsky? Tsk, tsk," she said, clucking her tongue. "You could also do with a little of that Grecian Formula stuff. Women don't like gray hair. Well, they do if the guy is *rich*. But you aren't rich, Puff. And, you are never going to be director of the FBI. Just to set the record straight, I suspected it was you when you sneezed back there on Twenty-seventh Street. Plus, no one runs in wing tips."

"It's Acting Associate Director Lapufsky to you, Star. That means I do all the work and the acting director gets all the credit. I'm freezing. Can you turn up the heat?"

Quinn blinked. "Acting associate director? When did that happen?"

"Six months ago. Guess you missed the announcement, huh?"

Six months ago she'd been in Europe for a month-long vacation. "Yeah, guess I did miss that particular announcement. Congratulations!" How bitter and angry her voice sounded to her own ears.

"Yeah, yeah, so are you going to turn up the heat or not?"

"No, I can't turn up the heat because I'm leaving for class, and I always turn the heat *down* when I leave the house. Waste not, want not," she said sweetly. "Spit it out, Puff. What is so important that you resorted to stalking me? I'm waiting." She tapped her foot irritably on the black-and-white tile in the foyer.

"I'm here to offer you the job of your dreams."

"And that would be . . . *what?*"

"I told you, the job you always wanted. I came to offer you a job on the Secret Service detail at the most famous address in the world: 1600 Pennsylvania Avenue."

"Yeah, well, thanks but no thanks. You're years too late. I have a lucrative law practice, and I teach law at Georgetown. I gave up that dream a long time ago." She moved to open the door but stopped when Lapufsky's arm shot out.

"I'd like you to reconsider."

"Okay." Quinn tapped her foot ten times. "All right, I reconsidered, and the answer is still no." She knocked his arm out of the way and opened the door. A wild, wet gust of rain washed into the foyer. Puff sneezed as he stepped aside to get away from the cold wind.

"Nice place you got here. Real . . . homey. Do you cook?" he asked wistfully.

"Sometimes. I'd like you to leave. I have to get to the university, or I'll be late for my class."

Puff shut the door. "Listen to me, Quinn, this is an opportunity of a lifetime. You were the first person I thought of when the order came in. I'm trying to make it up to you. You could at least hear me out."

"Like I said, you're years—eight years—too late." She opened the door again.

Ezra Lapufsky shut the door a second time. "Hear me out, or I really will drag you downtown. The first lady of the United States needs a two-man team of agents. Women this time. She asked for you by name. I was asked personally by the president to find the best agents to guard his wife. Are you listening to me, Quinn?"

Quinn laughed so hard she had to sit down on the hallway steps to compose herself. "That's your offer?" She finally managed to gasp before she went into another fit of laughter.

"What's so funny? You're acting un-American, Agent Star. I find that highly suspicious. Once an agent, always an agent. Didn't you read your contract? We can call you back into service anytime we want to."

"What's funny is that Lettie Jaye, the first lady, is nuttier than my aunt Birdie. I read the papers, Lapufsky. I am not now nor have I ever been a Secret Service agent even though I put in my time at Treasury, and you know it. Okay, you said your piece, and I had my laugh for the day. I can't believe you came here to ask me to *babysit* the first lady. That's what it amounts to, and we both know it. You can leave now."

"You're turning down the president of the United States! This is your patriotic duty. It's what you always said you wanted, and I'm giving it to you on a silver platter. Do I have to remind you how much the government spent on your training? This is payback time. You can't possibly turn your back on such a plum assignment. The president himself read your file, and he picked you at the first lady's request. You, Agent Star."

"Knock it off, Puff. We both know I'm not an agent no matter what you say. If you feel I bilked the government, then send me a bill. Now, are you going to leave peacefully, or do I have to kick that fat ass of yours out of here?"

"Quinn, Quinn, Quinn, what do I have to do to convince you?"

"Don't even try playing on my sympathy, you son of a bitch. I said, no, and I mean no. You are the last person in this world I would ever try to accommodate. You can stand there forever, and the answer will still be no. If you want to stay here, be my guest, but I'm leaving." To make her point, she opened the hall closet for her warm, lined raincoat. She fumbled in the corner for her umbrella when she suddenly remembered where she'd parked her car the night before. She yanked out a pair of red boots with ladybugs on the toes. She slipped them on. She had shoes in the car; no need to go upstairs for her heels.

"She's old and frail, Quinn. On top of that, she's sickly. Look, we both know your aunt and the first lady are old friends. Mrs. Jaye, because of that friendship, specifically asked for you. Over the years it would seem your aunt bragged about you and your accomplishments, and the first lady remembered every single detail. She wants you and won't take no for an answer. The president said she's teetering on the edge. Think about your Looney Tunes aunt and double that where the first lady is concerned. Your aunt is lucky because she has you. The first lady has no one but strangers to look out for her. You could become like a daughter to her. Someone has to care. Someone has to help that poor soul. The president is counting on you."

"You're absolutely breaking my heart. Is this

where you pull out the American flag and wave it in my face? No! Do you want it in the other four languages I speak?" She buttoned up her raincoat and jerked at the belt. "If you're planning on staying, do not, I repeat, do not turn up the heat. I have electric heat, and it costs a fortune to heat this house."

"What will it take for you to agree to come on board?"

"Lots of money, an ironclad contract signed by the president, a full-page ad in the *Washington Post* in which you admit that you screwed me royally. I think that might do it. See you around, Acting Associate Director Lapufsky."

Quinn closed the door behind her and walked down the steps. She heard the door open behind her but didn't break her stride.

"How much money?" Puff shouted to be heard over the pouring rain as he followed her.

Quinn's umbrella opened with a snap. "A hundred thousand signing bonus. What I earn in the private sector—three hundred grand should do it. All up front, of course. I get to take all my personal belongings, my computer, my files. I want time off. I also want to hand-pick an agent to work with me. I get to have guests sleep in the Lincoln Bedroom. Time off. I said that, didn't I? No twenty-four/seven for me. I want that contract to be airtight. I have a friend who's a federal judge who will look it over. It's got to be signed by both the president and the first lady. We renegotiate every thirty days. Call it a thirty-day trial if that will make you feel better. I can resign with only twenty-four hours notice. Take it or leave it," Quinn shouted above the roar of the rain as she stomped into a big puddle that splashed upward, sprinkling dirty water in Puff's face.

"When did you become so hateful, Quinn?"

Quinn turned and glared at him. "Just for the record, I'm not hateful, I just hate your guts, Acting Associate Director Lapufsky."

"The next time you say it, say it with some heart. I'll get back to you."

"Don't bother. I'm not doing it. Find yourself some other sucker."

Quinn clicked the remote on her key chain and lowered her umbrella all at the same time. A second later she was inside her car with the door locked. She didn't look at the FBI man again as she started her car up and inched into the early-morning traffic.

She didn't start to shake until she turned the corner onto Reservoir Road. She grew light-headed from the hot air spewing out of the heater. She pressed the button to lower the window and took great gulping breaths of air.

Was he serious? He sounded serious, or was this some kind of ploy to screw up Alex's nomination? Puff was jealous. He knows about Alex and me, and this is his way to derail the nomination, the very nomination Puff himself had coveted for years. Absolutely, he was jealous. The thought pleased her. *Good God, what if he agrees to all my outrageous demands? I have to call Birdie, Alex, and Sadie.*

Thirty minutes later she was informed that her class was canceled because of local heavy flooding. So much for Sadie's weather report of heavy rain later in the day. She packed up her briefcase and left the university. Her destination, Birdie's house on Connecticut Avenue. Maybe Birdie would cook breakfast. She needed something in her stomach even if it was some of Birdie's cooking, which usually defied description.

It took her all of an hour to drive to Birdie's. She parked and sloshed her way around to the kitchen door. She peered through the window and saw her aunt reading the morning paper. She rang the bell and waited. Winnie barked and sat up on her rear end, her front paws dangling in front of her.

"Lord, child, what are you doing out on a morning like this? Is something wrong? Of course something is wrong. Why else would you be here at nine o'clock in the morning? What can I do? How can I help? It isn't Alex, is it?"

Quinn slapped her raincoat down on one of the chairs. She watched as Winnie sniffed at the ladybugs on her boots before she kicked them off. The basset nosed them into a corner, so they were out of the way, and promptly flopped down on top of them.

Birdie peered over the top of her reading glasses. "I don't think Winnie likes your boots. Aren't you kind of old to be wearing galoshes like that?"

Quinn threw her hands in the air. "Birdie, you bought them for me from some catalog. You told me they were whimsical, like me."

"Oh. They are colorful. Sometimes you have to be daring in life. You know, a trendsetter."

"How about some breakfast?"

"Yes. That would be nice, dear. I would like pancakes. Maybe some bacon to go along with them. Or sausage? Maybe some eggs on the side. Winnie likes scrambled eggs. Yes, let's have everything I just mentioned. Leroy Ellis passed away. No one told me. I had to find out in the paper. That daughter of his is a spook. I'm going to have to go over to the funeral home as soon as it stops raining. You should probably make some fresh coffee, baby. I can't dwell on Leroy right now. He's gone. Tell me what brings you here."

Quinn told her as she slapped bacon into the fry pan. The moment it started to sizzle, Winnie was underfoot, dragging her food bowl over to the stove. Quinn giggled as she started to recount the morning's events. She ended with, "Do you believe that guy, Birdie?"

"Oh dear, what will I wear to the wedding. Maybe I can have something made up," Birdie dithered. "We are talking about Alex, aren't we? It's a good thing you told me now. Maybe I can track down your parents."

"Wear the dress with the yellow daisies all over it. That way all you have to get is a yellow hat. Maybe you shouldn't try to track down . . . what I mean is, I'm sure they won't . . . Oh, God, what if they actually show up? Alex . . . Alex is never going to . . . oh, go ahead, they won't come. At least we'll know we invited them."

Quinn whisked the eggs into an angry froth as she stared at her aunt.

"Look at it this way, baby, they'll add some merriment to the affair," Birdie said as Winnie nipped at Quinn's big toe in anticipation of breakfast. Quinn shook her foot. Winnie yelped. "Go get your baby, Winnie," she said, trying to divert the basset's attention.

"Now why did you say that? She's going to drag every toy in the house plus anything else she can lug out here to the kitchen.

Twenty-one trips later, the mound of toys was as high as the cabinet door under the sink. Quinn filled both breakfast plates, but Winnie was too exhausted to eat. She filled her bowl and waited to see what would happen. When the dog didn't move, she eyeballed Birdie.

"She wants you to hand-feed her. It's your fault; you told her to get her baby," Birdie said as she chomped on a slice of crisp bacon.

"You spoiled this dog, Birdie." She dropped to the floor and proceeded to hand-feed the basset, who looked at her with soulful eyes. When she was finished eating, she wiggled onto Quinn's lap and waited for her belly to be rubbed. Quinn obliged, her own breakfast forgotten.

"You didn't say anything about my morning visitor, Birdie," Quinn said as her aunt continued to eat. "What do you think?"

"I think it's a crock is what I think. Are you going to take the job because you think it's your duty, or are you going to take it because it's what you always wanted and because Lettie asked for you personally."

"Birdie, I wanted to guard the president, not babysit the first lady. Do you have any idea what a boring detail that would be? Agents kill each other to get out of that detail. I have a life now, and that isn't going to be part of it. I just find it strange that all these years later, they come to me. Something seems fishy. When was the last time you saw the first lady, Birdie?"

Birdie's brow furrowed. "About a month ago. And, come to think of it, she used to call about once a week, usually late in the evening, but I haven't spoken to her in a week or so. Lettie's terribly lonely. She absolutely hates Washington and living in a fishbowl. I don't think she'll ever get used to it. I hope Jimmy doesn't decide to run again.

"I understand why Lettie would request you to guard her. She's known for years about your dreams of being a Secret Service Agent. Before she moved into the White House, we talked several times a week. She'd call; then it would be my turn, that kind of thing. Both Lettie and I followed your career when you were with the FBI. She wants and needs someone she knows is honest, brave, and will treat her as a person, not just as the first lady. You, Quinn, meet those criteria. Are you going to take the job?"

"Nope. I'm going to go shopping for a wedding outfit. I might even get a head start on my Christmas shopping. Can I get you anything while I'm at the mall?"

"No, baby, but you can walk Winnie for me before you leave. I'll clean up since you cooked. Where is that dog? She was here a minute ago."

"Never mind Winnie, where are my boots?"

"Oh dear, I think Winnie took them. You know how she likes new things. We'll never find them unless she wants us to find them. They're with her

other treasures. You can wear a pair of mine, baby. I
think you should take the job."

Quinn's jaw dropped. "You do? Why, Birdie?"

"Listen, baby, everyone has a dream, and not
everyone gets an opportunity to realize that dream.
This is your chance to make your dream come true.
Your parents, the happy wanderers that they are,
are out there following their dream, and they didn't
let anyone stand in their way. Even you, sweet
angel that you were, couldn't deter them. Of course
they don't know the first thing about responsibility.
You, on the other hand, know all about taking
responsibility. You'll always wonder what doing
the job would have been like if you don't take it.
You'll kick yourself seven ways to the middle if you
don't at least give it a fair shot. If you find it isn't to
your liking, then you can resign. It's what you
always wanted to do. Maybe you can make a difference. Lettie's flaky. She's a talented painter. All
those artsy people are, and she's no exception. She
likes to go to museums, art shows, music festivals.
She loves to write poetry and little stories. She's a
reader and keeps up with what's going on in the
world, and she can hold her own in discussing the
latest best seller. She used to belong to two different reading groups, she taught painting, and she
plays the harp. She was in several recitals. Lettie is
an all-around kind of gal but she's being stifled in
Washington. She's very nice; don't get me wrong.
Jimmy Jaye is sharp and shrewd with great insight.
It can't hurt to have your picture taken with both
Lettie and Jimmy so you can hang it in your office.

Think about what an impression that will make. What does Alex say, baby?"

Quinn flopped down on one of the kitchen chairs. She ran her hands through her curly hair. "I haven't told him yet. When I do tell him all he's going to hear is Puff's name. I'm thinking he might get a little pissy."

"I'm thinking he might get a lot pissy," Birdie said ruefully. "I told you not to tell him about your affair. Even that lovelorn columnist says never tell. What did you do? You went right ahead and told him. You even gave him details. This is what they mean when they say your chickens come home to roost."

She shook her head, then raising her voice she called, "Winnie, I want you to bring Quinn's boots out here. Right now!"

Winnie waddled over to her blanket by the pantry door and lay down, but not before she threw her head back and howled, her ears horizontal.

"How much did you say you paid that guy Bash to train this dog?" Quinn asked.

"Three thousand. It was worth every penny, too. Buying the soup bones cooked in garlic was worth it for that alone. Winnie has never been so happy. She walks like a lady when we go out."

"She waddles, Birdie. And she smells like garlic. I guess she isn't going to fetch my boots, huh?"

Birdie stood up and adjusted her reading glasses on the tip of her nose. "Maybe tomorrow. She'll probably want to sleep with them. She does that when she finds something new. What are you going to do, baby?"

"I was going to go shopping, but I think I'll swing by the office, then go home. I need to think about all this a little more before I call Alex. I haven't even told Sadie yet. I think I'll run it by her first to see what she has to say."

"Did you feel anything when you saw him, baby?"

"Scorching anger. I wanted to smash his face in. Then I wanted to knee him. Then I just wanted to plain out kill him. I've been sick to my stomach ever since I saw him. My heart has been beating extra fast."

"I see."

"What do you see, Birdie?"

"Anger like yours tells me there's a part of you that still loves the man. Maybe Alex Duval isn't the man for you."

"You aren't always right, Birdie, and this time you are dead wrong. The whole time I was talking to him I kept wondering what it was I saw in him. I was dumber than dirt back then when it came to men and relationships. I'm borrowing your boots. I'll bring them by next week, okay? Can I do anything for you before I go home? Winnie's sleeping, so there's no point in my waking her for a walk. She'll just pee wherever she wants to anyway."

"Winnie has a small bladder. Sometimes she can't hold it. Winnie and I are fine. Call me."

"Love you," Quinn said, planting a big kiss on the top of her aunt's head.

3

She could see him standing on her stoop, shivering under a large, black umbrella. The idea of returning to her warm parked car suddenly appealed to her, but she knew he'd hunt her down. Obviously, he'd followed her all day and knew she was about to arrive home. Otherwise, he would be sitting in his own warm parked car. Double-parked, of course. When you were an FBI agent you could pretty much do what you wanted, including double-park.

Neither Quinn nor Puff greeted the other as she made her way to the top of the steps, but their umbrellas collided, hers forcing his back over his shoulder. It was her stoop, her doorway, why should *she* get wet.

"Lose your boots along the way?"

"What are you doing here, again? My boots are none of your concern. I don't have to let you into my house. My house is my castle, and there are laws pertaining to private property," Quinn said, fiddling with the key to postpone the moment when she would have to open the door and let him inside to drip on her carpet.

"Will you open the damn door already! I'm freezing. I need something hot to drink, and some aspirin. C'mon, c'mon, can't you see I'm soaking-wet? I'm probably developing pneumonia if I don't already have it." Lapufsky sneezed three times to make his point.

"This isn't a restaurant, and it isn't a drugstore either. This is my home, and I don't want you here. I thought we settled all of this earlier." Her heart beat furiously at her declaration.

"I need to clarify a few details. We're prepared to give you what you want. Turn the heat up," Lapufsky said, stepping past her to get into the warmth of the house. He immediately shed his raincoat and wing tips. "Do you have any dry socks?"

"No."

"Then put these," he said, peeling off his socks, "in the dryer."

Quinn hung her wet coat on the door to the hall closet. "Do I look like your maid? The dryer is in the pantry off the kitchen. Do it yourself."

"Where do you want me to put my coat?"

Quinn stared at the man she'd once loved. She smiled as she reached out to take the heavy, soaking-wet coat. She dropped it on the floor and stepped over it. Damn, surely he wasn't here to tell her Treasury had agreed to her outrageous demands. Her stomach proceeded to tie itself into knots. Her heart continued its furious beat.

On the way to the kitchen, she flipped the thermostat to seventy-six degrees. She watched out of the corner of her eye as Puff searched for the pantry. A second later, she heard the whir of the dryer as it kicked on. "Your feet are purple."

"That's because they're frozen. I remember the night when you sucked my big toe. I sucked yours, too. Interesting position as I recall. And it was your idea. How about some tea or coffee with a couple of shots of something in it. Don't forget the aspirin."

Quinn filled a bright red teakettle and set it on the stove. She put two black rum tea bags into two heavy mugs. She knew he took three heaping teaspoons of sugar in his coffee or tea, but she wouldn't give him the satisfaction of letting him know she remembered. "Do you take sugar, I can't remember?"

"Three, and you're lying. There's not a thing you don't remember about me. Why don't we cut to the chase here and clear away all that old garbage so we can get down to business. I like this kitchen. It's . . . cozy and warm. Like you used to be. My aunt Millie had a kitchen like this, all bright red with lots of green plants on the counter. Do you spend a lot of time in here?"

"Sometimes. You thought of me as . . . cozy and warm." She set the mug of tea in front of him. "Brandy or cognac?"

"Cognac. Yeah, yeah, you were like that in the beginning. Then you turned into someone I didn't know. In the end you were hostile, hateful, and downright ugly."

Quinn sat down. It was true. In the end she had been all those things and more. "For every action, there is a reaction. I reacted to how you treated me. How many times did I do the job and do it better than anyone else and yet you gave the credit to your buddies?"

"Twenty-seven times."

Quinn blinked at his ready response.

"And how many times did you lie to me?"

"In the beginning, never. At the end, all the time."

Quinn snorted as she fixed her gaze on a luscious green fern hanging over the sink. She couldn't remember if she'd spritzed it earlier. "Why?"

"Because you were unbearable. Agents work in teams. You wanted to do it all yourself because you were smarter, brighter, quicker. Yeah, you did work harder than the others, but they weren't slouches either. You wanted glory and there's nothing wrong with that providing everyone gets his due. You weren't a sharing person if I recall.

"I never denied you were the brightest and best in the section. You were. I hoped it would rub off on the others. I'm only as good as the people working for me. They were all top-notch agents, but they had personal lives, and you didn't. None of them slept with the flag wrapped around them like you did. You ate, slept, and drank the FBI. I didn't want you going to the White House. It's that simple. You would have been wasted there. To this day I still believe I did the right thing."

"You had no right to sidetrack me the way you did, and you damn well had no right to make decisions about what was best for me and my career. Dammit, Puff, you had no right!"

"You're right about that, too. Our section had the highest rating overall while you were with us. Once you were gone, we never attained it again. We did okay, but we weren't where we should have been."

Quinn could feel her chest puff out with pride. "You're telling me this . . . why?"

"To clear the air. I wanted to do it after you left. I used to stand outside your apartment at night trying to get up the nerve to ring your bell. I never did."

"You should have. Do you know how many nights I hid out and cried all night long?"

Lapufsky stared at her as though she'd sprouted a second head. "I didn't know you knew how to cry." He looked so baffled, Quinn took pity on him and poured more cognac into his tea. While he drank his tea, she fetched his warm socks from the dryer and tossed them to him.

"Ohhh, God, that feels good," he said, pulling on the socks. He leaned back in the chair and fixed his gaze on hers. "I guess you want to talk about *us*."

"What *us*? There was only you. It was always about you. It was never about me. You made that clear in the beginning. I was dumb as dirt back then and believed everything you said. You should have told me there were rules. I always go by the rule book."

"I did love you, Quinn. I wasn't ready for marriage any more than you thought you were. I did want you to succeed. I wanted to succeed myself. Marriage would have changed all that. We had a good thing there for a while. Then it went sour. You brought the job home with you. I never did."

"The hell you didn't. You used to arrange my cases around your libido, and don't try telling me different. You used to get a perverse kind of pleasure out of kicking me out of bed to go relieve someone on a stakeout after we made love all night. Don't even think about denying it. All I wanted was a commitment, even if the wedding was years down the road. That was all I wanted, Puff."

Puff flinched at her words. He decided to ignore her last statement just so he could breathe comfortably and not think about its meaning. "You had the least seniority, Quinn."

"And I was a woman. Go ahead, you can say it. You were on a power trip, and we both know it. You squashed me like a bug under your shoe and ripped my dream to shreds. You had too much power over me."

"You allowed it, and you accepted it, Quinn. What you don't know is I did ride those guys' asses where you were concerned. They knew we were sleeping together, and no, I never told anyone, so don't add braggart to your list of grievances against me. I was never a kiss-and-tell kind of guy. You had your chance to file a harassment suit when you left. You said you were going to. I gotta tell you, the whole section was in a state of chaos for a full year, waiting for that lawsuit. Everyone was so busy covering his ass, and writing down a chronology of events, that the director himself paid us a visit. The rumors were out there. Every so often, I'd drop something and say I heard the suit was going through, blah blah blah. It was all I could do, Quinn. You have your beliefs, and I have mine. You were wrong about some things and right about other things, just the way I was. I do have a question. Why didn't you file the harassment suit you threatened?"

Quinn knew that sooner or later the question was going to come up. "I didn't want to do anything to hurt you," she said sadly.

"I'm sorry, Quinn. You know what they say, the past is prologue."

"You took my dream away from me in order to further your own career. You must be feeling a little disgruntled, what with a new director about to come on board. That was your dream, wasn't it?"

"Yeah, that sums it up pretty good. I can say I'm sorry if that will make you feel better. One of these days I *will* be nominated as director. My turn is coming. Everything in this town is about politics as you well know. I came up through the ranks on my own. I don't have a political family nor are any politicians indebted to me. Duval has connections and clout. He won't cut it, though. He's all facade, no back bone," Puff said smugly.

"Do you have any soup? I can't seem to get warm. Do you think we could go into your living room and light a fire? You could bring me the soup."

Quinn felt her shoulders slump and didn't know why. "All right. But as soon as you've warmed up, I want you out of here. Don't go getting any ideas about staying over. I'll turn the heat higher. Why don't you just go home and go to bed? You look flushed, like you're running a fever."

"Because your place is nicer than mine, and my heat is on the fritz. The only place I can go is a hotel or back to headquarters. Don't forget the soup."

Quinn threw some logs on the fire, struck a match to the gas starter, and watched the kindling spark.

"Don't sit on that chair and don't sit on that couch either," she said, pointing to the two pieces of furniture in her small living room she didn't want him to sit on.

"Where do you want me to sit? I may be getting a cold, but I don't have any rare, life-threatening diseases."

"Sit on that Queen Anne chair. Push it over by the fire and stretch your legs out." She grudgingly tossed him an afghan Birdie had made for her when she was in college.

"Quinn."

"What?"

"I don't blame you for leaving the Bureau. For you it was the right thing to do at the right time. I never would have . . . thrown you to the wolves." He grimaced. "Just so you know."

"Yeah, well, that was then, and this is now. I'm not a fool, Puff. I knew you'd never process me to Secret Service. That's why I quit. I'll get you the soup; then I want you to leave."

When she got there, Quinn looked around her cozy, warm kitchen. She felt like she'd just been run over by a double-decker bus. Her hands were shaking when she opened a can of Campbell's Chicken Noodle Soup and poured it into a pot. She fixed a tray, added a napkin and salt and pepper shakers to the tray.

Why am I doing this? Why don't I just kick him out of my house? God, what if Alex pops in unexpectedly. How am I going to explain Ezra Lapufsky sitting in the living room eating soup I heated up for him. Alex would never understand. Hell, I don't understand either.

After adding saltine crackers to the tray, she carried it into the living room, using her shoulder to open the swinging door leading into the dining room.

She stopped in the doorway to the living room when she saw Puff stretched out on the rug in front of the fire, the afghan wrapped around him. He was sound asleep. She turned around, backed up, and set the tray on the dining room table before she dropped to her knees alongside her old lover.

How many times had she stared at him in sleep? Hundreds, probably. He looked so vulnerable. Boyish. Peaceful. She fought with herself not to stretch out alongside him. How sad to see the streaks of gray at his temples and the fine wrinkles around his eyes and mouth. He was still trim and fit, though, even with the few pounds he'd put on. He'd always paid attention to his diet and worked out religiously. Once, she'd loved him so much her heart ached with the feeling. Her heart continued to thump in her chest.

Her hand almost reached out to brush the hair back from his forehead. She clenched her fists, got to her feet, and bolted upstairs, where she changed into warm sweats and fuzzy slippers. She freshened her lipstick and brushed her hair. At the last minute she dabbed some sinful-smelling perfume behind her ears.

Downstairs, Ezra Lapufsky continued to sleep peacefully in front of the fire.

In the kitchen, Quinn picked up the phone to call Sadie, who answered on the first ring.

"Guess who's sleeping in front of my fire?"

"This is just a wild guess. Puff," came the response. "How did you know?"

"It just figures is all. What's Alex going to say about all this?" Sadie asked.

"Probably a lot. I'm hoping he's out of here before Alex comes over. Sadie, he offered me a job at the White House, on the first lady's Secret Service detail. He said I could pick my own partner. I made all these outrageous demands and literally kicked him out of the house. I never thought they would agree to those demands. He just got here and said they, and I don't know who the *they* are, agreed to all my demands. *All* my demands. Puff said there were a few points to fine-tune. I don't want to do this. I thought if I was outrageous enough, they'd cross me off their list. The man can make me so angry, and yet I felt such a sense of loss when I was watching him sleep. Can you see me babysitting Letecia Jaye? I-don't-think-so."

"Maybe you should reconsider, Quinn. Working Secret Service in the White House has always been your dream. Maybe that's why it's taken you so long to commit to Alex. You know, unfinished business, that kind of thing. The gig is three months on and three off. Can you handle that?"

"I suppose I could try it for a few months. Are you interested, Sadie?"

"Hey, it will look good on a résumé, which I might need if I fail at this business. It can't hurt to say you worked on the White House detail as a Secret Service Agent. If you want to take a crack at it, I'll go along for the ride. I can recruit my brother to work here full-time. He knows more about the business than I do anyway. Listen, I have to go, a customer just walked in. I'll call you later."

Quinn stared at the phone in her hand. It rang just as she was about to put it down. "Hi, Alex, how's it going?"

"It's hairy. I'm just calling to tell you I can't make it tonight. The whole town is flooded, and traffic is backed up everywhere for miles. I'm probably going to play catch-up and sleep on the sofa in my chambers. Are you okay?"

"I'm fine, but I'll still miss you."

"I'm going to miss you, too. I promise to dream about you all night long." The sudden relief that she felt at his words overwhelmed her.

"Me, too. Talk to you tomorrow."

I should have told him about Puff. Well, it's too late now. Quinn looked at her watch. Time to think about dinner. There were no leftovers of any kind in her refrigerator, so that meant she had to cook from scratch. If she made a pot roast, she could eat it the rest of the week. Alex loved hot roast beef sandwiches. So did she.

Thirty minutes later, the roast was simmering as she added carrots and small new potatoes. She dusted her hands dramatically as she whipped out her portable mixer and a set of bowls. A chocolate cake was in order. Tomorrow, she would drop half of it off at Birdie's just so she wouldn't eat it all herself. Birdie loved chocolate cake. So did she . . . and Alex.

Quinn turned on the small television set on the counter and watched the ominous weather report as she whipped the batter for the cake. Classes would probably be canceled the next day, too. Maybe she could sleep in for a change.

While the pot roast simmered and the cake baked, Quinn worked on her laptop at the kitchen table. The brief she was writing wasn't due for a week, but she had never been one to procrastinate. She worked diligently until she was satisfied with what she was seeing on the screen in front of her. Her neck felt tight, and her shoulders ached from sitting in the same position for so long. She stretched her neck and rolled her shoulders up and down until the tightness eased.

Eight o'clock!

In ten minutes' time she had the gravy made and the cake iced. While the coffee brewed, she cut up a tomato-and-cucumber salad.

Outside the rain came down in torrents, beating and slapping at the kitchen window. She shuddered, grateful that she was indoors and not driving home on the flooded roadways.

Quinn was setting the table when she felt a tap on her shoulder. Spinning around, she found herself looking into Puff's dark brown eyes.

"Thanks for letting me sleep by your fire. If you tell me where my shoes are, I'll leave," he croaked, his voice barely audible.

Quinn debated with herself for all of three seconds. "I can't believe I'm saying this, but you can't leave. All the roads are flooded. Besides, you don't look like you're in any condition to drive anywhere. I was just going to have dinner. Are you hungry?"

"Yes, actually, I am hungry. This looks nice," he said, pointing to the table set for one. "You always used to make the table look pretty when you cooked for me. I remember the first time you did it. I was so used to eating out of cartons and paper bags, it made a strong impression on me. I remember how the wineglasses sparkled, how the candles smelled like vanilla."

"You remember that?" Quinn asked in awe.

"I remember everything, Quinn."

Flustered, Quinn turned back to the stove. "The bathroom is behind the pantry if you want to wash up. There's a packet with a toothbrush and comb under the vanity. I'll set another place. How do you feel?"

"Like hell. I haven't been sick in years. My resistance must be down. I'll be right back."

The place mats were real linen, the napkins matching. The silver was sterling, the crystal Baccarat, the dishes Spode, all compliments of Birdie, who said Quinn needed fine things because she lived in a fine area with a fine address. She used these fine things every single day. She was glad that her table looked pretty. At the last second she opened the cabinet door of her buffet and pulled out two pretty blue candles that smelled like the first blueberries of summer.

Puff returned and took his place across from her. They stared at one another, old memories floating to the surface. Puff was the first to look away. *Your loss*, she thought smugly.

"You're a good cook, Quinn."

"Birdie made sure I learned early."

"Is there anything you *can't* do?"

"I suppose there are a few things. For some strange reason I could never master roller-skating." She paused before adding, "And I wasn't able to convince you to let me go to the Secret Service. That's two things."

"Well, I can't roller-skate either. Or ice-skate. Weak ankles. So, have you made a decision about the job?"

"Yes. I don't think I want it. I have a nice life now. I'm going to . . . I need more time."

Puff gulped at the wine in his glass. "By the way, who's that guy who hangs out here with you? The one I saw leaving the other morning. He looked familiar. Are you two serious?"

Quinn chomped down on a slice of cucumber. He looked like he really didn't know and was just asking out of curiosity. Should she enlighten him? "I guess you could say it's serious. His name is Alex." She waited for a reaction, and, when none was forthcoming, she settled back in her chair. "Why are you asking?"

"I guess I just wanted to know what he has that I didn't have. Other than that fancy Mercedes Benz he drives."

"Are you telling me you didn't run his license plate?"

"Now, why would I do that? So, what does he have going for him?"

"Puff, his name is Alexander Duval, and, as you know, he's just been nominated to head up the FBI."

"You don't mess around, do you?" Puff said, placing his knife and fork across his plate. "You could have told me sooner. Okay, I screwed that one up. Bendecci was the one who ran the background check on you. His report said that you were seeing some preppy looking jock named Alex Dovel. Obviously his typing skills aren't what they should be. Does that explain why I didn't know?

"I told you earlier, Duval won't last if he really does get the position. You're only as good as the people who work for you, and our guys are no longer satisfied with pretty boys with no background in law enforcement. There's no way he can pull it off. Plus, the guy doesn't even act like he wants the job. Someone is doing someone else a big favor by getting him nominated. The scuttlebutt is it's probably his father pulling strings. Guess you didn't want to hear that, huh? Are you embarrassed because you know I'm right? It all comes back to my original question, why didn't you tell me?"

"It's none of your business, Puff. I don't owe you any explanations. Just because you barge in here and offer me some prestigious, high-level job doesn't mean I owe you anything. My relationship with Alex isn't a secret and never has been. We're getting married in February."

Quinn felt suddenly sick to her stomach at the look on Puff's face.

"Is he the reason you're turning down the job offer?"

"No. I don't want to babysit the first lady. I'd go out of my mind doing that. I told Sadie I would consider it. Well, I considered it and the answer is no."

"Listen, thanks for dinner and the little trip down Memory Lane. I'll be leaving now."

"Don't you want some cake and coffee?"

"Maybe some other time. I'll take about four aspirin, if you have them."

"Sure." She tossed him the bottle from the kitchen cabinet. "Take them with you. You're running a fever."

"Yes, I am. I'm hot all over. Don't concern yourself."

"Okay, I won't. Your shoes are by the front door along with your coat. They're soaking-wet, Puff." Suddenly she felt like crying and didn't know why.

She did cry when she heard the front door open and shut. Hard sobs shook her shoulders as she sat at the table, her memories threatening to choke her. Her clenched fists pummeled the kitchen table. "I hate you, Puff. I hate your guts. I will always hate you for what you did to me. I don't ever want to see you again. Do you hear me, I hate you!"

She felt hands on her shoulders and knew instantly who was touching her.

"You were right; the roads are flooded—the water was up to my knees. You have crappy drainage here in Georgetown. It looks like you're stuck with me until the water goes down. I'm sorry you hate me. I'm sorry about lots of things, Quinn. I really am. Listen, I'm feeling kind of wobbly right now. Do you think I could sleep on your couch by the fire? I'm having some bad chills. I won't bother you."

Quinn took a deep breath and composed herself. "Okay, come on. You can sleep in the guest room, but first you should take a really hot shower. I'll make you a hot toddy. Maybe you can sweat it out. The heat is as high as it will go. There's an electric blanket on the bed, so that will help. Can you make it, or do you need help?"

"My legs are like wet straw. I think I need your help. Don't read anything into this that isn't there, okay?"

"Yeah, okay. Tomorrow you need to see a doctor."

"Yeah, okay. I've never felt this sick in my entire life," he groaned, as Quinn helped him up the stairs and into the bathroom. "Take off your clothes and hand them to me. Turn the water as hot as you can stand it. What's your feeling about sleeping in one of Birdie's old, oversize flannel nightgowns?"

"I'm all for it. Is it like her dresses, full of flowers?"

Quinn blinked. "Yeah. Purple pansies. You do have a phenomenal memory, don't you?"

"Goes with the territory. Modesty prevents me from talking further. I'm down to my jockeys."

Quinn slammed the door and walked across the hall to the guest bedroom. The first thing she did was turn the electric blanket to HIGH. She turned down the bed and fluffed up the pillows.

It was a pretty room, decorated for Birdie when she spent the night. She'd painted the furniture herself and even covered the old, antique rocker with a fabric that matched the comforter. Birdie did love violets. Just by chance she'd found a wallpaper border with exactly the same pattern. It had been just the right touch, bringing the room together. In the corner was Winnie's dog bed, also done in a washable violets cover. The bookshelves, painted white, held some of Birdie's scrapbooks and pictures of the two of them throughout the years. It was a comfortable room, warm and cozy. *Warm and cozy.* How many times had Puff used that expression? Several.

She'd never thought of herself as warm and cozy. More like hard as nails and mean as the devil. *Warm and cozy.*

"Where's the damn nightgown, Quinn?" Puff croaked from the bathroom.

Quinn grinned as she pulled one of Birdie's nightgowns from the dresser drawer. She handed it through the crack of the door. "Such modesty," she chirped. "I've seen it all before, or did you forget?"

"I didn't forget, but I thought you had."

"Do you still have the chills?" Quinn asked, ignoring his comment.

His teeth chattering, Puff padded into the guest room and slid into bed. "God, this feels good. If I lie real still, I don't shake. Do you think I have pneumonia?"

"Don't you cough with pneumonia? I'm no doctor. I'm a lawyer."

Puff reared up in bed. "That guy Alex, he didn't sleep . . . you didn't . . ."

"This is Birdie's room when she stays over. It's for guests. I'll be back in a minute with some aspirin. You need to sleep."

Puff swallowed the pills, his hands shaking badly as he brought the water glass to his lips. "I called the office from the bathroom and gave them this number and your number. The battery is low on my cell phone, so calls might come through to you. Sift through them, okay?"

"Sure. I'll make you a hot toddy; then you should sleep. This really is above and beyond the call of duty. I just want you to know that."

"I do know it. I'll find a way to make it up to you."

"I don't want you to make it up to me. I just want you out of here."

"You are hateful," Puff sniped. "What's that guy like?"

"Shut up. Why couldn't you lose your voice? That guy is none of your business."

Back in her warm, cozy kitchen, Quinn looked around at the mess she still had to clean up and groaned. She worked with quiet efficiency, the way she did everything. The concoction she prepared was poured into a soup cup with a heavy wide handle. "This will either cure you or kill you," she muttered as she made her way upstairs.

"Jesus, what *is* this?" Puff said, sniffing the brew.

"Just drink it, and don't ask questions?"

"Your ass will fry if you poison an FBI agent," Puff said, gagging on the mixture in the cup. "What the hell is this?"

"Onion slices, sugar, and water, simmered until syrupy—also good for sore throat and croup—with or without honey and lemon juice."

"What?"

"You heard me. Drink it and shut up. By morning you'll be dancing out of here. It's one of Birdie's old-fashioned remedies. Do you want me to grease your chest with Vicks?"

"That means I would have to pull up this nightgown."

"Yep, that's what it means."

"Can't you do it from the neck and work down to my chest?"

"Nope."

"Forget it then. Will it help me?"

"I don't know. Birdie always greased my chest when I got sick. Is *it* all *shriveled* up?"

"You are ugly *and* hateful. Let me be to die in peace. Close the door when you leave. The answer is no!"

"If I am, it's because of you," Quinn muttered under her breath as she made her way down the stairs.

It took her over an hour to clean up the kitchen and put away the leftovers. She eyed the chocolate cake sitting in the middle of the table. Testing her willpower, she covered it with a domed lid.

The coffee in the pot was hot and bitter from sitting so long. She drank it anyway as she waited for the eleven o'clock news to come on.

It hit her like a bolt out of the blue as she was watching a commercial for Pedigree dog food. What if this was all a setup to get at Alex? Puff said he gave the office her home phone number. Her *unlisted*, private number. If she took his calls, people would know he was here. Alex would find out. The president's men would find out. It would be on the news, and that would be the end of Alex's nomination.

Puff was sick, she reminded herself. That much was real. He'd left, but because of weather conditions, he'd had to come back. *Damn, done in by the weather and my own stupidity in keeping Puff's presence here a secret from Alex.*

She unplugged the phone. When she stared at the empty jack, her head started to pound while her stomach heaved. She ran to the bathroom behind the pantry and gagged.

Limp as a wet noodle, she made her way to the sofa, where she flopped down and buried her head in a pillow that smelled like Alex.

4

Quinn rolled over in her warm nest of covers, squinting with one eye at the red numerals on the bedside clock. A moan of disgust escaped her lips. She'd promised herself to sleep in this morning, and here she was, bright-eyed and bushy-tailed at five-thirty in the morning.

She propped herself up on her elbows and looked out the window. She'd been so tired when she went to bed, she hadn't bothered to draw the drapes across the long, narrow, floor-to-ceiling windows. It was a dull, gray morning, but it wasn't raining. Typical November weather. She wondered if the streets were still flooded. When she didn't run in the morning she always felt guilty.

The word *running* brought back the events of the previous evening. She flopped back onto the pillows. Ezra Lapufsky was sleeping in her guest bedroom. How had she ever allowed that to happen? She beat at the pillows with her clenched fists as she visualized her life as she knew it going down the drain.

Quinn leaped from the bed to race over to the bedroom door. A heavy sigh escaped her lips when she realized she hadn't been too tired to lock it. She continued to stare at the narrow door. Everything in the house was narrow or skinny. A house shoved between two normal houses. Early on she had surmised that this skinny piece of property had once been a garage or a carriage house of sorts. Birdie called it a Jack Sprat house. But the right colors and accessories had worked wonders and opened up the rooms, giving an illusion of spaciousness.

Should she take a shower first or make coffee? Maybe she should check on her houseguest. The possibility that he had departed during the middle of the night brightened her outlook.

Alex was never going to understand any of this. Never in a million years. Well, that was going to be Alex's problem, not hers. She hadn't done anything wrong. No decent human being would cast a sick person outside in last night's cruel weather. Actually, she had done just that, but Puff had come back and she'd realized how sick he was. Quinn looked at the digital clock again, wondering why Alex hadn't called her.

"Damn!" she said succinctly when she remembered unplugging the phone in the kitchen earlier in the evening. Oh, God, if Alex found out about Puff staying the night with the phone turned off, he would think what any other man would think, that the two of them were bumping *uglies* in the night.

Quinn grabbed her robe from the foot of the bed and raced downstairs to the kitchen, where she plugged in the phone. It rang almost immediately. She took a deep breath, and said, "Hello?"

"Hi, honey. How was your night? I missed you."

"Oh, me, too, Alex," Quinn mumbled as she rinsed the coffeepot and filled it with fresh coffee. "What's the weather like outside?"

"The rain stopped at around four. I wouldn't venture out until later this morning if I were you. Let's have an early dinner and take in a movie this evening if the roads are okay."

"Sounds like a plan to me. Call me later, okay?"

"You sound jittery, Quinn. Is everything okay?"

"Everything is fine. I just woke up."

"Okay, see you later. Love you."

"Uh-huh."

She replaced the phone, her eyes on the dripping coffee. She turned when she saw the kitchen door move. Puff stood in the doorway, freshly showered and dressed.

"Do you think you could give me a cup of coffee to go?"

"I think I can do that if you wait a few minutes." Such a brilliant retort.

"Did any calls come through last night?"

"I didn't hear the phone ring once all night." It was the truth. "How do you feel, Puff?"

"Like I was kicked in the gut by a horse, then run over by a train. I'm up and I'm moving. I don't have chills, though, so that's a plus. That poison you gave me last night must have worked. I'll pick some stuff up at the drugstore."

Quinn reached into the cabinet for a cup just as the phone rang again. She scooted across the kitchen to pick it up. Her greeting was cautious. She listened, her face going white. "It's the president of the United States, and he wants to talk to you," she hissed, handing over the phone. She listened to Puff's end of the conversation, her heart kicking up a beat.

"Yes, Mr. President, what can I do for you this morning? I'm sorry you couldn't reach me last evening. Yes, the storm was ferocious. No, Mr. President, I don't have her answer yet. You want to speak with her yourself? Hold on, Mr. President."

Quinn reached for the phone, her eyes murderous as she glared at her former lover. She listened to the silky words, the pleading tone. Her head bobbed up and down until she realized the president couldn't see her. "Yes, yes, I know the first lady is a lovely person. Yes, my aunt Birdie has told me many times what a fine friend she's been all these years. I understand, sir. I need more time, Mr. President. I have a business, and I teach at Georgetown. More money? Well, Mr. President, I've never been one to turn down money. Name my price? You want to know what that price is right now? Triple sounds fine to me. Is that a problem, Mr. President? Then I will certainly consider your offer when I make my decision. You need to know today because the first lady is *ragging* on you? Yes, yes, I understand. I think I can give you my answer by the end of the day. Yes, it is nice talking to you, too, Mr. President. Would you like to speak with AAD Lapufsky now?" She grinned evilly as she handed the phone back to Puff. She watched as his face turned white, then red, before he clicked the OFF button.

"Triple what we first offered you! You're blackmailing this country and the president of these fine United States!"

"Oh, stuff it, Lapufsky. What difference does it make? I'm not taking the job, so just forget about it."

"What do you mean you aren't taking the job? You just told the goddamn president of the United States that you wanted triple the original offer. Are you saying you lied to the president of the United States? I don't believe this!" Puff said, his outrage turning his face red.

"You haven't changed one bit, Puff. Don't you *ever* listen? I said the higher offer would play a part in my decision. I never said I would take the offer. I don't want it. There's also a little matter of that full-page ad in the *Washington Post.* All right, here's your coffee," she said, handing over a plastic Slurpy cup from 7-Eleven, filled to the brim.

"You lied to me. You said there were no calls last night. I could haul you in right now for lying to the AAD of the FBI. The president said he tried calling here all night long. The president was calling me all night long! God only knows what *he* thinks. Just you wait till he finds out you lied to him, too." His voice was so smug, Quinn flinched.

"Again, AAD Lapufsky, you weren't listening to me. I said I didn't hear the phone ring all night long. I didn't say it didn't ring. It's time for you to leave, and please, forget where I live and don't come back."

"I'll be back at five o'clock for your answer. The president is going to call you at that time, so don't try weaseling out of it. You set yourself up, and you're going to see it through to the end. Think about this today. I wouldn't be a bit surprised to find out, if you turn down the offer, that the IRS will audit you as far back as they can. Do you have any idea what kind of hell *that* would be? They might even sic themselves on your aunt for good measure."

"You're blackmailing me, you louse. I'll tell. I swear I will. You can't get away with this!"

"Get away with what? I'm FBI, not the IRS. Those people have minds of their own. And don't for one minute believe they are a warm and fuzzy IRS like it says in the papers. Even the IRS has public relations people. All I said was, I wouldn't be surprised. Thanks for your hospitality. The next time you get sick, you can come to my place."

"I wouldn't set foot in that roach-infested hovel you live in if you paid me my weight in gold. Get out of my house. Now!" Quinn sputtered.

Quinn walked around in circles for twenty minutes as she tried to sort through her jumbled thoughts. Her whole life was changing right in front of her eyes. She zeroed in on the chocolate cake sitting on the counter. Who was she trying to kid? She'd made the cake for Puff because she knew he loved chocolate cake. Instead of reaching for the cake, she picked up the phone. She needed to talk to Birdie.

"Baby, baby, what's wrong? Don't try telling me nothing, because I can hear it in your voice. Come on now, tell me all about it. Winnie is on my lap, and we're both listening."

"Puff came back again yesterday, Birdie. He told me that they would meet my conditions for taking that job with the Secret Service guarding the first lady. I told him no. I really blasted him for . . . for, you know, the past. He was sick, and I let him stay the night. Birdie, I cooked for him; I let him use my shower. I even gave him one of your nightgowns to wear because he had the chills. I made him a hot toddy. I . . . I didn't tell Alex. I should have, but I knew what he would think and say. Telling him now, after the fact, will make it look like I did something wrong. I swear I didn't, Birdie.

"On top of all that, I unplugged the phone last night so I wouldn't have to take any calls for Puff. Then this morning the president called him. He called here at the house, Birdie, and asked to talk to me. Me. He begged me to take the job, and said he'd pay me triple what I asked. What should I do, Birdie?"

"What do you *want* to do, baby? By saying no to the job, are you trying to get back at Ezra? Or are you afraid of the demands and the responsibility of the job? It's what you always wanted. It would seem to me that the only way to find out if what you wanted all those years is *really* what you want is to try it. Maybe down deep, you are trying to get back at Ezra by rejecting the job he's offering you."

"What about Alex?"

"What about him? He's a big boy. I don't see why you have to fess up at this stage. Since nothing went on other than the man's sleeping in my nightgown, I'd suggest you keep mum. Dump that gown in a sealed bag to preserve whatever hairs came off his body. DNA, that kind of thing. You just never know what the people in this crazy town are up to. Everyone wants to think they're players, and most of them don't even know the name of the game. They could be setting you up, but I don't think Lettie would allow that. Assuming she knows. The papers are full of all that garbage concerning the FBI. Just today they're saying that a small group of senior FBI executives, who protect one another at all costs, resist change, and retaliate against anyone who challenges them is to blame for the agency's recent debacles. Current and former Bureau officials told all of this to the Senate Judiciary Committee. I'm quoting from *USA Today*. They said the agents in the field call those guys 'the club.' This might interest you. They said they rule the FBI through petty office politics and derail the careers of anyone who investigates one of their pals. You might want to ask Ezra if he knows anything about the missing laptops that had top secret information on them. They're missing a lot of guns, too. Maybe they're concerned that if Alex gets in there, he might want to clean house. Be careful, baby."

"I'm always careful, you know that. I think you just told me more than I wanted to know, Birdie. How's Winnie?"

"Well, you know we had all that rain yesterday, and she's pretty low to the ground. She hates getting her tush wet, so she's been peeing on the carpet by the back door."

Quinn laughed. "She always pees on the carpet by the back door. You didn't go out last night, Birdie, did you?"

"No, I didn't. Things are all fouled up. Funerals are all backed up. The graves are full of water. Even when you're dead you have problems," Birdie said cheerfully.

"Yeah, guess so. You're sure you're okay?"

"Very okay. Which gown did he wear?"

"The one with the purple pansies." Quinn giggled. "He made my stomach jittery, Birdie."

"That means you aren't over him. You might want to postpone that wedding a few months until you're *absolutely* sure. You're going to take the job, aren't you?"

"I think so. I've been fighting with myself. I want to, and I don't want to. Like you said, I'll never know unless I try. I just hate giving Puff the satisfaction."

"Tell him it's all about money. Also, the sooner you tell Alex that you are taking the job the better off you'll be."

"Okay. I'm going to call him now. Puff said I was blackmailing the country and the president by raising my salary demands."

"That's nonsense. You always go where they pay you the most. If you want the job, then I say go for it."

"I don't know what I'll do if Alex pitches a fit, Birdie."

"It's your life, baby, not his. Just follow your heart, and you'll be fine."

The connection broken, Quinn stared at the phone in her hand. She could feel her heart thumping in her chest at the prospect of telling Alex about her offer and her decision.

Not ready to make the call, Quinn walked upstairs and into the guest bedroom, where she stripped the bed and remade it. She blinked at her reaction to the faint aftershave smell on the pillowcase. "You are one sick puppy, Quinn Star," she muttered to herself as she carried the bedding downstairs to the laundry room. She looked down at Birdie's nightgown and frowned. Should she do what Birdie said or not? Why not? As her aunt said, in this town you couldn't be too careful. She wadded up the gown and stuffed it into a Ziploc bag. She pulled the zipper tight and tossed it into the back of the overhead cabinet behind two large bottles of Cheer detergent.

She picked up a pile of yellow towels from the top of the dryer and carried them upstairs, where she jammed them into the narrow linen closet, wishing she had a roomier closet or, better yet, a walk-in one. One of these days, maybe after her detail at the White House ended, she would take her money and invest in a bigger house, one with walk-in closets and garden bathrooms. Maybe. Maybe she would move to Boise, Idaho, buy a farm, and hang out in the barn away from everything.

The day yawned ahead of her, and it was only midmorning.

In her bedroom, she picked up the phone to call Alex. She was put through immediately. Her head started to buzz the moment she heard her fiancé's voice. Literally gasping for air, she dived right in. "Alex, the most unbelievable thing has happened. I've been asked by the FBI if I would work the Secret Service detail guarding the first lady. I spoke to the president this morning. The president of the United States, Alex. He actually called my house. Do you believe this?" she gushed.

The five-second silence on the other end of the phone did not go unnoticed by Quinn. She sucked in her breath and crossed her fingers the way she'd done when she was a child.

"You told them what they could do with that offer, didn't you, honey?"

"I said I would have to think about it. They expect my answer by five o'clock this afternoon. When they first approached me yesterday, I said no. I made outrageous demands, thinking they would never meet them and that would let me off the hook. I didn't want to make any enemies." *God, who is this lame-sounding person?* "The demands really were outrageous, what I was making in the private sector, a signing bonus, and a partner of my choosing. Just in case, I asked Sadie if she's interested, and she's all for it. She said it would look good on a résumé. There are details to work out. Then when the president called he agreed to triple, *triple*, Alex, the original salary they offered. I would be a fool to turn this down. Agents work three months on and three months off. The first ninety days will be a trial period. If I decide it isn't for me, then I just won't sign on after the ninety days are up, assuming they want me to stay on. They'll take care of the university, and I can assign my cases to other lawyers I know. I guess my question to you is, will this help or hinder your nomination? I see it as helping. Birdie agrees. So does Sadie."

"You spoke to Birdie and Sadie before telling me. Why, Quinn?"

Oh nuts. Why indeed? "I'm not sure, Alex. I guess I

was excited and wanted a woman's opinion. You didn't answer my question, Alex."

"Have you definitely made up your mind to take the job?" His voice was so cool, Quinn could feel the frostbite starting to form on her ear. She could also feel a headache starting to form at the base of her skull.

"You know what, Alex," she said, her own voice just as cool, "I think I have made up my mind. Guarding the first lady was not what I had in mind back when I had dreams of working the White House detail, but it will do. If I don't take the job, I'll always wonder if I missed the greatest professional opportunity of my life. I thought you would be happy for me."

"If this is what you want, then, yes, I'm happy for you."

He didn't sound happy. He sounded furious. She said so.

"I think you're misinterpreting my tone for surprise. Truthfully, this is the last thing I expected to hear. As for your question, I just don't know if your joining the White House detail will hurt my chances of being confirmed. Only time will give us the answer to that question. Right now the media are crucifying the FBI. I don't know if it's justified or not. You did say you were never going back, didn't you?"

"To the FBI, Alex. I never said I wouldn't take a job with the Secret Service."

"Did someone recommend you for the job?"

There it was. The question she'd been dreading. "I

imagine it was one of my superiors at the FBI. I'm not sure. I can ask if you think it's important. I would like to think I was chosen for my abilities."

"That's all right. I was just curious."

Don't ask. Please don't ask. "I don't know what to tell you about this evening, Alex. With so much going on, I don't know if I'll be up for going out. I'll call you later if that's okay."

"Call me anytime. I am, after all, your fiancé."

Quinn stared at the pinging phone. Angry, she redialed the number and waited to be put through a second time. The moment he said hello, she blasted forth. "Did you just hang up on me, and did we just have our first fight?"

"Someone just walked in. The answer is no and no. I'll talk to you later."

Liar, liar, pants on fire. At least he hadn't asked her outright if Ezra Lapufsky was the person who'd contacted her. He'd said when the request came in, she was his first thought. That didn't mean he'd recommended her. More than likely he had. She had evaded, but she hadn't outright lied.

Her headache had blossomed into full-blown agony. She gulped aspirin, then stripped down to take her shower. "I hate men. I hate all men," she muttered as she lathered up under the steamy spray. *Why do all men come with an attitude?*

Quinn sat at the kitchen table, her eyes on the bright red, apple-shaped clock. The coffee cup in her hand had a bright red apple painted on the side, one of six Sadie had given her as a gift. She liked things that matched in her comfortable kitchen. It was her third cup from the present pot, her sixth cup of the day. Before long, her nerves would be twanging all over the place.

Sadie was late, but then Sadie was always late unless it was a do-or-die situation. Would Puff really show up at five o'clock? Of course he would. If the president was going to call, she guessed he would be five minutes early. Puff was hell on wheels when it came to punctuality.

Quinn closed her eyes. Whom should she think about? Puff or Alex? If she was smart, neither one. When it came to matters of the heart, as Sadie was wont to point out, she was dumber than dirt. Two days ago her life had been normal. She had a routine, a job that earned her more money than she needed, a satisfactory love life, her own house, and good, loyal, kind friends who rounded out her life. Now, thanks to Ezra Lapufsky, her life was in turmoil.

Puff had asked her what Alex had that he didn't have. If she had known the answer, she would have told him, but she didn't. Alex had been a top-notch attorney before becoming a federal judge. In areas of the law, he was brilliant. He looked good, worked out, and was always impeccably dressed even when they were jogging. He treated her well, bought her gifts, some expensive, some silly, some just because. He sent flowers regularly, just because. He spent hours planning little weekend getaways or day-trips that were always memorable. And, he never, ever, allowed her to pay or even leave the tip. As she told Birdie, he was spectacular in bed. At times. He was going to make a wonderful, *predictable* husband. If he had a flaw, it was his jealousy. He'd always been jealous of Puff from the minute he'd tricked her into telling him all about her real reasons for leaving the FBI. He was fond of saying, "Okay, let's hear the real deal, Quinn." At times he was an obsessive-compulsive person.

Puff, on the other hand, was loose as a goose, and no matter what time of day or night, he always managed to look disheveled. He was handsome in a craggy kind of way with unruly, dark, curly hair that was graying at the temples. Alex was handsome, too, but in a preppy way. In terms of intellect, they were evenly matched. Puff was Yale, and Alex was Harvard. Puff had worked his way through school, not having the luxury of being born into money the way Alex was. As for gifts, he liked to give gag gifts that made her laugh. It wasn't that Puff was cheap; he just didn't have a clue as to what to buy. Once, though, he'd given her an alabaster unicorn that still sat on her night table. And he'd given her a spray of cherry blossoms he'd picked along the Tidal Basin during the Cherry Blossom Festival one year. She still had it, too, pressed between the plastic pages of her scrapbook. Their lovemaking had been beyond spectacular, as each of them marveled at the pleasure the other could give. As far as she knew, he'd never been jealous.

Quinn jumped off the chair. *Damn, why am I doing this to myself? Am I a masochist? After all, I was the one to dump Puff, not the other way around. Why am I putting myself through all this angst eight years after the fact?*

Maybe Birdie and Sadie were right. Maybe Puff had sneaked into her heart, carved out his niche, and that little part of him would be with her forever and ever. How could she marry Alex if Puff was still in her heart? She remembered all too well how she'd felt when she'd stared at him yesterday while he was sleeping by the fire. She'd been caught off guard. She would never let anything like that happen again. Ezra Lapufsky was out of her life, and she planned to keep it that way.

He banged on the glass pane on the back door, opening it at the same time. To Quinn, he looked just as sick as he had when he'd left earlier that day. She said so.

"I'll live," he croaked. "What was that stuff you said you wanted to rub on my chest?"

"Vicks; do it when you go to bed. You should gargle, too. If I get your germs, I'm coming after you. My whole house is probably riddled with whatever it is you have."

"I'd like you to make me one of those toddies to go when I leave. Please," he added as an afterthought. "Okay, here is the contract. You sign on the yellow line. Where's Sadie?"

"She's running late. I'll look over her contract. Hey, I'm not signing this today. I want to run it by the head of contract law at Georgetown first. The money gets wired to my account, and when I see it there, then you get this," Quinn said, tapping the contract on the table.

"C'mon, Star, it's cut-and-dried, straightforward."

"Look me in the eye and say that. This is sixteen

pages of crap, fourteen of which I'm going to weed out. When it comes to government, nothing is simple. It's my way or the highway, AAD Lapufsky. Just remember this, I don't need this job."

"The first lady wants to have breakfast with you a week from tomorrow. First thing tomorrow, you and Sadie are to go out to Quantico for a full week's refresher course. We should be able to wind this up by then."

"Why the big rush?"

"I think they just want her comfortable with a female agent. Everyone is happy with you and Sadie starting work a week from Monday. The first lady isn't well. They used the word *fragile* a lot. You take the bullet for her just the way you would for the president. That's how important this detail is. Get it out of your head that it is a babysitting job. It isn't."

"When does the money go into my account?"

"Whenever you say you want it. All I have to do is make a call."

"Sadie?"

"Same deal."

"Okay, do it now, then. When it's confirmed, I'll run this over to Georgetown and fax it back to you. You are going to take care of my teaching job, right?"

"I did that earlier this afternoon. The dean understands he's giving you up to the White House, and your job will be waiting no matter how long it takes."

"Why did you stand me up in Vail that time?"

To his credit he didn't pretend not to understand her question. "It was NTK, and there was no time to call you."

"Need to know, my ass. I heard you were in Cancún, and don't deny it. With your buddies." Even after all these years she was surprised at how bitter her voice sounded.

"That's where the job was. You don't tell the director no, as you well know. Do you think he would have cared if I told him we had that ski trip planned for seven months? No, he would not have cared. You really hold a grudge, don't you?"

"Actually, no, I don't. I just like to have things clear in my head so when I slice off your balls, I'll feel good about it, knowing I'm not making a mistake."

Puff gurgled something that sounded impossible to her ears.

Quinn raised her eyes to the clock just as the phone rang.

"The president is always prompt," Puff said, reaching for the phone. A wicked grin spread across his face. "Me? I'm AAD Ezra Lapufsky, FBI. I guess you want to talk to Quinn. Just a minute, and I'll get her.

"Miz Star," he drawled elaborately, "a *Mister* Alex Duval is on the phone for you. Cut to the chase, the president is about to call," he hissed in her ear. The wicked grin remained on his face as he watched her take a deep breath.

"We have to make this quick, Alex. The president is about to call. No, honey, I can't make it. I have to take this employment contract over to Georgetown so the head of the contracts department can review it for me." She lowered her voice to a bare whisper, knowing Puff could still hear her. "I have no control over whom the FBI sends over here. Yes, I told him we're getting married. He doesn't care. Stop being so ridiculous. I'll call you when I get back. If that's the way you feel, then you call me when you have some free time. Good-bye, Alex.

"I hate it when you do stuff like that, Lapufsky. You didn't have to tell him who you were. Why did you do that?"

"Because he's a stuffed shirt who thinks he's hot spit, that's why. I can't believe you're engaged to that guy. I checked him out," he said imperiously. "He matches. Everything he wears matches." His voice was so full of awe, Quinn found herself smiling inwardly.

"That guy is going to be the next director of the FBI. A ten-year appointment, I might add," Quinn observed. "Have you guys found all those missing guns and laptops yet?"

"We're on it. As for you and Judge Duval, go ahead and make the biggest mistake of your life, see if I care."

"My biggest mistake was you," Quinn snapped back. What was happening to her? She wasn't a mean-spirited person. She was only that way with Puff.

"Why don't you make me that toddy so I can leave the minute you finish talking to the president?"

"I'm not making you anything. Go to a doctor and let him prescribe something for you."

"I don't have time since you won't sign this contract as is. That means I have to shuffle around and make changes and shuffle some more, then come back here."

"You're coming back here *again?*" Quinn asked, opening the cabinet for a pot, which she banged down on the stove. "Send someone else next time."

"You know it doesn't work that way. We at the Bureau see things through to the end. I will be escorting you to Quantico tomorrow, too. I'll pick you up a week from tomorrow to take you to the White House."

"I want you out of my life, Puff. Remember, I answer only to the president and the first lady. We're going on a three-month trial basis. I don't see any of that stuff in this contract. You weasel, you better damn well get it all in there, or I'm not going anywhere, and neither is Sadie. I'm still waiting for you to make that call."

"You're giving me a headache. Can you just shut up for a while. I'll take care of it. Do you have any idea how sick I am?"

"Ask me if I care," Quinn snapped. "Do you have any idea how badly you hurt me?"

"Back then, no. Now, yes," he croaked, his eyes full of misery. "Look, I concede I was a jerk. You were the best thing that ever happened to me and to the Bureau, and I screwed it up. I apologize. I'm sorry. I wish I could turn back the clock and undo all the things you think I did. I'm trying to make it up to you the only way I know how. I know how much you wanted the White House. I'm giving it to you on a silver platter. Can't you cut me some slack here?"

Quinn poured cognac into the pot. "Are you the one who recommended me to the Secret Service?"

"I gave you such a glowing report they actually

thought . . . hell, I don't know what they thought, but they did say no one was as good as I said you were. However, bear in mind, the first lady requested you personally." He looked down at his watch and sneezed four times in rapid succession. "He's late." Quinn pointed to a box of tissues on the counter. He blew with gusto. "That cake looks pretty good."

"Yeah, it does, doesn't it? Do you want some?"

"Yeah."

"Then why didn't you ask for some. Why do you always have to talk around things instead of saying what you mean?"

"Can we have a truce here?" Puff asked, sneezing again.

"Sure. When are you going to wire that money into my account? This is the third time I'm asking you. You get the cake after the call."

Lapufsky fished around the inside of his jacket for his cell phone. Quinn watched as he pressed numbers, then croaked, "Do it now. Call me back with a confirmation number. What part of, do it now, don't you understand? *Now* means now."

"Sadie's goes into my account, too. I told you that last night, didn't I?"

"No, you didn't tell me that last night. This is highly irregular."

"Since when do you guys ever do anything that is *regular*? Make the call." He did.

Quinn swiveled around to pick the phone up on the second ring. "Yes, sir, you have the right number. Just a moment." She handed the phone to Puff and mouthed the words, "It's the president."

"Yes, Mr. President, this is AAD Ezra Lapufsky. Ms. Star and Ms. Wilson are willing to come aboard. Yes, Mr. President, both agents will be happy to have a late breakfast with the first lady next Monday after their refresher training course. Yes, the money is being transferred as we speak. Yes, both agents are worth every penny. Yes, I agree, Mr. President, they don't come any better than Agents Star and Wilson. I would consider it an honor to have breakfast with you and the first lady and the agents. Good-bye, Mr. President."

Quinn watched as Puff grabbed for a pile of tissues to mop at the sweat running down his face. His cell phone rang. "What the hell took you so long, Kaminsky? It was a simple wire transfer that was okayed by Treasury last night." He motioned with his hands for pencil and paper. "Okay, repeat the confirmation number." He scribbled and handed the slip of paper to Quinn.

"*Thank you* would sound nice," Quinn said.

"You are one hateful, unforgiving lady. Now, can I have that cake? No, no, no. I don't want it on a paper plate. I want it on one of those pretty ones with the shiny silver. See, you did rub off on me. I used to love you so much my toes hurt."

"Your toes! That certainly sounds romantic."

"Not only are you hateful and unforgiving, you're scary, too. Are you like this with that guy Duval, or is it just me?"

Quinn leaned across the table until her nose was almost touching his. "Now read my lips, Lapufsky. You ruined my career; you used me to your own advantage. Then you added insult to injury and abused my feelings for you. I was young, dumb, and stupid back then. I was so in love with you, I couldn't see straight. You know what, I got glasses after I left the Bureau, and I see pretty well right now. I was practically suicidal back then, which doesn't say much for me, but I'm okay now. I don't want to hear any more of your confessions either. Now, eat your damn cake and get out of here."

"Okay. You must think that guy is going to come over here tonight, is that it?"

"Something like that."

"Look, there is one little hitch to this deal. It's out of my control. You said you and Sadie would only report to the president. That wouldn't fly. I tried. They met every one of your demands but that one. You report to me. Reports come to me. Daily. It shouldn't be this way, but that's what the powers that be want. It's the God's honest truth, Quinn. Okay, I'm outta here. I'll be back later this evening with the revised contract as soon as you fax it over to the office." He let himself out the back door without another word.

Quinn scribbled a note to Sadie and stuck it on the front door. Sadie knew where she kept the spare key.

She slogged her way down the wet street to her car. With luck, she should be back from the law school in ninety minutes.

5

Quinn let herself into the house by way of the kitchen door. She looked around in confusion. Every light in the house appeared to be on. The kitchen was just the way she'd left it—messy. She whirled around when she felt a cool draft near her ankles. "Winnie! Hey, girl, what are you doing here? Where's Birdie?" Winnie turned around and waddled through the kitchen to the dining room, then to the living room.

"Wow! Are we having a party or something?" she asked, looking around in surprise at Birdie, Sadie, and Alex. Winnie, she noticed, trotted over to the bottom of the steps and howled, her ears going vertical, something she'd just recently learned to do.

"Or something," Sadie mumbled.

"I just stopped by to see if you had any water damage," Alex said, getting up from his special chair to kiss her lightly on the cheek.

"I just dropped by to ask if you'd watch Winnie tonight. I'll pick her up at six in the morning," Birdie said from the couch, a highball glass in her hand. Alex, she noticed was drinking a bottle of Corona and Sadie was swigging from a bottle of Coca-Cola.

"Can all this wait a minute? I need to talk to Quinn about something," Sadie said, heading for the kitchen. Quinn looked back over her shoulders at her guests and shrugged as she followed Sadie into the kitchen.

"What's up? It's all done. I've got the contracts right here in my purse. I just have to fax them to Puff, and we're at Quantico for a week; then it's the White House for breakfast a week from tomorrow. You look funny, Sadie. Oh, no, don't tell me you're backing out of this."

"No, nothing like that. Listen to me, Quinn. Puff is upstairs in the guest room. When I got here, he was slumped over the wheel of his car, which was double-parked across the street. I got him into the house. He fought me, but it was either that or 911. I didn't know what else to do. Quinn, the guy has a 104 fever. He belongs in the hospital, but he won't go. You know how men are. It's a macho guy thing. John is the same way. They think they're indestructible. He wanted me to make him one of those drinks you make. He said you put *onions and sugar* in it. He . . . ah, is . . . what he's doing is . . . he's . . . wearing one of Birdie's humongous nightgowns. The one with the orange tiger lilies all over it. He knew right where they were, too. If I were you, I'd get Alex out of here before Puff coughs or something. He must have sneezed fifty times. Winnie already knows he's up there. Alex isn't dumb, Quinn."

"I don't believe this! He can't be upstairs! Are you sure he's running that high a fever?"

"I took his temperature. He's got chills again, and

he's red as a beet. I ran out to the drugstore and got those cool pads for his neck and forehead. You have to get Alex out of here. By the way, Birdie doesn't know Puff is up there. Her dog is smarter than she is."

Quinn threw her hands in the air. "Why me? Why am I under this black cloud?"

"What do you want me to do?"

"Well, for starters, go upstairs and sit with him. If he coughs or sneezes, put a pillow over his face, but don't smother him. Shut the door, too."

"What *are* you two up to?" Alex asked, poking his head in the door.

"Just talking about our gig at the White House, honey. I didn't think you were coming over tonight. I have a lot to do, Alex. I need to pack, because we leave for training in the morning, plus I have all these faxes that I have to send. You're more than welcome to stay, but I'm going to be busy."

"No, I'll get out of your way. I can see that I'm outnumbered. Call me tomorrow and let me know how it's all going."

"Okay, honey."

Winnie scooted into the kitchen, looked at everyone, then turned around and started to bark when Puff, attired in Birdie's tiger lily nightgown, walked into the kitchen. Birdie, behind him, was assessing the length of the gown on his tall frame. Alex's jaw dropped, as did Quinn's. Sadie sat down on the floor next to Winnie, who was doing her best to crawl up Puff's leg.

He looks pitiful, Quinn thought. *And sick.* The man really was sick, and he belonged at home or in the hospital. At the very least in some doctor's office. For the first time in her life she was speechless.

Puff drew himself up to his full six-foot height and looked around. "I didn't mean to interrupt. I just came down to make myself one of those drinks you made for me last night. I can do it. I know where everything is. I'll be out of your way in a minute. Cute doggie." Winnie nipped his ankle, then tried to crawl up his leg again. Unable to attain her goal, she managed to latch on to the edge of the tiger lily night-gown and tugged. It ripped up the side seam. Winnie continued to tug, then tugged again, not liking this strange man wearing her mistress's clothing.

Without missing a beat, Puff reached for a pot, slapped it on the stove, and turned to Birdie. "I'm sorry about your nightgown. I'll buy you a new one." His voice was so hoarse, Quinn wondered if she was the only one who understood what he was saying.

His eyes ice-cold, Alex looked around, and said, "Good night, everyone."

Quinn found her voice. "Alex, wait . . . it isn't . . . I can ex . . ."

"I don't think there's any way you can explain that," Alex said, jerking his head in Puff's direction.

"What's that supposed to mean?" Puff de-manded, his hands on his hips, his face bulldog angry.

Alex ignored him as he threw open the kitchen door. Winnie ran over to him and bit his ankle. He tried to shake her off, but she held on until she worked his loafer off his foot. She grabbed it in her teeth and waddled quickly into the dining room, Alex on her tail. Birdie stiff-armed him. "It's hers now. I'll send you a check for a new pair. We *never* take anything away from Winnie. Never."

Puff guffawed. He sounded like a bullfrog in acute distress.

Sadie grinned.

Quinn sat down, her eyes burning with unshed tears.

Birdie reached for the pincushion in the kitchen drawer and proceeded to pin the sides of the tiger lily nightgown.

The sound of the kitchen door slamming was so loud, Quinn shuddered.

"You damn well better hope you die in the middle of the night, Lapufsky, or I will kill you myself! Why did you come down here? You knew my fiancé was here, didn't you? You did this on purpose. You . . . you . . . FBI snake!"

"Yeah," Sadie said, echoing her friend. "By the way, orange is not your color."

It looked like Puff was about to make a retort when he fell back against the side of the cabinet, his legs going out from under him. He slid gracefully to the floor. Winnie moved as fast as her fat little legs would carry her and hopped into his lap. She nuzzled the tiger lily gown into a bunch under her chin and closed her eyes. Puff groaned.

"I think we should just take him to the hospital," Quinn said.

"Okay by me. Do you think we should change his . . . attire first, though?" Sadie asked.

"Nope."

"Between the three of us we should be able to get him on the sofa, where he can rest for a bit," Birdie suggested, and the three women proceeded to support him as he limped into the living room. "Sadie, fetch some bedcovers from my room," Birdie ordered. "It's all right, Winnie, you can sleep with him. Yes, yes, he's wearing my nightgown. It's all right. That's a good doggie. Now where did you put that man's shoe?"

Winnie threw back her head and let out a fierce howl. "All right, you can have it. I just asked where it was."

"I'm sorry, Quinn," Puff said. "I really didn't know he was here. I didn't know what to do, so I bluffed it out. Wouldn't you have done the same thing if you looked like I looked back in that kitchen? The guy actually *saw my ass!* How's that going to look if he becomes director? The first thing he's going to do is have me transferred to Timbuktu or someplace where I'll never be heard from again. Now, do you really think I'd set myself up for something like that? Where's that *smarmy* concoction you were going to make for me? I'm dying here, Quinn," Puff gasped as he coughed and sneezed over everyone, including Winnie, who was looking up at him adoringly.

Quinn couldn't help but notice. Winnie was usually a sterling judge of character. Until she stole his loafer, for some strange reason Winnie had never gone within ten feet of Alex.

"We're going to take you to the hospital, Puff.

You're too sick to be here, and I don't want you to die in my house," Quinn said.

"I'm not going to die, and I'm not going to the hospital either, so get that idea right out of your head. Just make me that drink and make it a double. Do you have the contract? Let me look at it. I need my cell phone, too. Let me get warm first, though. Boy, that's a humdinger of a fire, Birdie."

Quinn bristled. Where did he get off addressing her aunt as Birdie, like they were bosom buddies? Even Alex showed her aunt respect and called her Miss Langley.

"Thank you." Birdie preened. "I do love a good fire in the winter. So does Winnie. She loves to lie on the hearth and toast herself. I think it has something to do with being so low to the ground."

"Don't go cozying up to my aunt thinking you can get to me, you son of a bitch. You just ruined my life. I'm going to get you for this if it's the last thing I do," Quinn snarled.

Puff looked over at Birdie, his eyes pleading with her. "Your niece has a mouth like a longshoreman. You should caution her on her speech. If she marries that stuffed shirt, her every move and every word is going to be in the paper," he said virtuously. Winnie wiggled her fat little body upward and curled herself around his shoulders and neck. "AWK!"

"She seems to have attached herself to you, Ezra. Take good care of her. I have to leave now. O'Leary's never starts their viewing until I get there. I hate to keep the deceased, not to mention the bereaved, waiting."

"Tell whoever it is, I said good-bye," Puff said solemnly. Winnie barked in his ear.

Quinn burst into tears as she fled to the kitchen.

Sadie watched, her eyes big and round, as Quinn poured and dumped stuff into the pan on the stove. "Do you know what you're doing, Quinn? You could kill him with all that . . . slop."

"I should be so lucky," Quinn sniffed. "In one minute, he ruined my life. One lousy minute. Did you see Alex's face? Oh, God, what am I going to do?"

"Nothing. You're a victim here. Did you ever hear of the word *trust*? Alex is teed off, so what. John gets like that on a weekly basis. Just ignore him. Let him come to you. You didn't do anything wrong. Now that you mention it, Puff did look rather funny. I liked the part where Winnie ripped the gown. He does have nice buns. Who knew?" she quipped.

Quinn clapped her hands over her ears. "I don't want to hear any more. Good, it's boiling. I hope he burns his damn gullet."

"He still loves you, Quinn," Sadie said quietly. "You know what else I think. I think you're still in love with him, too."

"Well, you're wrong." Quinn burst into tears again. Sadie handed her a dish towel to wipe her eyes.

The living room was so hot that Quinn gasped. The fire was roaring, and someone had turned the thermostat to ninety degrees. "It's like a sauna in here without the steam," she muttered.

"Here's your drink," she said, handing the tray to Puff, who was curled into a ball on the sofa under a mound of blankets and quilts.

"I'm starting to like this dog. Look how she loves me. Don't you have a straw? If I move, she'll have to move. Get the straw and hold the cup."

"Kiss my butt, Lapufsky. Stop giving me orders."

"When, precisely, do you want me to do *that?* I'm up for whatever makes you happy," Puff croaked hoarsely.

"Sadie, get this jerk a straw."

"What did you take out of the contract?" Puff asked.

"Fourteen pages of this and that. It's as good as it's going to get, so suck it up. Where do you want me to fax it?"

Puff rattled off a number. Quinn copied it down. Sadie returned with a straw.

"You made this all wrong; it won't go through the straw," Puff complained. Winnie raised her head and glared at Quinn.

"Would you like me to spoon it into your mouth, or how about I just dump it on your head?" Quinn asked sweetly as she handed the oversize cup to her former boss. He gulped at it, tears running down his cheeks as he valiantly tried not to gag. Winnie licked at the rim of the cup each time Puff took a breather.

"God, this is worse than the other one. Did you change the recipe?"

Sadie looked on smugly, while Quinn rattled off the contents of the contract.

"Does it meet with your approval, AAD Lapufsky?"

"It'll do. Sign it, and fax it off now. The president

and the first lady are waiting for it. This is the *real deal* now, right?" Puff peered into the cup as though he couldn't believe he'd actually finished the evil concoction Quinn had made for him. Winnie sighed as she took one last lick at the bottom of the cup.

"I'm going to do it right now. Go to sleep. I don't want to hear another peep out of you till morning. Do we understand each other, Lapufsky?"

"I love it when you talk tough. It gives me the shivers," Puff said, snuggling under the weight of the covers. "What more could a man want? Warmth, the love of a good dog, two women who care about . . ."

"Okay, he's out! Let's do what we have to do. He's going to have one hell of a hangover in the morning. If he isn't dead." Her voice was so smug; Sadie laughed out loud.

In the kitchen, her laptop open and ready, Quinn sat down and flexed her fingers. "Okay," she whispered, "this is what we're going to do. I had them wire your money as well as my own into my bank account. Good, it cleared. Isn't it amazing how those guys can do whatever they want when they're nailed to the wall. Start thinking about a password. We're wiring this money to numbered accounts in good old Switzerland. Alex showed me how to do this last year. I opened the accounts today, and they're ready to receive the money. Oh, Sadie, look at those numbers. You'll never have to work again if you don't want to. If you invest wisely," she added hastily. "Okay, here goes!" A blizzard of numbers raced across the screen the minute she typed in her password. "It's your turn now. Type in your password and make sure it's one no one can ever figure out. You have to type it twice. Hit SEND, and your money is on the way. We're doing this because . . . because I know how they can confiscate funds in seconds. There it goes! Done. Now, we fax the contracts. A hard copy stays with Puff."

"Are we really, officially, Secret Service Agents now?" Sadie asked in awe.

"You better believe it. In a million years I never thought this could happen."

"Puff made it happen for you, Quinn. Did you thank him?"

Quinn ran her fingers through her hair. "No, I was too busy being mean to him. I don't know, Sadie, there's something that doesn't feel right about all of this. Think about it. They're paying each of us almost a million dollars to guard the first lady. Agents don't get anywhere near that amount of money. Even if the first lady is sick and frail, there are other agents that have to be as good as we are . . . or were. They were just a little too quick to give in to all of my outrageous demands. The president himself called. Don't you think that's a little strange?"

"Not really, considering that the first lady and the president trust your aunt. Hey, they agreed, we agreed, we're rich, and a week from tomorrow we're having breakfast with the first lady. Like Puff said, it doesn't get any better than that. I didn't eat anything today. You got anything good?"

"How about a hot roast beef sandwich with sliced tomatoes on the side and chocolate cake with vanilla ice cream for dessert? You can get it ready while

I fax these off. I'm going to try and call Alex, too."

"I hear you. Go, go," Sadie said, making shooing motions.

Quinn walked upstairs to her second guest bedroom, where her fax and copy machines were located. She called the room her minioffice. If and when she had more than one houseguest, the sofa opened into a bed.

She looked at the two-page contracts in her hand. Did she really want to do this? More to the point, why was she doing it? Was it because of Puff? Was it because of her lifelong dream? Puff said it was the real deal. Before she could change her mind, she slipped the four pages into the fax machine and punched out the numbers. The moment she heard the high-pitched squeal, she hit the SEND button. Her task at an end, she folded the papers and left the room to walk across the hall to her bedroom, where she closed the door and dialed Alex's number.

Six rings later she knew the answering machine would come on. It did. "Alex, it's Quinn. I'm not calling you to apologize, but I am calling to explain. Ezra was sick. I couldn't turn him out in that horrible weather. I did what anyone would have done. I let him spend the night. But it doesn't mean anything. I will admit, it did look strange. There was no way in hell I was going to give him a pair of *your* pajamas. My God, I wouldn't even let him sit on the furniture. All I could think of was giving him one of Birdie's nightgowns. I'm sorry you took things the wrong way. I don't feel I should have to explain or apologize for anything. If you don't feel that way, then something is wrong, and we need to talk about it.

"Sadie and I are going to have supper, then we're going to bed. We'll be leaving for the week's training course at Quantico early. I'll call you when I know what my schedule will be. Have a nice evening, Alex. I am sorry about your shoe. Birdie will replace them. She's just so protective of Winnie, and you know the rule—if Winnie gets it, it's hers. Night, honey."

Quinn wiped at the perspiration dotting her brow with the back of her hand. She fell backward on her bed, the knuckles of her hands pressed against her eyes. She longed for a mother with a comforting bosom to cry on. Everything seemed impossible. Besides, crying never solved anything. All you got from crying were red eyes and the hiccups.

She rolled over and swung her legs over the side of the bed. *Shift into neutral, Quinn,* she told herself. *Focus on dinner with Sadie. Don't think about Puff on your sofa and don't think about Alex sitting in his living room listening to your message. Think about tomorrow morning and finally making your dream a reality. Put one foot in front of the other and go downstairs.*

Quinn followed her own instructions and made her way downstairs. She made a point of going through the living room instead of down the short hallway and into the dining room.

In spite of herself, she smiled at the sight of Puff and Winnie on the couch. One of Puff's arms was around the dog's fat middle, while Winnie was nestled, half on his shoulder, a quarter on his neck, and a quarter on his chest. The dog opened one sleepy eye, then closed it. Puff looked better already. It wasn't quite as hot as it had been earlier, mainly because the fire had died down to smoldering red ashes. She turned down the thermostat to seventy-five degrees before she added two cherrywood logs to the fire and headed for the kitchen.

"It's ready whenever you are," Sadie said. "Did you check on our patient?"

"He's sleeping peacefully with Winnie. He doesn't look as flushed. Actually, he looks a lot better. I called Alex," she said, fiddling with her napkin. "I got his answering machine. I had this vision of him sitting there listening to my message. On the face of it, it is rather childish. Alex . . . Alex always likes to get his way."

"And you let him, is that what you're saying?"

"Sometimes. I pick my issues and defend them vigorously."

"Kind of what you used to do with Puff, huh?" Sadie said, sitting down and shaking out her napkin. Her expression was guileless when she stared across the table at Quinn. "Isn't it peculiar that Winnie took to Puff? Whoever would have thought that would happen. That dog is almost human sometimes. Why doesn't she like Alex?"

"He's not an animal lover like me and Birdie. Animals have dander, and they shed. Sometimes they have accidents. One time he saw Winnie pee on the carpet by Birdie's back door. He was appalled."

"I bet you have a whole list of things about him that irritate you, huh?"

"Whose side are you on here, Sadie? What is this, let's get Alex night?"

"No, of course not. I just don't think he's exactly who you think he is. Oh, he's nice, he's charming, he's all those good upper-crust things women always think they want in men. But you know what, Quinn? When you look in his eyes, nothing comes back at you."

"Why are you saying these things to me now? Are you trying to play matchmaker with Puff? I thought you liked Alex."

"I do like him. Believe it or not, John is the one who pointed out these things to me. I was as ready to accept him as you were. I just started to pay attention to him when I was in his company. John's a homicide cop. He notices stuff like that. "

"I thought John and Alex were friends."

"Yes, but not like you and I are friends. They talk law, sports, and politics. John said they never talk about anything personal. They pound a few beers in fancy glasses, and that's it. To be real friends like you and I are, you have to go way back to childhood. Those two guys just met up a few years ago. I've always told you that you gave Puff a bum rap. Take him away from the Bureau, and he's okay. Have I mentioned to you how obnoxious you've been these past two days?"

"You don't have to tell me because I'm having a hard time believing it myself. It's Puff. He brings out the worst in me. I feel it in my gut that he's setting me up for something. I can't shake the feeling."

"Quinn, how *do* you feel about him. I know seeing him was a shock, but what did you feel?"

Quinn suddenly lost her appetite. "My heart jumped around a little. I thought about the good memories, the bad memories. What might have been, that kind of thing. Then the anger took over, and I reacted. He really hasn't changed that much in eight years."

"Puff is a guy's guy. Everyone likes him. Alex is just Alex. I wish I could explain it better. Women probably look at both of them. A lot. Alex looks chiseled. Puff looks . . . *raw* and . . . *wild*. But he cleans up good. I'd like to see Alex out in the wilderness all messed up."

"Shut up, Sadie. You make all this sound like I have to make a choice. I don't."

"Hey, what are friends for? I fixed dinner, so you clean up. Whom did you make that cake for?"

"I made it for Puff, okay? No, I don't want any, but I will have some more coffee."

"None for me. I think I'm going to head upstairs to bed. Do you mind if I borrow one of your tee shirts? My stuff is all packed in my bags. I don't feel like carrying them in and upstairs."

"Help yourself. You know where they are. Night, Sadie."

After Sadie went upstairs to bed, and Quinn was finishing up with the dishes and tidying up the kitchen, it occurred to her that just around the corner in the next room was the man she'd once thought she was going to spend the rest of her life with. If she wanted to, she could go into the living room, drop to her knees, and kiss him full on the mouth. If she wanted to, she could whisper in his ear all the things she felt about him. She could tell him how he'd hurt her, how she'd cried herself sick over him. She could tell him she'd excelled, worked her ass off, not for herself but for him, just so he would praise her. She'd done everything but prostitute herself for him.

When she was finished in the kitchen, she turned the light on over the stove and took one last look around before turning off the overhead lights. At the last second, she went into the pantry for a stack of newspapers, which she spread by the back door for Winnie.

She tiptoed when she entered the living room to turn off the lights before heading upstairs.

"Quinn, is that you?"

"Yes. I was just going up to bed. Do you need anything before I do?"

"No. I'm okay. Actually, I think my fever broke. I want to thank you for letting me stay and for taking care of me. I know you hate my guts. I'm sorry about your guy, too. I'll make it right with him. I just wanted you to know that. I think I love this dog. I always wanted two golden retrievers, but with my crazy hours I can't have dogs. It wouldn't be fair to them."

Quinn sat down cross-legged by the couch. "I don't hate your guts, and don't worry about Alex. I'll straighten it all out. Do you really feel better?"

"I do. I'm suffocating under all these covers. Earlier I felt like I was freezing. You're okay, Agent Star. I've been meaning to ask you, did you ever hear from your folks?"

Quinn shook her head. "No. I think they forgot about me. Maybe someday they'll come back, and if they don't, that's okay, too. How about your family?"

"You know how Polish families are. Big and boisterous. They're all okay. My mom still asks about you. I go to the farm once a year or so, and my parents come down here, usually in the late fall when it cools off. My dad had knee replacement surgery last month, so they didn't come down. I'm thinking of going up for Christmas. Mom said it was my turn to go out to the field this year with all the nieces and nephews to chop down the tree. I'm looking forward to it. The pond might be frozen, and if it is, we'll have a game of ice hockey. If there's snow, we'll go skiing. My mother still can't believe you actually carried a gun and knew how to shoot it. My dad gets bent out of shape if he sees me stick my gun in my pants instead of the holster."

Quinn wrapped her arms around her knees. "I really liked your family. Any new little ones?"

"Yeah. My brother's wife just had a baby last year on the Fourth of July. They called her Independence. I'm not kidding. They nicknamed her Indy, but, yeah, that's the kid's name. Mom pitched a fit."

Quinn giggled. "Imagine going through life with a name like Independence. That's going to be tough on a little kid. Plus, she's going to have to learn how to spell it."

"I'm thinking she'll probably grow up to be the first female president of the United States." Puff guffawed. Winnie opened both eyes and licked at Puff's cheeks before she closed them again. "I want this dog!"

"Don't go there. Birdie would kill you if she even thought you had those kinds of hankerings. Are you sure you don't want anything before I go upstairs? Maybe some juice or a soda pop."

"Do you know what I would really like? An ice-cold beer. Do you have any?"

"Yes. I'll get you one. Do you want a glass?"

"The bottle is fine."

Quinn returned with the bottle of beer and handed it to him. "Night. Puff?"

"Yeah."

"Are you setting me up for something?"

"What?"

"With the Secret Service job."

"No, Quinn. I'm just doing my job. By the way, don't marry that guy. He's all wrong for you."

"You need to mind your own business, Puff. My personal life is none of your concern."

"I'd say the same thing to any old friend."

"We aren't friends, Puff, old or otherwise. You ruined all that. Just mind your own business, and I'll mind mine, okay?"

"If that's the way you feel about it, okay. I warned you, so my conscience is clear. We'll see you in the morning, won't we, Winnie, old girl." Winnie's long ears wiggled as Puff snuggled against her.

At the top of the stairs, Quinn looked down over the hallway railing. She could see Puff rubbing Winnie's belly. Tears welled in her eyes.

Sometimes, life just wasn't fair.

6

Quinn was up, showered, and dressed by five o'clock. Her bags were packed, her gear piled up by the front door. She heaved a sigh as she recalled how she'd unpacked everything the minute she'd returned from Quantico and her week of intensive training, then repacked everything for her stint at the White House. Puff called the week at Quantico a refresher course. She snorted at that unlikely term. Then again, she and Sadie had aced everything, to Puff's surprise. She snorted again. It was easy to surprise Puff these days. For some reason, she took great pleasure in surprising him.

Today she was reporting to the White House—1600 Pennsylvania Avenue, the most famous address in the world.

She sat on the edge of her bed and stared at her feet. For some reason, she always stared at her feet when she was troubled. Why was Puff involved in her assignment? Once he gave his recommendation, that should have been the end of it as far as the FBI was concerned. Why was she reporting to Puff and not the Secret Service? Was it even remotely possible that because she'd played hardball on the offer, that the powers that be, decided Puff was the one to convince her to take the job? Obviously, but once she was committed, he should have vanished from the picture. Did this unusual arrangement have something to do with Alex's nomination to head up the FBI? Why exactly was this assignment short-term? No one had defined exactly what short-term was in terms of days or months. More important, why were they willing to pay such an outrageous sum of money to her and Sadie to guard the first lady?

What *exactly* was wrong with the first lady? If anything. She tried to remember what Lettie's interests were, what she did during the day at the White House. First ladies always had causes. Did Lettie Jaye have a cause? She racked her brain trying to remember everything Birdie had said about her old friend, the first lady. Lettie wasn't the same old Lettie. She'd said that sometime last week, when she spoke to Quinn at Quantico. Birdie said Lettie had called personally to tell her how delighted she was to have Quinn and Sadie on board. Birdie had also said the first lady assured her she would treat the two women like daughters even though they would be guarding her with their lives. Birdie had also told her that Lettie wasn't her normal exuberant self but had summed it up as White House pressures one could only imagine. Then Birdie had started to pepper her with all sorts of questions and she said she couldn't answer because of security. Birdie had sniffed and said she understood, but she didn't, not really.

Quinn looked at the bedside clock. Alex should

have already called her to wish her luck. She sighed when she remembered Puff talking about his family. His mother had liked her. Which brought Alex's family to the forefront of her mind. They were brusque and professional, much like Alex. Conrad Duval, Alex's father, was the retired governor of the state of Virginia. He was tall and stately, with a glorious head of snow-white hair. He wore a brocade smoking jacket with a white silk ascot in the evenings, which complemented his steel gray eyes. Ardeth Duval, Alex's mother, was a tall woman, slim and graceful. She always wore a strand of pearls, and her hair was just as white as her husband's. She wore Chanel suits. Neither of Alex's parents was warm and fuzzy, and on the few occasions she'd seen the three of them together she hadn't witnessed any Kodak moments. She summed them up as cool and distant.

Alex's sister Allison was her mother's clone and owned a pricey antiques store in Georgetown. Allison was single and four years older than Alex. Alex always said he got along with his family because he rarely saw them. Birdie referred to them as *upper-crust*.

A smile tugged at the corners of her mouth when she remembered the first time Puff had taken her home to meet his family. The moment they entered the warm, cozy house, Sophie Lapufsky had hugged her son so tightly, Puff had bellowed for mercy as the family dog barked for his share of attention. While Puff tussled with the dog, Sophie had hugged Quinn, too, then pulled her into the kitchen, where she handed her a knife, a pot, and a bag of potatoes.

"We're running a little behind, so if you don't mind, I'd appreciate some help."

Puff came up behind her and whispered in her ear. "Peeling potatoes in Mom's kitchen means you're in. It means Mom likes you. She *never* lets anyone do anything in her kitchen. By that I mean guests. You don't mind, do you?"

Quinn smiled. "No, I don't mind, Puff." The truth was, she felt honored.

Quinn remembered how special she'd felt at that moment.

Time to go downstairs to make some coffee. She noticed Winnie on the sofa, next to Puff, who had stayed last night after their late arrival from Quantico.

Birdie, who had come over with Winnie to see them off to the White House, was already in the kitchen, and the coffee was almost finished.

"Where'd my dog get to?" Birdie demanded.

"She's on the sofa with Puff. I guess I should wake him up. I got up early because I knew you were coming over. I think Sadie is still sleeping, too. Birdie, does the first lady have any causes?"

"You mean the kind that make the papers? She sponsors young artists. She's into stuff like that because she paints. Rather well, as a matter of fact. She hosts luncheons from time to time, but that's about it. She doesn't like Washington. She goes back home to South Carolina every chance she gets. She was president of the Junior League, the Garden Club, the Historical Society, and she had a small art gallery on Charlotte Street. Her paintings hang in all the banks, the hotels, and even restaurants in Charleston.

Lettie is a true Southern belle, and no bunch of Washingtonians are going to change that. She might be a little . . . ah . . . flighty, as we would say in our time, but she's sharp as a razor. Get to know her, and you'll like her. Tell her I said hello. Call me and let me know how it's all going. Now, I'd like my dog, so I can get on with my day."

"Birdie, is there anything else you can tell me about the first lady? How's her health, do you know? I read just about everything I could find on her. I came away with the feeling this lady is no one's fool, she's feisty and she's forthright, or am I wrong here?"

"Lettie is Lettie. I don't know how to answer you, Quinn. As far as I know her health is just fine. She always makes a little joke when we talk about not being ready to be worked on by me. She refers to my . . . vocation as a special calling. She's sharp, and she's shrewd. Just like Jimmy Jaye. There are those who say she's a little too artsy, too caught up in her selfish desires. I read that in some article. Lettie just laughed about it. Does she have quirks? I suppose she does. We all have quirks. She likes to go barefoot and wear bib overalls when she paints. Does that count as a quirk?"

Quinn shrugged as she followed Birdie into the living room. Man and dog were sleeping peacefully.

"C'mon, girl, time to leave," Birdie said.

Winnie opened one eye, then closed it.

"Come on, Lapufsky, it's time to rise and shine," Quinn shouted. She clapped her hand over her mouth when Puff's arms and legs flailed the air. He finally landed on the floor.

"Damn you, Star, I was having a great dream. Couldn't you have shaken my shoulder?"

Winnie perched on the edge of the cushion and showed everyone her teeth. "Look, you scared this precious dog, too!"

"It's time for that precious dog to go home," Quinn muttered.

"Let's go, Winnie," Birdie said, dangling the basset's leash.

Winnie sat down and stared at everyone. Puff, propped up on his elbows, shrugged.

"I'm calling you, Winnie. We have to leave now," Birdie pleaded.

Winnie jumped off the couch to land on Puff's stomach, knocking the wind out of him. He fell backward. Winnie bellied up to his neck and started to lick his face and ears. "Didn't I tell you this dog loves me. I love you, too, Winnie, but you gotta go with Birdie."

Winnie's ears flapped as she showed her teeth a second time. She growled when Birdie tried to fasten the leash onto her collar.

"Why are you both looking at me like that? She knew I was at death's door last week, when she stayed with me all night and decided she saved my life. Now she sees me hale and hearty and *knows* that's what she did. You hear that all the time on television about how a dog's body warmth saved someone. Now she thinks . . . I don't know what the hell she thinks," he mumbled defensively.

Winnie continued to lick and nip at Puff's bristly chin.

Birdie, decked out in a brilliant dress festooned with red and purple tulips, sat down on the end of the chair, her dress spreading out like a crinoline, her worn Birkenstocks tapping the floor. A tear rolled down her cheek as she pleaded with the basset to come to her.

"I'll carry her out to the car, Birdie. Once you get her home, she'll be fine. She's a real sweet dog. I like dogs. I guess she could tell. Where are you parked?" Puff asked.

"I double-parked in front, right behind your car," Birdie said unhappily.

"I'll take her out, unless, of course, you want the good citizens of Georgetown to see you in that getup," Quinn said.

"Fine with me."

Winnie snapped and snarled as Quinn grabbed her around the middle. She gave her rear end a no-nonsense swat. Winnie threw back her head and protested before she tried to wiggle out of Quinn's arms. "Shake it, Birdie, this dog is heavy. Open the door!"

Puff jogged over to the door and thrust it open.

Back in the house, breathless with the effort of getting the dog into Birdie's car, Quinn eyeballed the AAD of the FBI, and said, "Birdie hates your guts, and she said you are never allowed to wear her nightgowns, ever, as in ever again. She is pissed off big-time."

Puff snorted his way to the bathroom, slamming the door behind him.

All Quinn could do was shake her head from side to side as she made her way to the kitchen.

• • •

Sixteen-hundred Pennsylvania Avenue. The most famous address in the world.

Quinn could feel her palms start to sweat. She could feel her heart pounding inside her chest. She wondered if Sadie felt the same way. Probably.

Puff was the lead car, she was second, and Sadie was behind her as they drove up to the security gate. While they waited to be cleared, Quinn looked upward. The flag was flying over the White House. It meant the president was in. In all the years she'd lived in Washington, she'd never toured the White House. Birdie said she'd taken her once when she was little, but she couldn't remember the trip. She'd never gone to the Capitol, the Lincoln Memorial, or the Washington Monument either. She had gone to the Vietnam Memorial with Alex. Afterward, she thought of it as a life-altering experience, the way in which it had brought home to her the reality of the Vietnam War.

Puff was so comfortable in these surroundings, but then why shouldn't he be. As AAD of the FBI, he probably spent a lot of time there. She could tell that he knew his way around, and the way he was chatting with the guard made her more certain than ever that he was a frequent visitor to the White House. Alex had never mentioned being to the White House. But as the nominee to head the FBI, he must have conferred with the president. And surely he would have been there when he was nominated to be a federal judge.

They were moving. She was officially on the White House grounds. Her heart lurched in her chest.

They parked their cars. Puff got out of his car first

and waited for them. "We're going in through the West Wing. The first lady's secretary is going to meet us and take us up to the family quarters. Stay close and don't talk to anyone."

"You're getting off on this, aren't you? Coming here must be a power trip for you."

Puff didn't bother to respond. Sadie rolled her eyes. "This is exciting, isn't it? I can't wait to see the Lincoln Bedroom," Sadie said.

Puff halted. "Sit," he said, motioning to twin Queen Anne chairs.

Quinn bristled. "Don't tell me to sit like I'm a dog."

"Would you please take a seat. I have to check in with the first lady's secretary. Don't touch anything."

"Just what kind of clearance does Puff have?" Sadie whispered.

"I was wondering the same thing myself. High, very high would be my guess. He is the AAD of the FBI and that carries its own clout. Sit and don't touch anything," she quipped.

Puff, Quinn noticed, had disappeared. He didn't reappear for thirty-five minutes. "Follow me. You're having breakfast in the family quarters instead of the dining room. It's much more informal and Let . . . the first lady feels more comfortable among her own things."

"You sound like a tired tour guide," Quinn snapped.

"I am tired, but I feel good. Whatever bug I had last week, I hope you don't get it. Look sharp now. I really sang your praises, so don't go making a liar out of me. That goes for you, too, Sadie."

"Gotcha," Sadie said, snapping off a smart salute.

She appeared out of nowhere, a slim little lady in a swirling chiffon dress the color of a summer rainbow. With shoes to match. In November. Butterflies stuck on the ends of bobby pins adorned her gray hair, which was fashionably cut and styled. Pearls graced her long, thin neck. She wore a plain, wide, gold wedding band on her left hand.

Quinn's first impression of the first lady was, *she's beautiful but has the saddest eyes I've ever seen. A hundred and two pounds soaking-wet* was her second thought.

"Ma'am, this is Special Agent Quinn Star, and this is Special Agent Sadie Wilson. Agents Star and Wilson, this is Mrs. Letecia Jaye, the first lady of the United States." His voice was so solemn, so respectful, Quinn blinked in surprise.

"You can leave now, Mr. Lapufsky. I can take it from here," the first lady said. "The president won't be joining us as planned. It seems he had a meeting with the Secretary of Labor he forgot about.

"How would you like me to address you?" the first lady asked the two agents.

"Quinn and Sadie will be fine, Mrs. Jaye."

"I'd like it if you would call me Lettie in private. Hearing my name helps me to remember I'm a real person aside from being the first lady. Please, sit down and help yourselves. I shooed all the help out. There's no need for them to know my business so they can write a book about it. My hands are a little shaky this morning, so I would appreciate it if you'd pour the coffee and juice. We have everything. Grits, eggs, Jimmy Dean sausage, bacon, muffins, toast, and fresh fruit. The White House chefs prepare everything.

"Mr. Lapufsky . . . I guess I should refer to him as Acting Associate Director Lapufsky, sent me such glowing reports on you two agents. My husband was especially impressed. The AAD called you the cream of the crop. It's a sterling compliment in my opinion.

"I think you young ladies are going to do just fine. I can tell just by looking at you that we're going to get along well. By the way, how is Birdie? I haven't talked to her for a while. Is she still doing that . . . that . . . mortuary thing?"

"My aunt is fine, ma'am, and she sends her regards. Yes, she still . . . helps out at the various mortuaries."

"That must be a calling of some kind. I consider it a . . . vocation. She does that, and I paint. Later, I'll show you some of my paintings. I can't paint here. Did they tell you no one wants to guard me?" She fiddled with her wedding band, sliding it up and over her knuckle, then sliding it back down. "I requested you girls personally. Birdie told me she explained it all to you."

"No, ma'am, no one said anything about no one wanting to guard you, and, yes, Birdie did explain it all to me."

"I got rid of all of them. They couldn't relate to me, and I couldn't relate to them. They were a cold lot. You two look like you have some spunk. Do you?"

"Yes, ma'am, we have spunk," Sadie said.

"I know your whole story, Quinn. I called Birdie a while back. That's why I asked for you. I'm told you two struck a hard bargain. I applaud that." The first lady chuckled.

"Yes, ma'am."

"May I ask why," Lettie said, stirring the grits on her plate.

"You said you read our files. AAD Lapufsky had something to do with it, ma'am, and I wasn't sure I wanted to babysit you," Quinn said honestly.

Lettie's fist shot in the air. "I knew you would tell me the truth. I knew it! AAD Lapufsky said you would probably talk around it and not own up to the truth. We can get down and dirty, if we have to, girls. I'm one of you. Those other agents were like blisters on my rear end."

"No kidding," Sadie said in awe.

Quinn chewed on her Jimmy Dean sausage, her mind racing. She risked a glance in Sadie's direction, but her partner was busy filling a side dish with fresh fruit, her own face a mixture of surprise.

"We can talk some more later. I'm rather tired, so I think I'll take a little nap. When I wake up, we can take a walk in the Rose Garden. I try to get some fresh air every day."

"What time do you get up, ma'am?" Quinn asked.

"Around seven. This morning I woke up at seven-thirty. If you'll follow me, I'll show you to your rooms; then you can come back and finish your breakfast. I'm going to want to see your guns later, too. Perhaps you could teach me how to shoot. I want to make this a fun experience for you."

Quinn looked down at the watch on her wrist. It wasn't quite nine o'clock. *A fun experience.* Puff's warning of, "Don't take your eyes off the first lady," rang in her ears.

"Ma'am, we'll be right outside your door. Would you please keep it ajar."

"If I do that, the smoke will spiral out into the hall. I burn cinnamon in the bathroom so you can't tell. I fibbed, okay. We used to do that all the time. A Southern belle, that's what they call me, never lets anyone see her smoke. I'm addicted," she mumbled around the cigarette hanging from her mouth. When her eyes started to water, she took the cigarette out of her mouth. "Can you imagine what the newspapers would say if they knew I smoked. They've been on me about the way I dress, my hair, and my Southern drawl. All they want to do is change me. They say I have to conform to the images of other first ladies. I don't want to be like the other first ladies. I just want to be myself. They make jokes about me on those late-night talk shows. I know about it because I watch those shows. I'm a fitful sleeper."

"You need to tell us things like that, ma'am. Why don't we all go back to the dining room and have a cigarette and . . . talk. We can burn the cinnamon in the kitchen. From now on you don't have to worry about hiding *anything* from us. Sadie and I are going to be twelve and twelve. I'm taking the first shift, and she gets the second. Every three days, we'll alternate. We might change that or switch up. We're going to play it by ear."

"Birdie said you were smart. Let's do that. I didn't know you girls smoked. It's not good for you. You need to give some thought to quitting."

The first lady puffed furiously. "If I promise not to be any trouble, can you both stay with me. You can sleep when I sleep. If that will cost more money, I think we can arrange it."

Quinn poured more coffee into her cup. She was enjoying her cigarette, too. She felt her scalp start to prickle. "This detail only calls for one agent. Is there a reason, ma'am? Sadie and I will try to accommodate you any way we can."

The first lady pursed her lips and mouthed the words, "We'll talk when we go for our walk." She crushed out her cigarette and lit a second one. "I get a chest X-ray every six months," she blurted. "So far so good. Does Birdie smoke? Everyone I know who quit smoking has died."

"How strange," was all Quinn could think of to say. "Birdie, Sadie, and I quit at the same time," she added, puffing as furiously as the first lady. Sadie looked like she wanted to be somewhere else as she, too, puffed away on her cigarette. "Sometimes we cheat," she said through a cloud of smoke.

"Jackie Kennedy was a secret smoker. I think it's better than being a secret drinker. I do drink, though. Sometimes. Not a lot. Well, sometimes a lot. Like when the press goes after me. Then I drink AND smoke. All I want to do is go home. I can do what I want when I'm home. They keep telling me I can, and then they say I can't. I hate it here. I absolutely hate it here."

Quinn looked into her coffee cup, trying to come up with something intelligent to say. When she couldn't come up with anything, she lit a second cigarette. She was afraid to look at Sadie.

"Do you know how I know when my husband is

here? You know, my husband, the president? I go outside to see if the flag is flying overhead. He's always gone in the morning when I get up, and I go to sleep before he does, so I hardly ever see him. He must be here because the flag is flying. All right, I'm done smoking. Let's light the cinnamon and go outside for a walk. Dress warm. It's cold. I never had children. I wish I had a daughter. A son would be nice. Maybe one of each. Jimmy Jaye wanted a boy, and I wanted a girl with blond curls. I just love those little black patent leather slippers little girls wear with the white ruffled socks. Should we bring the cigarettes or not? I used to have a mind of my own. I don't know what happened to it," the first lady dithered. "I never used to talk this fast either. Probably the same thing that happened to my husband. He's not my husband, you know," she whispered. "Maybe they put something in the water."

Oh my God, Quinn thought.

"Ma'am, neither Sadie nor I know the way around here yet. AAD Lapufsky gave us a floor plan, but we haven't had time to study it. Can you wait a few minutes?"

"Oh for heaven's sake, it isn't hard once you get used to it. I'll lead the way. Do you want to peek into the Oval Office? We can stroll right by it. Just pretend you're not looking. That's what I do when I feel like spying on *them*."

It took Sadie three tries before she could clear her throat, and she wasn't smoking.

Quinn slipped into her coat, feeling as if she were about to enter the Twilight Zone.

Outside in the crisp November air, the three women walked abreast of each other. "The newspapers say I'm reclusive. Did you know that?"

"No," both agents said in unison.

"I'm reclusive because they won't let me out of here. They say I have severe allergies, and I'm incapacitated. I don't have any allergies. I want to go home. I'm going to. I want to be in my own house for Christmas. I want to see my friends. They won't allow me to invite them here. They're an embarrassment, they said."

"Who is they?" Quinn asked. *I'm going to kill you, Puff.* "Trips have to be planned in advance, ma'am. As you know, the house, the grounds—the entire area—have to be secured and the local authorities have to be notified."

"I know all that. When we first got here, they let me do anything I wanted. It's just these last ten months or so that things have gone awry. I said I wanted to go home back in September. Jimmy Jaye said I could go, then he said I was needed here. He didn't say why, though. He never gives reasons, and as the wife of the president of the United States, I have to listen. If I decide not to listen, I'll have to get a divorce. I love Jimmy Jaye. Everyone loves Jimmy Jaye. They say he's like Will Rogers. I gave up Jimmy Jaye to our country. I'm sorry I did that. We had a nice life before we moved here. He types me notes. Jimmy Jaye doesn't know how to type. He does have lovely penmanship, though. We learned those ovals and pushpulls back in grade school. That's why our script flows. My own is almost as good as Jimmy

Jaye's. It's almost Thanksgiving. I'd like to be back home for all the holidays. I can come back after the New Year. Can you talk to them and arrange it? I'd like to go as soon as possible. I'm a prisoner here," the first lady said breathlessly.

She's a babbler, Quinn thought. *How can she talk so much and not take a deep breath in between sentences,* she wondered as she digested the information Letecia Jaye had just spouted. Was she mentally ill? If that was the case, somehow, Birdie would have gotten wind of the fact. Were *they,* whoever *they* were, afraid she would speak out of turn, say something to embarrass the president? Or were the mysterious *they* a figment of the first lady's imagination? What was the problem?

"I'll put the wheels in motion, ma'am. Is there anything else you think we should know?"

"Anything else? It would fill a book. You can't repeat or say anything I'm telling you. You know that, don't you?"

Both agents nodded.

"I'm telling you, the man who says he is president is not my husband. What I mean is the president is my husband, but there's someone else who looks and acts like him. He's here, too. I think he lives here. You don't believe me! I can see it on your faces. At first, I couldn't believe it either. I know my Jimmy Jaye. Sometimes he calls me on the phone and says silly things. They make me laugh. They want everyone to think there's something wrong with me. There's nothing wrong with me. I should know my husband, shouldn't I?"

"Of course," Quinn said.

"Are you on any medication, Mrs. Jaye?" Sadie asked.

"I knew you were going to ask me that. I take an aspirin a day, and I take a pill for my cholesterol, a low dosage. That's it. I am not crazy, but they want you to think I am."

"Why?" Quinn asked.

"I don't know. Maybe it's because that man isn't my husband, and I know it. I think that's why they try to keep us apart. I heard them talking, and one of them said not to worry about me because I was a dumb Southern belle gone to seed."

"Ma'am, who are *they?*"

"The people who are around my husband all the time. When we first got here, most of his advisors were friends that Jimmy Jaye hired or appointed. You have to do that because of all the help they gave during the campaign. One by one, they left or were ridiculed so much they just couldn't take it anymore. Everyone in my husband's administration now is new. I don't even know their names. The ones who left, Jimmy Jaye's and my friends, never call us anymore. That's another reason why I want to go home. I want to find out why. *They* don't want me to do that."

"Do you ever see your husband? Do you have conversations with him? Do you have dinner or breakfast together?" Quinn asked desperately, her mind going in all directions.

"Of course we see each other. We're married. Just because we have separate bedrooms, it doesn't mean we don't live together. We had separate bedrooms back home, too. Jimmy Jaye snores and is a poor sleeper. It works for both of us. We had dinner yesterday. Then Jimmy said some ambassador was coming by at around eight-thirty, and he had to go back downstairs. They budget my time with my husband. Sometimes I don't see him for days. That's why I always have to check to see if the flag is flying. I've tried to go to the Oval Office, but they always tell me he's in meetings or he can't be disturbed.

"We talked about home, my painting, and all our old friends. Jimmy Jaye was really sad that all our friends deserted him. He said he called a few of them, and, do you believe this, they wouldn't take his calls. They wouldn't take a call from the president of the United States!" Her outrage was palpable.

"What do you think is going on?" Quinn asked carefully.

"I think there's one big conspiracy going on. This isn't polite to say, but we're all girls here. Everyone is covering their asses."

"But why?" Sadie demanded.

"I don't know," the first lady wailed. "They listen to my phone calls, too. I know they do. Our telephone lines are down a lot. I think they just unplug them somehow. In the White House, how can phone lines be down? It would be in all the newspapers and on the television news in a minute. I wanted to go to a drugstore, and they said there were no drivers available. If I want to go somewhere, I have to make it known weeks in advance. If I don't get away from here, I'm going to lose my mind."

"Why don't we have a cigarette?" Sadie said

soothingly. "We can sit right here on this bench, and you can light up."

"That's a splendid idea. Now, aren't you glad I brought the cigarettes? If they catch us, they'll probably make us put them out."

"Over my dead body," Quinn said.

"Oh, I like your attitude!" the first lady said, firing up her cigarette with a butane lighter. "When I spoke to Birdie last week, she said I was going to love you girls. She said you wouldn't let anything happen to me."

"Our Quinn is a lean, mean, fighting machine. She graduated first in our class at the Academy. She could take on all those guys standing over there outside, what's that, the Oval Office?" Sadie said proudly.

"Really? Knowing that makes me feel so *safe*. Yes, that's the Oval Office. Do you think I'm a nutcase?" the first lady asked bluntly.

"No!" both agents said at the same moment.

Lettie Jaye literally purred her contentment as she puffed away on her menthol cigarette.

"Company at two o'clock," Sadie said.

"Oh dear," Letecia Jaye said, swallowing a mouthful of smoke. She coughed and sputtered.

"I'll take care of it, ma'am," Quinn said.

Palms out in front of her, her coat opened to reveal her shoulder holster, Quinn took two steps forward and stopped. "And you would be?"

"Agent Martin."

"I'm Agent Star. What can I do for you?" Quinn eyed the tall agent with the dark glasses. She watched as he removed them to see her better. He looked like all the other agents, confident, alert but relaxed. She was surprised at his bright blue eyes for some reason. He looked to be about forty or so, with a receding hairline. Those blue eyes were staring her down. She had a wild, crazy thought. With her refresher course behind her, she knew without a doubt that if she had to, she could take this guy to the ground and not break a sweat. Agent Martin looked like he was thinking the same thing.

"I'd appreciate it if you would put your cigarettes out. It doesn't look good for the first lady to be smoking where she can be seen."

"The first lady's husband knows she smokes. I agree it's not a healthy habit, but they are her lungs. She lives here, Agent Martin. As I see it, as long as she isn't harming anyone or anything, I think she can do pretty much whatever she wants to do, and that includes smoking cigarettes. The first lady is my responsibility as of eight-fifteen this morning. What that means is, buzz off, Agent Martin, unless you want to bring it to a test."

The agent's eyes narrowed when Sadie stood up, her coat open just the way Quinn's was. The first lady puffed, smiled, and waved to the agent. Three perfect smoke rings spiraled upward. To Quinn's relief, Agent Martin retreated.

"Oh, I'm so glad I have you two. It's time to go back to the house. The light is halfway decent right now," she said, looking upward. "I think I'll paint for a while. I guess I'm not going to take a nap. All this crisp air has given me energy. No more cigarettes till after lunch. I'm trying to cut down. Maybe I'll even quit. One of these days."

"That sounds like a plan. I have a few calls to make, ma'am, and I want to set up my computer. Sadie will be with you. Do you have a problem with that?"

"No. Will you see about getting permission for me to go home?"

"I'm going to get right on it, ma'am."

"Do you like it here, girls?"

"We haven't been here long enough to know that yet, ma'am," Sadie said. "I have to say it's a very prestigious address. I imagine the grounds are beautiful in the spring and summer."

"Would you like to walk by way of the South Lawn? That's where Marine One lands. Oh, let's do that another time. They take away all your rights when you move in here. I don't have any money in my purse. Do you know why that is? It's because I can't go anywhere to spend it, so their thinking is why should I have money. Back home in Charleston, I used to go to the bank every Monday morning. Then I'd go to the dry cleaner and from there to the grocery store and the produce market. Sometimes I would meet friends and we'd stop for a glass of sweet tea. They don't even know what sweet tea is here. It's sad," Lettie said. "I didn't know it was going to be like this. I didn't know I was going to have to lie and pretend my way through four years. I didn't know the people of this country were going to make fun of me. They don't even know me. How can decent people do that? I won't let them make me into something I'm not. That would be cheating the very people who voted for Jimmy Jaye to run this country and to make things better for them. He's done a wonderful job. Everyone wins but me," she cried pitifully.

They entered the family quarters. Quinn looked around, noticing the furnishings for the first time. All the rooms looked like they were straight out of *Southern Living.*

Quinn shed her coat and reached for Sadie's to hang them up. The first lady carried her coat back to her room. She waved as she made her way to her assigned bedroom. She was stunned to see her computer set up and plugged in. All she had to do was unpack and make her calls. It took her all of fifteen minutes to empty out her suitcase and overnight bag. Her cell phone was in her hand a second later. Who to call first, Alex or Puff? Since she was on the job, she should call Puff first. She punched in the numbers and waited.

"Acting Associate Director Lapufsky."

"You better tell me what the real deal here is, or I'm walking out," Quinn hissed into the phone. "Is she a mental case or not?"

"Honest to God, Quinn, I don't know. They said there was some kind of problem between her and the president. She gets vague, can't remember things, and wants everything done yesterday. They want her watched twenty-four/seven. Whatever you do, don't take your eyes off her."

"She wants to go home. How do I handle that? She said they won't let her go. She said a lot of things I'm having trouble with. You better be leveling with me, Puff."

"When does she want to go?"

"The sooner the better. Two days, three. Four at the most. Don't even think about stalling me on this. I know my job description. She's ready to go *now*. By the way, she says the guy that's president isn't her husband. I think she thinks there are two presidents. Do what you want with that one. You tapping this phone?"

"It's the White House, for God's sake. It's the most secure building in the world. Why would they tap your silly cell phone? Stop worrying."

"You didn't answer my question? Are they?"

"Yeah."

"What about my computer? Did they program something onto it so they can monitor it?"

"Probably."

"You know what, she's right; it is like being in a prison. That's a violation of my privacy. You can't invade my privacy. I'm an American citizen."

"They can do whatever they want when you're in the White House. Suck it up, Agent Star."

"Strange ears listening to this conversation prevent me from telling you what you can do and how you can do it, Lapufsky!" Quinn clicked the OFF button. She sat down in an old Charleston rocker. She kicked off her shoes and stared at her feet. When she didn't receive any form of enlightenment, she allowed her gaze to sweep across her new home away from home. Everything was either yellow or lime green mixed with white. On a sunny day with the draperies open, she would need sunglasses. On this dreary November day, it was almost cheerful.

She saw them then, Letecia Jaye's paintings. And they were beautiful. The lines were clean and strong, the colors blended perfectly. Birdie was right, the first lady had talent.

Time to call Alex. She wondered if he would take her call this time or have his secretary tell her he was unavailable.

7

Ezra Lapufsky mopped at the perspiration dotting his brow. He felt a moment of panic when he realized he might be suffering a relapse. While he'd felt like crap all day, he had been able to function satisfactorily much to his own surprise.

He looked around his cluttered office. He needed someone to come in and straighten it up. But if he did that, he'd never be able to find anything. A tired-looking rubber plant sitting in the corner drew his attention. Usually he was pretty good about watering it. Even though he had his coat on and it was hot in the building, he walked down the hall to the water fountain to fill a Styrofoam cup. To his delight, he carried it back without spilling it. Tomorrow he would trim off the dried, yellow leaves and give it another dose of water. At the moment, he just wanted to go home and sack out. He could pick up some Chinese and maybe some Tsingtao beer. Some aspirin, a nice hot shower, and he'd hit the sack.

Normally, he was the last to leave, but now that he was calling it a day at five o'clock, the elevator was crowded with chattering women discussing the freezing weather conditions, icy roads, turkey recipes, and Julia Roberts's latest movie. He couldn't remember the last time he'd gone to the movies. He knew it was cold outside, but twenty degrees for November was a bit much if the chatty ladies were correct. As for turkey, his mother always took care of that. He hoped he could make it home for Thanksgiving. He did love stuffing, and those little carrots his mother made that were sweeter than honey.

Puff stood aside as the gaggle of people exited the elevator. His ears perked up when he heard a joyous, high-pitched bark. He saw the whirlwind, felt the air stir when Winnie beelined for him. He saw Birdie standing off to the left, resplendent in a bright orange-flowered dress, her coat over her arm. He immediately dropped to his haunches to cuddle the dog. His eyes were full of questions as people stopped to smile and grin.

"Is something wrong, Birdie? Did something happen to . . . ?"

"No, no, nothing's wrong. Well, yes, something is wrong. Quinn is fine. She called today from the White House. It's Winnie. All she did was cry today. She sat by the kitchen door and wailed and howled till I thought I would go out of my mind. She was fine last week, but seeing you again has done something to her. I never should have brought her over this morning. We have a problem here, Ezra."

"Birdie, I'm sorry. I'm really sorry. What do you want me to do?"

"I don't know. I thought your being an FBI bigwig, that you could come up with something."

Puff shrugged helplessly.

"Would you consider coming home with me and perhaps staying over for a few days? I have a nice leg of lamb in the oven with little new potatoes and mint jelly. My house is warm, the way you like it. It breaks my heart to see Winnie so unhappy. Look at her. She's lying on your feet. She loves you."

Leg of lamb sounded better than Chinese out of a carton. He didn't live that far from Birdie. "Okay, Birdie, it's a deal. What about tomorrow, when I have to go to work?" Loved by a dog. Did it get any better than that?

"Winnie is very smart. If she sees you in the guest room and your things are there, she'll know you're coming back. So, will you spend a few days with us?"

"Sure. Should I follow you or go home first and pick up a few things?"

"I guess you should take Winnie with you and meet me at home. I'll have dinner ready by the time you get there. I have to go out tonight, so it's good that you can make it. Winnie hates being left alone."

"Okay. Birdie, does this mean I have to wear your nightgown again?"

"I don't know. Let's play it by ear." A lone tear rolled down her wrinkled cheek. Puff stared at her, unsure of what he should do. In the end he put his arms around her, and whispered, "We'll work something out. Winnie is your dog. She loves you, and I won't steal her away."

"You might not have a choice, Ezra."

It all happened within five seconds of exiting the Hoover Building. One minute, Birdie was ahead of him by two steps, her Birkenstocks slapping the pavement; then she was flat on her back. Winnie yelped and dragged him sideways before he could trample her. He was on his knees a second later, cell phone in hand. The moment he heard her cry of pain, he pressed 911.

"Easy, Birdie, easy. I called nine-one-one. Don't move. You didn't hit your head, did you?"

"No. It's my leg. I slipped on a patch of ice. If it wasn't ice, then my leg just went out from under me."

He could see she was in pain. Five minutes later, the ambulance screeched to a stop, and the EMS workers hit the ground running. The cursory examination took all of five seconds. In the blink of an eye they had Birdie on a stretcher that they lifted into the back of the ambulance. "I'll go with you," Puff said lifting one leg to step into the back of the vehicle.

"No dogs, sir."

"Yes, dogs. FBI," Puff said, flashing his badge.

Birdie spoke through clenched teeth. "No, Ezra, they won't allow you to take Winnie into the hospital. You'll be without a car. Take her home. I'll be fine. I needed a new hip anyway. I heard them say it's broken. That happens to people my age. Take care of Winnie and don't tell Quinn. Promise me."

"Sure. Sure," Puff said, backing out of the ambulance.

"Ezra?"

"Yes."

"Will you stand in for me at McNally's tonight?"

"McNally's. Sure, be happy to. What about Winnie?"

"You can take herrrrr with youuuuu."

"The shot is working. Move it, mister. FBI or not,

we have a job to do here," one of the EMS workers said, grabbing the door to close it.

"Yeah, yeah, okay."

"We need a statement," one of DC's finest said.

Puff gave his name and told the policeman what had happened. He was sweating again as he scooped up Winnie and carried her to his car in the parking lot.

Forty minutes later, Puff walked around to the back of Birdie's house. *Some FBI agent I am. I didn't think to ask Birdie for her key.* Winnie whined at his feet. "No key, girl. I guess I have to break one of these panes of glass. I sure hope your owner doesn't have her alarm system on." He looked around for a rock. Winnie waddled over to a small iron bench and started to bark. "I'm working on it, girl." Winnie threw back her head and howled, a sound that carried up and down the street. "Jesus, Winnie, what was that all about? What? Oh, okay. Good girl!" Plastered to the back of the bench was steel gray electrical tape that held a key to the kitchen door. "We're in business, baby. Whoever said dogs were dumb? Maybe you should pee or something. That's a nice-looking bush over there. Go for it, Winnie."

Puff waited while Winnie debated the situation, then huffed and puffed her way inside, where she squatted on the carpet by the back door. Puff shrugged. His old dog Jack used to do the same thing even though his mother denied it.

Inside the warm kitchen, Puff shed his overcoat and gloves, tossing them on a chair next to the dishwasher. Winnie eyeballed the gloves, and, when they didn't fall off his coat, she rammed the chair sideways. The gloves slid to the floor. She scooped them up and trotted off, her long tail swinging from side to side.

Puff sighed as he looked around. Birdie's kitchen reminded him of his mother's kitchen. It smelled the same way. He sniffed. Yep, he could smell lemon, vanilla, roasted meat, and cinnamon. His eye fell on a still-warm pie sitting on the counter. He hoped it was apple raisin with little bits of chopped pecans in it.

He opened the oven door and removed the roasting pan. His mother always said to let meat sit before you sliced it. She never said what you were supposed to do while you were letting the meat "sit."

Then he took his cell phone out of his shirt pocket. He called George Washington Hospital, identified himself, and waited. Within minutes he was told Birdie was in surgery. He needed a game plan here. Before he could think twice about his promise to Birdie, he punched in Quinn's cell phone number.

Quinn identified herself in a no-nonsense manner. He rattled off the events of the past hour. He listened to her squawk her outrage at not being notified. "Listen to me, Agent Star, you are now a Secret Service Agent. Your personal life no longer exists. You have a job to do, and you leave when and if I say you can leave. Birdie is in surgery. She made me promise *not* to call you, a promise I've just broken. I'm going to go to the hospital after I go to McNally's and stand in for her. What am I supposed to do? Do you know? First, though, I'm going to eat and feed Winnie. I guess I'll be staying here unless you have some objections, and if you do, I'll probably just ignore them."

Puff listened to Quinn's explanation of what he was supposed to do at McNally's, and his face went white. "I can do that. Hell, yes, I can do that," he muttered. "Of course I'll call you when I get back here. All right, I'll call you from the hospital. I'll arrange for a private duty nurse. Two? Okay two. See, see," he bellowed. "This is a perfect example of why you weren't ready to go to the Secret Service years ago. You're getting emotional. There's no room for crying and emotion. You are now a Secret Service Agent, so start acting like one. That's an order, Star. Your aunt is fine, and I'm going to make sure she stays that way. I'll take care of the dog, too. Stop worrying. I'm getting a little tired of hearing you tell me to kiss your butt. Put up or shut up. How's Alex?" Puff reared back when he heard the click in his ear. Emotional females!

Time to eat!

He sliced and mashed, then gorged. He was just about to cut into the succulent-looking pie when Winnie made her appearance. She looked up at him with soulful brown eyes. "I have your plate all ready, Winnie. See, I cut the lamb up real small, mashed it in with the potatoes, and string beans. I even put a little gravy on it. We used to do that for Jack, and he lived to be nineteen. It was the *vegetables*. Okay, okay, I'm going to sit down here with you and eat my pie. I used to do that with Jack when he'd get sick. Mom did, too. Birdie's coming back, Winnie. It's a sort of vacation. I'm going to stay here with you. I'll go to the office a little later and come home a little earlier. I don't want you getting separation anxiety. I heard about that on *Animal Planet*. You want some pie? I gotta take the nuts out. Nuts aren't good for dogs. You get the crust.

"I'm sitting here on someone else's kitchen floor

eating pie and talking to a dog. Then I'm going to a . . . funeral home to . . . to view some dead bodies, after which I will pass on my opinion. Then I will go home to my apartment to pick up some stuff, go to the hospital, and come back here. I might be able to go to bed at some point tonight. I forgot. I'm also going to have to listen to Agent Star ream me out again. You know what, Winnie, she got better-looking. She's full of herself, though. She hates my guts, too. Is she grateful that I got her the job at the White House? No, she is not. Okay, time to get this show on the road."

Winnie sat up and waited expectantly. "Look, girl, this is the way it's going. We're going upstairs and pick out a room. I'll turn down the bed so you know where I'm sleeping. I'm coming back." Winnie's tail dropped down between her legs, a signal she wasn't buying his story. He remembered Birdie's words to leave his clothes behind. Hell, he could do that. All he had to do was borrow something of Birdie's and change when he got to his apartment.

Upstairs, he chose a room at the end of the hallway with its own bathroom. Later he would check out the decor. First, he had to find something to wear. He stripped down to his boxers before he trotted back down the hall to what he thought was Birdie's bedroom. In the closet he found a gray sweat suit that he immediately donned. He looked into the pier glass and, in spite of himself, burst out laughing. The sleeves of the sweatshirt came only to the middle of his arms, the pants to a little below his knees. No one would notice once he put on his overcoat.

Puff looked around for Winnie, who was nowhere

to be seen. He whistled for her as he made his way back to his room. She wasn't there either. His shoes and socks were gone. In their place was one of Quinn's red ladybug boots and Alex Duval's left shoe. He turned around and looked at Winnie, who was sitting in the doorway. "I get it. I really get it. Shoes are for walking. If you keep my shoes, I'm coming back. Okay. Listen, my stuff is here. You wait right here till I get back."

Winnie barked and barked. With approval or disapproval, he didn't know.

Forty-five minutes later, Puff sailed into his apartment building to the amusement of the other tenants, some arriving, some leaving. "I'm undercover," was the best thing he could come up with as he flashed his credentials and bolted for the elevator.

It was the witching hour when Puff was finally led to Birdie's hospital room. He felt something tug at his heart when he stared down at the little lady he'd always liked. "Don't talk, Birdie. I just wanted to hang around long enough to tell you the doctors say you're going to be fine. They put a pin in your hip. They say you're going to need a hip replacement at some point, but that's down the road, so we don't have to worry about it now. You're going to need some recovery and rehabilitation time, but I think you can handle it.

"Winnie's fine. Your dinner was excellent. I'll clean up when I get back. I can stay at your house as long as you want me to. I don't want you to worry about Winnie. I can go home at lunchtime to check on her. I . . . ah . . . went to McNally's like you wanted me to. Miss Olong looked . . . hell, Birdie, she looked . . . *dead.* I guess that's because she was dead. They painted her up some, and she had on a purple dress. I think it was purple. I signed your name in the book and got one of those little cards for you. Mr. McNally's son said they put those sparkly things in her hair like you told them to. I forget what you call them. Mr. McNally senior said to tell you he hopes you have a speedy recovery. He said he's wary of setting someone out until *you* look them over. The nurses want you to sleep, so I'll be going."

"Quinn?" Birdie said sleepily.

It was a question. "I told her, Birdie. I had to. She's all right, and everything else is fine. I'm sorry I broke my promise, but Quinn would never forgive either one of us if we didn't tell her you're in the hospital. If I can't get here tomorrow, I'll call you."

On his way to the car, all Puff could think about was how relieved he felt that Birdie hadn't asked him to stand in for her again at McNally's. He didn't want to think about *that.*

With almost no traffic at that hour of the night, Puff made good time returning to the yellow house on Connecticut Avenue.

He was dead on his feet when he finished cleaning up the kitchen. All he wanted was a hot shower, a cold beer, and a comfortable bed. All were within his reach as he marched up the steps and down the hall.

Winnie was waiting on the bed for him. She'd pulled down the covers and was lying on one of the pillows. He burst out laughing when he saw the nightgown he'd seen earlier at the foot of Birdie's bed. Winnie must have dragged it into his room. God, if he could only see inside her mind. He swigged on the cold Budweiser in between brushing his teeth and unpacking his bag. Winnie watched his every move.

While he gargled, Winnie howled as she pawed the pillow. "I have to do this," he explained. *You're talking to a dog, Lapufsky. You're verging on delirium.*

"I'm not wearing that nightgown even if you bark all night. What we're going to do here, is wad it into a ball and stuff it between our respective pillows. That way you won't miss her so much."

Clad in pajama bottoms and white tee shirt, Puff climbed into bed. He was asleep within seconds. The minute he started to snore lightly, Winnie hopped off the bed. She trotted down the steps and out to the kitchen, where she peed by the back door. She looked around, then proceeded to walk through all the rooms before padding back upstairs. She stopped by Birdie's room, walked in, circled the bed, sniffed at her slippers, then waddled back down the hall to the guest room where Puff slept. She hopped up onto the trunk sitting at the bottom of the bed and onto the bed. She bellied up to the pillow, shoved at the quilt, and lay down next to Birdie's nightgown, one paw on Puff's shoulder.

Man and dog slept peacefully.

On the morning of her second day at the White House, Quinn listened unashamedly outside the door of the first lady's sitting room. She motioned for Sadie to join her.

"What's going on?" Sadie hissed.

"Steven Ballinger, the head of the Secret Service, is in there. I'm only getting every third or fourth word. It seems he isn't too happy that we're actually living in the quarters. The first lady just read him the riot act and is about to boot him out. The chief of staff, Lawrence Neville, was just here, while you were getting dressed. She made short work of him, too. I heard her say she wanted to have lunch with her husband."

"What did the chief of staff want?" Sadie hissed a second time. Quinn shrugged.

Sadie headed for the dining room, where breakfast was laid out on a sideboard. She helped herself to toast and coffee. Quinn chose a slice of melon and a bran muffin. They nibbled in silence until they heard the outer door slam shut. Lettie Jaye appeared almost immediately.

"They don't like you two girls being here," she said happily as she sat down. "You did say it was all right to smoke, didn't you?"

"Whatever you want, ma'am. Is anything wrong?"

"Everything is wrong. I'm trying not to be ungrateful, but I don't like it here. I don't like cold weather. Do you know right now the camellias are blooming in my garden at home? We always had a huge centerpiece on the table at Thanksgiving. Everything is barren and brown here, just like our lives. Jimmy Jaye and I believed them when they told us he was the only man who could turn the country around. People knew Jimmy Jaye, loved and trusted him. That's how he won the election. They made it happen. All he had to do was agree to appoint certain people from something they called the A-List to various posts in the administration. Good, solid men and women. Two women," she snorted.

"Last year they said was a banner year. Jimmy Jaye made good on all his promises. Well, almost all of them. He's still working on some of them. Then I don't know what happened. I spent a lot of time back home, so I didn't *see* what was going on.

"In the beginning I didn't know how things worked. I lived with it because I had no other choice. Do you know Jimmy Jaye is always surrounded by agents? Even when he walks up here from the West Wing, there's a detail with him. I'm hardly ever alone with him. It wasn't like we were joined at the hip back home. Jimmy Jaye had his friends and activities, and I had mine. We also had a third group of friends, a political group. We would attend functions together and more or less meet up on Sunday mornings. We'd have breakfast together, go to church together, come home and read the papers together. Sunday was always our day to spend together."

A smoke ring circled Lettie's head. "Now, we see each other in the hall and wave. Then I won't see him for days. In the beginning, I thought that's the way it was supposed to be. Then I started reading up on first ladies and their families. I started to pay attention to things and to ask questions. I asked a lot of questions. The only problem was, the answers I got were at best vague and sometimes outright lies. I gave up my husband to the American people, and this is what I get. Did you tell them I want to go home?"

"Yes, ma'am, I did. Do you mind telling us why it is that Sadie and I report to the FBI instead of Mr. Ballinger, who is head of the Secret Service detail here at the White House? It's rather . . . unorthodox," Quinn said, searching for just the right word.

"Obviously, I'm not as important as my husband. I told you, I kicked up a fuss; then I remembered Ezra. I met him six years ago at the Governor's Ball. We hit it off. He remembered me when I called him. He came into my gallery in Charleston one day after the ball and bought four of my paintings for his mother for her fortieth wedding anniversary. I thought that was so nice. We had a glass of sweet tea out in my little courtyard off to the side of the gallery. He told me he was with the FBI and how much it meant to him. He said someday he was going to be the director. He told me all about his family, and they sounded so nice. When you don't have children, it's nice to hear about close-knit families. When he left with his four paintings he said, and I remember it all so well, 'Ma'am, if you ever find yourself in trouble, you call me directly.' So, I did. And here you are," she said brightly. "Oh, by the way, Jimmy Jaye adored Ezra. I asked him to appoint Ezra to head up the FBI, and he said he would. Then I heard on the news he appointed some elegant-looking man whose father is a former governor. His father either owns or is involved somehow in those hateful HMOs. I saw the judge being interviewed on *Sixty Minutes*, and he has very cold eyes. That isn't good. I don't care if he is a federal judge."

Quinn almost choked on a mouthful of coffee as

she tried to digest the information the first lady had just divulged. She couldn't help but wonder what other nuggets of information the first lady had stored away in her head. Alex's father involved in HMOs! She didn't know what to make of that. Maybe she would ask Alex *if* he ever called her back. Well, she wasn't going to think about Alex and his stuffy attitude where she was concerned. "So don't call me, see if I care," she mumbled under her breath.

Her fingers tapping on the table, Sadie stared at a picture on the wall over the buffet, a picture of the first lady and the president standing in the Rose Garden.

Quinn reached for a cigarette. Sadie flicked the first lady's lighter with shaking hands.

"What else do you want to know?"

"Well, I . . ."

"Is Acting Associate Director Lapufsky capable of being in charge of the FBI?" Sadie asked.

"My goodness yes. Jimmy Jaye had him investigated up one side and down the other. He's more than capable. Even your aunt Birdie agreed. Birdie and I talked it over. That's what good friends do, talk to one another, ask each other for advice. She did know Ezra quite well if you recall. She so enjoyed the time you two were 'courting.' Even though she didn't show it, she was quite broken up when you and Ezra parted company. She said Ezra was an honest man and could see both sides of any issue, which is paramount in law enforcement. Politics! I hate it! We almost had it in the bag, and then, poof, he was out of the bag," the first lady said dramatically. "Everyone always thinks the president has all this authority, but it isn't true. You girls aren't saying anything. Why is that?"

"Ma'am, we're just here to guard you. We can't get involved in your personal life. We can, of course, be sympathetic, which we are," Quinn said, an edge to her voice.

"Ezra called me this morning to tell me about your aunt's accident and surgery. I want to go to see her in the hospital. You'll take care of that, won't you? I'd like to go this afternoon. Maybe they'll let us stop at Starbucks for coffee. Do you know any newspaper reporters who you trust?"

"No, ma'am," both agents responded simultaneously.

"Oh, well, we'll ask Birdie when we see her. We need one on our side. We'll just keep that to ourselves and not mention it to Ezra. These grits are terrible. I must have told them a hundred times how to make them. That's what I mean; no one listens to me! All the food they serve me has the same taste, no matter what it is."

Sadie and Quinn exchanged meaningful glances.

"Ma'am, I'm from Alabama," Sadie said. "I grew up cooking grits for my brothers and sisters. I can make collard greens and Hoppin' John that will make your mouth water. My pecan pie and sweet tea are the best in all of Mobile. Even my mother says so. Would you like me to make some for you, ma'am?"

"I would dearly love that, Sadie. Can I go to the grocery store with you to buy all the ingredients?"

"Only if you want to wait three weeks for clearance. I thought I could run out today and get everything or have someone from the kitchen staff get it for us. I could make it for you for dinner this evening."

"Will we have time, Sadie, if we're going to go to the hospital?"

"We'll have plenty of time, ma'am."

"If you'll excuse me, I have to call AAD Lapufsky to arrange our outing," Quinn said.

In her bedroom with the door closed, Quinn called Puff's cell phone. The moment he answered, she said, "The first lady wants to go to the hospital to see Birdie. No, I did not tell her about the accident. She told me *you* told her. So, AAD Lapufsky, arrange it for this afternoon. The first lady seems to be taking some heat here this morning from the COS and the head of the White House Secret Service detail. Do you know anything about that?"

"Your job is to guard the first lady and lay down your life to protect her if necessary. That means anything else is none of your business. I don't know anything about it. I'm still trying to figure out why I was chosen to handle all this. What time do you want to go?"

"One o'clock. The first lady would also like to stop at Starbucks. Let's plan that stop for two-thirty to be on the safe side. They clear the place for twenty minutes; what's the big deal?"

"The big deal is a whole detail of agents. As it is, Ballinger hates my guts. Three cars. All to buy a cup of coffee. It won't fly."

"Be persuasive, Lapufsky. Feel free to spend my taxpayer dollars. Are you working on her trip home? She's getting impatient. The lady has a mind of her own. She's going to go if she has to walk. Keep that in mind, okay?" Quinn clicked the OFF button before Puff could respond.

Back in the dining room, she made her announcement. "I think it's going to be okay. We should be able to leave at one o'clock with a stop at Starbucks at two-thirty. The wheels are in motion."

"Oh, this is so wonderful," Lettie said, her eyes filling with tears. "This will be the first time I'm going out in over a month. Those little luncheons in the dining room don't count. I have to decide what to wear. What should we take to Birdie? Maybe we could stop at Victoria's Secret to pick up a little something."

"Well that will certainly spice up the front page of the *Washington Post* tomorrow morning," Sadie quipped.

"Do you think so, Sadie?"

"Yes, ma'am, I do."

"Then let's do it! I'm going to run down to the Oval Office to get some money."

Quinn held up her hand. "You can do that, but you have to wait for us."

"All right, all right, but don't dawdle," the first lady said as she headed for the door, Quinn and Sadie on her heels. Quinn deliberately avoided looking at Sadie, as they walked down the steps, then down a long corridor that led to the Oval Office.

"Mrs. Foster, isn't Mrs. Tappen here today?" Without waiting for a response, the first lady continued, "I'd like to see my husband."

"Mrs. Tappen had a dentist appointment. I'm afraid that the president isn't available right now, Mrs. Jaye. He is in a meeting with his top-level advisors."

"Well, will you please interrupt him and tell him I need some money. I'm going out this afternoon."

"You are!"

"Yes. I would like the money now, please."

Quinn thought it a reasonable request.

"Mrs. Jaye, I can't disturb the president. I'll call Mr. Ballinger for you," Mrs. Foster said.

Quinn frowned at the receptionist's response.

The first lady's shoulders stiffened, and her jaw set grimly. Quinn and Sadie both backed up three steps and waited.

Steven Ballinger looked like a Sumo wrestler dressed in a power suit and tie. Lettie got right to the point. "I need some money. Since I can't go to a bank like a normal person, I would appreciate it if you would do it for me. Now, sir!"

"May I ask why you need this money?"

"No, you may not."

Ballinger reached inside his jacket for his wallet. He withdrew a fifty-dollar bill and handed it to her.

The first lady's shoulders stiffened even more. "I don't want your money, Agent Ballinger. I want my *own* money. It galls me that I even have to ask for it. What do you think I can do with fifty dollars? Not much, I can tell you that. I'll go to the bank myself. Better yet, I'll use my credit card. I do have one, you know."

Ballinger, his eyes on Quinn and Sadie, clenched his jaw. "How much money would you like, Mrs. Jaye?"

"Five hundred dollars," the first lady responded smartly. "Not a penny less."

"I'll bring it up to your quarters, Mrs. Jaye."

On the way back to the family quarters, the first

lady turned around. "How'd I do back there?"

Quinn hid her smile. "He's bringing you the money, so I'd say you did okay." Sadie nodded.

"I wouldn't have had the nerve to do that without the two of you standing there. You could have taken him, right?"

"Well . . ." Quinn hedged.

"He is big," Sadie said.

"He's all fat. Can't you tell? Fifty dollars!" The first lady laughed. "You can't buy anything in Victoria's Secret for less than a hundred dollars. Besides getting a gift for Birdie, I might want to buy something for myself. I am so excited."

Quinn pulled out her cell phone. "This is Special Agent Star. The first lady wants to go to Victoria's Secret." She held the phone away from her ear when Lapufsky started to squawk.

Sadie grinned from ear to ear.

"Are you talking about that skimpy underwear store with the pink bags?" Puff asked in an incredulous tone of voice.

"That's the one!"

"No!"

"That's what she wants, Puff. If you want to tell her no, then you call her and tell her no. She has her heart set on this outing."

"That store is in the damn mall. It's going to be a hassle, and it will be in the papers tomorrow."

"Yeah," Quinn drawled. "I thought about that. I guess she doesn't care. What's it gonna be?"

"I'll get back to you. What's she gonna buy?"

"Maybe she just wants to look. They have a wide

array of . . ." She laughed out loud when she heard the click on the other end of the phone.

Ten minutes later a knock sounded on the door of the family quarters. Quinn opened it, hand on her holster. "Agent Ballinger. What can I do for you?"

The big man was about to step over the threshold when Sadie blocked his way. "You only come in here if the first lady invites you. I'll tell her you're here." Quinn closed and locked the door, while Sadie ran back to Lettie Jaye's bedroom.

"Ma'am, your money is here."

"Oh, good," the first lady called. "I'll be right out." And right out she came, trailing a silky crimson dressing gown that could only have come from Victoria's Secret. Or Frederick's of Hollywood. She winked at the two agents. "I have a bunch of this stuff. Jimmy Jaye used to like it." She opened the door, reached out, snatched the envelope from Ballinger's hand, and shut the door. She rifled through the money faster than a bank teller. "It's all here. I can't wait to put it in my purse. It's going to take me a while to get ready. Watch television or something," she said, closing the door to her room behind her.

"Do you think she's nuts?" Sadie whispered.

"Nope. I think she just has cabin fever," Quinn whispered in return.

"That must be Puff," Sadie said, as Quinn clicked the ON button of her cell phone.

"Okay, you can go to Victoria's Secret. What are *you* going to buy?"

"Something you only dream about, Lapufsky." Quinn ended the call before he could say anything more.

8

"What is it this time, Agent Star?" Lapufsky snarled.

"A slight change in plans, *sir*. We just realized, Mrs. Jaye wants to go to Victoria's Secret *first*, before going to the hospital. She wants to buy something for Birdie. I said I had to check with you first." Quinn's voice turned syrupy sweet when she said, "I told her you were the man who could make the old switcheroo. So, what's it gonna be, Acting Associate Director Lapufsky?"

"Why do you always make my name and title sound obscene? I'll call the store. They might not want to change the time of her visit. What's your best guess as to how long she'll be in the store?"

"I have no clue. She hasn't been out for a while. She might want to look at *everything*. When it comes to silk and satin, women like to feel it, touch it, imagine what it will feel like wearing it, and they might want to try it on. That all takes time. Ninety minutes tops. It should be worth the publicity alone for the store. I think our ETA would be around one-twenty."

"I'll get back to you."

Quinn turned to her partner. "He's going to get

back to me." She walked over to the window to stare down at the Rose Garden. She made a promise to herself to take the spring tour when the roses were in bloom. She turned when the phone rang. Sadie picked it up on the second ring. She listened to her partner's brisk, professional voice. She grinned when she saw Sadie mouth the words, "It's the president's press secretary. He wants to know if the first lady is really going to Victoria's Secret?" Quinn's head bobbed up and down.

The moment Sadie hung up the phone, a knock sounded on the door, and Quinn's cell phone rang. Quinn tossed the phone to Sadie as she headed for the door. "Agent Ballinger, how can I help you?"

"Where's the first lady?"

"She's getting dressed, sir." She watched Sadie click off the cell phone from the corner of her eye. When her friend gave her a thumbs-up, she knew the store manager at Victoria's Secret had okayed the change in time. "I'll see if she can come to the door, sir." She jerked her head in the direction of the first lady's bedroom.

Sadie was breathless when she returned to the door. "She said she's too busy and for Agent Ballinger to put whatever complaint he has in writing and for him not to forget he's the one who was overheard saying she was long in the tooth. She said to say it verbatim," Sadie hissed.

"I can do that," Quinn muttered as she opened the door and delivered the message. The agent's face went from white to red to purple, then back to white when he stomped off.

The next phone call was from the first lady's secretary. Sadie again raced down the hall to Lettie Jaye's bedroom. She sprinted back, and said, "She said to tell her yes, she's going shopping, and if she wants her to fetch something back to make a list. She's going to buy whatever tickles her fancy." Quinn repeated the message.

"Who's left?" Sadie grinned.

"The eight-hundred-pound gorilla, that's who." Quinn laughed.

"Do you mean the prez himself?"

Quinn looked at her watch. "In about seven minutes."

"Wow! Do you think she'll cave?" Sadie asked, nibbling on her lip.

"No. She's going to Victoria's Secret come hell or high water. Having us here seems to give her courage. I don't think that's a bad thing, Sadie."

"I don't either. I think I hear the president's elevator. You're losing it, Star," she gurgled. "Six minutes!"

Five minutes later the president strode into the room, an agent flanking him on each side. He was an imposing figure, dressed in charcoal gray with a red tie. Quinn and Sadie remained where they were. None of the three men acknowledged either of them. The president looked around as though he was trying to get his bearings. Quinn's eyes narrowed as one of the agents took the president's elbow and herded him down the hall to the bedroom where Lettie Jaye was dressing.

Exactly nine minutes later, still wearing the crimson dressing gown, Lettie Jaye walked out of her room, her arm linked with her husband's. "I want you to meet my new agents, Jimmy Jaye. They are so nice to me, not like those others you had guarding me. They're going to take me shopping. Isn't that nice, Jimmy Jaye?"

"Very nice, darlin'." The president extended his hand to Quinn, then to Sadie. "Take good care of my wife. She means the world to me. It's a pleasure to meet you two in person," he said, shaking Quinn's and Sadie's hands. He shook off one of the agent's hands and stepped away from him. The other agent moved closer, but he slapped him away, too. "Be sure to take an umbrella and dress warmly. Do you think you ladies could bring me back some peanut butter fudge?" He twinkled.

"Of course we can. Jimmy Jaye, I'm going to go home in a few days. Is that all right with you?"

"Of course, darlin'. Whatever you want is fine with me. If I can get away, I'll join you. I miss the cat. Why don't you bring her with you when you come back." If Quinn hadn't been staring at Lettie, she would have missed the sudden change in her expression. The two agents moved in and started to usher the president toward the door. Lettie ran to her husband, but one of the agent's stiff-armed her.

Quinn and Sadie moved as one, their hands on their holsters. "Try that again, and you'll be looking down the barrel of this gun," Quinn said, shoving the first lady aside.

"I just wanted to kiss my husband," Lettie Jaye wailed.

"By all means, ma'am, kiss your husband. The

agents will wait while you do that," Quinn said gently.

"Mr. President, Mrs. Jaye wants to kiss you good-bye," Sadie said loudly.

"My wife? Where is she?"

"I'm right here, Jimmy Jaye. You always kiss me good-bye. You forgot."

"Now how could I forget something so important. Oh, my, you smell good, Mama."

Lettie was twitching like there was a bee in her undies when the door closed behind the agents and her husband. "See, see, that's what I mean. They won't let me get up close to him. What's wrong with kissing my husband? That was my real husband, too, by the way. Did you notice how he says silly things? The cat's been dead for twenty years, and I'm not his mama. You don't think it was some kind of code, do you? He's not a silly man. I think he's afraid of those agents. They aren't supposed to hold him up. He can walk. They walk in front of you and behind you. Sometimes on the side, but they never crowd you. Those are the rules. They broke them all. They aren't supposed to be in here either. These are our private quarters. In 180 years the White House has never been penetrated. By evil people. What they don't say is there *might* be evil people already inside. Let's talk about this later. I have to finish dressing."

Quinn and Sadie watched the first lady literally skip down the hall to her bedroom.

"What did I miss here?" Sadie grumbled. "Did the president come up here to talk her out of going shopping?"

"If he did, he changed his mind once he got here. I heard him, you heard him, and so did those agents, not to mention the first lady. He thinks it's nice that she's going shopping. That's the absolute in clearance as far as I'm concerned. Do you agree?"

"Yep," Sadie said. "So what do we do now?"

"We sit and wait. The glamorous life of a Secret Service Agent; stand or sit around and wait. Kind of like the army. Do you have your two-way?"

"Yes. And you?"

"In my fanny pack. I think I'm going to get one of those animal print bras with the matching panties."

"Sounds good to me," Sadie said. "I like black lace myself."

"What do you think *she's* into?" Quinn whispered.

"If you're looking for a wild guess, I'd say red. She told me she's in her red period. She showed me some of her paintings yesterday. They were just smears of red paint. I guess artists go through color periods. I don't know anything about paintings, but what I saw were just globs of color. Then she had a blue stack for her blue period. She tried to explain it to me. The blue period is depression. The red period means there might be hope. Her yellow period was when they first arrived and everything looked sunny. Her brown period meant each day was worse than the one before and the one to come. Wait till you hear this one. She said her orange period came a year after she got here. That was when she wanted the place to catch on fire with all the people in it except her and Jimmy Jaye and what she called the good people. Her old paintings are beautiful. I think the first lady is very talented, and she feels like she's being wasted here. No one in this town has been kind to her. I can understand her giving up and hunkering down. I think I might do the same thing."

"You're right; they haven't been kind to her. Sometimes the press gets ugly. They attack the weak. Are you really going to cook dinner tonight?"

"I am. Mrs. Jaye said we have Mrs. Clinton to thank for the kitchen in the family quarters. I called down to the dining room and told them what I wanted. They said they would have everything brought up by four o'clock."

Fifteen minutes later, Quinn and Sadie both stood up, their jaws dropping when the first lady walked into the living room. "What do you think, girls? Do I look all right? Or do I look like Southern white trash?"

"Oh, no, ma'am, you look . . . beautiful," Quinn said.

And she did look every inch a regal first lady in her navy blue Dior suit with matching tam perched on the side of her head. Her bag and shoes were Chanel. Pearls graced her neck and earlobes. As she twirled around for effect, she pulled on black leather gloves.

"Is my makeup all right? One time they said I looked painted. I really worked on it."

"It's flawless, ma'am," Sadie said. "And you smell . . . heavenly. I'll call downstairs and tell them you're ready."

Six agents stood outside the doors of Victoria's Secret, which were closed and locked the moment the first lady and her two agents entered the store. Quinn's eyes were everywhere, as were Sadie's, as their charge strolled through the store. Salesclerks stood discreetly against the wall, their eyes on the first lady.

"Sadie, tell one of the clerks what we want and let them bring it to you. I'll follow Mrs. Jaye. I'm a 36-B cup. Remember now, no thongs."

Quinn grinned to herself as the first lady homed in on the red bras and panties. She picked up two sets, one trimmed in red lace and one trimmed in black lace. Both were skimpy and racy. Her gaze shifted to the pile of lingerie the first lady had already set aside on the counter. Black thigh-highs, red thigh-highs. Black fishnets with sparkles in the corners of the diamonds. For Birdie there was a flannel nightgown full of fluffy white clouds on a blue background.

"Did I miss anything, Quinn?" the first lady asked forty minutes later.

"I don't think so, ma'am. If you did, it wasn't worth buying. These are my things," Quinn said, pointing to a meager pile of undergarments. "These are Sadie's," she said, indicating a pile similar to her own.

Her money in her hand, the first lady tapped her foot. "I can't wait to go home to try these on," she whispered.

"Me, too," Quinn whispered in return.

The manager of the store rang up Lettie Jaye's order, smiled, and said, "That will be $749.86."

Hoping to avoid embarrassment for the first lady,

Quinn deftly reached for her arm and drew it downward. "Put everything on this card," she said, holding out her platinum Visa card. "Ma'am, wait over there with Sadie, please. I'll take care of all these purchases and see that they don't get mixed up."

"Didn't she have enough money?" the manager asked smugly. Quinn could see it as a headline the following morning.

"On the contrary. She was going to pay cash, but I just remembered how much trouble I had when I returned something that I paid cash for. It's always better to use a credit card." She scrawled her name on the charge slip and pocketed the receipt.

"Girls, girls, let me carry some of these," Lettie Jaye said, reaching for a couple of the bright pink shopping bags. "My goodness, we have eleven of them!"

"Smile, ma'am, there's a reporter with a camera," Sadie said.

Lettie Jaye smiled and waved, two of the bags dangling from her wrist.

Quinn heard one of the agents mutter, "Christ Almighty, this will be fodder for at least a week. Whose bright idea was this anyway?"

"It was all my idea!" Lettie Jaye chirped as she was rushed along to the waiting limousine.

Inside the car, Lettie buckled up and immediately handed over her wad of bills to Quinn. "I appreciate what you did for me back there. I didn't know what to do. One time I went to the grocery store and didn't have enough money. It was a long time ago, but I remember how embarrassed I was when I had to put things back. I'll get you the rest of the money tomorrow if that's all right."

"It's fine, ma'am, don't give it another thought," Quinn said.

"Do you think Birdie will like the nightgown? I thought it was rather serene with the clouds and blue sky, and it felt so soft. Birdie is serene in her own way. At least that's how I always think of her. I get flustered and tongue-tied. I'm always afraid I'll say the wrong thing and embarrass Jimmy Jaye and this fine country. He always said I should speak my mind. I tried to do that in the beginning, but the reporters just twisted my words. Sometimes I feel like a whipped dog."

Quinn fought the urge to put her arms around the president's wife but knew that was not an option.

"Don't you worry, ma'am. You have backup now," Sadie said staunchly.

"Then I won't worry. I'm so excited to see Birdie again. I do hope she likes the gift. Maybe she would prefer red flowers."

"No, ma'am. Birdie is into nightgowns. She just lost . . . got rid of two of her favorites a couple of weeks ago."

The first lady brightened as she settled herself more comfortably in the limousine.

The moment the three-car caravan stopped in front of the hospital, the agents swarmed out, two-way radios in hand. Quinn and Sadie waited for the all clear before opening the door. They stepped out first, the first lady following them. "I'll be in front of you, ma'am. Sadie will be behind you. The other agents are up ahead securing the elevator. Birdie is going to be so surprised!"

Surprised was hardly the word to describe Birdie Langley's reaction to seeing the first lady of the United States at the foot of her hospital bed.

"Good God, Lettie, is it really you? Who sprang you?"

"Your niece, that's who. Go outside now, girls. Birdie and I have some catching up to do."

Quinn winked at her aunt, who could only stare at her in amazement. She blew her a kiss and winked again.

Outside in the hallway that was deserted except for six agents, Quinn leaned against the wall away from the other agents but close to Sadie. "I think we pulled this off. I really do. All we have to do is get through Starbucks, and we can go back and collapse. I feel like my eyeballs are standing at attention." All six agents turned to stare at her when her cell phone rang. She knew it would be Puff even before she clicked the ON button.

"How's it going?"

"We're at the hospital now. Actually, Sadie and I are out in the hallway with six other agents. The first lady enjoyed shopping. I guess I should tell you there was a reporter outside in the mall, and he took our picture. I suppose it will make the front page tomorrow."

Quinn knew Lapufsky was clenching his teeth.

"What did she buy?"

"Stuff," Quinn hedged.

"What kind of stuff?"

"You know, stuff. Underwear. Fancy underwear."

"Describe it."

"Don't go there, Lapufsky."

"Do you want to tell me about your encounters with other White House staff and Ballinger?"

"No, actually I don't. I handled them. Rather well, I might add."

"Yes, you did, and I'm proud of you. Don't let them intimidate you. They'll try. Just remember, this is a special assignment, and you work for me. Don't be afraid to mention that from time to time."

"Okay, Puff. The first lady is enjoying herself. She told me there were times when she felt like a whipped dog. I don't like hearing stuff like that."

"I don't either. There's no controlling the media, Quinn. Remember that. Call me when you get back to the White House. Oh, tell Birdie, Winnie is doing just fine. She slept with Birdie's nightgown. The one that was at the foot of her bed. She dragged it into my room. Tell her the dog misses her."

"Okay, I'll tell her. Why are you being so nice to me all of a sudden?" Quinn asked suspiciously.

"Because I like you, that's why," Lapufsky said, breaking the connection.

"Imagine that," Quinn muttered.

It was ten minutes past four when the trio entered the family quarters of the White House. Lettie Jaye kicked off her shoes and tossed her bag and hat on a chair. "I'm going to take a nap. I'm exhausted. Just leave the bags where they are. I'll look through them later. Thank you for a lovely afternoon. I know it was above and beyond what you normally do, and I appreciate your going to bat for me. I'll let you know if Jimmy Jaye is going to be joining us for supper. I guess this is downtime for you both, is that right?" the first lady said, yawning elaborately.

"I'm going to cook dinner. I can see everything was brought up while we were out," Sadie said.

"I'm going to go on the Net," Quinn said.

"She sleeps a lot," Sadie whispered. "Two naps a day, then she goes to bed at nine and is up at seven, give or take an hour either way. That's an awful lot of sleep if you want my opinion."

Quinn stared down at the grocery bags on the kitchen counter. Her eyes were thoughtful as she poked into the bags. "I felt sluggish myself today. Last night, too," she whispered in return.

"It's funny you should say that. I felt the same way. I was actually starting to wonder if I was coming down with the bug that felled Puff," Sadie continued to whisper.

The agents stared at one another. "Are you thinking what I'm thinking, Sadie?"

"I'm on the same page, Agent Star." Sadie put her fingers to her lips, then waved her arms about. She mouthed the words, "I think these walls might have ears." Quinn nodded.

In her room, Quinn clicked on her computer. She pulled up everything she could on the first lady of the United States. She spent the next two hours going from site to site and making notes and printing out what she could. Everything looked normal, the transition from private life to public life and all the little snags that were to be expected were evident.

One reporter chastised Lettie for not having a cause. Lettie immediately chose the arts and proceeded to spout chapter and verse on how hard it was for a young artist to be taken seriously and recognized. She held teas and luncheons and hung unknown artists' work in the family quarters. They called her own work mediocre at best, something Lettie took personally and retaliated against, with some unflattering words on reporters and their view of the arts. It was all downhill after that. They picked on her hair, her clothes, her style, which they said was no style at all, and, of course, her Southern drawl. She speaks like she has a mouthful of grits. And, she pronounces dog *doag.* They really went to town and crucified her about the way she said, you all, pronouncing it *yawl.*

One columnist went so far as to say, Letecia Jaye was no Hillary Clinton, Nancy Reagan, or Jackie Kennedy, nor would she ever come close.

That's when Letecia struck back by granting her first and only up close and personal interview. She invited three reporters, two women and one man, and did the interview in the Blue Room. Quinn laughed out loud as she read the interview.

For starters the feisty first lady struck home with the comparisons the press had made. "Well, ladies and gentleman," she drawled, "my husband never promised you a two-for-one presidency. I am not an empress, nor do I aspire to be one. You, the press, dubbed Mrs. Clinton Empress Hillary. And who was it that said she was a false feminist? Someone from *The New Republic?* I'm sorry we don't have a Whitewater in our background to make things more interesting for you. Would you rather I be a congenital liar the way William Safire said Mrs. Clinton was? I suppose you're going to say there is something about me that pisses people off the way Sally Quinn wrote in the *Washington Post* about Mrs. Clinton. Should I apologize for my husband being faithful to me? No, I don't throw lamps because my husband was never discovered in *flagrante delicto.*

"Nor do I want to be like Queen Nancy, the marzipan wife. You all called her the Iron Butterfly, the Evita of Santa Barbara. Let me ask you, did I spend $900,000 on a White House makeover while my husband slashed the welfare budget? No, I did not. Did my husband and this administration suggest that catsup could do as a vegetable for the poor folk of this country? No, he did not. Did I spend $200,000 on china? No, my husband and I often eat off paper plates. Paper plates that we pay for out of our own money. It's been reported that just one of Mrs. Reagan's handbags cost more than the annual food stamp allowance for a family of four. Mrs. Reagan said that the reason no one liked her was because they resented her size four figure. I'm a size twelve. Be sure to write that down.

"The Queen of Camelot, Jacqueline Kennedy, refused to attend congressional wives' prayer breakfasts, and she couldn't be bothered with a luncheon the wives held in her honor. She made the comment,

'Why should I traipse around to hospitals playing Lady Bountiful when I have so much to do at the White House just to make it livable.' She had no interest in the professional life of the president. She was an ex-Republican and, until she met JFK, had never bothered to vote. She was quoted as saying, 'People have told me ninety-nine things I had to do as first lady, and I haven't done any of them.'

"I am who I am—Letecia Jaye. This is the only interview you will ever get from me, so go to town on it. What that means is, don't call me, I'll call you."

Smiling to herself, Quinn continued to read. When she was finished, she sat back on the swivel chair and propped her stocking feet on top of the desk. *Misunderstood* and *maligned* were the words that came to mind in regard to the first lady.

To her credit, Lettie Jaye hunkered down and continued to invite young artists to the White House. She refused to change the way she dressed and wore her hair. And her Southern drawl became more pronounced until one reporter said they needed a Southern interpreter to understand what she was saying. From that point on, Lettie Jaye shut her mouth and only smiled. Another reporter said a muzzle was on his Christmas list for the first lady.

Next she read the first lady's bio and was suitably impressed. She closed out the site she'd been viewing knowing the woman she was protecting with her life was worthy of such a sacrifice. She was a kind, caring woman who donated endless hours to worthwhile causes like animal rights, the homeless, abandoned children, and funded college scholarships for those in need of higher education. She served on hospital boards, the library, was an officer in the Historical Society and Garden Club as well as the Junior League. She gave art and harp lessons free of charge on Saturdays to anyone who cared enough to learn.

Quinn gathered up the pile of papers she'd printed out to give to Sadie.

"Everything's ready," Sadie said, sitting down on a stool. "We just have to wait for Mrs. Jaye to get up. Do you want to try one of my flaky, light-as-air biscuits? I outdid myself. I think my mother would be proud. The gravy looks pretty good, too. I know you don't like collard greens, but you're gonna love mine because I put bacon in them. And a lot of pepper."

Quinn grimaced. She was an iceberg lettuce kind of gal, but she would eat the collards to make Sadie happy. Nor was she into Southern cooking. Maybe she would acquire a taste for it.

"I think I'm going to call Birdie and Puff. I wonder if he's made any progress with the first lady's trip home."

"I hope so. I could do with some warm weather. It was cold out there today," Sadie said, uncapping a bottle of Coca-Cola. "I don't know what it is, but I've been so thirsty since I got here. I see you swigging at something all the time, too, Quinn. Mrs. Jaye also has something in her hand all the time. They must use a lot of salt in the kitchen."

Quinn chewed on her lower lip.

Both women reached for their guns when they heard the first lady scream. They were at the door of her room in seconds, guns drawn when Sadie kicked open the door.

Lettie Jaye stood in the center of the room, her index finger pointing at the television, where her husband was speaking about the environment. "That's not my husband! That's not Jimmy Jaye!" she cried hysterically. "Jimmy Jaye couldn't give a speech like that without cue cards or a monitor. He can't rattle on like that off the cuff. That's not my husband!" At the agents' skeptical expressions, she yelled, "I'm telling you, that's not my husband."

"Ma'am, how can you be so sure?" Quinn asked, her heart skipping a beat.

"Because, Jimmy Jaye was just up here in our quarters a few hours ago. We sat on the edge of the bed, and I told him he needed a haircut. His hair is gray, but it isn't *that* gray. You're trained to be observant, didn't you notice his hair when you were introduced?"

Come to think of it, the president's hair did look grayer on TV, Quinn thought. Before she voiced her thoughts she realized that if the walls did have ears, as she and Sadie suspected, those ears now knew what the first lady was saying. She looked over at Sadie, who nodded, proof that she was thinking the same thing.

Quinn's index finger went to her lips. "Follow my lead," she whispered. "The lighting isn't that great in here, ma'am. I think it is your husband. Take another look."

Quick on the uptake, the first lady took her cue. "You're right, Agent Star. I think it is the lighting. Oh dear, I feel like such a fool. Well, that's nothing new. I'm sorry I got you so rattled over nothing. I guess Jimmy Jaye got himself a haircut this afternoon. He always listens to me when I tell him things like that. He is a handsome man; there's no doubt about it. My husband is a constant surprise to me. Imagine memorizing that whole speech! I could never do something like that. I think he's every bit as charming as Bill Clinton, don't you?"

"Yes, ma'am. We were just about to come for you to tell you dinner is ready," Sadie said, motioning with her hands for all of them to leave the room.

An hour later the first lady tossed her linen napkin on the table. "That was such a good dinner, girls. I can't tell you how I appreciate eating down-home food. I could cook myself, but I'm always so tired, and it seems like a lot of trouble for just one person. It's rare that Jimmy Jaye and I dine together. I'm going to save this for him and leave a note on his pillow. He does like his midnight snacks. The best thing that happened to me since coming to the White House is having you girls assigned to me." The first lady beamed her pleasure.

"Coffee, ma'am?" Sadie pointed to the fresh can of Folger's coffee sitting on the counter.

"I would love a cup of coffee. Afterward, I'd like to take a short walk outside. I know it's cold, but we can bundle up. Did you hear anything about my trip?"

"I'm working on it, ma'am," Quinn said. "Did you have a nice visit with my aunt?"

Lettie Jaye fired up a cigarette and blew out a long

stream of smoke. "I had a wonderful visit with her. You don't have a thing to worry about. She's going to be just fine. She is worried about her dog, though. I told her if things got dicey, we'd bring him here. I'm the first lady. I can do that. We talked about old times and how old we're getting. We shared a few secrets . . . from our youth," she added hastily. "She loved the nightgown, and said it felt cloud soft. I thought that was nice." She offered up a sly wink for Quinn and Sadie's benefit.

"Did you like the grits, ma'am?" Sadie asked, fishing for a compliment.

"They were as good as they get. Didn't you see how much I ate? You'll see, in the morning, they'll be gone. Jimmy Jaye will eat them when he comes up. Or, maybe he'll have them for breakfast. The good part is we don't have to clean up. Get your jackets, girls, we're going for a walk now. I have the cigarettes."

After dinner, the three women went out for a walk. Outside in the icy-cold November air, Lettie Jaye waited until they were away from the White House and walking over the frozen ground near the garden before she spoke. "That was not my husband we saw on TV tonight. In order for Jimmy Jaye to get a haircut, he has to make an appointment, and a barber comes in. It usually takes a week to arrange. My husband is charming. The man speaking on the environment was at ease, but he lacked Jimmy Jaye's charm and famous smile. That man didn't smile. Do you know why he didn't smile? I'll tell you why. Because his teeth are different than Jimmy Jaye's teeth. What do you have to say about that, girls?"

9

Quinn squinted at her small travel alarm clock. How could it be five o'clock already? It felt as if she'd just gone to bed.

Within seconds she was out of bed and in the shower. Her game plan was to go on the Net to garner more information on the first lady as soon as she'd had her morning coffee. Her instincts were in high gear. Something was not right; she could feel it in her bones.

The steamy shower felt good on her tired body as she let her mind race. She and Sadie had gone to their respective rooms at midnight, and up until that point there had been no sign of the president. Did he snooze in his office? Did he work twenty-four/seven? Was he even in the family quarters?

Ten minutes later she was in the kitchen watching Sadie make coffee. "Is the president up yet?" she whispered.

"He's not here," Sadie whispered back. "I peeked into his room. I know, I know, don't say it. The bed wasn't slept in. What does it mean, Quinn?"

"I really slept well last night, Sadie," Quinn said

in her normal voice, an indication that Sadie was to follow her lead. "I'm going to call Birdie in a little while to see if she had a good night. Alex hasn't called. I need to give him a call, too. Mrs. Jaye told me she'd like to look at some videos today. I made a list. She's partial to martial arts movies. Do you think you could pick some up? She doesn't want to go to the White House theater to watch them but prefers to be here in the family quarters. You could also pick up some hair spray for me. I don't know how I could have forgotten to bring mine with me."

"I'll do this stint," Sadie said. "I just looked over the first lady's day planner, and she has a busy morning. Unless she kicks up her heels and cancels everything. She's supposed to attend a luncheon with the president given in honor of a contingent from Uganda. You do what you have to do, and we'll switch up this afternoon. By the way, the flag is fly-ing, so the president is definitely here even though there is a question mark next to his name for the luncheon. I'll check this morning to see if the two Marines are guarding the Oval Office. Mrs. Jaye said that's another way to tell if the president is in. Who knew?" Sadie quipped.

"If you need me, I'll be in my room on the com-puter. It's an indoor day, I take it."

"Yes."

Quinn waved to the first lady, who entered the kitchen, her cigarettes in hand. The first thing she did was reach for her cell phone to call Alex Duval, who picked up on the third ring. "Hi, honey, how are things going?" Quinn asked brightly. She took a deep breath as she waited for her fiancé's reply.

Alex's voice was cool and professional. "If you're referring to the nomination, it isn't the slam dunk we all thought it would be. There appears to be some Senate opposition to me. Some of the senators object to the platinum spoon they say I was born with; others are saying the nomination is a party favor. And still others are saying my background doesn't fit the job. I now know I was not the first choice. But then, I'm sure you already know that."

"How would I know that, Alex? What are you talking about? Are you saying you could be rejected?"

"That's what I'm saying. Your old lover was the first choice, but I guess he had even less support than I do. Don't tell me you didn't know."

Quinn picked at a string hanging off her suit sleeve. She rolled the thread between her fingers and yanked at it. "It's politics," she said lamely. "No one ever seems to get one hundred percent approval. You're going to make a wonderful director." She wondered if Alex would pick up on her loyalty. He didn't.

"When are we going to see each other?" he asked coolly.

"I wish I knew the answer to that, Alex. I'm waiting now to see if they okay the first lady's trip back to her home. She wants to be home for the holidays."

"Speaking of the holidays, my parents invited us for Christmas."

"Alex, I can't make any promises right now. Besides, you know I always spend the holidays with Birdie when I can. The holidays have always been special to Birdie and me. Can we talk about this later, honey?"

"What about Thanksgiving?" Alex persisted.

"If the first lady's trip is approved, I won't be here, Alex. Perhaps, with her approval, you could join us. Will you at least think about it? I would think a trip south at the first lady's request would look good in print." Quinn wondered why she was feeling so jittery? Was it Alex's tone or what he'd actually said? Was this the beginning of the end of their relationship? Suddenly she felt sick to her stomach.

"I'll have to see how my schedule shapes up. I can't promise anything at this time, Quinn."

"Alex, will the Senate vote before the holiday recess, or will you have to wait till January?"

"Right now it looks like the Senate will vote in January. As I told you, it is not a slam dunk. In fact, according to my sources, it's starting to look murky. I have to run now. Call me when you have some free time."

Quinn stared at her phone for a long time before she clicked the OFF button, then clicked it on again to call her aunt. She was assured by Birdie's private duty nurse that she was fine and was walking up and down the hall with the aid of a walker. "I'll give her your message when she gets back."

Quinn's next call was to Ezra Lapufsky. "Are you getting anywhere with the first lady's trip?" she asked.

"What's with you, Star? These things take time. The holiday season is the most important time of the year at the White House. The first lady is supposed to be in residence to accept the Christmas tree when it's delivered from wherever the hell it's coming from this year. She is supposed to pick out a theme, oversee the decorations, and a lot of other things all other first ladies have done in the past. It's called carrying on traditions. There are parties and receptions she's supposed to attend. How would it look if she's down South picking magnolias? I just heard she canceled all her engagements for the next few days. What the hell is that all about?"

"Magnolias bloom in the summer. I don't know how it's going to look. I didn't know she canceled her engagements. She must have done it before she left her bedroom. I guess she's thought this through and made her own decisions. Maybe she wants to enjoy a few Kodak moments at home and get up close and personal with her friends instead of strangers. I met the president yesterday, did I tell you that? He's very imposing. Is there a reason why he doesn't sleep in the family quarters? I always thought first families dined together, or at least had breakfast together. I suppose sleeping could be considered optional considering the demands of his job."

"Whatever you do, don't let the first lady see the paper this morning. They did a cartoon of her decked out in . . . risqué attire. It is not flattering. You don't look so good either. Those goddamn pink bags show up like beacons. You'll be happy to know your little excursion made the front page. Animal print underwear, eh?"

Quinn threw the phone across the room and watched as it bounced back onto the teal-colored carpet.

She turned on her computer and brought up the front page of the *Washington Post*. She didn't know if she should laugh or cry when she stared at the grainy picture on her computer. In living color no less. The pink bags bearing the name, Victoria's Secret, had been blown up somehow to dwarf the first lady, herself, and Sadie, making them look like Lilliputians. The contents of the shopping bags along with the price of each item in them were listed neatly in two columns. The bottom line read, "Special Agent Quinn Star, owner of the animal print undies, paid for all the purchases with her platinum Visa card."

She was almost afraid to scroll down to the Op Ed page but scroll she did, and then she gasped when a five-by-seven-inch square showed a caricature of the first lady wearing sunglasses, decked out in spike heels, fishnets, garter belt, and lacy bra straining to cover her voluptuous bosom.

"No, no, oh no, no, no," Quinn groaned. She printed out both the article and the picture. They didn't look any better coming out of the printer. She stomped her way to the kitchen, where she handed the papers to the first lady.

Lettie Jaye read the article and looked at the picture. She burst out laughing. "I should only look this good," she said, pointing to the picture. "Jimmy Jaye is going to get such a kick out of these. That's if they let him see them. Girls, girls, relax, I'm not upset. You two look so pretty. They mentioned you each by name and listed what you bought. I imagine your beaus will be excited when they read this. Goodness, the phones will be ringing any minute now. My secretary," she said, lowering her voice, "will not appreciate the article or the picture one little bit. She's the schoolmarm type."

Quinn gulped at her coffee as she stared at a grinning Sadie. The phone rang just as Quinn set her cup down. She swiveled around to pick up the phone and listened. "It's for you, ma'am, it's the president."

Both agents walked out of the kitchen but were within hearing distance of the first lady. They listened to her conversation, their eyes locked on one another.

"For heaven's sake, Jimmy Jaye, it's just a picture. Well, maybe if you spent more time with me, I wouldn't have to go shopping. I might just as well be a prisoner in this house. I don't care if it is the White House. When was the last time you shared my bed? You don't even remember, do you? Well, I remember. I bought those . . . *duds*, as you call them, to entice you. I know how you like racy things. Keep this up, *Mister President*, and I'll be heading for the divorce court. You didn't stay in our quarters last night either. I left food for you, and it wasn't touched. I don't want to hear about all your meetings. No one, not even the president, has to work twenty-four/seven every day of the week. Unless there is some sort of crisis, and there is no crisis anywhere in the world that I am aware of. I'm getting sick and tired of this whole thing. Actually, I'm getting *really* damn sick and tired of this whole thing. I absolutely will not issue a statement to the press, and you better not have the press secretary issue one either, Jimmy Jaye. That will only add fuel to the fire.

Nothing's gotten into me, Jimmy Jaye. I'm the one who should be asking you what's gotten into you. Now tell me this, when am I going to see you? You are my husband even though you sometimes tend to forget that. I can talk to you any way I please. We're married. Married people have discussions all the time, and, no, this is not a fight. If we were fighting, you would damn well know it, Jimmy Jaye."

"Talk about belching fire. I didn't think she had it in her," Sadie whispered.

"Sadie, I don't think we've seen half of what this lady is capable of. Sshhh."

"I'm still waiting to hear about my trip, Jimmy Jaye. You listen to me now. You call up the head of the Service and you okay that trip right this minute. If you don't, I'm going to call the *Washington Post* myself, and you aren't going to like what I say. Let the vice president and his wife handle all the Christmas duties. Let him earn his money for a change. Going to funerals is not my idea of a worthwhile job. I'm going home for the holidays, and that's final. You just stop right now with that allergy business. I don't have allergies, and you damn well know it. Don't even think about bringing up my fatigue. You and your people ran me ragged, so I had a right to be tired. I do have an itch right now to come down to the Oval Office and pop you right in the nose. This isn't like you, Jimmy Jaye. And stop calling me sweetheart. You always call me darlin'. I hate being called sweetheart. I'm giving you ten minutes, Jimmy Jaye. You aren't my husband, are you? You're that other one they parade out from time to time,"

Lettie Jaye said as she finally ran out of steam.

Quinn winced when she heard the first lady utter a few choice cusswords before she slammed the phone back onto the cradle.

"Are you all right, ma'am?" Sadie asked.

Her eyes on her watch, the first lady mumbled, "I'm fine. That wasn't my husband," she whispered. "For a minute he almost had me fooled. You can't live with someone for forty years and not know the way they talk and the little comebacks that are part of your daily life. There's some kind of *conspiracy* going on here. Even Birdie thinks such a thing is possible. I told her everything. I had to tell somebody," she said defensively.

The agents watched as the first lady tapped her foot to an imaginary countdown. The phone rang. "Nine minutes and fifty-six seconds," Sadie said out of the corner of her mouth.

The phone rang again. Lettie Jaye compressed her lips into a tight line before she said, "Which one are you? The real one or the imposter? What was the cat's name, Jimmy Jaye? You can't answer that because you don't know. I want you to stop thinking I'm stupid. Stop it, Jimmy Jaye, or whoever you are. I am not being foolish either. What do you mean I can't go at this time? I'm going. What part of, 'I'm going,' don't you understand? I'm not coming back either. You put that in your pipe and smoke it, *Mister President*."

The first lady burst into tears. "That imposter said I can't go home. They can't stop me, can they? I told you he was an imposter. He didn't even know the cat's name."

"Ma'am, I don't know. I'll find out though," Quinn said, whipping out her cell phone. This was all too mind-boggling.

"He doesn't own me. I'm talking about my real husband, not that wanna-be president. When I married him, we became a set. You know, like salt and pepper shakers or a pair of socks. We went together just perfectly. We were a unit and always respected one another. Jimmy Jaye didn't buy me. He got me *and* a wonderful dowry. We do things like that in the South. Well, maybe not now, but back then we did. I'm going to want all that back when I file for a divorce. I'm going to go to one of those tabloids and spill all the beans. They even pay you for dishing up dirt. Every little thing around here is a secret. It's not supposed to be like that."

"This is Special Agent Star, AAD Lapufsky. The president, the one *without* the warts, told the first lady over the phone that she can't make the trip. Are they reconsidering or is it carved in stone? It *is* carved in stone. I'll tell her."

"I heard," Lettie Jaye said sweetly. "I need a cell phone. Give me the one you took from Birdie yesterday. It's in her purse," she whispered. "Go ahead, try the phone. It will be dead. So is the other one connected to the White House switchboard. Our private line *never* works. If you don't believe me, try it. They do this to me all the time. I told you, I'm a prisoner here."

Quinn ran to her room and fished through Birdie's handbag until she came up with her cell phone. She handed it to the first lady.

"I know this number by heart. I've been tempted to call it a thousand times, but I never could quite get up the nerve. I have that nerve now," the first lady said grimly as she pressed a series of numbers.

"Who . . . who . . . are you calling, ma'am?" Sadie dithered

"The *National Enquirer*, who else? I'm going to give them the straight skinny, and what I don't tell them they can make up to suit themselves. You know how that goes. It's all about selling newspapers."

"Ah . . . no, I don't know how it goes, ma'am. I don't think you should be calling a tabloid," Sadie said, her eyes wide with horror at the possible ramifications. "This isn't in our job description, is it, Quinn?"

Quinn shrugged.

"What can they do to me that they haven't already done? It's too late, the call is going through. Yes, this is Letecia Jaye, the president's wife. Yes, the *real* wife. As far as I know there are no others. Do you know something I don't know? Never mind. I'm calling you because you have millions of readers, and I want them all to know . . . how badly I'm being treat—

"Line's dead. Oh well," she said, shrugging her shoulders, "they'll be sniffing around here in about two hours. Maybe an hour, give or take a few minutes. They can get the dirt on anyone or anything. The ladies in my bridge club back home used to bring all the tabloids to our meetings. We always said we were playing cards, but we were reading those awful papers, then discussing them. I'm going home, and that's my final word."

Quinn clicked on her cell phone. "It's dead," she said in awe. "Sadie, check yours."

"Mine is dead, too."

"Now do you believe me?"

The two agents stared at one another, nodding at the same time.

"We have the radios." Quinn pointed to the earpieces they both wore and the radios attached to their belts. She clicked on the frequency used to contact Agent Ballinger.

"This is Agent Star in the family quarters. Our phones aren't working. The first lady wants to make some calls. You're working on it!"

The first lady snatched the radio out of Quinn's hands. "You listen to me, you fat weasel, I want my phone connected. This is not going to look good in the press. Don't tell me to calm down. I want to see my husband. He is the president. I am his wife. That gives me some kind of seniority over you. My agents need their phones. It's none of your business whom I call or when I call them. You are involved in this conspiracy, and don't tell me there is no conspiracy. I do not need a doctor."

While Lettie Jaye continued her tirade against the head of the White House Secret Service detail, Quinn drew Sadie aside. "You own a high-tech security firm. Isn't there something you can do? We need to get Puff over here. She's not crazy, Sadie. Maybe a little high-strung, but I'm starting to think she's right. Just look at her, she isn't *droopy* like she was when we first got here. I think she might be right that something is going on. It's not all *that* far-fetched to think they might have been putting stuff in her food to . . . to . . . slow her down. She was sleeping a lot like you said. She's bright-eyed and bushy-tailed now."

Sadie ran to her room and opened her duffel bag. The array of gadgets she carried with her were the latest in high-tech equipment. They'd been checked and cleared when she'd entered the White House. She pawed through her gear until she found a cell phone guaranteed to withstand anything, and one that could be used underwater and not be traced. She had never tested it out and still didn't believe it worked, but she was willing to try anything. She dropped the stopper in the sink and filled it with water. A moment later she punched in Puff's number.

"Where the hell are you? It sounds like you're at the deep end of the ocean." Sadie laughed hysterically. "You need to get over here. The first lady is going three rounds with Ballinger, and they cut off all the phones and our cell phones. Bye."

Sadie dried off the phone and released the water in the sink. She looked around frantically for somewhere to hide her latest high-tech gizmo. She finally settled on a roll of toilet paper, stuffing the slender cylinder down the middle of the tube.

Sadie nodded to Quinn when she returned to the living room. Quinn released her breath in a loud *swoosh.*

The first lady paced and puffed on a cigarette. "I'm going to quit smoking when I go home. I quit so many times, but then they would do something to rattle me, and I'd start all over again. Jimmy Jaye smokes, too. His daddy used to grow tobacco. My daddy grew cotton. Smoking is better than taking drugs. Well, not better, but at least I have my wits about me when I smoke," she babbled.

"Yes, ma'am," Quinn said.

Quinn and Sadie both watched as the first lady took a long, deep breath, squared her shoulders, and marched to the middle of the room. "I want both you girls to go outside in the corridor and wait for me," the first lady said. "I'm going to lock the door. I don't want you to come in until I call you. Do you understand?"

"Ma'am, we can't do that. Our orders are to stay with you and not let you out of our sight."

"Oh shoot, I forgot about that. All right, I guess you can stay. You can watch me, but don't interfere. That's an order. Stand over there against the wall."

"Ma'am . . ."

"Do what I say. They'll be here soon. Go on now."

"An order is an order," Sadie said.

They watched in bug-eyed amazement as the first lady set about smashing up the family living quarters with her husband's prize baseball bat, given to him by Mickey Mantle.

"She's really venting," Sadie said, as the first lady hacked and gouged, banged and pounded the furniture, the knickknacks, and the glass-topped tables. She upended furniture and banged out windows before she headed for the kitchen, where, in one fell swoop, she had dishes, glassware, and silverware flying in all directions. Coffee grounds, sugar, and flour sailed through the room like confetti. On her way down the hall she stopped long enough to turn the stereo volume to high. Noise thundered and reverberated throughout the quarters.

"This ain't no gone-to-seed Southern belle," Quinn said, trying not to laugh. "I'd say she's one pissed off lady."

"I'm just wondering if we should be trying to stop her. It is her stuff, though. I'm doing just what she said; I'm standing here. How long do you think it will take someone to come up here to see what's going on?"

"Just about . . . now," Quinn drawled. "God, she isn't even breathing hard."

"Someone is ringing the bell!" Sadie shouted, to be heard over the noise.

"You can open the door, but don't let anyone cross the threshold. That's an order, girls!"

Quinn pulled out her gun. Sadie did the same thing. The first lady swung her baseball bat to the right and left. She looked as professional as Sammy Sosa.

Sadie snicked back the lock and stepped back.

"Don't come any closer," Quinn said.

"What in the damn hell is going on here?" Ballinger snarled.

"I'm redecorating," the first lady said, swinging the bat in her hands for emphasis. "I did not invite you here, so stay right where you are. As you can see, I'm in no danger. I told my agents to shoot you if you try to come in here." She moved to the left to turn down the volumn on the stereo.

"Now, now, Mrs. Jaye, just calm down. I have Dr. Iverson here with me. We're just going to come in and talk to you." Ballinger took a step forward at the same moment Quinn and Sadie dropped to a half crouch, their guns drawn. The sound of both agents pulling back the hammers was so loud it sounded like thunder.

The first lady walked calmly over to the door and slammed it shut. She then locked it. Her shoulders slumped as she leaned the Mickey Mantle bat against the wall. She started to cry. "They're going to give me those shots that make me sleep for days like they did the last time. I lost whole blocks of time. They said I had a nervous breakdown. I didn't have any such thing. It all started when Jimmy Jaye started acting silly. I think he's the one having the nervous breakdown, and they don't want anyone to know.

"In the beginning, I did everything I was supposed to do. I read everything I could on all the other first ladies. What makes me so different from Bess Truman? She didn't let them bully her. I stood still for it because that's the way I thought it was supposed to be. I memorized everything, so I wouldn't make the same mistakes they did. I tried so hard I made myself sick. By the end of the second year I just gave up, like I'm giving up now. I thought if you were here . . . you're so different, so kind and caring, I thought it might be better. I'm sorry you had to get involved in my problems. You can't talk about any of this. I guess you know that."

"Yes, ma'am. Don't worry about Sadie and me. We have jobs in the private sector we can go back to when it's time. It isn't time yet, ma'am. We're here to guard you, and that's what we're going to do."

A discreet knock sounded on the door. The agents looked to the first lady, who nodded. Quinn opened the door, her gun at her side, Sadie to the right of her. "AAD Lapufsky," she said, relief ringing in her voice.

"He can come in, no one else," the first lady said.

"Will somebody please tell me what the hell is going on here? The switchboard is overloaded and crashed. The e-mail crashed right afterward. There must be a thousand reporters out front, most of them from tabloids. They said the first lady called and was going to give them the lowdown on what was going on here. Somebody say something," Lapufsky bellowed.

"I want to go home. They say I can't go. I was trying to get their attention. I thought if I smashed up my stuff, and it is my stuff, somebody might actually listen and pay attention. I'm the one who called the *National Enquirer.* They cut me off, though. I know there's a doctor on the other side of the door just waiting to give me a shot of something to knock me out. It's just like the last time. There's nothing wrong with me. All I want to do is go home. Give me one good reason why I can't go. Just one."

"Yeah," Quinn said *sotto voce,* "give her just one good reason." She raised her voice slightly. "I'd also like to know who your boss is. How is it that you supersede the head of the White House Secret Service detail. Who do you report to, Puff?"

"The highest person in the land, that's who. Drawn up by White House counsel and witnessed by three unbiased witnesses. Senate and Congressional approval just for kicks. Just ask Mrs. Jaye."

"Yes. My husband signed the order. It was a trade-off, Agent Star. I got you, and AAD Lapufsky was dropped from the list of candidates for director of the FBI. He gave up his nomination so I could have you two girls guard me. Jimmy Jaye has always been concerned with my safety because he loves me. He promised me I could go back and forth to Charleston anytime I wanted. Jimmy Jaye never goes back on his word. He didn't like taking the nomination away from Ezra and inserting Judge Duval's name because he's an honorable man and never goes back on his word. He did it because of me."

Quinn gasped as she stared at her old lover. Puff had stepped aside for all the right reasons. She wondered if Alex would have done the same thing. "I thought the presidential family, especially the president, couldn't decline protection."

"That's true, they can't. In this case we just added on to what was already in place. It was all done with the first lady's comfort level in mind. As the president said, a happy first lady is a contented first lady. The president's two main concerns at this point in time are the country and his wife. Peace and harmony within the White House are paramount. When one half is not happy, the other half suffers. Do you get my drift?

"I just came from the Oval Office, ma'am. The president said you can go home the day after tomorrow. He apologized for your heartbreak and said the vice president and his wife will gladly stand in for both of you over the holidays. He's planning on joining you as soon as he can free up some time, even if it's only for a few days. He said he'll talk to you over dinner this evening at seven o'clock."

Quinn's eyes narrowed, as did Sadie's. "That's so sweet. The first lady was just telling us earlier that she's been dying to cook something for her husband. All his favorites. Isn't that right, Mrs. Jaye?"

Always quick on the uptake, the first lady nodded.

It was Lapufsky's turn to narrow his eyes. "Ma'am, you might want to make some kind of statement about that tabloid you called up before things get out of hand."

In the time it took Quinn's heart to beat twice, the first lady was in Lapufsky's face. "Are you telling me this is another trade-off? If that's the case, the answer is no. If I comment, I give them fodder, and it will never go away. Not to mention how foolish I'll look. That political cartoon this morning is about all I can handle right now. Ignore it, and they can speculate all they want. What did my husband say?"

"Actually, he thought it was rather amusing. His exact words were, 'That's my Lettie.' He said you remind him of Mamie Eisenhower and Bess Truman all rolled into one. I think he meant that as a compliment."

"They had guts, so, yes, I will take that as a compliment. Are we talking about the tabloids or the political cartoon?" the first lady asked.

"I heard him tell the COS he couldn't wait to see all those *goodies* you bought."

"Did he now?"

"Ma'am, I know you have a lot of packing to do. Why don't you get started, and I'll clean up this mess," Sadie said.

"That sounds like a plan to me. AAD Lapufsky

and I have some things to discuss . . . *outside*," Quinn said. "You might want to think about ordering the ingredients for dinner this evening."

"You're absolutely right. I'll take care of it right now," Sadie said.

Outside in the frigid air, Quinn huddled inside her wool coat. "What's going on here, Puff? This is like no detail I've ever seen or heard about. Mrs. Jaye is a very sweet lady, and she loves her husband very much. She has these . . . *ideas*. Sadie and I just listen, but I have to tell you, I'm starting to wonder if maybe she's right. She never sees her husband. I find that really strange. She says there are two presidents. One with warts. He's the real one. The other one has no warts. She calls him a wanna-be president. She did call the *National Enquirer*. She would have told them all the stuff she's been telling Sadie and me, but she was cut off. Puff, she knew the number by heart and said she'd wanted to call them a thousand times but never had the nerve. If something is going on that I should know about, you better tell me now. How can I do my job if I'm kept in the dark, and don't give me that need-to-know crap either."

"If they cut off all the phones, how did Sadie get through to me?"

Quinn snorted. "She owns a high-tech firm, small but elite. Some young kid developed this cell phone, probably in his garage, that works underwater. If you want a reason as to why the kid developed it, probably because he could. Maybe he's some kind of teenage genius. Don't look at me like that. It worked, didn't it? The kid even has a patent on it. Sadie is thinking about manufacturing them. Does the president have a stand-in, Puff?"

"Don't be ridiculous. The first lady has cabin fever is what the problem is. It never should have gone this far. They should have let her go home when she wanted to. The president said she has these terrible allergies that act up here, then make her cranky and miserable. When she goes home, the allergies go away. Don't go making this a case of national security."

"Get off it, Lapufsky. I've never heard the first lady sneeze or even blow her nose. She said she doesn't have any kind of allergies. She said she sleeps a lot. I think they were putting stuff in her food to make her sleep. Sadie thinks so, too. Sadie cooked last night, and this morning, too. What you saw in there was the result of the first lady being up to snuff. There's something going on here. The first lady uses the word *conspiracy* a lot."

"You've been watching too many movies. I bet you watched that movie, *1600 Pennsylvania Avenue*. Trust me, there's nothing going on here except one hyper, cranky first lady who wants to go home. Your job is to guard the first lady, and that's it. Don't go getting involved. It's against the rules, and you can start by being civil to Ballinger. Pulling a gun on him is not going to win you points."

"Stop being a jerk, Puff. I was doing my job, and you know it. How was I supposed to know the White House wasn't being penetrated? I *was* guarding the first lady. He had no right to cross that threshold. She was standing right there, and he could see she was fine. I admit she had a baseball bat in her hands. That might not have looked real good. And Ballinger had no right to bring a doctor to see her. If she wants a doctor, she'll tell us she wants one. That alone sent up a red flag to both Sadie and me."

"Let it go and do your job. You won this round. The first lady is going home."

"Guess what! She ain't coming back either. I'm just the messenger, so don't shoot me."

"Doesn't look like your boyfriend is going to get the votes he needs to head up the FBI. Are you heartbroken over that, Agent Star?" Puff said, changing the subject.

"No. Why should I be? He would make a good director. Maybe not as good as you, but good. If you weren't so damn in your face and knew how to keep quiet, they probably would have gone with you. Somehow they would have worked things out where the first lady was concerned. You don't always have to be as mean as a junkyard dog."

He kissed her then. One minute she was shivering, the next minute steam was coming out of her ears. It was no gentle kiss, no featherlight touch to her lips. This kiss rocked her world and sent an electric shock through her entire body. It was the bells-and-whistle kiss that romance novelists wrote about.

Puff released her abruptly and walked away. He called over his shoulder. "I thought so. I just wanted to be sure."

"Thought what?" Quinn said, running after him, her face flushed.

"You still love me. That's okay, because I never stopped loving you."

"I do not. You do!"

"Yeah, you do. Now stop bothering me and do what you're supposed to do, guard the first lady.

"You . . . you . . ." At a loss for words, Quinn could only sputter.

"Tell Sadie if that phone really works and she manufactures them, we'll order fifty thousand of them. See ya, Agent Star."

Back inside the family quarters where life was more or less back to normal, Quinn sat down, her face burning. She watched with glazed eyes as Sadie and the first lady stared at her over their glasses of sweet tea.

"Do you want to share with us why you look like you do," Sadie gurgled.

"You look like you were soundly kissed," the first lady said. "Is there going to be a wedding? We can have it in my courtyard back home. In the spring, when the azaleas are in bloom, or in the summer, when the magnolias are out. My garden is lovely. Wouldn't it be nice to say, 'I got married when the lilacs were in bloom'? The air will be scented for miles around, like when the honeysuckle blooms. I'll arrange everything. Oh, Birdie was so right. She just adores that young man. He's so kind to us old people. That's so important. He got approval for me to go home. He will have my undying gratitude forever and ever. I know this wonderful lady named Vera Wang, who makes wedding dresses, and a good friend of mine makes one-of-a-kind wedding cakes. She can make Birdie a dress, too. This is so wonderful. I know Jimmy Jaye would be honored to give you away. Imagine being given away by the president of the United States. I'll be happy to take care of everything. Of course I'll consult with Birdie. There aren't too many men who would give up their heart's desire for my well-being. Well, I know you girls must have a lot of talking and planning to do, so I'll just get back to my packing. I'm so happy for you, dear," the first lady said, kissing the top of Quinn's head.

Quinn closed her eyes and shook her head at the same time. "Did she just say what I think she said?"

"Uh-huh. He kissed you, didn't he?"

"Yes, and he said he still loves me. He wants to order fifty thousand of those cell phones that operate underwater if you decide to manufacture them."

"Wow! Do you love him, Quinn?"

"Of course not. I'm engaged," she said, wiggling her ring finger under Sadie's nose.

"I get it. You're going to make him grovel, right?"

"Yeah."

10

Judge Alex Duval stared out of the Oval Office window that offered up a view of the famous Rose Garden, the site of so many historical events. Today it was brown and drab, wintry-looking. His reflection in a gilt-edged mirror by the window told him he looked tense. How could he relax when he knew that there was every possibility that his world could crash around him at any given moment?

He was forty-four years old and never once, during his life, had he ever taken a chance on anything unless he knew the outcome ahead of time. It was just one of the many lessons he'd learned from his aristocratic father.

Aside from his tenseness, his reflection told him he looked like he belonged in these hallowed surroundings. Dressed in a Savile Row suit, a pristine white shirt, and a cashmere overcoat, he looked as polished, if not better than anyone he'd encountered at the White House so far that morning. The images in the windowpane told him two things—that someone was approaching him from behind and his fiancée was kissing the acting associate director of the FBI in the Rose Garden.

"Judge Duval, good of you to stop by on such short notice. Take a seat. Coffee? Tea?"

"No, Mr. President, I'm just fine."

"That's good. I just wanted to take a minute to tell you we've hit a bit of a rough patch on your nomination. However, I'm confident we can swing things around. I want you to be patient. We'll be working the phones until the Senate goes into recess for the holidays. As you know, things change on a dime around here. I'm hopeful that things will go our way. Thanks for coming by."

Alex wondered if he looked as dumbfounded as he felt.

"Chester, show Judge Duval out."

Alex was about to offer his hand when the president moved swiftly to return to his desk.

"It was nice seeing you, Mr. President. I want to thank you for your vote of confidence."

"You weren't my first choice, Judge Duval, but we're living with it. But then you already know that since you accepted the nomination. Don't take that the wrong way."

Stung to the quick, Alex turned to follow the president's aide. He knew he wasn't going to get the approval he needed to become director of the FBI. He might as well call his father and get it over with.

The man created his own breeze as he strode down the hallway, his overcoat flapping on both sides. "Judge," Puff said, acknowledging Alex.

Duval half turned as he nodded curtly. Lapufsky didn't have an escort. He asked why.

"The AAD comes and goes at all hours, sir. He has top clearance. He knows his way around quite well. Here's the elevator, sir. Have a nice day."

At one time his own father had had White House aspirations. Aspirations that didn't have the backing he needed for a run for the presidency. Maybe his mother had something to do with it, or maybe it was her family's background she didn't want investigated. It looked like the chickens were coming home to roost. He dreaded telling his cold-eyed father what had just transpired.

Alex exited the White House amid hordes of reporters and photographers and walked over to Independence Avenue, where he'd parked his car. He'd been nervous and jittery earlier when he'd first arrived. He thought a brisk walk in the frigid air would clear his thoughts. He turned on the engine and the heater before he called his father.

"Sir, it's Alex. I really have nothing to report. Hell, the man didn't even shake my hand. It was a three-minute meeting, maybe two. He said there was opposition but didn't say what it was. He did say they were going to work the phones to generate support. He also reminded me that I wasn't his first choice. Have you heard anything? Call me if you do. Yes, it's true, Quinn is guarding the first lady. I was just going to call her to see if we could have dinner. By the way, as I was being escorted to the elevator, I saw the acting associate director breezing down the hall. The same acting associate director who was the president's first choice. I don't know if that means anything or not. Tell Mother I said hello."

That was another thing. Early on, probably when he'd learned to talk, he'd been instructed to refer to his mother as Mother, never Mom, the way his friends had referred to and called their mothers Mom. Maybe that was because she'd never acted like a real mom. His father hadn't acted like a dad, either, and was always addressed as sir. Most of the time, though, he thought of him as Father. *Damn, why am I thinking about stuff like that now?*

Alex leaned back against the seat. He closed his eyes. He had to think about what he had seen in the Rose Garden as well as the scenario he'd witnessed in Birdie Langley's kitchen.

Quinn Star would make the ideal wife. She was beautiful, bright, articulate, and knew her way around Washington. So what if she had a weird aunt and absentee parents who traipsed around the world. Quinn was responsible, had her own law office, and taught law at Georgetown. Serving as a Secret Service Agent guarding the first lady of the land only added to her already impressive credentials. She owned her own house in prestigious Georgetown and stood to inherit a mighty fortune when her aunt Birdie went to the Big Obituary in the sky. Quinn was a class act. His parents weren't too fond of her, saying her blood wasn't blue enough. That was okay; his parents didn't like anyone but themselves. Hell, he'd never been sure if they liked him.

His stomach started to rumble when he thought

about what they would say if the nomination didn't go through. He wasn't good enough, didn't measure up. The press would have a field day. Hell, they were already having a field day. CNN and MSNBC must have called his chambers a hundred times asking for interviews or to go live on their respective shows.

Alex jerked at his tie as he dialed Quinn's cell phone. She clicked on after two rings.

"Quinn, it's Alex. How are things going?"

"Rather well, Alex. How about you?"

"Everything is pretty much the same. I just left the White House. I was hoping to see you, but I wasn't anywhere near the family quarters. The president assured me they're all working on the nomination. Listen, can you manage dinner?"

"No, Alex, I can't. The president will be in the family quarters having dinner with the first lady this evening, and Sadie and I both have to be here. We will be going to South Carolina the day after tomorrow with the first lady. She received permission today to make the trip."

"How did you manage that?"

"I didn't have anything to do with it. The Service handles all of that."

"I saw your old boyfriend when I was in the White House. He looked like he comes and goes whenever he feels like it." How snide his voice sounded. How petulant.

"I wish you would stop referring to Acting Associate Director Lapufsky as my old boyfriend. I've been asking you for years to stop it. You never listen to me, Alex, and I'm getting tired of it. He has a job to do just as I do and you do. He and I were involved a long time ago. This is the last time I'm going to tell you not to bring it up again. I mean it, Alex."

"I feel like we're drifting apart, Quinn. One day we were getting married, and the next day Lapufsky is standing in your kitchen wearing one of your aunt's nightgowns. Within hours he manages to get you a cream puff job, and, bam, you're in the White House. What do you expect me to think?"

"What you think is one thing. What you say is something else. If you loved me, you'd trust me."

"I do. I guess I'm just a bit overwhelmed right now. By the way, what *are* all those reporters and camera crews doing outside the gates? There must be ten satellite vans jockeying for position."

"Now, Alex, stop and think about what you just said. How would I know what they're doing out there? Why didn't you ask them yourself? Reporters love to talk to people. I have to go now. I'll call you later this evening."

Alex sat in his car with the engine running for a full ten minutes before he slipped it into gear. He turned once to look back over his shoulder, wondering if he was losing the best thing that ever happened to him.

"That was Alex. He sounded funny, Sadie. It was almost like he knew something and wanted to mention it but didn't, that kind of attitude. He said he was just here, talking to the president, I guess. He also said it's a zoo out front." Sadie grinned. "I think I'll have some more of that sweet tea you made earlier."

"Are we going on Air Force One to Charleston?" Sadie called from the kitchen.

"Not the big plane. There are other smaller planes called Air Force One. When a member of the first family wants to use one of the planes, they have to pay for the usage out of their own personal funds. I guess Mrs. Jaye will have to pay for this trip herself. I had no idea she was as knowledgeable as she is in regards to past administrations and the White House. Just look at that bookshelf, Sadie. Those books aren't there for looks. They've been read, marked up, pages turned down, and spines broken. I think Mrs. Jaye really did study up on what was expected of her. I think she tried, too. They didn't cut her any slack, that's for sure."

"Are you just babbling out there so you don't have to think about Puff kissing you?" Sadie said as she dropped ice cubes into the glasses on the counter. "I can't believe this kitchen was once Margaret Truman's bedroom. Do you suppose she knows it's a kitchen now? That's kind of sad, isn't it, Quinn?"

"Puff was just being a smart-ass, and no, I am not thinking about it at all. I don't think Margaret Truman cares that her old bedroom is now a kitchen. I can't imagine that she was very happy here if her mother was so miserable. Children react to their parents. The critics weren't very kind to her, either, with her music career. I can't help but wonder if any of the first families were happy here. You know, really happy?"

"Do you think the president will really come for dinner?" Sadie asked.

"I do. What's on the menu?"

"The first lady said the leftovers. She said if he'd come up the night before, he wouldn't be eating leftovers. She said she wasn't knocking herself out at the last minute with the possibility he might not show up. I guess he's done that before."

A knock sounded on the door. Sadie and Quinn looked at one another, but it was Quinn who went to the door. "Yes?" she called through the door.

"It's Chester, miss. I have a note for the first lady from the president."

Quinn opened the door and accepted the envelope. "Does the president require a response?"

"No, miss."

Quinn carried the note down the hall to the first lady's room. The door was open, with suitcases and trunks scattered about the room. The first lady was humming under her breath as she tossed things into the trunks and suitcases. Quinn noticed that the pink-striped Victoria's Secret bags were all lined up in a neat row on a chaise longue. "Ma'am, Chester, the president's aide, brought up a note for you. He said it didn't require a response."

"Would you mind reading it to me, Quinn. Right this minute I don't have a clue as to where my glasses are."

"Ma'am, are you sure you want me to read something written by the president. It's personal."

"Goodness, child, it's from my husband. Forget that Jimmy Jaye is the president, so go ahead and read it."

Quinn cleared her throat as she withdrew the single sheet of paper from the envelope.

Roses are red. Violets are blue.
I love you. See yawl tonite and let's not brawl.
                                    Jimmy Jaye

The first lady burst into laughter. "That's my Jimmy Jaye. If you stop to think about it, it is kind of poetic." She reached for the letter. "This was written by my husband. The real one," she whispered. "See this," she said, withdrawing a sheaf of letters tied with a pink string. "These are from Jimmy Jaye. These," she said, indicating another pile, "are from the imposter. They're typed, and Jimmy Jaye never typed anything in his life. He doesn't know how to type. I'm saving all of them the way Nancy Reagan did. When we're finally away from here, I'm going to write a book and include all these little notes. I'll use the money I get for the book to set up a foundation for aspiring young artists." She held the note against her breast.

Quinn smiled. "Is there anything you want us to do, ma'am, while you're packing?"

"No, dear. Just having you and Sadie here is a big help. I feel like my old self again. If you like," the first lady said shyly, "I'd like to give you and Sadie one of my paintings. Go through the rooms and pick the ones you like. Who knows, maybe someday they'll become valuable. I do my own framing, too. I can't wait to get home, so I can get into the swing of things again. I have so many exciting ideas. Christmas in the South is so wonderful. Thanksgiving, too. I'm going to invite Acting Associate Director Lapufsky. Do you think he'll come? We do our turkeys in a deep fryer," the first lady added.

Quinn nodded as she left the room. Now what was she going to do if Alex found out that Puff was going to join them. Of course, Puff probably wouldn't go, preferring to visit his parents the way he usually did. Then again, that was the old Puff. This new Puff was something else. It would be just like him to take the first lady up on her invitation.

"Now what? Why are you looking like that, Quinn?" Sadie asked.

Quinn told her.

"That could indeed get sticky. You know what? In the end neither one will go. So what are we supposed to do now? Just sit here?" Sadie asked, draining her glass of sweet tea. "I think it's entirely possible to lose your mind on a detail like this. I'm just not a sedentary person. If we stay on this job, we could start to atrophy."

"Let's take a look at some videos of the president," Quinn whispered.

"Great idea," Sadie whispered in return. "If you can take over, I'll go to the nearest library and take out some videos on the prez. Then I'll go to Blockbuster and rent a few videos, okay? I'll switch the cases and leave the Blockbuster videos in my car," Sadie whispered.

Quinn nodded.

Quinn and Sadie stood away from the door when the president entered the family quarters. "Wait outside," the president ordered his two agents.

"But, Mr. President . . ."

"Outside," the president said imperiously.

"Mr. President . . ."

"I'm having dinner with my wife. Now, stand outside and wait for me."

"What about these two?" one of the agents said, pointing to Quinn and Sadie.

"That's up to my wife. Darlin', will you feel more comfortable with the girls in or out?"

Lettie Jaye winked at her agents as she linked her arm with her husband's. "They need a break. So let's let them wait outside. Now, Jimmy Jaye, let's you and me do . . ."

Outside in the hall, Sadie and Quinn stood on one side of the door, the president's agents on the other side.

"How is the first lady doing?" one of the president's agents asked.

"Just fine. How's the president doing?" Sadie asked.

"Just fine," the agent responded.

"I guess everything is just fine then," Quinn said, a smile in her voice as she walked a little farther away.

"What did you think of the *Post* this morning?" the second agent asked, a wicked expression on his face.

"I thought it was just fine," Quinn said.

"I thought it was just fine, too," Sadie said. "Give me a break," she muttered under her breath. "They're visualizing you in that tiger print underwear."

"I know." Quinn grinned.

Quinn stared up at the paintings on the wall. History had never been something she was really interested in, but seeing the different paintings in the White House made her suddenly want to know more about her famous surroundings. She said so.

"Not me. I don't like old stuff. I know history has its place, and that's the way it should be. I like the here and now. What good does it do to hark back? The future is where it's at, and what we're doing now for the future. Hey, it's how I feel. Do you think I should manufacture those phones that work underwater?"

"Why not? You proved they work. The FBI is going to be your first customer. I can't imagine a real need for them, but you never know. I guess in the end it will depend on your costs and the profit margin. How long do you think the president will be in there?"

"As long as it takes." Sadie grinned. "She has eleven Victoria's Secret bags, or was it nine? Ninety minutes tops would be my guess."

Quinn adjusted her earpiece, and the tiny microphone attached to her sleeve that all agents use to send messages.

"Are you going to take up the first lady on her offer to have your wedding in her garden?"

"I'm not sure there is going to be a wedding, Sadie. Besides, the first lady thinks I'll be marrying Puff, not Alex. Are you *ever* going to marry John?"

"Not right now. I want to spread my wings. I'm not ready to settle down, with kids that we'd have to adopt and a white picket fence. I want to get my company off the ground. John isn't in a big hurry either. Homicide detectives aren't the best catches in the world, you know. What we have right now works for us. You're having second thoughts, aren't you?"

Quinn shrugged, her eyes on the hands of her watch. "That is the *real* one in there, isn't it?"

"The first lady seemed to think so. Last night I was watching a rerun of that program *JAG* and saw how an imposter impersonated that good-looking naval lawyer. They make a mold, then a mask and use spirit gum. It was interesting."

Quinn's eyebrows drew together. She found herself clenching her teeth. "I'm not ready to buy into all that just yet. Ask yourself why the president's staff and the Secret Service would go to such lengths. I certainly don't have a clue. And to what end?"

"I'll bet Puff knows," Sadie said. "So what was it like to kiss him again after all these years?"

Quinn was about to offer up a sharp retort and thought better of it. "For one little minute there, I thought I could soar with the eagles. I heard the bells and the whistles. Then I wanted to cry."

"You were comparing him to Alex, weren't you? That's a natural thing to do. You're going to have to make some hard decisions, my friend. Don't go off half-cocked the way you did when you blew Puff off the first time."

Sadie put her wrist up to her ear. "Heads up, Quinn, the president is about to leave the family quarters."

"Good evening, ladies," the president said, strolling past the two agents.

"Mr. President," Quinn and Sadie said in unison.

When they entered the living quarters, they saw

the first lady sitting at the kitchen table sipping a glass of ice tea. An empty glass and plate sat across from her. "Sit with me, girls." She lit a cigarette and blew a perfect smoke ring. "Jimmy Jaye will be joining us for Thanksgiving. Isn't that wonderful?"

"Yes, ma'am," the agents said.

"What are you going to do this evening while I finish my packing?"

"We thought we would watch a few videos, unless there's something you would like us to do."

"No, dear. Your job is to watch me, and that's it. I was told I was never to ask the agents for favors or have them do things for me. I don't want to take advantage of you. Did you know Mamie Eisenhower never got out of bed till noon? She didn't have any causes or pet projects either. She said it all sounded like a terrible chore. The *Washington Post* slammed her for her inactivity. Do you know what she said? She said, 'It's simple, I'll just stop reading the paper.'" Lettie Jaye snorted when she said, "She also made the comment that she never knew what it was that women wanted to be liberated from. They said she was the best rested president's wife in history. For heaven's sake, the woman didn't even know how to cook. Ike cooked. All she knew how to make was fudge.

"Well, girls, I'm going to leave you now. Enjoy your evening. I promise not to stir out of my room again."

There was something almost eerie about the presidential quarters once the first lady retired and the lights were turned down low.

Both agents settled themselves in front of the family television set. Sadie slipped in the first presidential video she'd gotten from the library. Notepads and pens in hand, they watched the president of the United States make speech after speech. They paid close attention to the scenes that featured the first lady, the president's advisors, his Secret Service detail, and some of the dignitaries he had met with since taking office.

Quinn dropped her voice to a bare whisper. "Everything looks normal the first year. The president made nine trips, three back to South Carolina. All were working trips. He and the first lady both looked normal at the state dinner for the Emperor of Japan. Mrs. Jaye's dress is fashionable. I thought she looked charming. Are we in agreement that the first year is okay? He looks the same in all the videos. Do you agree?"

Sadie nodded.

"Okay, we're into the second year. The NATO anniversary dinner in the East Room looked okay to me. He looks as charming and dashing as he did the year before. He had a fresh haircut for the dinner. Then just five days later he's walking across the South Lawn to get on board Marine One. His hair was longer but not much. His shoulders didn't seem as straight. He was on his way to Camp David, and Mrs. Jaye was back home in Charleston. I didn't see that easygoing, loose-limbed stride he's famous for. Did you?"

Sadie shook her head.

"That's the first change, eleven months into the

second year. Remember the brief shot of the president in the Green Room staring up at the Georgia O'Keeffe painting of Bear Lake, New Mexico? He thanked Mrs. Jaye, who as we know is into the arts. The painting is the first by a contemporary woman artist to hang on the State Floor. The first lady didn't look too pleased. The president wasn't standing very close to her. Actually, he didn't go near her. There were no close-ups of the president. It was like he popped in unexpectedly. He didn't seem comfortable to me. If Mrs. Jaye's theory is correct, then I'm thinking the imposter, not the president, was in the Green Room that day, and the first lady knew it. How am I doing?"

"Just great. I'm with you here. No close-ups of him for the next few months, and we're into his third year in office, this year. Except . . . except the one last month, where he entertained a group of Scouts for thirty or so minutes. He wanted an exhibition of knot tying. He said he was a Boy Scout. One of the boys was about to show him his skill when he was interrupted and whisked away. That was the real president, the one with the warts. Make a note, Sadie, to ask the first lady if the president was ever a Boy Scout.

"There were shots of him where I thought his ears were bigger, his nose shorter, and he was smiling without showing his teeth. It could have been the lighting. I think he has liver spots on his forehead. Of course, pancake makeup covers that when he's being photographed. I did see those same spots on his forehead when he left here earlier this evening. I don't know, Sadie. I suppose anything is possible. The big question is why? He's got a year to go. I haven't heard a thing about him possibly running again. He's popular. He's effective. It's also possible he has a wife with an overactive imagination. None of which is our business, I might add. We're here to guard the first lady, and we're playing detective, which is not in our job description. Where do we go from here?"

"South Carolina," Sadie whispered.

"I wonder how Birdie's doing. I think about her a lot. Winnie, too. It's hard for me to believe Puff is staying in Birdie's house taking care of the dog. I didn't think he had it in him," Quinn mused.

"Why don't you call? I'm sure he's still up. If not, oh well." Sadie grinned. "I'm going to turn in and think about all this. I want to know the why of all this. Night, Quinn."

"Night, Sadie. Listen, I'm going to snitch one of the first lady's cigarettes and go outside to smoke it. I need to clear my brain, too. I think we're missing something, but I have no idea what it is."

"Go ahead, my door will be open. We're settled for the night. Remember, there has been no penetration of the White House in 180 years."

"I wonder why that doesn't give me great comfort," Quinn said, shrugging into her coat.

Quinn walked out into the hall and down the steps. She spoke curtly into the microphone attached to her sleeve. "This is Agent Star. I'm going outside for a breath of air. I'm at the doors now. Acknowledge please."

"You're free to go, Agent Star," a faceless voice said briskly.

Quinn looked at the cigarette in her hand. She really didn't want it, so she stuck it in the pocket of her coat that held her cell phone.

It was a cold night, the sky full of stars. Even though it was midnight, lights shone from the windows in the West Wing. Were they ever turned off? She made a mental note to ask someone.

She thought about Alex and Puff. The cold, brisk air wasn't helping her thoughts one bit. Before she could change her mind, she whipped out her cell phone and called Birdie's house phone. Puff picked it up on the third ring. He sounded sleepy. Quinn grimaced.

"I'm calling to see how Winnie is and to ask if you stopped by to see Birdie."

"Do you know what time it is, Agent Star?"

"Yes, it's after midnight. Why should you sleep when I can't?"

"Because I'm me, and you're you, that's why. Winnie is fine. She's sleeping right here next to me. I didn't get to go to the hospital, but I did call your aunt. She's doing fine and can't wait to get home. Now can I go back to bed?"

"Do you know the name of the president and Mrs. Jaye's old cat, Puff?"

"No. Should I know that?"

"Do you know if anyone knows?"

"Is this one of those trick questions, or is it a question that's really important?"

"It's a simple question, Lapufsky. Can't you answer it without asking another question?"

"I personally have never come across that little tidbit. No one has ever mentioned it to me. Hell, I didn't even know they had a cat. I'm a dog man myself. Is there anything else, Star?"

"You're obnoxious. How can I find out?"

"Ask somebody," Lapufsky grunted. "Don't call me again tonight."

"I thought you said you loved me."

"That was then; this is now. I spoke too hastily. Forget I said that. Good night, Agent Star."

"Shove it, Lapufsky," Quinn said, slamming the cell phone shut. She dropped it back in her pocket. Her teeth were chattering, and she could feel tears on her eyelashes. Angrily, she reached into her pocket for the cigarette. She took two drags before she crushed it out under her boot. She picked it up, wrapped it in a tissue from her pocket, and dropped it back next to the cell phone.

"Like I believed you even for one minute," she said, her voice husky with unshed tears as she made her way back to the family quarters. She spoke into the microphone on her sleeve. "This is Agent Star. I'm entering the building and will be going upstairs to the family quarters."

"You're free to enter, Agent Star."

11

Quinn eyed the first lady and Sadie as they sipped sweet tea at the kitchen table. A mixture of emotions ran through her as she watched them unobtrusively from her position in the doorway. She was glad she was leaving the White House although it was just for a few hours. Even if it was just for a short time to pack her clothes for what was now a three-month stay in the South, leave instructions with the housesitting service, and other odds and ends. She also wanted to stop at Birdie's house to say good-bye and to see how her aunt was faring. Her clients had been switched to other lawyers, and her replacement at Georgetown University would do just fine, so there was no concern there.

Guarding the first family and working in the White House had been a long-held dream. The way things were going or not going, the reality was more like a nightmare. Had Puff been right years ago when he'd said she wasn't cut out for this kind of job?

She'd always been a mover and a shaker, but these days she was almost immobile. She missed going to the gym, missed running early in the morning. She missed her students and her clients. She missed the routine of her life. Secretly, she agreed with the first lady. You really were a prisoner if you lived or worked in the White House. With just a few days under her belt she already knew that this would never be a life of her choosing. She also understood the first lady's feelings and felt sorry for her.

Quinn was shaken from her reverie when the first lady said, "There you are, dear. So you're leaving us?"

"Just for a few hours, ma'am. I should be back by dinnertime or shortly thereafter; then Sadie can do what she has to do. You aren't upset that I'm leaving, are you?"

"No, dear, not at all. Sadie has promised to take her gun apart and show me how it works. I have a little Derringer in my dresser drawer. Jimmy Jaye bought it for me one year for my birthday. I keep it in a pair of rolled-up socks," she whispered for their benefit.

Quinn nodded. How had the Secret Service missed that? "Sadie, may I talk to you for a minute?"

"No, no, don't get up, Sadie. I'm finished with my tea, and I'm going back to my room to finish the last of my packing. I'm going to do a little painting afterward, so you girls just talk all you want."

"How much time will you need, Sadie?" Quinn asked as she waved good-bye to the first lady.

"Two hours tops. John's out of town on a case, so I just have to pack and turn down the heat. Take all the time you need. I've got it all covered," Sadie said, waving her arms about. "I might even whip up something for dinner. Mrs. Jaye seems to like my cooking. I'll save you some. Quinn?"

"Yes."

"Are you going to see Alex?"

"I don't know. I'm thinking about it. I'll see you later."

Outside in the brisk November air, Quinn struggled with her emotions. Suddenly, she felt free. If she were a bird, she would have flapped her wings and flown away. Instead, she shivered inside her coat and turned on the engine of her car. It would take just a few minutes for the heater to start blasting warm air. The car in gear, she drove through the security gates. The moment she swung onto Pennsylvania Avenue she felt as if she had entered Never Neverland, with the television trucks, satellite dishes, and hordes of reporters and cameramen hovering like vultures. She turned her head the minute she noticed one of the camera crew pointing his long-range camera in her direction. She knew within two minutes they would have her name and address once they ran her license plate.

Damn, she should have read the morning paper. Why hadn't she? Because the first lady wanted to sit and gossip at the table, after which she insisted on a tour of the West Wing. "Because," as she put it, "we aren't coming back, and you might not get to see everything I'd like you to see." Then it was lunch and more gossip, followed by Lettie Jaye's monologue on first ladies, protocol, state dinners, and various dignitaries, those she liked and those she didn't like. Well, she could always stop at a newsstand once she got to Georgetown. Her instincts told her the gaggle of people outside the White House were there because of Lettie Jaye's shopping trip and her call to the *National Enquirer.*

On the other hand, if the headlines were bad, Puff would have been on the horn the minute the paper hit the street, possibly even before. Unless the headlines were spectacularly bad, and he was temporarily left deaf, dumb, and blind. She shuddered at the prospect.

Ten minutes later, Quinn maneuvered her BMW two doors away from her skinny house in Georgetown. She walked down the street and around the corner to the local newsstand, where she picked up a copy of the *Post.* She folded the paper and stuck it under her arm as she ducked her head to ward off the biting wind.

Inside her house, she ran to the thermostat and turned it as high as it would go. Hot air blasted out of the registers as she made her way upstairs.

Hands on her hips, Quinn eyed the contents of her closet. Lettie Jaye had told her November in Charleston was cool but not cold the way it was in Washington. With that in mind, she chose thin-knit, long-sleeved sweaters and light flannel slacks with matching jackets. At the last second she tossed in some jeans, a few sweatshirts and sweatpants. Sneakers, shoes, underwear, nightclothes, and one party dress were the last to go in her travel bag.

Because she was one of those rare females who did not like to shop, Quinn's linen closet revealed an abundance of toothpaste, toothbrushes, shampoo and conditioner, her favorite soaps and bath powders. These she tossed into an overnight bag. Her blow-dryer, curling iron, hairbrush, and various combs, along with her setting gel were already at the White House.

Her bags were packed, zipped, and locked in under eighteen minutes. She used up another ten minutes going from room to room disconnecting appliances, checking the windows and the locks on the back door as well as the door in the kitchen that led to the basement. She turned down the heat to sixty-two degrees, activated the alarm system, left instructions about her plants for the housesitting crew, and left her house.

Outside, she breathed a sigh of relief as she headed to Birdie's house. Once she got there, she could call the newspaper to stop delivery, then remembered she'd already done that. Why else would she have had to buy a paper. "I must be losing it," she muttered, as she stowed her gear in the trunk of the car. All she had to do was fill out a forwarding address for her mail and she was good to go. Thank God she didn't have pets to worry about. She knew Birdie wouldn't mind accepting her mail on a short-term basis and would send it on.

On the short ride to Birdie's house, Quinn let her mind wander to Alex and Puff. She felt like she was on a downhill treadmill watching her life skid by. She loved Alex, didn't she? If that was so, why had she gone weak in the knees when Puff kissed her? What kind of husband would Alex make? Would he ever putter in a garden, clean up dog poop, or step outside looking anything but suave and debonair? There was nothing serendipitous about Alex at all. Then there was his cold, austere family. She wouldn't be marrying them, she told herself. How would they take to Birdie and her dedication to dead people? Not well at all was the answer. The big question was, did she love Alex heart and soul? Would they ever sit on a front porch in rocking chairs when they got older? Probably not, because Alex had a thing about bugs and night air not being good for a person.

Puff was totally different. He still had his old sneakers, jeans, and sweats from his college days. All were full of holes but deeply comfortable. There was no reason to think Puff had changed his habits in the years they'd been apart. Puff was a creature of habit and comfort. The more holes a piece of clothing had in it, the better he liked it. He liked what he called his "comfort zone," and old clothing and old shoes fit into that particular zone. He wouldn't have a problem cleaning up dog poop because he'd had Jack, whom he loved. Puff's idea of getting dressed up was jeans, tee shirt, and sports jacket. He wore a suit to the office with a white shirt and tie that was always askew, but he hated it and took his jacket off every chance he got. Once she'd seen him in a tux with his hair slicked back. She'd gotten so lightheaded she almost fainted. Back then she had loved him heart and soul. There was nothing she wouldn't have done for Ezra Lapufsky. Puff was born serendipitous. She smiled to herself at the thought of him being born.

She liked his rambunctious family, all the confusion as well as the busy kitchen with the tantalizing aromas his mother created. How she'd loved the way his mother had wrapped her arms around her and kissed her cheek. She remembered thinking at the time that Mrs. Lapufsky looked and smelled just the way a mother was supposed to look and smell. They were a good-natured, happy, loving family. She'd hoped to belong to the family one day, but Puff hadn't wanted to commit to any long-term relationship.

Quinn squirmed inside her coat when she thought about Alex's lovemaking versus Puff's lovemaking. Alex was methodical, his moves down to a science. He was not the least bit experimental. Puff, on the other hand, was known to whoop and holler, and he did love to experiment. He didn't have one bit of trouble walking around in the buff, whereas Alex slipped into a robe the minute he swung his legs over the side of the bed. And he wore slippers. Puff liked a cigarette and a beer after sex. Alex had to *wash up*. She'd mentioned the washing-up bit once, and he'd just looked at her, and said, "Maybe you should think about doing the same thing."

Puff liked to cuddle, as did she, after sex. Alex, on the other hand, on more than one occasion had wanted the sheets changed. She'd done it, too. There was something about changing the sheets after lovemaking that never sat right with her. She'd lied to Birdie and herself when she'd said their lovemaking was spectacular.

Alex was champagne and caviar, and Puff was beer and pretzels.

What was she?

She was saved from answering her own question when she pulled into Birdie's driveway. She groaned when she saw Puff's car at the entrance to the garage alongside Birdie's car.

The moment she stepped from the car she could hear Winnie barking. She smiled. There was nothing nicer than being greeted by a loving dog. She frowned when she opened the kitchen door. In DC you locked your doors and kept your alarm on. It was common sense. She said so as she watched Puff wolf down a slice of pizza.

Winnie was seated on a chair at the table, chewing on a pizza crust. She barked once by way of greeting, then went back to her lunch.

"Take a load off, Star? Want a slice? No anchovies. I'm FBI," he said, by way of explanation for not locking the kitchen door. "How's it going at the most famous address in the world? You having the time of your life?" He guffawed at his words. Winnie barked in agreement.

Quinn took off her coat and threw it over the back of the chair. "It's cold," she said indignantly as she bit the end off a slice of pizza.

"If I had known you were coming, I would have kept it hot. Since I didn't know you were coming, I let it get cold. Winnie doesn't have a problem with it, and neither do I. Actually, I like cold pizza. Sometimes I eat it for breakfast right out of the box. If you warm it in the microwave it gets soggy. Don't go getting too comfortable, Star. I want to know about that circus outside the White House."

"You're FBI, you figure it out. Where's my aunt? Why are you here in the middle of the afternoon? I thought she was coming home today."

"I came by to check on Winnie. I need to eat from time to time. Do you have a problem with that?"

"I have a problem with *you*, Lapufsky. Where's my aunt?"

"She was moved to rehab this morning. Five days, then she comes home with a private nurse and a walker. She's doing fine. She asked me to stay here, Quinn. How could I say no? I like Winnie. You couldn't take her, and I hate boarding a dog. When you take them home from the kennel they hate you, and they're never the same. Do you think I'm contaminating this house or something?"

"Of course not. All I did was ask where Birdie was."

"And I told you. By the way, she's conducting business from rehab just the way she did from the hospital. The funeral directors are messengering her photos, and she's on the phone with them constantly. She was having a real problem with McNally's using a number three rouge when they should have used a number two, and the lipstick was too waxy and pink. Peach Glow works perfectly on all lips. I'm on top of it all. She wants the cosmetologist who does the hair fired. Says everyone's hair looks like corkscrews, even the men's. She said it's supposed to be soft and flattering. She said to tell you not to worry about her; she's just fine. I took care of all that in between making sure the FBI continues to run smoothly so that your boyfriend can settle in comfortably. But it's looking more and more like he isn't going to squeak by," Puff said happily.

"You wouldn't have anything to do with that,

now would you, Lapufsky?" Quinn said, chomping on the cold pizza.

"Nope. His old man is supposedly trying to do some arm-twisting. I guess you can do that when you're a former governor with an impressive Rolodex. I don't think it's going to work, though. That's the scuttlebutt."

Quinn looked around the kitchen. She loved the rag carpets by the stove and sink. Birdie had taught her how to braid the old rags in strips during the winter months when they sat by the fire. They were old and almost threadbare, but Birdie refused to throw them away. She used to do her homework at this very table, with a plate of cookies and a glass of milk. They weren't homemade cookies, though, but store-bought. Birdie wasn't into baking even back then. As a child Quinn hadn't known the difference. Puff's mother baked cookies that melted in your mouth and tasted totally different from the store-bought kind.

"I love this kitchen. Actually, I love this whole house. I feel like crying, and I don't know why," she blurted.

Puff stared at her.

Winnie slapped one of her paws on the tabletop for attention. Puff handed over another crust. "You aren't supposed to give dogs tomatoes, turkey, or nuts. See, I was careful to scrape off the sauce," he said.

It was Quinn's turn to stare across the table.

"Did you read the paper today?" Puff asked.

"I've been so busy I haven't had a chance to yet. Why?"

"That tabloid rag said they did a voice analysis on the telephone call that came from the White House, and it was the first lady who called them. They're sniffing around big-time. Don't go getting paranoid now when you read the paper. The first lady's press secretary issued a statement saying Mrs. Jaye is returning to South Carolina due to health problems. A kinder, gentler climate, so to speak."

"That's a lie, and you know it. There's nothing wrong with her. Why are they doing that?"

Puff slapped both hands on top of the old wooden table. Winnie stopped chewing long enough to look up at him. She cocked her head to one side, then the other, before she went back to the pizza crust. "Look, Quinn, there are . . . people who are expected to act in certain ways. Presidents' wives do not shop at Victoria's Secret, and they do not call up tabloids. First ladies do not snub the press and do not make off-color statements to the press. They do not thumb their noses at the White House and the staff who work for the president. She's a very nice lady, but they consider her a loose cannon. They say she's irrational. She can be kept quiet and under control in her own environment. It's the only place where she's happy. Keep your thoughts to yourself and do your job."

"This whole thing sucks."

"Sometimes it does." Puff looked down at his watch. "I have ten minutes. Do you want to talk about *us?*"

"What us? There is no us," Quinn snorted.

"Yeah, there is. You just don't want to admit it. Denial is a terrible thing. All it does is make for misunderstandings and unhappiness. Alex Duval is a jerk and not worthy of you. He doesn't sweat. Ask yourself why that is. Everyone sweats. If you were half as smart as you claim to be, you'd see all that," Puff said, a smug look on his face.

"His socks match. He doesn't wear one blue and one black one like you do."

"Now that is really earth-shattering. I did that once. Once! The lightbulb burned out, and I just grabbed two socks. Unfortunately, they didn't match. Get your facts straight. It was one black and one brown, not blue and black."

"Whatever."

"I guess I better be on my way if you don't want to talk about us," Puff said, getting up to put on his coat. Winnie hopped off the chair and ran to the door, where she whimpered and whined. Puff dropped to his haunches and cupped her head in his hands. "I'll be back tonight. We'll have hamburgers." He pretended to drop his glove on the floor. Winnie had it in her mouth in a heartbeat. She waddled away to her lair.

"See this," Puff said, pointing to the rag rug by the stove. "This strip is from the dress you wore the first day of kindergarten. This strip is from your shorts when you went off to summer camp for the first time. This one is from your junior prom dress, and this one is from the senior prom. This strip is a ribbon from your christening bonnet, this one is from your dress from your first birthday party."

Stunned, Quinn gaped at Puff. "How . . . how do you know that?"

Puff smiled. "Birdie told me. I don't know exactly why, but I thought it was important for me to remember. If you want to read something special into that, be my guest. My mother does things like that. Birdie is like her in a lot of ways. You are lucky to have her because she loves you dearly. The same way I do."

Quinn could feel her shoulders start to sag. There were so many things she wanted to say, so many things she wanted to ask, but she didn't. Later, she knew, she would regret it. Tears burning her eyes, she did her best to smile when she said, "the hem of your coat has Winnie's pee on it." This was definitely a Puff and Quinn moment. Oil and water. He loved her dearly. That's what he'd said. Puff didn't lie. Well, hardly ever, and never about the important things. He loved her. Dearly.

Puff shrugged. "It's not important." Then he was gone.

Quinn ran over to the stove and sat down on the rag carpet and burst into tears. She cried as she rocked back and forth, hugging her knees.

In the living room, Winnie's ears flapped sideways at the strange noises coming from the kitchen. She trotted out to the kitchen and wiggled her way into Quinn's lap. Quinn hugged the dog until she squealed.

"I wish you could talk, Winnie. I know you like Puff. I also know you don't like Alex. Alex isn't a pet person, but that doesn't mean he isn't a good person." Winnie wiggled off her lap to waddle over to the sink, where she flopped down on the rag carpet. Her paws picked and dug at one of the braids on the rug. Quinn swiveled around to watch her. "That's the one from my Girl Scout uniform." She started to cry again.

Winnie dropped her head on her paws and closed her eyes.

Quinn ran to the bathroom, where she washed her face and combed her hair. How flushed her face was.

Back in the kitchen, she looked at her watch. She had plenty of time to straighten up the kitchen. She also had time to make dinner for Puff and Winnie if she wanted to. If she wanted to. Winnie loved stew. So did Puff.

Quinn pulled out Birdie's Crock-Pot. Frozen cubed chuck already packaged went in, along with a package of frozen carrots. She peeled potatoes and an onion, added some celery, and dumped them on top, adding a can of beef bouillon and a can of mushroom soup. She covered it and set the timer. By the time Puff got home it would be ready. It was certainly better than hamburgers, and this way Winnie would get her vegetables.

A frozen peach cobbler went into the oven. By the time she was ready to leave it would be done. *Little Miss Homemaker,* she thought sourly. The truth was, she loved cooking and keeping house. She delighted in spraying her bedsheets with lavender and other delicious scents. She liked a pretty bedroom with fresh-cut flowers on the dresser, and she loved eating off pretty dishes and drinking from crystal glasses.

She wondered if she was going to turn out to be an old maid. Her eyes started to burn at the thought.

She eyed the timer sitting on the stove. She pried the top off a can of soda pop as she rummaged in her bag for her cell phone. She dialed Alex's private number. He answered on the third ring, sounding breathless. "It's Quinn, Alex. I'm over at Birdie's. I stopped by my house to turn down the heat and to pack some clothes. I came over here to check on Winnie. By the way, do you like Winnie? I just wanted to give you a call before I head back to the White House. How is everything?"

"I'm not fond of animals. They shed. My court-room is under control. The weather is atrocious for this time of year, and it's beginning to look more and more like I won't get the nomination. Does that cover everything?"

"Are you angry at me, Alex? Are you having second thoughts? I think we need to talk."

"Right now that doesn't sound possible, does it? You're leaving, and I'm up to my eyeballs in politics. It sounds to me like you're the one who is having the second thoughts."

"That's not true, Alex. Things happened, and they snowballed. Working on the White House detail was always something I wanted to do, Alex. I had hoped you would be happy for me just the way I was happy for you when you were nominated to head up the FBI. Your tone of voice is telling me you aren't the least bit happy for me."

"I am happy for you, Quinn. It's the selfish side of me that isn't happy. I'm never going to get to see you. Three months is a long time even if we call each other every day. Talking isn't the same thing as feeling and touching."

"You could come south on weekends. I'll have time off. The pressures won't be as great at the first lady's home as they are here in Washington. And there will be other agents working the detail. I miss you." The moment the words rushed past her lips she knew they were a lie. She didn't miss him at all.

"I miss you, too." The words sounded just like words. Was he lying, too? She thought so.

"What's on your agenda for this evening, Alex?"

"Dinner with my parents. My father has some ideas he wants to run by me. My mother just wants to go to a classy restaurant so she can be *seen*. I'm not looking forward to it if that's your next question. What are you going to do? By the way, where's your old boyfriend?"

"How would I know where he is, Alex, and please stop referring to him as my old boyfriend. I don't like it when you do that. As to what I'll be doing this evening, I'll probably watch martial arts movies with the first lady. She's really into that karate-chopping stuff. She can get verbal when the going gets tough."

"I've read she has *simple down-home tastes*. I also read that she's addicted to those sudsy soap operas," Alex said. Quinn thought he made the words sound obscene. He might as well have used the term Southern white trash.

She was going to let his statement go but changed her mind. "You know, Alex, Mrs. Jaye is a lovely woman. She's kind, she's caring, and she's worked like a dog to help her husband get to where he is today with no thanks from his political cronies and the public. So what if she likes martial arts movies. I like them myself because of the action. All those spinmeisters out there have no real clue as to what she's all about. You like James Bond movies," she said pointedly.

"At least they have a plot. Ian Fleming was a wonderful writer. The adaptations don't stray from the books. Jackie Chan is a clown."

Quinn bristled. "Jackie Chan probably makes more money on one movie than you'll earn in a lifetime. We're fighting here, Alex, and it's silly. Each of us has different likes and dislikes. That's why we're individuals. I'm thinking we should hang up now before one of us says something we'll regret."

"Was this a duty call, Quinn, made out of guilt? Is Lapufsky there?"

"That does it! Good-bye, Alex," Quinn said, breaking the connection.

"I didn't want to get married anyway," Quinn said, knuckling her eyes as she walked over to the carpet by the stove and sat down again, this time crossing her legs Indian fashion. She picked at the braids making up the oval carpet. There were so many memories tied to the carpets. Wonderful memories, sad memories, funny memories. In a million years, Alex would never understand the meaning of the old carpets. How strange that Puff did. Birdie must like him a lot to share things like the carpets with him. How weird that she hadn't known that. Her slender fingers traced the tartan braid that had come from her first miniskirt. She'd worn that skirt with different blouses and sweaters until it fell apart. Her fingers searched for and found the navy braid from her first school uniform.

Memory Lane was a sad place to travel.

"You're going to make a lousy FBI director, Alex," she muttered as she got to her feet. She knew without a doubt that Puff would pack it in if Alex got the nomination. That was sad, too. Puff would have made an excellent director. Everything was sad. "You would probably make a lousy husband, too, Alex. Well, guess what, the wedding is off." She wondered why she didn't feel anything as she made the declaration.

When the timer went off fifteen minutes later, Quinn turned off the oven, removed the peach cobbler, and set it on a trivet. The stew was bubbling nicely. She added some dry parsley, a few cloves of garlic, some fresh ground pepper, and a dry bay leaf before she covered the Crock-Pot. The last thing she did was scribble a note that read, DO NOT EAT THE BAY LEAF AND, WHATEVER YOU DO, DO NOT GIVE IT TO WINNIE. She signed the note with a large Q.

She was on her way to her car when she turned around and headed back into the house, where she set the table with Birdie's favorite place mats and dishes. The place mats were yellow linen, the napkins the same but with appliquéd green tulips in the middle. The dishes, one of Birdie's rare finds, matched the mats perfectly along with a matching bouquet of colorful tulips in the center of the plates.

The last things to go on the table were a water dish for Winnie and a crystal goblet for Puff's beer, and the salt and pepper shakers.

Quinn felt like sixteen kinds of a fool when she reset the alarm and locked the door. Her eyes were misty when she climbed behind the wheel of her car. "I didn't do it for *him*. I did it for Winnie and because I'm a nice person." *Liar, liar, liar,* her conscience roared, as she drove over to the rehab facility to say good-bye to Birdie.

The drive was short, with little traffic to slow her down. Her mind raced with thoughts of Puff, the things he'd said and how she'd felt. He still loved her. The thought boggled her mind. It was obvious that he knew what her feelings were even though she'd denied them for so long. Oil and water.

Light snow was falling as Quinn locked her car. She sprinted around the building and up the walkway leading to the main entrance. Inside, she looked around before she followed the bright yellow arrows to the wing where Birdie was in residence.

Quinn knocked softly on the door, then opened it. Birdie was sitting upright in a leather chair by the window. She held out her arms and Quinn leaned over to kiss her aunt.

"You're lookin' good, Birdie. I just came from the house, and Winnie is fine. She was sleeping by the stove when I left. I had lunch with her and Puff. I just came by to say good-bye. We leave in the morning for Charleston. He said he loves me, Birdie. Puff. Puff said that. I'm babbling here. You like him, don't you?"

Birdie motioned to the bed where Quinn perched. "I always liked Ezra. But it's not important if I like him or not, it's what you feel. Judge Duval is a fine man. A bit of a stuffed shirt but most men in politics are stuffed shirts. Puff is a real person. So what if he's untidy. Winnie loves him. Dogs are shrewd judges of character as you well know. Follow your heart, baby.

"Charleston, eh? Beautiful city. Lettie will be a different person once she gets there. Living in the South is relaxing, and Lettie thrives on it. Give her my love and tell her I enjoyed reading about her in the paper. Tell her to call me anytime."

"Okay, Birdie. I'm sorry I can't stay longer. I'll call you when we get to Charleston. Don't worry about Winnie, and for heaven's sake, don't worry about me either. Do what they tell you, Birdie, and you'll be a hundred percent before you know it."

Quinn leaned over to hug and kiss her aunt. "I'll miss you, but I will call."

Birdie returned the kiss and hug, then waved Quinn to the door.

It was 9:23 when Ezra Lapufsky let himself into Birdie Langley's kitchen. He immediately locked the door and armed the security system before he dropped to his haunches to cup Winnie's head in his hands. The dog stared up at him adoringly. He tussled with her to the dog's delight until he became aware of the tantalizing odors wafting from the Crock-Pot on the counter. It was then that he noticed the table setting and the note Quinn had left him.

Peach cobbler. One of his favorites. He lifted the lid of the Crock-Pot. Ah, stew, another favorite, along with a loaf of crusty French bread still in its freezer wrap.

Puff looked around the empty kitchen and felt a sudden sense of loss. There should be someone standing on the carpet by the stove. Someone who smiled at him and asked how his day had gone. Someone who would help him off with his coat and kiss him soundly, saying she missed him. Instead, he had a fat little dog who was hugging his ankles and who had lathered him with wet kisses. A dog to sit at the table the way she sat with Birdie when no one was around. A dog who would love him forever and ever and never once question him about anything. A dog who would accept him with all his faults and still love him. The way Quinn had loved him once. Totally and unconditionally.

He felt awful when he threw his coat over the back of one of the kitchen chairs.

Puff walked over to the sideboard, where there were family pictures. Once he'd been on the sideboard. Now Alex Duval was on it. He picked up the picture of Alex and Quinn under one of the cherry trees along the Tidal Basin. Duval looked slick and dapper in his creased khakis with his crisp white shirt rolled up twice on each arm. A Rolex graced his left wrist. Brooks Brothers shoes, the ones with the tassels that lasted forever, were on his feet. He looked fit and trim, and Puff knew he worked out in one of Washington's most prestigious gyms.

Quinn looked . . . like Quinn. She was smiling into the camera, her arm around Duval's waist. They must have asked a tourist to take the picture. She was dressed stylishly in tailored slacks and a matching blouse. When they used to go to Rock Creek Park to picnic they wore scruffy clothes and carried their picnic in a grocery bag with a couple of old towels for a blanket. His eyes started to burn at the memory. He knew in his gut Duval had one of those wicker picnic hampers that came with a Range Rover complete with utensils, tablecloth, and napkins.

"Take a look at this guy, Winnie. What's he got that I don't have except money?" He waited for Winnie's reaction. He watched until she waddled out of the room, returning with Alex's shoe. Puff burst out laughing when he saw the dog had chewed the toe off right down to the sole. "Attagirl, Winnie, you are a girl after my own heart. C'mon, let's eat, but first I have to wash my hands. My mother was hell on wheels about us kids washing up before dinner." Winnie barked as she struggled to get up on her chair. She turned to Puff, who grinned and lifted her onto the padded seat full of cushions to enable her to eat at the table. "Ya know what, Winnie, Judge Alexander Duval would split a gut if he could see you sitting here eating off this fine china and drinking from this fine crystal bowl. Do we care? No, sir, we do not care!"

Puff was on his third helping of stew and his second beer when he noticed Winnie had not eaten the carrots or the potatoes. "No, no, I promised Birdie you would eat your vegetables so eat. All of them, Winnie. Then we'll go for a walk. I need the exercise as much as you do."

Winnie obediently ate the carrots and potatoes before she hopped off the chair and ran to the door.

Puff sighed as he shrugged into his coat before disarming the alarm system. A man and his dog. Birdie's dog actually. It didn't get any better than this. Did it?

12

Judge Alexander Duval turned onto Pennsylvania Avenue and headed for the 2800 block where the Four Seasons Hotel was located. The superdeluxe Aux Beaux Champs in the hotel was his mother's idea of the finest restaurant in town. A place to be seen and whispered about. He turned the keys to his car over to the valet. He walked inside to see his parents waiting for him in the lobby, looks of impatience on both their faces.

As always, he was struck by his parents' regal bearing. His father looked every bit the retired politician, right down to his snow-white hair, recent eye lift, and custom-cut suit. His mother, statuesque, patrician features glowing with expensive makeup, was dressed in the latest Paris fashions. There was nothing even remotely welcoming in either of his parents' expressions. His Rolex told him he was two minutes late. He decided not to offer up traffic as an explanation for his tardiness.

The Aux Beaux Champs was known for its inventive Continental cuisine with a strong French accent. He looked around, knowing his mother approved of the elegant dining room with its lush greenery and Chinoiserie. He knew his father would order the finest, most expensive wine, and his mother would order the spectacular three mignons of veal, lamb, and beef with the three different sauces that the restaurant was known for. His father would order and make a pretense of eating the creamy Breton cake. His mother would nibble on her dinner, as would his father, their way of saying the outrageous price of the dinners didn't matter. He himself would order from the low-cholesterol, low-calorie menu. Thanks to Quinn and her constant nagging about eating healthy.

Alex realized as he stared across the table at his parents that he hated these mandatory family dinners. He tried to conjure up some kind of emotion in regard to his parents, but it wouldn't come. They were just people sitting across from him, people he really didn't know. How could he know them? He'd had nannies from the day he was born until he was ten, at which point he was shuffled off to a private school and only returned for holidays. Summers were spent at a prestigious, sleep-away camp. Then it was prep school, and eventually college and law school. Summers were spent traveling, either alone or with a group of friends. There were never any family outings. They'd never even gone to the Washington Zoo as a family.

"You look tired, dear," Ardeth Duval said briskly as she brought her wineglass to her lips.

Something long held in check, snapped in Alex. "You were never a mother in the past, so don't try to act like one now. I work long hours, and yes, I am tired. I'm assuming we're here to discuss the lack of enthusiasm for my nomination. Let's get to it, sir." That was another thing. He never called his father Dad or Father. It was always sir when addressing him. His mother was Mother, never Mom.

"I don't think you're going to get the nomination, Alexander. I called in all my favors on both sides of the aisle. There's strong opposition to you. I'm thinking it's because you do your job too well. You're known as a fair-minded, impartial federal judge. Sometimes, Alexander, you have to skirt the edges a little."

"That's unethical," Alex snapped. "I can accept whatever happens. My life doesn't depend on being the director of the FBI, *sir.*"

"How is that going to look, Alexander?" his mother asked. "You'll be known as the man who didn't make it. It will be embarrassing."

"For whom, *Mother?*" He felt a blatant satisfaction when he saw his mother flinch at the word *mother.*

"You should be out there campaigning, trying to sell yourself. Your mother and I aren't sure that your fiancée . . ."

"What about Quinn?" Alex asked coldly.

"She *works,*" Ardeth Duval said just as coldly. "Good heavens, she used to be an FBI agent. She's had affairs. Now she's guarding the first lady, who is a mental case if I ever saw one. All that can't be helping you. By the way, Thanksgiving dinner is at four this year."

"I'm sorry, but I can't make it. You'll have to talk

to one another at the table since Allison is going to be in Europe."

"What exactly is that supposed to mean, Alexander?" the senior Duval snapped.

"What don't you understand? I won't be there. That means you will have to talk to one another at the table or eat in silence. In the past, all you've ever done is fawn over Allison and discuss all the ways that I have disappointed you. I don't care to hear it any longer. I won't be joining you for Christmas either."

"You're being childish, Alexander," his mother snapped.

"How could you possibly know what is childish and what isn't? You never allowed me to have a normal childhood. Isn't it wonderful that I can speak four languages and am fluent in Latin. Latin." His lip curled to show what he thought of that statement.

"*That* woman, with her crazy aunt, has rubbed off on you, Alexander. I will not tolerate disrespect from you, and neither will your father."

"That woman's name is Quinn. Her aunt isn't crazy either. You don't even know her, so don't condemn her with your holier-than-thou attitudes. *Respect* is just a word. If you want it, you have to earn it. I just realized I'm not hungry after all. If you'll excuse me, I'll leave you two alone now."

"Just one minute, Alexander," Conrad Duval said as he reached into his inside breast pocket. "I've taken the liberty of setting up some private meetings with some of the senators who can help you. They've assured me they're willing to go out on a limb."

There was such disdain on Alex's face, the elder Duval turned away.

Alex stormed out of the restaurant, his anger in check. In his car with the heater running, he thought about his unhappy life. An unhappy life until he'd met Quinn. She'd brought sunshine and laughter into his dark, miserable life. And he finally realized that with his stuffed-shirt attitude, he was in danger of losing her. Maybe he needed to loosen his tie once in a while when he was around Quinn, or maybe he needed to stop taking himself so seriously. Then again, maybe he needed to develop a liking for animals, dogs in particular. Maybe what he needed to do was be a little more spontaneous and earthy, like Ezra Lapufsky. He groaned at the thought.

He drove aimlessly in the dark night and, before he knew it, he was outside the Shanghai Garden, Quinn's favorite Chinese restaurant on Connecticut Avenue, a short distance from her aunt Birdie's house. He parked the car and went inside, where he ordered Quinn's favorite, Peking duck with taffy apples and bananas for dessert.

It was almost ten o'clock when he walked back to his car. Instead of turning the car around, he continued down Connecticut so he could ride past Birdie Langley's house. He was stunned to see the house lit up. Quinn must still be there. His heart quickened at the thought. He roared up the driveway and parked the car.

In the backyard, Puff was shivering inside his warm coat. The night was cold and clear, with millions of stars blinking in the heavens. On the fourth lap around the yard, Winnie finally found the spot she was searching for and squatted. The moment she was finished, she tugged at the leash to return to the house.

"Oh, oh, what have we here?" Puff muttered as he walked up to the kitchen door, where Alex Duval was about to ring the bell. "Kind of late to be visiting, isn't it, Your Honor?" Puff asked as he pulled Winnie closer to his leg and opened the door. "Come in, it's cold out here."

Puff watched as Duval's gaze swept across the kitchen table, taking in the place setting for two and the two empty beer bottles. *He thinks Quinn is here. He probably thinks she's upstairs getting ready for me, dressed in that animal print underwear. It would simply never occur to the judge that an animal, no matter how loved, would be allowed to sit at the table.* A devil perched itself on Puff's shoulders. "What can I do for you, Your Honor?"

"You're right, it is late. I thought Quinn might still be here. I'm sorry I bothered you," the judge said coolly.

That was when he was supposed to say, Quinn isn't here. Supposed to. "Oh, it's no bother, Your Honor."

"I'll say good night then."

Winnie chased him to the door, nipping at the heel of his shoe, obviously hoping to get a mate to the one she'd already confiscated and chewed. She showed her teeth and barked when the shoe remained on the judge's foot.

Puff was so pleased with the dog's performance,

he broke off a piece of the crust from the peach cobbler and handed it to the dog. Puff swore under his breath. Duval was the show horse, and he was the workhorse. "That was a rotten thing I just did, old girl, and you weren't so ladylike yourself, but we aren't going to let it bother us, and we sure as hell aren't going to lose any sleep over it either. I'm going to clean up here, then we're going to hit the sack. Get your gear ready and put it by the steps."

Winnie's gear included a ragged blanket, a yellow stuffed cat with one eye and whiskers, a duck that squeaked, and a bunch of Christmas bells tied to a shoelace.

The last thing Puff did before turning out the kitchen lights and arming the security system was to turn the picture of Alex and Quinn so that it faced the wall.

The only way to describe the first lady of the land the morning of her departure from the capital was to say she was ecstatic to be finally going home to a place she loved. She beamed, she glowed, she smiled, and she danced around the family quarters like a young girl. "Girls, the temperature in Charleston is a very nice sixty-eight degrees, thank you very much. It will seem like the height of summer after this weather. I'm packed. Come see my closet, there's nothing left. I've packed everything. I'm leaving my paintings, but I'm taking my paints and brushes."

Quinn blinked at the emptiness of the first lady's bedroom. Obviously, she meant what she said. There wasn't so much as a hairpin lying around. She felt her stomach tie itself into a knot. What would the ramifications be if the first lady made good on her promise not to return to the White House?

"Oh, just two hours to go before we board the plane. I did tell you, didn't I, that Jimmy Jaye and I will be billed for this flight. We pay for so much that the public doesn't know about. For instance, your salaries for this special assignment. I'm going to go down to the Oval Office to say good-bye to Jimmy Jaye. He came into my room this morning at five-thirty and kissed me on the cheek. That's not a proper good-bye. I was still asleep. He likes to go to the Treaty Room early in the morning when he gets up early like that. He started using it as his second-floor office right after we got here. It was nice having him so close by. We were able to sneak in little ten-minute visits almost every day." She sighed at the memory.

"There is *one* thing I am going to miss when I leave here. There is such a sense of magic and beauty that is unmatched when late at night I look out at the Washington Monument and the Jefferson Memorial across the fountain. I am not going to miss our private bowling alley. I never bowled even once. I'm not going to miss the sixty-seat theater either even if it does have its own popcorn machine. I never used that hot tub Gerald Ford had installed on the lawn, and neither Jimmy Jaye nor I ever used the heated pool. It's all such a waste. I tried to tell that to the accounting office, but no one would listen to me.

"Goodness, how I had to fight to get the Secret

Service detail moved farther away from our quarters. They were so . . . so *invasive.* The moment Jimmy Jaye leaves our quarters, he is surrounded by Secret Service. He hates it like I do," Lettie Jaye prattled on.

The moment she took a long, deep breath, Sadie asked, "Do you have a staff to cook and clean in Charleston, ma'am?"

"Lord, yes. Actually, just Cassie Franklin and her husband, Jacob. They've been with me for years and years. Forever it seems. Recently, her nephew helps them with the heavy cleaning, running errands, and the like. This new regime wanted me to pension them off, but Jimmy Jaye and I both refused. Cassie hates the Secret Service because they go with her to shop and they watch what she cooks. You girls wouldn't like living like this. This political life literally sucks everything out of you.

"Come along, we're going to go down to the Oval Office to see my husband. I want a proper good-bye, and I want to make sure Jimmy Jaye isn't upset with me. You'll see that privacy is at a premium when it comes to the Oval Office. They have peepholes in the doors so the staff can check to see when a meeting is over or about to be over. There's a private dining room and Jimmy Jaye's private study. He's in there a lot. He said the Oval Office was intimidating. I agree with him on that. When he can, Jimmy Jaye scoots out to the little patio that's off his dining room. It's just precious and is sheltered by trees and shrubs. If it wasn't for the Secret Service, it would be perfect. They don't talk, you know. My husband and I like to talk. They're like robots you wind up. They answer in clipped sentences or words, and they look at you as much as to say, don't talk to me. Neither of us could get used to it.

"The Secret Service doesn't do things like open doors, hold packages, or hold a purse even if it's just for a second. One time another first lady said, and this is supposedly a quote, 'If you want to remain on this detail, get your rear end over here and grab those bags.'"

Sadie gasped. The first lady smiled.

"One first lady who shall remain nameless called the Secret Service 'trained pigs' and insisted they stay ten yards away at all times." Sadie gasped again.

"I know all this because I read a lot," the first lady explained. "There is nothing I don't know about 1600 Pennsylvania Avenue. When the Clintons were in office, this address was called the campus because of the president being a baby boomer and his staff was baby-faced. The staff had their own radios and coffeemakers and wore casual clothing. George Stephanopoulos chewed bubble gum at his first press conference. George Bush stopped all that.

"Did you know there is a 27-million-dollar phone system installed for the entire White House? That's outrageous. That's so staff can dial direct and have voice mail. Half the time the darn thing doesn't work. Or so they say," the first lady said sourly.

"Wait till you meet Mrs. Tappen, Jimmy Jaye's secretary. She's like a bulldog. You have to go through her to get to Jimmy Jaye. Even I have to go through her. My own secretary is afraid of her. I'm not afraid of her. Everyone sucks up to her. Isn't that a crude statement? It is, I know."

She's like a runaway train, Quinn thought. *Or she's on speed.*

"All right, ladies, we're about to beard the lion, Mrs. Tappen." Lettie Jaye opened the door and walked over to the secretary. "I'd like to see my husband, Sylvia. All I need is five minutes. Today, not tomorrow or the next day. Right now to be specific."

"Mrs. Jaye, you know the rules. You should have called down earlier and requested time. The president is in a meeting, and the minute it's over he has to go on to another meeting followed by a briefing. I don't see how I can possibly arrange even five minutes."

"Find a way, Mrs. Tappen. I'm not leaving here till I see my husband. Pencil me in between meetings. The world won't come to an end if you do that."

Sylvia Tappen pursed her mouth. "You're being difficult, Mrs. Jaye. I just explained to you that it is impossible right now."

Lettie Jaye walked around Sylvia Tappen's desk and over to the door to look through the peephole. She turned and looked the secretary in the eye. "The only people in there are the press secretary and the COS." In a flash she had the door open and was saying, "Jimmy Jaye . . ." before she was stopped by two Secret Service Agents. It was so slickly done that Quinn found herself backing up a step.

"I came to say good-bye, Jimmy Jaye. Your . . . your *goons* are touching me. Aren't you going to do something?"

"Of course I'm going to do something. Sit down, sweetheart, and I'll come around and kiss you good-bye. You know the rules. You should have called, or I would have come upstairs. We aren't back home, sweetheart. This is the White House, and we do things differently here. I wish you'd cooperate a little more fully, Lettie."

Lettie Jaye clucked her tongue in disgust. "You aren't my husband. Where is he?"

"I'm right here. Are you having one of your bad days again, Lettie?"

"Actually, whoever you are, I *was* having a good day until I came in here. Where is my real husband? What's the cat's name, Jimmy Jaye?"

The president threw his hands in the air. "Lettie, let's not do that cat thing again. I was your husband when I got up this morning, and nothing has changed since then."

"What did you do when you got up this morning, Jimmy Jaye?" the first lady persisted, her tone angry, her stance that of a pugnacious bulldog.

"I got up at five, peeked in on you, but you were sound asleep so I showered, shaved, dressed, and was in the dining room at five-thirty, where I had scrambled eggs, sausage, toast, and coffee. I had a briefing at six and have been on the go ever since. As much as I love this little respite, and love seeing you, I'm afraid we have to say good-bye so I can get back to running the country. Now, let me give you a kiss."

"That will be the day. No one but my *real* husband kisses these lips. There's a conspiracy going on here. You might be able to fool some of these people, but you can't fool me. You aren't my husband! Those tabloid people out front are going to figure it out. *They're smart!*"

"Mrs. Jaye, if you so much as breathe around those people, there is going to be trouble," the chief of staff said. "You need to leave now with your agents."

"Did you just threaten me, Mr. Neville?"

Red in the face, the COS said, "Of course not. I was warning you that you can't trust those tabloid people."

"I think, Mr. Neville, that right now, I would trust them more than I trust you and this imposter who is claiming to be my husband."

One of the president's agents stepped forward to take hold of the first lady's arm. Sadie stepped forward, her arm outstretched. "That's far enough. The first lady is leaving."

Quinn stepped around the agent, her gaze sweeping the room, settling on the president in particular. The moment she had everything committed to memory, she followed the first lady and Sadie upstairs to the family quarters.

Tears ran down Lettie Jaye's cheeks. "That wasn't my husband. He didn't say he kissed me on the cheek this morning. He doesn't know the name of the cat. I told you, my husband never calls me sweetheart. He calls me darlin'. You heard him yourself. Where is he? Why are they doing this? What is that man doing standing in for my husband?" She wailed. "Oh, God, maybe I shouldn't go back to Charleston. What if they're drugging him or something equally evil? How will I know? I'm telling you, that was not my husband. I just hate leaving Jimmy Jaye behind, but what else can I do? My thinking is by leaving and causing all this ruckus, I can save him from back home. With me out of the way, I'm hoping we can flush out those who are . . . who are . . . doing what they're doing.

"Another thing, Jimmy Jaye's hair is *fluffy*. That man's hair is like straw. I know my husband, and that imposter was not my husband. I need a cigarette. And a drink."

Quinn looked at Sadie, who nodded.

"Is brandy all right?" Quinn asked as she walked into the kitchen.

"Brandy is fine. You believe me, don't you?"

"Mrs. Jaye, we don't know your husband the way you do. We do believe that you believe it isn't your husband," she hedged, trying to be tactful.

"So you think I'm crazy, too. I'm not. I have to get out of here. Jimmy Jaye will just have to fend for himself." She downed the fiery liquid in one long swallow.

Sadie's voice was hesitant when she said, "Ma'am, is it possible that your husband, the president, is . . . is in on whatever you think is going on? You need to think about that, ma'am."

"I have thought about it. That's another reason I have to get out of here. I don't feel safe here, and I don't care how that sounds. I'm going to my room to lie down for a while. Call me when it's time to leave."

"All right, Mrs. Jaye," Quinn said.

When the door to the first lady's room closed, both women looked at one another. "Was it the *real* one?" Sadie hissed.

"Not to my way of thinking," Quinn said, mouthing the words. "She's right about his hair, too." Sadie flopped down on a chair and rubbed her temples.

"Are you going to tell Puff about the president's hair?" Sadie asked, taking her cue from Quinn and mouthing the words.

Quinn shook her head. "He'd never believe it."

"Now what?" Sadie said.

"Now we wait until it's time to leave for Charleston."

The first lady, her eyes puffy from crying, apologized to Quinn and Sadie for what she called losing her cool. "I really am not going to miss *this place* at all. I don't know if you girls realize this, but I finally figured it out with a little help from some of my friends. Making me look bad, attacking me, makes the president look bad. People are careful what they say about a president, but his wife is fair game. Keep that in mind."

"Yes, ma'am," both agents said in unison.

Sadie spoke into the microphone attached to the cuff of her coat. "We're on our way."

"Wait," Quinn said. She ran back to the first lady's television and DVD and grabbed the videos they'd watched earlier. She dumped them in the Blockbuster plastic bag.

"Ma'am, you'll have to carry these. Our hands need to be free," she whispered in her ear. "We want

to study the president when we get to Charleston."
The first lady's eyes lit up as she reached for the bag.

She was upbeat now as she started a monologue
about Air Force One. "It's really only called Air Force
One when the president is on board. Actually, there
are two Air Force One planes, I mean, and the Air
Force maintains them at Andrews Air Force Base. It
cost $250 million to outfit each of them. Jimmy Jaye
was appalled at the cost. Of course they are lavish.
The truth is, each one of those planes is a flying
White House.

"Each plane has a presidential suite complete with
VIP showers, a private presidential office, a staff conference room that seats eight people, a separate section that can be converted to a complete trauma
center with a foldout operating table, another office
area with fax machines, computers, and copy
machines. In case the president wants to write a
speech or something.

"The planes have a guest area, a Secret Service
area, a fourteen-seat compartment for the press, and
seven bathrooms. Can you believe that, seven bathrooms? Jimmy Jaye and I were dumbfounded when
we saw that. We were just as dumbfounded to find
out each plane has eighty-seven telephones, some
white, some beige for classified conversations.

"The upper deck is for state-of-the-art communications gear. However, there is no escape pod, but
the planes have sophisticated antijamming and
antimissile gear, a tactical collision-avoidance system, wind-shear detection capabilities, wiring that is
protected against the electromagnetic effects of a

nuclear blast, and aerial-refueling capacity, should that be needed beyond the plane's initial range of ninety-six hundred miles. I memorized all of that knowing someday I would have the opportunity to repeat it. I hope you feel like you're learning something from me."

"We sure are, ma'am," Quinn said.

"Air Force One flies at six hundred miles an hour and costs thirty-five thousand dollars an hour to operate. Am I boring you girls? Jimmy Jaye said it was important for me to know all this. I don't know why. You girls are the first people I've ever talked to about the planes.

"The presidents gave the planes names. Did you know that? *Queenie* was the first presidential jet plane and carried Dwight Eisenhower to Germany. *Queenie*'s predecessor was *Columbine II*. It was junked, and they eventually restored and refitted it and called it *Columbine III.* Truman's plane was a DC-6 'Sam Fox' 7451 and was called *Independence*. Roosevelt's 'Sam Fox' was named the *Sacred Cow.* Jimmy Jaye calls ours, *Little Paint*. For me. That's just between us, girls. I guess that was more than you wanted to know."

"No, not at all, ma'am. I never would have known all those things if you hadn't mentioned them. Like you said, I like to learn new things. I don't think any other first lady was or is as knowledgeable as you are."

"For all the good it did me." Lettie Jaye dabbed at the corners of her eyes with her knuckles. "I read everything I could get my hands on, and I memorized it all. I did it for Jimmy Jaye. I didn't want to be an embarrassment to him or the administration, but they never let me get out of the box. They pummeled me from day one.

"Well, that's enough of that," the first lady continued. "We're going home now, and home is where my heart is. Let's talk about something pleasant, like your young men. Oh, yes, we also have a wedding to plan, don't we?" The first lady twinkled.

Sadie burst out laughing as Quinn squirmed in her seat.

The first lady smiled from ear to ear.

13

"We're home!" the first lady exclaimed as she craned her neck to look out of the limousine's window. "I feel like I've been reborn. Inside of five minutes, you girls are going to understand why I love this place so much. Just look out of the window. You can see people actually walking by. There are cars on the road with people in them. People. When we get out of the car you'll be able to smell the ocean, and from the front bedrooms upstairs you'll be able to see Fort Sumter. What *are* they waiting for? The weather is lovely. I can't wait to see Cassie, my housekeeper!"

"All right, ma'am, we're cleared to exit the car. Sadie and I go first, you follow," Quinn said as she eyeballed the people meandering down the street, her eyes everywhere. Sadie, her wrist close to her mouth, took her position on the right side of the first lady.

"Hello, how are you? Beautiful day, isn't it?" the first lady said to a young couple who nodded agreeably. She turned to Quinn. "They don't even know who I am. Isn't that wonderful?" Quinn thought about the statement as she ushered her charge through a mas-

sive wooden, steel-reinforced gate that was painted
Charleston Green. She listened as the three locks were
snapped into place and a Secret Service Agent took up
his position to the right of the gate.

"Feast your eyes, girls, and tell me this isn't one
of the most beautiful spots you've ever seen in your
life."

Quinn tensed as she looked around. She spoke
into the microphone on her wrist. "What's the security here?" she asked as she obediently looked
around the lush courtyard.

Coming to Charleston with the first lady was considered an out-and-out garbage detail for the agents.
Dan Zack's surly response affirmed his opinion of
the detail. "We have it covered, Agent Star. All you
have to do is babysit the first lady and sip tea."

"I asked you a direct question, Agent Zack. Don't
make me come out there," Quinn snapped.

The agent's tone changed slightly. "The security is
the same as at the White House. *Little Paint* is as safe
here as she was there. The house on the left is empty
and has been empty for years. It was owned at one
time by the president's brother and his wife. Their
names were Sue Ellen and Kincaid Ashwood Jaye.
The house and the property were willed to the president on their deaths nine years ago. The premises
have been secured. The house on the right is also
empty, and the government owns it. The government purchased the property the day after the president was inaugurated. Those premises have also
been secured. There are agents all along the perime-
ters of the three properties."

"Are we safe and sound?" the first lady questioned as she sat down on an iron bench to remove her shoes and knee-highs. She wiggled her toes, then dug them into the moss growing between the old Charleston bricks. "Ah, this is just perfect." She sighed happily. "So what do you think?" she asked, waving her arms about.

"Ma'am, I'm not up on courtyards or horticulture. Is this copied from a certain period or a special place?" Quinn asked.

"No. My great-grandmother loved the earth. She loved planting things, especially flowers. Each generation added something. The brick wall that backs up to the Ashwood Jaye house . . . it will always be the Ashwood Jaye house to me, is Jimmy Jaye's and my contribution. Actually, Jimmy Jaye laid the brick himself. It's all old Charleston brick, such a pretty pink color. We did the cutouts or shelves for want of a better word. In the spring we have beautiful clay pots full of geraniums and petunias, and they're like a rainbow the way they cascade down the wall. The tiered wall was my mama's design. She wanted ivy and moss to grow between the bricks, and, as you can see, it looks almost like a walled carpet. The tree was huge when I was a little girl. Even back then it shaded the entire courtyard. When we were just private citizens, we virtually lived out here in nice weather. Sometimes on really hot nights, Jimmy Jaye would sleep in his old Pauley's Island hammock. I'd sleep on the glider in the corner.

"We never had a Christmas tree. I know it's against tradition, but we did it anyway. Instead, we'd light up this old angel oak from top to bottom. Thousands of colored lights. It is the prettiest thing you could ever want to see. Cassie and I would drape the circular bench at the base of the tree with red velvet and pile the presents on top. It's so closed in that it never really gets cold, so we can pretty much enjoy this peaceful haven all year long. We rarely entertained inside. Everyone was more comfortable out here. Jacob, he's Cassie's husband, and you'll meet him when he returns from some trip he had to take, would bring chairs and little tables with beautiful candles for centerpieces. Our friends never wanted to leave when we would shoo them out at midnight. I never see those friends anymore. I'm going to call them tomorrow and find out exactly why they no longer want to claim us as friends," the first lady fretted.

"I also want to order my poinsettias from Dwayne Ward's nursery in Summerville. He'll bring them out here and set them up on the wall in all the niches and along the border. This little slice of paradise is prettier than the White House at Christmastime. Here in the South we start to decorate the day after Thanksgiving. It's a tradition.

"Did I tell you Jimmy Jaye and I own a house in Summerville? We do. It belonged to Jimmy Jaye's grandmother, then his mother, and finally it came to him. My grandmother, like many people back then, believed that life was healthier because of the pine trees. I don't believe it because the trees are so ugly. Anything that ugly can't be good for you. And they drop pollen. People back then were so misinformed.

We never go there anymore. It takes an Act of Congress to arrange it, and Jimmy Jaye and I just got sick and tired of trying to make arrangements to visit the house and the town only to be thwarted at every turn.

"I say we get settled in, girls, unpack, and come down here for tea. Tea will be a mint julep and munchies. Cassie will be making shrimp and grits for dinner with red velvet cake for dessert. Doesn't that sound grand?"

"Yes, ma'am," both agents said in unison.

"After I change my clothes, girls, I want you to go over this house with a fine-toothed comb to see if we're *bugged*. If we are, I want to know."

Both agents looked at one another as they followed the barefoot first lady into the house.

Sadie stared at the splendor of the antebellum mansion. "Oh, I love this! Someday, I want a house just like this. Ma'am, I can see why you love this place so much. Oh," she gushed, "these floors are beautiful, and look at all the old woodwork and the doors . . . they're breathtaking. I love the fireplaces. Everything is so . . . burnished and sparkly. I can see why you were happy living here. The staircase is exquisite. The foyer is bigger than my apartment. I read somewhere that people judge your house by your foyer. It's just perfect. Isn't it perfect, Quinn?" she asked, twirling around trying to see everything at a glance. Quinn nodded.

The first lady beamed her pleasure. "This is Cassie, girls. Cassie has been like a sister to me all these years. We were playmates from the age of three. When she finished school, she worked for Mama, then she came with me when Mama passed away. I wanted her to retire, but she wouldn't hear of it. She lives in the little guest cottage beyond the courtyard. Cassie, this is Secret Service Agents Quinn Star and Sadie Wilson."

Cassie Franklin's handshake was bone-crushing. Quinn winced at the little woman's powerful grasp. She was tiny, not quite five feet tall. She, too, was in her bare feet as she padded about the room in her pristine white apron. Her smile was infectious, her eyes full of merriment, and she jabbed a fork that was still in her hand as she led the way to the kitchen. "Are they going to be with us forever?" she asked the first lady, indicating the Secret Service Agents outside.

"It looks that way at the moment, Cassie. Ignore them like I do. I'm home now, and I'm not going back."

"Good for you, Lettie. How's Jimmy Jaye?"

"I don't know, Cassie. We'll talk about all that tonight when it's time for bed. I have so much to tell you. Did anyone call or write?" she asked wistfully.

"No, and no one stopped by either. I did see Miz Alice Prentice at the grocery store the other day. She nodded. I told you, Lettie, Miz Alice always had a high snoot factor. I made it my business to follow her down the cereal aisle and let her know you would be in residence as of today. She said, 'How nice.'"

Lettie Jaye bit down on her lower lip and turned away. "We're going to settle in, Cassie, then have juleps in the courtyard."

"Sadie and I will have tea or soda," Quinn said, looking around. "We can't drink on duty, ma'am."

"That's not a problem. I'll drink theirs, Cassie. I'm home now, and I can do whatever I damn well please. We have cigarettes, don't we?"

"I thought you quit, Lettie. Southern belles do not smoke, as you well know."

"I did quit, Cassie, but *they* got the best of me. I have to work up to quitting again. I need to be stress-free when I quit. One hour, and we'll all meet down here. Is it my imagination or is it getting cooler?"

"There's a cold front moving in, Lettie. I heard Ben Pogue say so on the early news this morning. You might want to wear a shawl or a sweater. You know you don't like to shiver. What *did* you buy at Victoria's Secret, Lettie?"

"You know about that! Good grief. I'll *show* you this evening. I bought something for you."

The housekeeper smacked her hands in glee. "Come along, girls, I'll show you to your rooms and give you a little history of the house."

Quinn looked over her shoulder to make sure the Secret Service Agent was still standing by the wall gate before she closed the door behind her.

"This kitchen has not had a lot of work done to it other than new appliances when the old ones gave out. The entire floor is all Charleston brick. I scrub it, and the patina is from years and years of wear. The fireplace works and is two-sided. Lettie likes to sit and rock after dinner. Those two rocking chairs belonged to her great-grandmother. The president couldn't sit still long enough to rock. He was always up and doing something, so it would be Lettie and me that did the rocking. Lettie is just a regular person. She's not like those other Southern belles she calls her friends. She helps me with the dishes and when it's time for spring and fall cleaning, she's always right there with the mop and bucket. When it comes to this old house, we do it all together because we both love it. I've lived here all my life. I guess I'll be dying here, too. See this old table with the claw feet. It takes six men to move it, that's how heavy it is. Lettie and the president, when he's here, like to sit at the table, drink their coffee, and read the *Post and Courier.* It's our local paper, but it carries national news, too. The president is partial to *USA Today* because the paper has colored pictures. I like it myself. The thing we all like the best is that you can see out the windows to the courtyard. We're all partial to the greenery. The camellias are blooming now. By Christmastime they'll all be in bloom. Lettie has this giant fishbowl that she fills with the snow-white camellias for the table on Thanksgiving. She sets a fine table. She told me those state dinners are the pits."

Quinn smiled, and Sadie giggled.

"The dining room is formal. All these old houses on the Battery have formal dining rooms. Here the floors are heart of pine and as old as the house. I have someone help me clean and polish them. Every room in the house has a working fireplace. Of course we don't use them all just like we don't use all eleven bathrooms."

"Eleven!" Sadie gasped.

"There are three full floors. The president had an

elevator installed several years ago. It was the best thing he could have done for these old bones. He did it just for me, but I suspect Lettie had something to do with it. That woman coddles me. I missed her so when they went off to Washington. It was an ugly thing they did to my Lettie. Just out-and-out ugly. Those newspaper and television people should all get pimples on their rumps. Lettie used to call me late at night and cry and cry. I tried to make her feel better, but I know it didn't work.

"On this wall are the portraits of Lettie's ancestors and the other side of the room are the president's. See how they glare at each other? The president hates this room."

Cassie led them into a larger room. This is the living room. The plantation shutters are originals. We get the full sun in these front rooms, and, as you know, during July and August the heat is brutal. We close the shutters tight, and it helps a little. The president insisted all of Lettie's pictures be hung in here. He hung some of them himself. He was always real handy with a hammer. Sometimes I just can't believe he's president of the United States.

"Lettie loves yellow, so, as you can see, all the sofas and chairs are yellow. They complement the paintings. The greenery is left up to me to tend. The tables are all cherrywood. We use beeswax to keep them looking nice. Humidity here in the summer is a problem.

"We have two sunrooms, and Lettie and the president each have a small office on this floor. There are two powder rooms off each of the sunrooms.

"This is the foyer and, of course, the staircase. The elevator is to the left. It looks just like a closet door. Like you said, Miss Sadie, they used to say a house and the hostess of the house were judged by her foyer. This particular foyer is larger than most on the Battery. It's eighteen by twenty-six, mostly to accommodate the staircase. The rugs are rare Orientals. The cabinets are from the president's family as are the crystal and the other antiques. Lettie's stuff is on the second floor. During Hurricane Hugo in 1989 the front of the house took the brunt of the storm and had to be done over. We kept it just the way it had been, didn't change a thing. This house is well over three hundred years old.

"My nephew already took your bags to your rooms, so we can just step into the elevator, and I'll show you your rooms. It will be just you two on the second floor. Lettie's suite of rooms is on the third floor because of the lighting. She has a small studio next to her suite. A verandah runs all around the first and second floors. There are agents posted everywhere, so don't be alarmed if you see someone walking about outside your windows. You can draw the drapes if you like. Well, here we are. I put you next to each other because there is a connecting door, and I thought you might like to talk to one another without running out into the hall. If you like, I can have my nephew build you a fire or you can simply turn up the heat. Over the years we had all new plumbing and wiring installed, so you should be very comfortable. If there's anything you need, just pull the bell cord. There's a dumbwaiter in each room and a laundry chute. Lettie and I used to slide and ride down both of them when we were little. We were hellions back then, that's for sure. Well, I'll leave you now to settle in," Cassie said breathlessly.

When the door closed behind the housekeeper, Quinn turned to Sadie. "This room is bigger than the entire first floor of my house in Georgetown. Would you look at that four-poster! Lord, three steps to climb into it! Alex's sister would get orgasmic if she could see all these antiques. Speaking of Alex, I should call him. Puff, too. Check out your room, Sadie, while I see if I can reach either one of them. Who has the videos?"

"I have them," Sadie said. Lowering her voice to a whisper, Sadie continued, "Quinn, the housekeeper will be able to back up the first lady's opinion on her husband if we show her the videos. I'm sure if the two women are as close as they appear to be, she'll know if it is or isn't the president. When are we going to check for bugs?"

"Just as soon as I make these calls," Quinn whispered in return. "I'm going to ask Puff if the house is bugged just to be on the safe side."

Birdie Langley woke from a sound sleep, her hands clenched into tight fists. She lay quietly, listening to the silence surrounding her. This might be a rehab center but it was just as quiet as a hospital in the middle of the night. Was it a noise? Did someone open her door to check on her? Did she have a bad dream?

She looked around in the dim light and decided

she hated the place as much as she hated the hospital she'd been in. It was then that she realized she'd fallen asleep with the television on. Evidently no one had bothered to turn it off, which also meant no one had checked on her during the night. So, what was it that woke her up? If she'd had a bad dream, she couldn't remember it. She looked up at the television. She'd been watching CNN earlier. All through the night they hashed and rehashed the daily news. She watched now as President Jaye spoke to reporters as he crossed the lawn to the helicopter that would take him to Camp David for some kind of meeting. She reached for her glasses and stared at the image facing her.

She knew James Madison Jaye almost as well as she knew Lettie Jaye. She couldn't remember Jimmy having such a long-legged stride, nor could she ever remember him moving so quickly. People from the South, and Jimmy was no exception, tended to walk more slowly than fast-track Northerners. Also, as best she could remember, Jimmy would always stop and face reporters and patiently drawl out his responses. This long-legged Jimmy was calling out answers over his shoulder. She really did wish he would get his hair color right. She had to remember to needle Lettie about the president using Grecian Formula. She cackled at what she thought would be the first lady's response.

Birdie leaned back into her nest of pillows and closed her eyes, but sleep eluded her. She felt wired, and didn't know why. Maybe it was this silent place and all the smells that went with it.

Why had she listened to that young doctor? She should have insisted on going home. She could afford to have a therapist come to the house to help her. She could also afford a daily domestic. The bottom line was she missed Winnie terribly. She needed to be home with her files, her computer, and her scrapbooks.

Scrapbooks!

She had hundreds of pictures of the president of the United States. Hundreds. Why was that important? Why was she even thinking about it?

Angry with herself for what she considered a senior moment, she pressed the button on the side of the bed to raise it. She turned the television back on and switched the channel to MSNBC and waited. Sooner or later, the news channel would show the president just the way CNN had.

She needed to talk to her niece. Why? Where did that thought come from? Maybe she should talk to Ezra. On the other hand, maybe she shouldn't talk to anyone. Too many questions for the middle of the night. She longed for Winnie, who was her best friend and confidante. Tears gathered in her faded blue eyes.

Her eyes snapped open. "I'm going home in the morning even if I have to crawl," she announced to the semidark room.

There was no place like home, and that's exactly where she was going.

Ezra Lapufsky nicked himself when he heard the sound of the ambulance siren. He nicked himself again when Winnie made a beeline for the steps and thumped her way to the bottom. "What the hell . . ."

Holding a washcloth to his chin, he loped down the hall and on down the steps in time to see Birdie Langley being helped in the front door. He watched, his bushy eyebrows shooting up to his hairline, as Winnie whirled and twirled, her ears flapping faster than an oscillating fan. Her encore was to sit up on her flat bottom and howl at seeing her mistress. He felt jealous.

"Now, that's a greeting if I ever saw one. I missed you, too, girl! Did you take good care of my dog, Ezra?" Birdie asked as she made her way to her favorite chair with the aid of her walker.

"Your dog is fine, as you can see, Birdie. You took it on the lam, didn't you?"

"Such powers of deduction. I guess that's why you're so valuable to the FBI. They can do the same thing for me here that they were doing in rehab. I have a Jacuzzi, and they're coming today to install one of those chair rails. I'm doing just fine. I have a nurse with me, as you can also see, and the therapist will be here shortly. I've got it covered, Ezra. I've been working on all of this since five o'clock this morning. An agency is sending over a housekeeper and a cook."

"Good for you. There's no place like home. My mother says that all the time. If you're sure you have it all covered, I'll finish up and get out of your hair."

"I'd like it if you'd stay on a while longer, Ezra. For Winnie. Of course, if you don't want to, I understand. I have some things I'd like to talk over with you this evening. I hope you don't feel I'm taking advantage of you."

"I'll help in any way I can, Birdie. I'll try to make it home by seven, eight at the latest. You take care of yourself. Call me if you run into any snags."

"Such a nice man. He's so perfect for my niece," Birdie mentioned to the stone-faced nurse standing next to her chair. "I'm just going to sit here in my chair and enjoy my home and my dog. Help yourself to anything in the kitchen." Minutes later, she was asleep, Winnie next to her on her chair.

It was ten minutes past eight when Ezra Lapufsky walked into Birdie Langley's kitchen to the tantalizing smell of dinner roasting in the oven. He tried to guess what he would be eating but gave up. He questioned Birdie, who was sitting at her little kitchen desk, papers and scrapbooks scattered all around her. Winnie was lying on the floor near the desk. She barked a greeting and went back to snoozing.

"Herb-roasted chicken with giblet stuffing and giblet gravy. Winnie is having chicken and rice along with carrots and peas. You're just in time, Ezra. Take off your tie and shoes, wash up, and we can eat."

"Yes, ma'am," Ezra said smartly. He knew an order when he heard one.

An hour later, Winnie gobbled her dinner and waited patiently for her dessert of blackberry shortcake. She looked adoringly at Puff and Birdie, trying to decide where she had the best chance of getting more than a teaspoon of the flaky cake. She waddled over to Puff, then backtracked to Birdie, who added another small square of cake to her plate along with a dollop of pure whipped cream. She licked every crumb before she trotted over to the carpet by the stove and lay down. "The best part is we don't have to clean up," Birdie said.

"It was a wonderful dinner, Birdie," Puff said, loosening his belt buckle. "I don't know how I'm going to adjust to eating out of cartons and paper bags when you kick me out of here."

"You can stay as long as you like, Ezra. It's nice to have a man in the house. It is going to be a problem with Winnie when you leave. Believe it or not, I do get lonely sometimes. Now, don't be telling that to Quinn, or she'll start to feel guilty. She comes by as often as she can, but she has her life to live. I did want you both to get together. You are much too stubborn, Ezra, and so is Quinn. Judge Duval is not the man I would choose for her. Sometimes he reminds me of one of my *stiffs*. He appears to be so uptight all the time. I don't think the man has a spontaneous bone in his entire body. You, like Quinn, have some piss and vinegar to you."

Puff felt his chest expand. He smiled. "I'm working on it, Birdie. Have you heard from Quinn since she got to Charleston?"

"No. I'm sure she's busy. Lettie Jaye can keep you hopping. I knew when she went to Washington that it wasn't going to work for her. Not that she didn't try. She did. Jimmy didn't have a bit of trouble. All in all, he's done well by the country. He inherited a mess with the economy and terrorism and all, but we're weathering it. What do you think of him personally, Ezra?" Birdie asked carefully.

"We didn't get up close and personal, Birdie. The closest I came to him was shaking his hand, then he retired to his desk and I sat on the sofa. I thought he would sit in the chair opposite me, but he didn't. The room was crowded with people. The president told me what he and the first lady wanted. I listened. Most of the people on his staff tried to dissuade him. He listened, then told all of them to stand down and he would make the decision, and since he and the first lady were footing the bills, there was no problem. He told the room at large that the first lady's happiness was his primary goal. He also chastised everyone for letting the media get out of control when it came to his wife. He wasn't a happy camper that first day. Ballinger, who's in charge of the Secret Service detail, was chewing nails and spitting rust. I liked the president because he was looking out for his wife and not taking any crap from his advisors. Does that answer your question?"

Birdie nodded. "How many times were you in his company?"

"Just one other time. We talked, one-on-one, about four times on the phone when Quinn wouldn't commit. The second time I met him he was in a pissy mood. Why are you asking me these questions, Birdie?"

"No reason," Birdie responded vaguely. "I couldn't sleep last night so I was watching the news channels rehash the day's political news. They showed Jimmy heading off to Camp David. It's like the man has two personalities and two hair colors. I wish he'd get his hair color right or his people would get it right. Women notice things like that. Doing what I do with the funeral homes makes me even more aware of hair coloring. It's important to remain consistent."

Puff shrugged as he made a mental note to pay more attention to the president's hair color.

"Do you find it a little strange, Ezra, that all the people he brought with him from the South defected? Lettie said they were forced out."

"Let's not go there, Birdie. Some people just don't have the makeup for twenty-four/seven scrutiny. Other people thrive on it. Now, is there anything else I can do for you before I retire. I'm bushed today. I can't seem to get a handle on this cold weather so early."

"There is one thing. I don't know what the mail procedures are at the Southern White House, so I was wondering if you could overnight a parcel with some pictures for Lettie and Quinn. I was going through some of my scrapbooks this afternoon, and I thought Lettie might like them. I didn't seal the envelope, so you can check it out to see that they are just photos. Can you do that for me?"

"Of course. Where is it?"

"The brown envelope on my desk. Be sure to overnight it. Now, what time will you be getting up in the morning? I can have our new cook make you breakfast."

Puff beamed as he riffled through the pictures in the envelope. He sealed it, scribbled his name across the flap, and laid it on top of his overcoat. "I get up at five. It's been a while since I had blueberry pancakes with blueberry syrup."

"Done!" Birdie said, smacking the tabletop. Winnie opened one sleepy eye, then closed it. "Sleep tight. Check out my chair rail. I had them put a side car on it for Winnie. We tried it out a few times this afternoon. She loves it. I'm going to teach her how to climb in and start it up herself."

"Do you want me to walk her before I go upstairs?"

"That would be nice, Ezra. Tell me something, what is your honest opinion of Judge Duval?"

"Are you comparing him and me where Quinn is concerned? If you are, he's the show horse, and I'm the workhorse. He understands Washington and the politics behind it. He has an impeccable background. There's no hint of scandal anywhere. So they took potshots at his mother, so what? It's his record that should count. I don't like him personally because I'm jealous. I can never be what he is. Nor do I want to be like him. I honest to God don't know what Quinn sees in him," Puff said as he fastened the leash onto Winnie's collar.

"He was there when you broke her heart. I think she was looking for someone who is the exact opposite of you. It's not too late, Ezra. I think you could still be in the running if you'd put on your running shoes."

Puff snorted as he opened the door and walked out into the night with Winnie at his side.

"Running shoes or not, old girl, I don't think I

stand a snowball's chance in hell with Quinn. What's your opinion?"

"Woof."

"Yeah, that about sums it up," Puff said glumly as he walked over the frosty grass and waited for Winnie to find her spot.

14

"If I have to look at one more video of the president, I'm going to puke," Sadie grumbled as she removed a DVD from the player. "We've been here for four days, and all we do is sit on our butts watching these things or watching the first lady tromp from room to room. I hate this job," she hissed for Quinn's benefit. "I thought she was going to be happy when she got here, but she's like a cat dancing on a hot griddle. You were right when you said this was a babysitting detail. For whatever my opinion is worth, I think she's getting ready to blow."

Quinn looked around the pleasant room filled with wicker furniture, green plants, and winter sunshine. It was a peaceful room, a room to come to for solace and rest. At least that's what the first lady said she used it for. However, she had yet to set foot in the room since her return, preferring to spend her time in her studio on the third floor or huddling with Cassie the housekeeper in the outside courtyard. Quinn looked over at Sadie and nodded in agreement.

"I couldn't sleep last night, Quinn. I lay in bed trying to figure this whole thing out, and, you know what, I couldn't do it. Figure it out, I mean. The president and his wife are paying us an exorbitant amount of money to babysit. Make no mistake, we are babysitting. I'm starting to get claustrophobic, so I can just imagine what *she's* going through. She's not talking to us either the way she did back in Washington. She's sweet and nice, don't get me wrong, but she's hatching something. I can feel it in my bones. Furthermore, Quinn, we aren't supposed to be watching these videos, and we aren't supposed to be doing half the things we've already done. Secret Service protects and stands guard. We're glorified first lady sitters."

"Who says we aren't supposed to be doing those things? We were hired by the Jayes. Yes, we're Secret Service, but somehow in hiring us they circumvented Ballinger and the other higher-ups in the Secret Service. That's what I can't figure out. Those tabloid reporters are out front, too. There's no real back way out of here other than to climb those walls and fences. To me that's scary. You know what else scares me, Sadie, the Derringer in her room that she keeps rolled up in a pair of socks. I also think there's a mountain of other stuff we don't know." Quinn's facial features tightened when she said, "The one thing I am certain of is there are two men in the White House who are acting as president of the United States."

Sadie ran her fingers through her frizzy hair, causing it to spike on the ends, making it look like corkscrews. She wrinkled her nose, making her freckles lump into a round ball on her cheeks. She slumped farther down into the softness of the sofa she was sitting on. "I hate this job! I mean I *really* hate this job."

"You're whining, Sadie. Think about how you can expand your business and make it more competitive in the marketplace with all the money you're earning doing this gig. It's short-term. Three months isn't that long."

"Three months can be an eternity. Dammit, Quinn, I have thought of that, and it isn't making the job any more palatable."

"Listen to me, girlfriend, there are two presidents in the White House. There is no doubt in my mind. There's one who walks fast and takes long strides because his legs are a bit longer. That one also has a different type of hair. That one tends to talk fast and actually appears to be trying to slow himself down. He can talk off the cuff and is fond of talking over his shoulder as he bounces along. He swings his arms when he walks. Long arms, too. His tux fits differently, as do his suits. When he's in khakis and a tee shirt walking the grounds, he doesn't seem relaxed. I think he's the imposter. The other president tends to move slowly; he walks like he has no destination in mind, stops to talk face-to-face. He oozes charm. His hair color around the ears is pure gray, whereas the other one's hair has some darkness to it around the ears. The first lady described it as fluffy. That has to mean it's soft. Sometimes when hair is turning gray it gets wiry, like Birdie's. It has more body to it. The real president, to my way of thinking, has a tone of voice that is mellifluous, and he never appears to be in a hurry and he likes to make jokes. He also likes to walk with his hands in his pockets. You know how I am with shoes,

Sadie. The imposter has *heels* on his shoes. I pointed that out to you in one of the videos. That has to mean he's a little shorter than the real president. The real one is *loose*, the other one is uptight. You can see it in his features. Does that make sense, Sadie?"

"I suppose so. Are you stirring loose a hornet's nest, Quinn?"

Quinn ignored the question. "Why do you suppose Birdie had Puff send me this packet of photographs?" she asked, waving the manila envelope. "There was only that little sticky scribbled note saying she thought the first lady might want to add them to her own scrapbook. Birdie *never* parts with her pictures. You know how she is with those damn scrapbooks. They're her life! I think Birdie suspects something's wrong."

"Do you think she's noticed the discrepancies in the president's appearance on different occasions?" Sadie demanded as she jumped up and started to pace the sunroom. "Oh, oh, she's on the move. I hear her on the steps. Up and at 'em, girl!" A second later, Quinn was on her feet.

Both agents gawked as the first lady sashayed into the sunroom attired in an elegant garnet, light wool dress that was so magnificently cut they knew it had to have cost a fortune. She wore an elaborate silver belt and matching pendant. Her silver-gray hair was upswept and held in place with decorative sparkly combs. Her shoes matched her dress perfectly and looked butter soft.

She's a knockout, Quinn thought. *She's comfortable in her own skin because she's on her home turf.*

"I'm having a luncheon guest today, girls."

"You look lovely, Mrs. Jaye," Sadie said. "Do you want us to stay out of sight? We can stay in the kitchen so that we're close by. Those are the rules, ma'am."

"I understand. Actually, I'm a little surprised that Mary Alice agreed to join me for lunch. Her husband Jonathan was my husband's White House counsel. Mary Alice loved Washington, with all the parties and important people. I just never thought they would pack up and leave. One day they were there, and the next day they were gone. I called and wrote, and she never responded. I called all our old friends the first few days right after we got here. Mary Alice is the only one who bothered to return my call. I'm nervous. I can't believe I'm nervous. Mary Alice and I were sandbox playmates. We were both presented at the St. Cecilia Society's Ball. We were such good friends, members of all the same clubs, including the Junior League. We shared secrets the way girlfriends do, that kind of thing."

"I'm sure it will all be fine, ma'am. You'll renew your friendship and make plans now that you're back here," Sadie said warmly.

"I certainly hope so. Without friends there's no point to my being here. Oh, I wish we had never gone to Washington. You have no idea how much I wish that. Everything changed the minute we got there. Every single person in that town has his or her own agenda, and there are those who would slit your throat for a nickel. Some would do it for free."

Quinn shuffled her feet, an uneasy feeling settling in the pit of her stomach.

"I want you girls to do something for me later. I think I know how we can prove what we were talking about earlier. We'll discuss it after Mary Alice leaves," the first lady whispered. "God, you don't think she'll talk to those tabloid people out there, do you?"

"Depends on how badly she needs the money," Sadie said sourly. At the look of dismay on the first lady's face, she added hastily, "I seriously doubt it."

"There's the doorbell. I guess the Secret Service cleared her. Hurry, girls, scoot into the kitchen."

Cassie looked up from her position at the counter, where she was putting the finishing touches on a succulent-looking vegetable tray. She put her hands on her hips and glared at the two agents. "This is not going to go well. I tried to warn Lettie, but she wouldn't listen to me. That woman Mary Alice hates my Lettie. She's green with jealousy. It wasn't always that way. I don't know why she's coming here except to cause Lettie grief."

Quinn shot Sadie a warning glance that clearly said, don't ask questions.

"Well, I guess I do know why. This is a small city, and everyone pretty much knows everyone else. When Mr. Prentice was appointed White House counsel, their noses went so high in the air they needed oxygen. Then when they came home in *diss-grace,* talk was they weren't good enough for Jimmy and Lettie. He *said* he resigned. The newspapers said differently. People in town said them Yankees up in Washington *whupped* his Southern ass. *Diss-grace* is a hard thing to live down. Lettie thinks she can make it right but she can't. *Mistah* Prentice," she drawled, "saw his legal practice go downhill. *Miz* Prentice wasn't as ladylike as she should have been. No, this isn't going to go well. Now, if you'll excuse me, it's time for me to do my part. Do I look spiffy? Befitting the first lady of the land and all that. I wasn't good enough to go north either," she said, trotting off to the dining room with the tray perfectly balanced in the palm of her right hand.

"Politics," Quinn muttered.

"They suck," Sadie hissed. "I think one of us should listen to what's going on in there."

"I think you're right. Cassie is serving off the sideboard, so why don't we just crack this door a little and listen in. If we're careful and don't open the door too wide, we'll be able to see both women. Who knows, we might learn something," Quinn said.

"Do it," Sadie hissed as she took up her position on the opposite side of the doorway.

"I am not staying for lunch, Letecia. I can't believe you would even expect me to sit at the same table with you after what you and your husband did to us."

"My husband didn't do anything to you or your husband. Your husband resigned, Mary Alice. He said he was resigning for the good of the country. How can that be my husband's fault? I had nothing to do with it, Mary Alice."

"You *are* as dumb as the papers make you out to be, Letecia. The only reason my husband resigned was because they were going to fire him. His resignation letter was *dictated* to him, and he was told to sign it. The whole world knows it. You shamed us. We can't hold our heads up anymore. You know what this town is like. Either you're in or you're out. Let's not forget Elba and Hudson while we're on this discussion. Fontaine and Elmore aren't fond of you and your husband either. Jasper and Ennis throw darts at your husband's picture. That's just the tip of things. We had to form our own little club just so we would have someone to talk to. Other than that, we're outcasts. Your people called us the turnip patch trash," Mary Alice Prentice screeched. "Don't even pretend you don't know what I'm talking about, Letecia."

"I thought you all resigned. Jimmy Jaye said none of you could take the criticism. He said he warned you all about the way Washington operated. He said you wanted to return home where people were real and normal. No one held your feet to the fire. Why are you taking it out on me? I hated it there, too. I couldn't wait to come back home."

"Dammit, Lettie, we had no other choice. Your husband, and I don't care if he is the president of the United States, is as crazy as a loon. He's like a Jekyll and Hyde. One minute he's one way and the next minute he's way out there in space. Jon said he looked absolutely stunned when he handed him his resignation. The day before he told him if he didn't have his resignation on his desk by eight o'clock the following day, the press secretary would announce that he was fired. Jon had no other choice.

"And another thing, Lettie. We lost all that money on the house we leased. So did the others. We incurred great expense in going to Washington at your husband's request. I had to buy clothes that really aren't suitable for here. Great expense," Mary Alice said, her voice ringing with bitterness.

The first lady shrugged helplessly. "Mary Alice, I'm sure . . ."

"Don't you Mary Alice me, Letecia Jaye. I don't want to know you anymore. Neither do the others. I was the only one dumb enough to return your phone call because I wanted you to know *exactly* how I feel. No one is impressed with you, so get that thought right out of your head." She eyed the sideboard and the wide array of food Cassie had spread out. "Are the taxpayers paying for all that food?"

The first lady ignored the question. "I thought you were my friend, Mary Alice. How can you say these things and how can you talk to me like this?"

"Because you damn well deserve it, that's how. I didn't know till I got here that those tabloid people were here. I'm going to speak with the others, and if they pay us enough to get back on our feet, we're going to give them an earful. Dennis Miller and Larry King will be begging us for interviews. Fontaine loves Jerry Springer, so we might even take a shot at that. What do you think of that, Letecia Jaye, first lady of the land?"

The first lady stared at her longtime friend. "We live in a democracy, Mary Alice." She straightened her shoulders as she prepared herself to utter the one word that would bring Mary Alice Prentice to her knees. "I guess you can do whatever you want, but it's so *tacky*. However, you should ask yourself how it will come out in print. You won't be doing yourself or the others any favors by going on the talk-show circuit. It will turn out to be a circus. Another thing, *everyone* will see how *tacky* you and the others have become."

Quinn's fist shot in the air. "Yessss."

"Who cares what they think? Money is money. What can be worse than being called turnip patch trash and having people snicker when they see you? That was not a good picture of you with all those Victoria's Secret bags in your hands. You looked . . . *slutty.*"

"I'd rather look slutty, Mary Alice, than stand accused of being *tacky.* What do you know about slutty or what the word even means? You had sex twice in your life because you wanted two children. I know all about your sex life because your husband complained to my husband years ago. I happen to like sex with my husband, and if a few skimpy undies can help, I'm all for it. I know you look the other way and pretend you don't know what's going on, so don't you go getting uppity with me, Mary Alice Prentice."

"Letecia Jaye! Well, I never! Are you implying that my husband has paramours?" Mary Alice screeched a second time.

"Hell no, Mary Alice. Why would I *imply* something when I know it for a fact?"

"Whoa!" Sadie said, grabbing hold of her sides so she wouldn't laugh.

"I'll see myself out," Mary Alice Prentice huffed.

"You'll do no such thing. This is the Southern White House, and we adhere to protocol here just the way we do at the White House. Cassie, show Mrs. Prentice to the door and have the Secret Service escort Mrs. Jonathan Prentice to her car."

"Way to go, Lettie," Sadie exulted.

Quinn grinned.

"Girls! Come to lunch!" the first lady called the moment the front door closed. "Cassie, set an extra place."

The first lady stared at the two agents, her eyes bright with unshed tears. "I'm not going to cry even if I do feel like it. Mary Alice is a shallow person. I guess I always knew that and didn't want to have to deal with it." Her crisp, linen napkin made a snapping sound when she shook it free of its folds. "And just for the record, I paid for this food. I always pay for our food when we're here. You can ask Cassie if you don't believe me. Jimmy Jaye and I don't feel the taxpayers should have to foot the bill for our food. It's a point of honor with us."

"Yes, ma'am," Quinn said as she dipped her spoon into a cold cucumber soup. She wondered how she was going to choke down the salmon mousse that was sitting on the sideboard.

"Jonathan Prentice was a *miserable* attorney," the first lady said bluntly. "However, he was very good at rallying support when Jimmy Jaye ran for office. He knows how to raise money. Neither he nor Mary Alice wanted to believe there were two ways of doing things. Our way and *their* way. I learned the hard way. I tried to tell them both, but they thought I was being *uppity*.

"Mary Alice couldn't wait to throw her first dinner party, and it was a disaster. She served she-crab soup, black-eyed pea cakes, a crab dish, fried okra, spicy collards, and Hoppin' John. Her dessert was a caramel mousse that slithered off the spoon. I understand the tablecloth, one of Mary Alice's grandmother's heirlooms, was ruined. The next day it was in all the gossip columns. Mary Alice never recovered from that. It seems the ideal menu would have been a clear consommé, stuffed quail, an arugula salad, glazed carrots, and a champagne sorbet for dessert. Washingtonians don't eat the same kinds of food that we're used to eating in the South. She might have been able to save the day if she hadn't taken it so to heart. Instead, she lashed back and talked out of turn. If you do that, the press puts its own spin on things. It was very sad. Jonathan, I'm told, just shuffled papers and had all his aides do the bulk of his work because he was out of his league so to speak.

"One night Jimmy Jaye wanted a dinner party with just our old friends. It was a lovely meal, and the chef worked very hard to make everything perfect. It was a very nice evening. We watched a first-run movie in the theater, and it was like old times. The next morning the paper was full of it. The political cartoons showed all of us 'turnip patch trash' in bib overalls chowing down on barbecued pig. Even I cried at that. The very next day Jimmy Jaye said we wouldn't be inviting our friends to the White House anymore because they were an embarrassment to the presidency.

"Mary Alice and the others thought they could

just stop by the White House for coffee and gossip anytime they felt like it. I tried to tell all of them they had to wait, to get a feel for the political scene, but they were determined to get their pictures in the paper so they could send them back home. They jumped in with both feet and didn't know how to swim against the current. They wanted to hobnob with all the socialites. They got slapped down before they got out of the gate." The first lady's eyes misted over again as she recalled the various newspaper articles concerning her friends.

"Then there is Hudson Drexel, the man my husband appointed as his national security advisor. Hudson couldn't find his way out of a paper bag. I told Jimmy Jaye he was making a mistake. Hudson lasted fifty-four days. The press said he wasn't even qualified to be a Wal-Mart greeter. Elba, his wife, got an attack of the vapors. That was just a rehearsal for a nervous breakdown that never materialized. Somehow or other Elba managed to get herself a ton of stationery that said, 'From the Office of the National Security Advisor' in gold leaf at the top, and proceeded to send letters back home to everyone in the phone book. Chatty letters saying how important she and her husband were. The postage alone caused a stir, and it made the front pages.

"I don't want you to get me wrong here. They were all nice people, kind people, caring people who got caught up in something they weren't equipped to handle. When it turned sour, they turned on Jimmy Jaye and me. It got very ugly."

Quinn looked down at her plate as she dug her

fork into the salmon mousse. She was learning more than she wanted to know. She risked a glance at Sadie, who looked fit to be tied.

The first lady wasn't finished. "Elmore Collins was the one who did the press briefings. Like I said, Elmore and his wife, Fontaine, are very nice people, just like the others. However, they both have a very thick Southern drawl. Elmore would not have been my choice, but no one asked me. One day the press decided to bait him or play a game, whatever, because they had to keep asking him to repeat things, and he would get annoyed. They said he spoke like he had a mouthful of grits. This one day one of the reporters from the *Post* brought in a man wearing this big sign on his chest that said, INTER-PRETER in big red letters. Every time Elmore would say something, the man would stand up, wave his arms for silence, and elaborately translate what it was Elmore said. Poor Elmore, he was almost in tears. That was fodder for the press for a whole week. They actually had the man pose for a picture with his sign. That's the way it was. I had hoped they would be a little more forgiving.

"I'm not even going to go into the Rebel flag business or that barbecue sauce fiasco because it would take a whole book to do that. Now, if you girls will excuse me, I'm going upstairs to change my clothes. I'll meet you in the sunroom in an hour. Cassie, make sure my cigarettes are in there, and I'd like a triple shot of bourbon on the rocks when I get there. I'd like some barbecue for dinner, and make it as sloppy as you can."

"Yes, ma'am." The housekeeper snapped off a salute that would have made any general proud. "She's *pissed* off! When Lettie Jaye gets pissed off, look out. It's about time, too," Cassie said, retreating to the kitchen. She poked her head back in the door a second later, and said, "Don't get the idea the first lady is a lush. She isn't. She only drinks when she's stressed beyond endurance."

"Uh-huh," Sadie said.

Quinn pushed her plate to the center of the table and reached for her coffee cup. "I feel like my name is Alice, and I just walked through the looking glass."

"The media can be too powerful at times, especially if they have it in for you. They used that power to ruin those people. Don't they have any recourse? It's a miracle that Mrs. Jaye didn't cave in the way her friends did. Quinn, did you believe that woman, Mary Alice Prentice, when she said she was going to talk to the others about selling their stories to the tabloids, and do the talk-show circuit?"

"Yes. When you're made a laughingstock, or your pride is injured, all you want to do is lash out and get even. Maybe the fact that Mr. Prentice is a lawyer will hold them in check, but if Mrs. Prentice calls the shots, I don't hold out much hope. That was pretty awful about the briefing, wasn't it?"

"I probably would have dug a hole and crawled inside. It sounds to me like the old conflict between North and South has risen again. Wonder what Mrs. Jaye wants to talk to us about," Sadie said. She made clinking sounds with her spoon against the side of the cup.

"Maybe it's about the cookbook she plans to write someday. You know, her Southern recipes that she took to the White House. The same recipes that were never used. She said she's going to tell a story for each recipe. Maybe she wants our opinion. It could be anything. Let's get some more coffee and head for the sunroom."

Thirty minutes later the first lady entered the sunroom. The garnet dress she'd been wearing earlier had been replaced with paint-stained slacks and a paint-stained smock. The sparkly combs in her hair were gone, too, replaced with a tortoiseshell clip in the back, and she was barefoot.

The first lady sat down, reached for her drink, and took a healthy slug. She smacked her lips approvingly before she reached for a cigarette.

The agents waited expectantly.

"Dental records!" the first lady said triumphantly.

"What about them?" Quinn said.

"Jimmy Jaye's dental records can prove there is an imposter in the White House. Teeth are like fingerprints. All we have to do is get them. You girls can do that, can't you?"

"Ma'am, how would you suggest we do that?" Sadie asked, her voice shaking at what the first lady was suggesting.

"At night after the office closes. How hard can it be to pick a lock?"

Quinn stood up, alarm written all over her face. "Mrs. Jaye, we can't do something like that. We swore to uphold the law, not break it. Why don't you just call the dentist and ask for your husband's records?

In fact, I'm sure your husband's dental records were transferred to Washington along with his medical records."

"If I ask, he's liable to tell someone. What excuse could I possibly give for wanting them? Are you saying you won't do it? I know Harvey Ladson. He might have turned over the records, but he would have kept a copy for his office. He's like that. Just in case Jimmy Jaye or I were here and needed a root canal or something. He's very, very thorough. He's not the type to have someone tell him what he *has* to do," Lettie Jaye babbled.

"Ma'am, we can't do it," Quinn said.

"Then I'm just going to have to find someone else to do it. You can't talk about this to anyone, remember that."

"Ma'am, if you do that, and the person gets caught, how is it going to look for you when they say you're the one who instigated the theft? They'll crucify you in the press." At the look on the first lady's face, Quinn threw in what she hoped was her big gun. "They might make you go back to Washington. Please don't do this. There has to be another way to prove it."

"Jimmy Jaye called me after I went upstairs. He said he misses me. He was the real one. He was so silly. I feel even sillier talking about it. He wanted to know why I came here without him. Do you believe that? He also said his people are trying to take away his power, and he wasn't going to stand for it. He asked about our old friends and wanted to know if they called or if I had called them. I told him about

Mary Alice and the tabloids. He said she was *squirrelly*, and no one would believe anything she said. He said she and Dennis Miller deserved each other. He had to hang up because he had to attend some oil meeting, and another one after that with some ministers. He did say he loved me very much."

"That should have made you feel better," Sadie said.

"It did for about five minutes. Then I realized how tired he sounded. He doesn't get nearly enough sleep. Jimmy Jaye is a man who needs a lot of sleep. There was a time when he could get by on three or four hours, but that was before we went to Washington. I'll see you at dinner, girls. I have things to do now."

When the French doors to the sunroom closed behind the first lady, the agents looked at one another. "This is not good. She does have a point, though. Dental records would prove her theory," Quinn said. "She's right about us not talking, too. You don't think she'll really find someone to . . . to do what she wants, do you?"

"Quinn, I have no clue. Her friends seem to have deserted her. Who else does she have besides Cassie and her husband, Jacob, and Cassie's family? Maybe her husband's family? I don't think there's any kind of family here, either on the first lady's side or the president's side. Money does talk, though, and she has plenty of that. The promise of big money can entice people to do things they wouldn't ordinarily do."

"Do you know what I think, Sadie? I think we're looking at this all wrong. The first lady told us there is a conspiracy going on. She truly believes that. I think you and I are leaning toward the same way of thinking based on what Mrs. Jaye has told us. We're thinking something terrible, like something global, something with awful ramifications. Typical spy stuff. You know, deadly serious goings-on. What if it isn't anything like that at all. Just think back to some of the things Mrs. Jaye has said to us about her *real* husband. What's the one word she uses more than any other when she talks about him?"

Sadie shrugged.

"Think, Sadie."

"She's always asking him the cat's name."

"No. Well, yes, that, too. I'm thinking of the word, *silly*. Obviously the president is not a silly man. If he was, he wouldn't have been voted into office. What does that tell us, Sadie?"

Sadie threw her arms in the air. "He's punchy from not enough sleep. He's getting warped. The pressure is getting to him? I don't know, Quinn."

"Maybe, just maybe, there's something wrong with his health or maybe his mind. His advisors wouldn't want the world to know that, now would they? At least not till next year, when he can say he doesn't want to run again. All kinds of bad things could happen if people found out the president was unwell or disabled for some reason. The stock market could crash. The terrorists might step up their attacks. I'm no politician, I'm just guessing here. There would be all kinds of turmoil. Vice President Waverly might not be strong enough politically to take over the job. People have agendas and work toward fulfilling them. You know, feathering their own nests for when the ax falls, and they have to move on. Most important is the power. Who would benefit from all that power? Power is the most powerful aphrodisiac of all. Mrs. Mary Alice Prentice and Elba Drexel are perfect examples. The women behind the men, that kind of thinking.

"Suppose there really is something wrong with President Jaye's mind. With the election next year, I suppose Adam Waverly would gain real support for the nomination if he had a year to serve as president and could run as an incumbent. But if the fake president, not the real deal, announces that he will run for reelection, right after the New Year, then the vice president doesn't get the chance to serve that long or prepare a campaign for the nomination.

"Suppose further that the people around the president now, the ones who took over from the president's friends, have a different person in mind. If he is able to jump in later next year, say in the late spring, when the president resigns because of his disability, since no one else will have prepared to seek the nomination, he'd be a shoo-in. And if he gets elected, how grateful do you think he'll be to the people who engineered the situation that got him the nomination?

"I'm just talking off the top of my head, Sadie. I'm wondering if I should call Puff, but he doesn't want to hear stuff like this. He says, do what I was hired to do, which is watch over the first lady."

"Do you think she's in denial? I think if I lived with someone as long as she's lived with the president, I'd know if he was acting peculiar. I don't think she's seeing what's right in front of her nose, or if she is, she's denying it. I'm talking about his mental state. She wants the dental records to prove what she's saying. Why isn't she questioning his medical records? The president must have had a doctor here whom he saw from time to time."

"He's now the Surgeon General, Quinn. Did you forget? If there is something medically wrong with the president, and the doctor didn't alert anyone, he's history, too."

"Yes, I guess I did forget that little detail. Do you think his records would still be in the office? Did he close it up or maybe sell his practice to another doctor? I don't know how stuff like that works. Do you?"

"No, and I don't want to know. I don't like that look on your face, Quinn. Don't go getting any ideas about all of this. None of this is in our job description."

"I know, but I can think about it. Think about all those recent videos we watched. Not the ones when the Jayes first moved to Washington. Everything is choreographed right down to the most insignificant detail. You were the one who said it looked staged and phony."

Sadie's tone was defensive. "That was just my opinion. That doesn't mean it's so. The man is the president of the United States. Mrs. Jaye told us how they prepare for an event, even a walk on the lawn has to be scheduled and mapped out. Nothing is left to chance."

"I'm going upstairs to check on the first lady. Then I'm going to call Birdie and Puff. Hell, I might even call Alex."

"Don't come back down here with any harebrained schemes because I'm not budging on that breaking and entering gig," Sadie hissed as she picked up the latest issue of *Newsweek* magazine with a picture of the president on the cover and started to leaf through it.

Quinn offered up a grimace as she left the room.

15

Ezra Lapufsky eyed the president's chief of staff with a jaundiced eye. He didn't like Lawrence Neville or his imperious attitude. In fact he didn't like any of the president's staff in the White House. He wasn't even sure he liked the president these days. He'd voted for him, but back then the man had been different. Everyone and everything seemed to be different these days. He picked at the cuticle on his thumb and wondered what the hell he was doing there. Command performances were something he hated with a passion.

His mind wandered to Quinn the way it always did when he was stressed. When she wasn't chewing out his ass, she could be the sweetest, kindest, most caring woman in the world. He hadn't slept a wink after her phone call. She'd been so cold, so matter-of-fact, so in control he had the feeling she believed what she was saying, which was that there were *two* presidents in the White House running the country. He'd reamed her out, but she'd held firm. And that business of the first lady's friends going to the tabloids and Jerry Springer made his hair stand

on end. It was a free country, and even in these times
people could do whatever they pleased as long as it
didn't interfere with national security.

The bottom line was the first lady was pissed off.
Not only was she pissed off, she was unhappy. A
chill of something he couldn't define raced up his
arms and back. Breaking and entering to steal the
president's dental and medical records was something he couldn't even begin to comprehend. He
knew in his gut he was going to be ordered to go to
Charleston.

Neville strode into the room, his back ramrod stiff.
"Coffee?"

"No thanks."

"I'm here to give you a heads-up. It's definite that
Duval will *not* be the next director of the FBI. The
president wants to nominate you right after the
Thanksgiving holiday. Duval himself called the president this morning and said he didn't want the job.
It was his way of saving face. We can guarantee it, if
you want it."

Puff could feel his shoulders start to twitch. Here
it was, the plum he'd wanted since the first day of
his FBI career. All he had to do was nod or utter one
little word. Yes. That's all he had to do. Did he even
trust himself to speak? Quinn's words last night ric-
ocheted inside his head. "In return for what?" *Christ
did I just say that?*

The chief of staff played with the knot of his neck-
tie. His neck was too fat, what there was of it. He
stretched his neck to try to loosen his collar a little. "I
like it that you're not one to play games, Lapufsky.

In return for your going down to the Southern White House to take care of things. The first lady is like a wild hare these days. The president is upset with her behavior. Her friends are threatening to go to those ugly tabloids and those ridiculous talk shows. We can't have those hayseeds making a mockery of this administration. As I said, the president is upset. You seem to have a special place in the heart of the first lady, and we know about your past relationship with Agent Star. Whip them into shape, Lapufsky, and we're not going to give you a lot of time to do it. I don't want to hear anything negative, just positive reports. The president wants happy, happy, happy. You're still virtually a young man. You have a long career ahead of you. I want you to think about that."

Puff's stomach churned at Neville's words just as the door opened and the president of the United States entered the room. Puff stood up immediately, and said, "Good morning, Mr. President."

Suddenly Puff was glad he'd spent the money and taken the time to have laser surgery done to his eyes several months earlier even though he had been scared out of his wits. He now sported twenty-twenty vision. He scrutinized the president just the way Quinn told him to. He memorized every little nuance, every little blink of his eyes, his lips, his nose, and the goddamn color of his hair. He wished he could see his teeth. Too bad he didn't know a sidesplitting joke that would make the man laugh. He looked down at the president's shoes. Inch-high heels. He sucked in air.

"What's your answer, Acting Associate Director Lapufsky?"

"I'd like to think about it, Mr. President. Can I get back to you later today?"

"Absolutely. Regardless of your response, I want you to go to Charleston. Consider it a presidential directive, Ezra," the president said, using his first name. Puff's stomach coiled into a tighter knot. "I'm worried about my wife. She's been behaving erratically, and I don't want word to get out. Sometimes I think poor Lettie is delusional. She just wasn't cut out for political life. You're going to have to be firm with her. I've tried talking to her, but my wife has a mind of her own. I know what she wants, and it just isn't possible at this point in time. I cannot resign after the people of this country voted me into office. They're depending on me to lead them through the darkness into the light. I'm doing that." His somber tone rang with such sincerity, Puff could feel the hairs on the back of his neck stand on end.

Reaching down, the president grasped a small American flag sticking up from a paperweight. After looking at it as if he had never seen a flag before, he shifted his grip to the little dowel threaded through its left-hand side. Waving the little flag high above his head to make his point, he intoned, "This is all about God and country and the commitment I made to the fine people of this nation."

Puff had the crazy urge to place his hand over his heart and salute the little flag, until he started to feel the bile rising in his throat. He waited, wondering if there was more to come. There was.

"This morning my wife called her secretary and the press secretary and said there was a conspiracy going on here. As I said, Lettie is agitated. It's not going to go any further than the White House on this end. We're sending down an additional detail of Secret Service. We're all hoping that you and the two female agents can rein Lettie in. If this can't be done, if you aren't the man to do the job, we'll have to resort to other means."

"What do you mean by *resort to other means*, Mr. President?" Puff asked bluntly.

"Ezra, the first lady will have to be hospitalized. For her own good. They have such wonderful medication these days . . ." he said, letting his words trail off into nothingness.

Puff looked down at the president's shoes again. Then he looked at the hair over his ears. He was still waving the little flag, his eyes cold and hard. *Now that's a threat if I ever heard one.* He could feel his skin start to crawl as he shrugged elaborately to show he understood clearly what the president was saying. He couldn't help but notice the little smirk at the corners of Neville's lips.

"I trust that I, and my administration, have your cooperation then, AAD Lapufsky."

"You're the commander in chief, Mr. President. Of course you have my cooperation." *Liar, liar, pants on fire.* It was one of Quinn's favorite sayings when she was angry and thought she had the goods on him. It fit the situation perfectly.

The door opened from the outside. The president swept past him but not before he handed the little flag to Puff. Neville reached out to take it back, but Puff was too quick and jammed it in his pocket. He forced a grin. "You never know, I might have kids someday, and I'll want to give it to them." There was nothing the chief of staff could do without making a scene.

Puff felt like his head was going to explode as he left the White House and made his way to his car. He thought about what had just transpired, Quinn's phone call, the work piled up on his desk, and his own family. The possible nomination was almost an afterthought. His parents would be so proud when he told them. *If* he told them. *If.* Then he thought about the packet of pictures Birdie had asked him to overnight to Quinn. Suddenly he felt sick to his stomach. Did everyone in the world subscribe to Lettie and Quinn's cockamamie theory? Then he thought about the one-inch heels, the darker, wiry hair around the president's ears.

Instead of driving to his office, he headed for Birdie Langley's house.

Thirty minutes later, Puff could hear Winnie barking inside the house. The sound alone made him feel better. There was something about a dog that could calm his twanging nerves immediately. All he had to do was sit with a dog, any dog, stroke him, talk to him, and his world settled right down. He hoped Winnie would work some magic for him.

The dour-faced nurse opened the door for him, then left the kitchen. Birdie looked up from her little desk in the corner of the kitchen, her eyes full of questions. Winnie stopped chewing on a soup bone that was as big as her head long enough to utter a sharp woof and went back to her bone.

"I was just at the White House," Puff said by way of explanation.

"Some people like going there. They think it makes them important for some reason," Birdie said. "The coffee is fresh, help yourself."

Puff shrugged out of his overcoat and threw it on a chair. He filled a cup and carried it over to the table. He positioned himself so he could face Birdie.

"Spit it out, Ezra. You didn't come here in the middle of the morning for my coffee. What's wrong?"

"You know what, Birdie. I think you know what's wrong. Why did you want me to send those pictures to Quinn? I want the truth. You're talking to the acting associate director of the FBI now, so be careful how you answer," he whispered.

Birdie took her cue from Puff's whispered tone. "Is this a professional or social call?" Birdie hissed. "Is this house bugged?"

Puff nodded. "It's whatever the hell you want it to be, Birdie. Now talk," he muttered, his lips barely moving.

"You can't scare me, you know. I'm too old to have some young buck come into my kitchen to give me the third degree. This is a free country. This is my castle. I'm allowed to think and have my own thoughts. I sent those pictures for Lettie. When you get old, you do things like that. You remember your youth and what might have been, that kind of thing."

"That's nonsense, Birdie, and you know it. I want the real reason."

"That is the real reason. Bring me some coffee. Put some milk in mine."

"The president offered me the job as director of the FBI. His COS as much as said it's a done deal. It seems Judge Duval withdrew from the running earlier this morning."

"What's the catch?" Birdie said, taping a picture of a snappy Springfield coffin onto the page she was working on in her scrapbook. "This casket costs eleven thousand dollars. Do you believe that? It's expensive to die."

"You can bury me in a cardboard box for all I care. The catch is I have to go to Charleston and muzzle the first lady. If I don't, they're going to hospitalize her because they say she's delusional. What do you think of that?" he hissed angrily.

Birdie closed the scrapbook with a snap, a murderous look settling on her face. "I think the question should be, what do *you* think of that?"

"I don't know what the hell to think, Birdie," he said loud enough so only she could hear. Then he walked to the sink and turned the faucet on full blast.

"Whatever she's doing, she's got Quinn and Sadie on her side. They all think there are two presidents in the White House. In this day and age, do you really think that's possible? Come on, Birdie, cut me some slack here."

"Anything can happen, so I'd say it's within the realm of possibility. Obviously, you think all three of them are wrong. Make that four," she said smartly.

"Jesus! You, too, Birdie?"

Winnie reared up, barked, and pushed her soup bone across the floor. She waited to see if anyone was interested enough in her treasure to take it before she pounced on it again and started to whittle away at the giant bone.

"Obviously you must think there's a seed of truth to it all, or you wouldn't be sitting here in my kitchen. Your problem is you don't know what to do about it. Suppose, Ezra, just suppose we're right and there is an imposter in the White House. How could we prove it? Let me show you something. Be patient with me now," Birdie whispered softly, just loud enough to be heard over the water splashing into the sink.

Puff watched as Birdie riffled through a stack of photographs, picked one out, and laid it on the side. She riffled through a second stack of pictures, chose one, and laid it next to the first one.

She reached for her sketch pad and pencil. He watched as she swirled and stroked until the first page was done. She ripped it off, turned it over, and started to draw again. "Now, you can look."

Puff stared down at two bodies in coffins that Birdie had sketched. His skin started to crawl. "Which one is the real president? The camera doesn't lie, Ezra. If you look at the two photographs, they look pretty much alike because they weren't taken up close. This is all the proof you need," she scribbled on a piece of paper. She tapped the two pictures she'd just drawn to make her point. "Everything in life leads up to the moment they place you in one of these," she said, pointing to a flyer that advertised the Springfield casket line. She threw her hands in the air. "Who knew?"

Puff felt dizzy. "Which one is he?" he scribbled on a piece of paper.

"You tell me, Ezra. Is it number one or is it number two? You just came from a meeting at the White House with the president. Surely you have some memory recall," Birdie scrawled across the bottom of the paper.

Puff's index finger pointed to the second drawing.

"Is that the one you had your meeting with?"

"Yeah. Yeah, the second one," Puff wrote.

"That's the imposter. Take this magnifying glass over to the table and study the two pictures, then study the drawings. Lettie sent me the picture of the imposter. I took the picture myself of the real Jimmy Jaye about seven months ago when I went to the White House to have tea with Lettie," Birdie whispered as she tried to contain her excitement.

Both Birdie and Puff were so engrossed in staring and comparing the pictures on the table, neither of them noticed Winnie pawing at Puff's coat. When it finally fell to the floor, she would have put a well digger to shame. She worked industriously until she had what she wanted, and then she woofed with pleasure as she trotted off, the little dowel the flag was attached to firmly between her teeth. The flag flapped in the breeze from the air vents.

"No, Winnie! No! Bring that back! I need it!" Puff bellowed.

"For heaven's sake, Ezra, I have a ton of those little flags in the pantry from the Fourth of July bazaar.

Let her have it for heaven's sake," Birdie said, forgetting to whisper.

"You don't understand, Birdie. The president . . . the imposter . . . whoever the hell he is, gave that to me. The COS tried to get it back, but I stuffed it in my pocket. Fingerprints, Birdie! Fingerprints!" Puff hissed in her ear.

"Winnie, baby girl, bring it back to mama," Birdie cajoled.

"She's ignoring you, Birdie. I need that flag. If you're right, that's all we need to prove your case. If she chews it up, we're dead in the water. Where does she stash her goodies?"

"Everywhere and anywhere. You know the rule, if it's on the floor, it's hers. She's stubborn. She knows we want it back, so we have to figure out a way to trick her. Be warned, she's smart. She might not look it, but she is. Does your interest in checking the fingerprints on that flag mean you believe us?" Birdie wrote on the paper.

"It means my mind is open. Dammit, Birdie, what if she chews it up?"

"Winnie does not chew up stuff. She'll give it back eventually. She either carries it around, or she hides it. Well, sometimes she chews things. Not often, though. She loves you, Ezra, so I don't think she'll chew it up. Go in the pantry and there's a box on the bottom shelf. Take a few of the flags out and let her see you putting them in your pocket. Maybe she'll take the bait," Birdie said, her pen flying over the paper.

Puff waited until Winnie waddled back into the

kitchen before he got up to do Birdie's bidding. He made a production out of stuffing three of the flags into his pocket, his eyes on the dog, who yawned, then stretched out on the carpet by the stove.

"I told you she was smart," Birdie smirked. "My goodness, it's sleeting outside. I wonder if it will turn to snow."

"It's only November, Birdie. Make sure you don't leave the house. I'm not going to be here to look out for you."

"Ezra, you can't let them put Lettie in the hospital. You just can't. There's nothing wrong with her. She gets her panties in a wad like we all do from time to time, but this time it's serious. All the woman wants is her husband. She's afraid, and that's why she's doing what she's doing. I'd be afraid, too, if I was in her position. Those people are very powerful. They can make people disappear, and you know it."

Puff massaged his chin as he stared down at the two pictures on the table. "Where do you suppose they came up with such a look-alike?" he scribbled.

Birdie reached for the picture of the imposter. Her charcoal flew over the page. "Now what do you think?"

"Who *is* that?"

"It could be anybody. Look, Ezra, I patch up corpses. When a person has been ravaged by a disease and the only alternative is cremation or a closed coffin, I do a little magic. Putty, spirit gum, and I can make the person's face look just like it looked when he was alive and well. You don't have to be a genius, you just have to know what you're doing. And you

can't stand under real bright lights. The bone struc-
ture of both men must be similar; otherwise, it
wouldn't work."

"Son of a bitch! Why, Birdie? Do you know?" Puff
looked down at the end of his pencil. It needed
sharpening.

"No, Ezra, I don't know. It must have something
to do with the administration getting rid of all the
men the president first appointed when he got here.
They're all gone, replaced with new people. It could
be anything. I thought he was doing a pretty good
job of running the country. The papers say the same
thing. Maybe he doesn't like the job. Maybe it was
more than he planned on. He has to be concerned
about his wife. Lettie and Jimmy had . . . have . . . a
strong relationship. They have always been very
close. This town will suck the blood right out of your
veins, and you know it. I don't think either one of
them was prepared for the cruelty and the backbit-
ing and the power mongers who invaded their nice
little life. You have to do something, Ezra. That's just
another way of saying they were out of their league."
Puff had to strain to hear Birdie's whispered words.

"I have to take orders, Birdie. A whole detail of
Secret Service Agents is on the way south as we
speak."

"I thought you were in charge of the first lady.
Doesn't that mean you call the shots?" Birdie fretted.

"It's true, Birdie, but guess who put me in charge?
The president. He can rescind his order anytime he
likes. If everyone doesn't make nice when I get there,
that's exactly what's going to happen. In the mean-

time, Birdie, see what you can do about finding that flag. If you do find it, this is what I want you to do. Call this number and someone will come here to pick it up. Make sure you put it in a brown envelope. Just in case someone is watching, have the guy stop at McNally's Funeral Home. The lab will check for fingerprints. I'm going to keep one of those flags in my pocket and see what develops. You never know. I'll put the remaining ones back in the pantry with the others. The day isn't over."

"This is like a really bad movie," Birdie said. "I'm worried about Quinn and Sadie. Lettie can take care of herself."

Puff's jaw dropped. "And you think Quinn and Sadie can't take care of themselves! Ha! Either one of those two could wrestle me to the ground and hog-tie me in three minutes flat. Maybe two."

"Really!"

"Only if I let them." Puff grinned. He apologized silently for the lie he'd just told Birdie.

"I'll call you from Charleston. If you do find the flag, pick it up with a tissue. Don't get *your* fingerprints on it."

After Puff turned off the tap and started to leave, Birdie rolled her eyes as she waved good-bye. Winnie continued to snooze on the carpet by the stove.

Birdie waited a full ten minutes before she dialed Quinn's cell phone number. "Hello, baby, how are you and Sadie? I've been sitting here thinking about both of you. It's sleeting outside. I think I'll have my new housekeeper make a fire for Winnie and me this evening. How's Lettie doing now that she's home?"

She listened to Quinn's tale of life in the Southern White House.

"Listen, baby, I just wanted to give you a heads-up. Ezra is being sent down to Charleston along with an additional detail of Secret Service Agents. He just left here. It seems Lettie was playing with the telephone this morning and everyone at the White House including the president thinks she might have to be hospitalized. I just thought you might want to know that.

"By the way, did I tell you that McNally's might be *relocating*. Dunwoodie is talking about retiring. I'm not sure if he's selling or merging. You know how rumors fly around in this town. I find it all very interesting, at the same time it is distressing. The new people might not want my services. You take care of yourself now, you hear? Give Lettie my regards."

Birdie looked over at the sleeping dog. "I hope she's half as smart as you are, Winnie, and she got my meaning," she mumbled. Winnie bounded to her feet and trundled over to where Birdie was sitting. She looked up at her expectantly. "I need the flag, Winnie. If you bring it here, I'll give you another one. Be a good girl. It's important. I know you took it upstairs because I heard the whir of the chair rail even over the sound of the water. I guess I hear better than Ezra does. Go get it, girl," she whispered.

Winnie waddled through the kitchen and out the door to the dining room. She was back in a few seconds with one of Quinn's socks. She laid it down at Birdie's feet. Birdie shook her head.

An hour later Birdie looked down in dismay at the

collection by her feet. A tea bag, an empty Animal Cracker box, Quinn's slipper, a small rock with the words, Dare to Dream, carved into it, a silver spoon, the earpiece from her old reading glasses, and a Nordstrom catalog covered her feet. "No, Winnie. I need the flag. Fetch it for me, baby. Go on, good girl. Get it for me. I won't give you vegetables tonight if you bring it to me. It's for Quinn. Get it, Winnie."

Winnie looked at her treasures, then at Birdie, then back at her treasures. The fat little dog marched off, her tail swishing importantly. Birdie's fist shot in the air when she heard the whir of the chair rail. When she heard it a second time, she held her breath until Winnie trotted into the kitchen, the flag between her teeth. She dropped it at Birdie's feet. She waited to be praised, and Birdie wasn't stingy with it. "Good girl," she said, picking up the flag with a tissue and depositing it in a manila envelope. A rawhide chew was Winnie's reward.

Mission accomplished.

Quinn relayed to Sadie what Birdie had told her. "Now what?"

"Do we tell her or don't we? This isn't in our job description, Quinn."

"If you say that to me one more time, I'm going to swat you. Birdie thinks we should *relocate.*"

"You can't be sure of that," Sadie groaned.

"Yes, I am sure. Alan Dunwoodie is only thirty years old. He's too young to retire, and McNally has been in his place forever. He owns the place. He's not going anywhere. Plus, McNally and Dunwoodie hate each other. That was just a red herring Birdie threw into the conversation in case anyone was listening. Do we tell her or not? We've already broken so many rules one more isn't going to matter."

"You're in charge. You make the decision," Sadie said.

"I say we tell her and let her decide what she wants to do. The truth is, I don't think she can do anything. We certainly can't stop them if they decide to take her to a hospital. Don't you get it, Sadie? Our services will suddenly cease to be needed. C'mon, let's go upstairs and see the first lady. This is her show all the way. She isn't crazy, Sadie."

"Dammit, I know that. All right, let's go."

The first lady was splashing paint with gay abandon and humming the words to "Sweet Georgia Brown" when they knocked on the partially open door.

"Girls, girls, come in. Tell me, how do you like this?" she asked, pointing to the canvas on her easel.

"It's very nice," Sadie said."

"Lovely," Quinn said. "Ma'am, Sadie and I were wondering if you'd like to join us in your courtyard for coffee."

"I'd like that very much. I'm just about done now anyway, the light is changing," she said aloud. "What's wrong?" she whispered anxiously.

"The paint smell in here is very strong. Doesn't it give you a headache?" Quinn asked, putting her index finger to her lips.

"Sometimes," the first lady said, cleaning her hands on a paint-stained towel. "I'm ready if you are. No, no, I'm not ready yet. I want to use the bath-room. Just wait for me."

Ten minutes later in the courtyard, seated on one of the decorative benches, the first lady took deep breaths to try to calm her nerves. Her face was white with shock. "You won't let them put me in a hospital, will you? Please, don't let them do that to me?"

"Ma'am, we can't stop them. We were hired to watch over you. That's it. Period."

"Oh, God, oh God! What am I going to do. Cassie!" she shrilled.

"For God's sake, Lettie, you're going to wake the dead," Cassie admonished. "What's wrong?"

The first lady told her. Then she stood up. Her whole body was trembling. "You're both fired as of this minute."

"Ma'am, you can't fire us. The president hired us. AAD Lapufsky . . ."

"My husband and I hired both of you together. Both our names are on the contract you signed. The money paid to you was wired out of *my* account. My *own personal* account. Cassie knows all about that. Call AAD Lapufsky right now, this second, and tell him I fired you. Do it! That's an order!"

Quinn had no other choice but to do what she was told. She held the phone away from her ear when she heard Puff snarling. "If you don't believe me, I'll let you talk to the first lady herself."

Quinn handed her cell phone to the first lady, who barked into the mouthpiece.

"I fired them. They're going to leave. I decided I

don't want or need agents watching over me. I'm willing to put up with the other agents as long as they stay out of my house. I can do whatever I damn well please. I'm the first lady of the United States. I want to hear you say you understand that I fired both your agents. Good. My housekeeper heard you say that. *I know how you people twist and turn things to your own benefit and even make people disappear.*" She handed the phone back to a stunned Quinn, who could only stare at her, her jaw going slack.

"Now, girls, I'd like to hire you back as my . . . companions. Do you accept the job?"

Quinn looked at Sadie, who nodded. "Okay," they both said in unison.

This is no dumb Southern belle gone to seed, Quinn thought hysterically.

Before either agent knew what was happening, Cassie was shooing them down the steps from the kitchen to what was once the summer kitchen in bygone years. "Just trust us, girls," the first lady whispered.

"Oh hell," Sadie muttered.

Quinn could only grin. "Now what?"

"We're taking it on the lam," the first lady said. "You are no longer agents of the government because I fired you. You can't get into any trouble. We're getting out of here. Hurry, Cassie."

The agents watched as Cassie Franklin literally crawled into the cavernous fireplace that had once been the main cook station. She swept away dust and debris until she found what she was looking for, a cast-iron trapdoor."

"Where . . . where does that go?" Sadie asked, her voice quivering.

"Just next door." Cassie giggled. "Hurry, ladies. Lettie knows the way. We used to play down there as children. Don't worry about a thing on this end. I know what to do. Lettie, please be careful."

"I will, Cassie. You are absolutely the best friend I could ever hope to have. You're better than the sister I never had," the first lady said as she hugged the housekeeper. "Make sure your nephew understands how important secrecy is. Even if they threaten you, don't tell them anything. Just don't let them scare or intimidate you. Start dinner preparations and act normal."

"Okay, Lettie. Good luck."

Quinn looked at Sadie. She ripped at the microphone and battery pack, holding it in her hand. Sadie did the same thing. Cassie jammed them into the pocket of her apron.

The cast-iron fireplace floor closed into place. Quinn felt like she was in a tomb.

"Hold my hand, Quinn. Sadie, hold Quinn's hand. It isn't far. The only problem is, we're going to have to stay in the tunnel until they search the house. The good news is there is a root cellar on the Ashwood Jaye side that's rather large. We'll be able to sit down and wait. I want to thank you for believing in me. You have no idea what it means to me. Birdie must be so proud of you, Quinn. And you, Sadie, I imagine your own mother is just as proud of you. I'm going to write them both a letter on official White House stationery once this is all settled. I'll have my husband sign it, too. His signature is worth more than mine."

"Mrs. Jaye, won't the agents check the summer kitchen?"

"Of course they will. They'll be like fleas on a dog. Cassie knows what to do. You aren't angry with me for firing you, are you? It was for your own safety. I have no doubt in my mind that they would shoot you first and ask questions later."

Quinn shuddered, knowing the first lady was right on the money. Sadie knew it, too.

Ten minutes later, the first lady said, "This is as far as we can go. This is the old root cellar. I have my cigarettes and lighter in case we want to smoke. Let's see what we have here. Well, not much, just some old wooden shelves that we can sit on and stretch out our legs. I suppose we should all take a nap. Maybe one at a time. There are some candles here on the shelf. I could light one, but they take up oxygen. I don't know how much air is down here. We used to play for hours, but the trapdoors were always left open, so we could scamper in and out. What do you think, girls?"

"There's air coming from somewhere," Quinn said. "At least I think there is. I feel a draft on my legs."

"Good, let's light one of the candles. I really hate the dark. So does Jimmy Jaye." The first lady started to cry. "I made such a mess of everything. The whole country, the *whole world* is going to hear about this. Mary Alice is going to split her sides laughing. Historians will put me down as the first nutsy cuckoo first lady in history. That's going to be pretty hard to live with. I'm already a pariah, so just imagine what I'll be when all of this comes out, and it will come out. Jimmy Jaye will probably divorce me. I'll have to get a cat to keep me company in my old age. Why couldn't I have been just stupid like the others? Why did I think I could be a *real* first lady like Bess Truman?" the first lady said unhappily as she flopped down on one of the makeshift shelves that served as a bench.

Quinn and Sadie made soothing noises. "Cassie will be your friend forever and ever. We will, too, ma'am," Quinn said generously.

The first lady wiped her drippy nose on the sleeve of her shirt. "Do you have any idea what it's like to wake up every day and know you have nothing to say about when or what you're going to do? They stole and plundered my life. Why couldn't they let me be me? Why did they have to try to make me into someone I'm not? If you back a dog into a corner, he's going to try to get free. That's just how I feel, like a tired old dog. I don't want you girls thinking I'm some crazy person. I want you to leave here thinking you met a nice lady who gave it all she had but her all wasn't enough. I want to know I can call you up sometime just to chat if I get lonely. Will you take my call and talk to me?"

"Of course we will," Quinn said, putting an arm around the first lady's shoulder. Sadie held the first lady's hand on the other side.

"I'd be real honored if you would call me sometime, ma'am," Sadie said.

The first lady sighed. "Let's talk about your wedding, Quinn."

16

Ezra Lapufsky let himself into his apartment. He stood on the threshold of the doorway and looked around. Did he really live in this awful mess? When was the last time he'd cleaned it? He shrugged, knowing he was lucky if he had time to take his clothes to the dry cleaners and the laundry. Dust an inch thick covered all the furniture. Two rubber plants that had once been beautiful had dry, yellow leaves that stood out like bright sunshine in the messy living room. He shrugged. They added color to the otherwise dreary-looking room.

He walked over to the fireplace and stared up at the pictures on the mantel that were lined up like soldiers. He'd taken the apartment because of the fireplace. He hadn't used it once in all the years he'd lived there. He reached up to pluck a picture of Quinn smiling into the camera. He used the palm of his hand to wipe the dust off the gilt frame and the glass. It was his favorite picture of Quinn, taken in his parents' backyard. Jack was sitting on her lap, looking up at her adoringly. Jack had loved Quinn, and he'd been jealous. Being an animal lover was one of the things that had endeared her to him.

He walked through his messy apartment seeing pictures of her everywhere. She'd die laughing if she knew he'd kept them all. They hadn't been a problem. When Quinn moved on, he'd never brought another woman there. It had seemed sacrilegious to do so. He snorted. Quinn would roll on the floor, busting a gut if she knew how he felt.

He gave himself a mental shake. There was too much going on for him to trip down Memory Lane just then.

He packed quickly, then groaned when he remembered all his shaving gear and toiletries were at Birdie's house. He'd just have to pick stuff up either at the airport or the nearest drugstore. He zipped up the garment bag and carried it to the front door, his duffel bag over his shoulder. At the last second, he set everything down and walked out to the kitchen. He was hungry. He opened the refrigerator and reared back. One look at the contents told him he probably had cures growing for every disease known to man.

He took an extra five minutes to call the management company to send over a cleaning crew while he was away. "Yeah, I want them to do everything, wash the inside of the windows, clean out the refrigerator, and change the sheets on the bed. Have them do the laundry, too, and lay a fire. There's wood in the basket. The bathroom is a top priority. Have them wash the carpets in there, too, and hang up clean towels. Yeah, just send me the bill. Thanks."

Forty-five minutes later he dumped his bags by his desk, hung up his overcoat, checking to make sure the little flag was still in the pocket. Satisfied that it was still there, he headed for the coffee machine, where he motioned for his agents to come forward. "Short briefing, guys. I'm on my way south. Malinowsky, you're in charge. Let's get to it. Duval is out of the picture, and the president is going to nominate me after Thanksgiving. I have to give my answer later today." He grinned as the handshaking and backslapping went on for five full minutes.

Back in his office, glowing with his agents' praise, Puff was about to stick his hand into his overcoat pocket when his cell phone rang. He snapped a greeting and waited. For one split second he felt like he was going to black out. "You better be trying to get a rise out of me, Agent Star. No, no, I don't want to hear that crap. You are the first lady's agents. She can't fire you! I don't give a good tinker's damn how many agents there are there. You stay until I tell you to go. Is that clear? What do you mean, *no?* Let me talk to the first lady.

"Mrs. Jaye, you cannot fire Agents Star and Wilson. I know you *said* you just did it. Yes, you and the president are the ones who signed the contract, and yes, I understand that the money was wired out of *your* personal account. All of a sudden you are now satisfied with the other agents and you don't need women agents any longer. Fine, fine. Do this for me, Mrs. Jaye, please. I'll be there by five o'clock. Keep Agents Star and Wilson until I get there. Will you do that for me? *No!*"

Puff stared at the cell phone in his hand. "Son of a bitch!" Angrier than he'd ever been in his life, he snapped the phone shut and threw it out into the hallway. Special Agent Jim Atkins leaped up and caught it in midair. He tossed it back.

"Nice throw, boss! Remember those anger management classes," the agent called over his shoulder.

Puff's middle finger shot into the air as he grabbed his coat and his bags. His destination: Charleston, South Carolina.

Three hours later Puff was looking up at the magnificent antebellum facade of the Southern White House. He took the front steps two at a time, a bevy of agents behind him. "All right, where are they?" he bellowed at the top of his lungs.

A tiny woman with a wire whisk in her hand and wearing a white wraparound apron appeared in the dining room, a frightened look on her face. Her arms shot upward. "Who . . . what . . . what do you want?"

Ezra Lapufsky flashed his credentials. "Where are the first lady and her agents? Are you the housekeeper?"

"I am the housekeeper," Cassie squeaked. "I think the first lady is napping. I guess the agents are with her. I haven't seen them all afternoon. I've been cooking and baking. Mrs. Jaye wanted chocolate cake and gumbo for dinner. I'm also making a pot of spaghetti. What's wrong? Who are all these people?"

"All these people are federal agents, ma'am."

"Mrs. Jaye doesn't like it when you agents track through the house invading her privacy," Cassie snapped imperiously as she remembered the first lady's words not to let the agents intimidate her.

"Ma'am, I can take a bath in the first lady's bathroom if I want to. Now, will you show me the way, or should I do it myself?"

"She's not going to like this," Cassie shot back as she went up the stairs. "Those two ladies might shoot you, so you better call up the steps that you're coming. For your information, Mr. Federal Agent, I would not allow you to take a bath in the first lady's tub. You remember that now."

"When was the last time you saw the agents or Mrs. Jaye?" Puff said, ignoring the housekeeper's words.

"After lunch. I cleaned up, and they all went upstairs. The first lady doesn't like people hovering around her. I know my place. I stay in the kitchen, where I belong. Don't you be shooting any holes in this beautiful old house." Cassie wagged a skinny finger to make her point.

"Mrs. Jaye, it's me, Cassie. There are some people here to see you!" the housekeeper shouted at the top of her lungs.

Puff cringed at the shrillness. "Okay, which room belongs to the first lady? Which ones belong to the agents?"

Cassie pointed out the agents' rooms as she clutched at her apron, balling it into tight little bunches to keep her hands still. "The first lady's suite of rooms and her studio are on the third floor."

When there was no response to his hard knocks on the mahogany doors, Puff opened each door and stepped inside. Both rooms were empty. He headed for the third floor. "Well!" he barked.

"Well what?" Cassie barked in return.

"They aren't here," Puff said pointedly.

"Are you saying that's my fault? I'm just the housekeeper, *sir*."

"Where else could they be? We're making enough racket here to wake the dead."

"Maybe they're in the downstairs sunroom. I don't know, sir. I told you I was in the kitchen and didn't see them this afternoon."

"What time is dinner?"

"Dinner is whenever the first lady says it is. Sometimes it's six, sometimes it's eight. With spaghetti and gumbo it doesn't matter what time you eat it. The longer it cooks the better it is."

"Are you sure they didn't go out somewhere?"

"How would I know that, sir? Ask the men guarding the house. Ask all those tabloid people standing outside. They don't miss a trick. The only way out of this house is through the courtyard, and you have agents stationed there, or through the front door, and there are agents stationed there, too, as well as the upstairs verandah. Talk to them. They did not come to my kitchen, and that's all I can tell you. Don't you be touching or breaking anything. I don't want to have to explain to Mrs. Jaye how her heirlooms got smashed up. I need to frost my cake."

Cassie walked back to the kitchen, then into the little lavatory off the pantry, where she sat down on a stool. She hugged her skinny arms around her chest and tried to breathe normally. The moment she heard movement in the kitchen, she flushed the toilet, washed her hands, and exited the lavatory, drying her hands on a decorative paper towel with the presidential seal in the middle of it. "Don't even think about touching that cake!" she said spiritedly.

"Where does that door lead?" Puff asked.

"To the old summer kitchen. No one has been down there for years."

"Are there any lights down there?"

"There were. The bulbs might be burned out by now. Just a minute, and I'll get you a flashlight. Stay behind me. I know where the rotten spots are on the steps. Step where I step," Cassie said as she fished a small flashlight out of one of the kitchen drawers. "Be careful, I don't want you falling and suing Mrs. Jaye and the president."

"Just lead the way," Puff snarled.

Cassie grinned in the darkness as she led the way down the steps, a line of agents behind her. She flicked a switch at the bottom of the steps. A dull, yellow light shone down on the old summer kitchen.

Cassie eyed her handiwork and felt pleased with the job she'd done. The old kitchen looked like no one had set foot in it for years and years. The pump at the sink was as old as the house and so rusty it was about to fall apart. The cupboards were full of old dishes and crockery, most of them badly chipped or cracked, but because they had once belonged to the first lady's ancestors, she refused to throw them away. The wire mesh on the vegetable and fruit bins was just as rusty as the old pump. A blue Schwinn bicycle minus a seat leaned against one of the walls, its tires flat. It belonged to the president's youth, and he refused to part with it. A vacuum cleaner and an old footstool along with a pile of luggage rested against another wall. Everything was covered by dust, grime, and cobwebs. A chopping block and an old kitchen table with an enamel top stood at one end of the fireplace, while a huge stack of cinder blocks stood at the opposite end. Cobwebs draped the opening to the fireplace and hung from the beams overhead. She'd used her blow-dryer to distribute the cobwebs just the way she'd seen them do on the Shoppers Channel when they were demonstrating Halloween techniques for a fun-filled night of fright.

"No one's been down here for years. It looks exactly the same as when we secured the building last week," one of the agents said. "The floor is brick and covered with layers of dust. It was like that last week, too. We might have disturbed it a little, but we didn't touch anything. It's all clear," another agent pronounced.

"Then where the hell are they? What about the two houses next door?" Puff demanded.

"They're being checked now, sir."

"Has anyone been here today?" Puff asked, zeroing in on Cassie.

"No, sir. We haven't had any deliveries other than the mail, and one of the agents brought that in. It's on the foyer table. Mrs. Prentice was here yesterday. She's the only one who came to call since Mrs. Jaye came back home. I don't like it down here. Do you mind if I go upstairs? You better follow me and step where I step," she cautioned, her heart thumping in her chest as she led the way back upstairs to the kitchen.

The agents stood in the kitchen, sniffing appreciatively and eyeing the chocolate cake sitting on the counter. They waited for further instructions from Puff.

"Go over this goddamn house again from top to bottom. Tig, you, Isaac, and Max scour the grounds. If they aren't here, where the hell are they?"

Puff homed in again on Cassie, who was busy changing her apron. "Do you have any idea where Mrs. Jaye might have gone if she left the house?"

"No, sir, I don't. Mrs. Jaye doesn't confide her personal business to me," Cassie lied with a straight face. She wondered how much trouble she could get into for lying to a federal agent. *I'm not under oath*, she told herself.

"Did you know that Mrs. Jaye fired Agents Star and Wilson?"

Cassie managed to look stunned. "No, sir. How could I know that?"

"Were you not present when Mrs. Jaye informed me that she had fired the agents? She said you were."

"I don't know what you are talking about, sir. I've never heard of you or heard you speak before today. But if Mrs. Jaye fired them, as you *say* she did, then they probably left."

"Then why are their belongings still in their rooms?"

"I don't know the answer to that, sir."

"Are there any secret rooms in this house?" Puff asked, his tone desperate.

Cassie snorted. "Not that I know of. Why don't you call up the president and ask him. For sure he would know."

"Now why didn't I think of that?" Puff said sarcastically. "They can't have disappeared into thin air. Jenkins!" Puff bellowed.

"Yes, sir?"

"I want you to talk to those sleazeballs out front. See what they're willing to part with."

"Denvers already did that. We're on top of it. No one has left this house today."

Puff stomped his way back to the kitchen. "Miss Franklin, my people tell me no one has left this house today. If that's true, the first lady and my two agents are still in this house. I want you to tell me where they are."

"I told you, I don't know," Cassie wailed. "I've worked here for forty years, and no one ever said anything about a secret room. Why don't you call the president and stop pestering me? They must have walked out the front door, and your people didn't see them. Or else they went through the gate in the courtyard, but they would have had to come into the kitchen to do that. They did not come into the kitchen. Don't blame me if your people fell asleep. Standing around all day doing nothing makes you sleepy. I see your agents yawning all the time. Maybe they went to a movie and forgot to tell me. The first lady loves movies."

"Where else would they go?"

"I told you, I don't know, sir."

"All right. I want you to go to your quarters and stay there. Do you understand?"

"Of course, I understand," Cassie said, turning the stove off under the gumbo and spaghetti. "I live in the cottage beyond the gates. If you're going to search it, I'd like you to do it before I get there."

"It's clear," Agent Atkins said.

Puff watched as Cassie filled a bowl with gumbo and clamped a cover on top of it. She cut herself a generous slice of cake and wrapped it, too, before she shrugged into her coat. It was then that Puff realized he was still wearing his overcoat. He knew before he stuck his hand in his pocket that the little flag was gone. He knew instinctively that one of his agents had taken it. Neville had spies everywhere. In the end it didn't matter. The real flag was back at Birdie's.

"Get everyone in here immediately!"

The detail of agents filled the old kitchen. Puff shrugged out of his coat and threw it over a chair. "The first lady and her two agents seem to have vanished. No one saw them leave. That means they're still in this house somewhere. Now, goddamn it, find them. Tap the walls, look at the floorboards, check that attic again and the summer kitchen. Now get on it!"

Puff whipped out his cell phone. Should he call Birdie or the White House first? He opted for Birdie. He felt his shoulders loosen the minute he heard her voice. "Have you heard from Quinn?"

"No, she hasn't called me. Why?"

"I was just wondering."

"I would love to talk to you, Ezra, but I have some business I have to take care of with Mr. McNally. There I go having another senior moment. I already took care of that earlier. I am getting so forgetful these days. Was there anything in particular you wanted, Ezra, or did you just call to ask about my niece?"

"No, that was it. Have a nice evening, Birdie." He felt a tad better knowing the flag with the president's fingerprints was on the way to a private lab for testing.

He couldn't put it off any longer. He dialed the chief of staff's personal line. He didn't mince any words. "The first lady and her two agents, whom she fired earlier, have vanished . . . sir. I would like to make a suggestion. Ask the president if there are any secret rooms or trapdoors in this old house. The housekeeper says she doesn't know of any. As far as we can tell, they're still inside somewhere."

"You lost the first lady? You damn well better be telling me this is some kind of sick joke. What the hell kind of Mickey Mouse operation are you running there, Lapufsky?"

Puff shivered at the man's tone. "Sir, I just got here about twenty minutes ago. The premises are secure. The Secret Service said no one left the premises. The gates are both secure. The structures on either side have been secured. They just vanished. We're checking the floors and walls in case there's a secret room. Old houses used to have things like that. We need confirmation from the president. The tabloids are out front, and they confirmed the Secret Service account that no one left the house."

"Jesus Christ, Lapufsky! We're talking about the first lady here. What do you mean she fired her agents? You almost managed to get yourself nominated to become director of the FBI, and you lose the first lady!" Neville screamed in his ear.

"I didn't lose the first lady. The Secret Service lost her. I told you, I just got here. Another thing, *sir*, I did not accept the nomination were it to be forthcoming. I haven't made my decision on that matter as yet. The first lady fired her agents. She can do that if she wants to. None of this was my idea, Neville. You and your people convinced me to take it on. If you recall, I said it was a bad idea from the get-go."

"She's a whack job. Find her before this gets out. The president is going to have a hemorrhage when he hears about this. This better not hit the air, Lapufsky."

Puff poured himself a cup of coffee. He stood at the sink drinking it, burning his tongue in the process. He cursed ripely. The fact that all three women were missing had to mean they were together. His gut told him the first lady of the land was in safe hands, Quinn's and Sadie's. Birdie had been careful to tell him Quinn had not called her. She didn't say that she hadn't called Quinn. Birdie would have felt it was her duty to let Quinn and the first lady know what was going down.

Ignoring his burned tongue, Puff kept drinking the coffee. He drained the cup and refilled it as he thought about the two charcoal sketches Birdie had made for him. He knew in his gut he didn't lose the little flag; someone had taken it. He let his mind backtrack. Someone could have taken it while his coat was hanging in the office. Or when the airline hostess hung it up for him. Or . . . when he arrived in Charleston. The only thing he was certain of was that he hadn't lost it—it was deliberately taken out of his pocket.

Knowing all that, he now had to pay serious attention to Birdie and the first lady's theories that there was an imposter in the White House. Why else would Neville use the threat of hospitalizing the first lady? He wished he was back home in his messy apartment. Anything was better than this.

"Sir, those media scumbags out front want to know what all the activity is about. They smell something," one of the agents said.

"Tell them company is coming. That's all you tell them, and, for God's sake, try to stay out of sight, okay?"

Quinn retraced her steps to the trapdoor in the old summer kitchen and strained to hear any sounds from above. She could hear people talking but couldn't make out the words. Was Cassie still in the kitchen or had she returned to her little cottage? She looked down at her watch. Ten o'clock. She scurried back down the tunnel to the root cellar.

"Well?" Sadie said.

"There are people in the kitchen, but I couldn't hear what they were saying. What now, Mrs. Jaye? It's ten o'clock."

"Then let's try the trapdoor. In the past, they've never stationed agents in the other houses, but they do stand guard outside. They consider this a compound of sorts, so it's all part and parcel of this house. If anyone sneezes, they know about it. Follow me and don't make a sound, and forget that I'm the first lady. Right now we're just three women trying to make sense out of something wicked. I have my gun and my diary."

"Oh my God! She's got a gun *and* a diary. I didn't even know she had a diary. They're gonna say we kidnapped her, you know that, don't you?" Sadie hissed in Quinn's ear, as they made their way up a rickety set of steps to the Ashwood house. "They'll shoot first and ask questions later."

"You're making me nervous, Sadie, so be quiet. I'll try to get her to give me the gun. As far as I'm concerned, we're still on the job, Sadie. We were told to watch the first lady and do what she says. That's exactly what we're doing. If she wants to call us her companions or her agents, it's all the same thing to me. We're both pretty good shots. We came in second and third in our sharpshooting class. Maybe she's one of those people who whips out a gun, closes her eyes, and squeezes. When this is all over, I'm personally going to kill Ezra Lapufsky."

"Not if I get to him first, and, guess what else, it doesn't make me feel one bit better."

"Girls, you have to be quiet now. I'm going to find the latch and lift the floor to the fireplace. I might need some help here. I think we'll need to use our shoulders. Voices will carry because the house is empty. There are agents everywhere. Trust me, I know how they work. I can't believe I finally got someone's attention. Push hard with your shoulder."

Sadie heard Quinn groan as she squeezed her slim form next to the first lady. They both gave a mighty shove at the same moment, but the old iron floor didn't budge.

"I think it's me. I don't have the upper body strength I once had," the first lady said. "Sadie, take my place or, if we can manage it, let's all three try it at the same time. Be careful, girls, these steps are very narrow. Fortunately, these old summer kitchens are underground, so the sound will be muffled. Now push!"

"It's moving," Sadie gasped. "Easy now. Quinn, try to hold on to the end so it doesn't fall down with a bang. This is an iron floor, and if we drop it, the sound will ricochet around the world. God, this thing weighs a ton. Okay, okay, I have hold of my end. Quinn, there's some kind of handle or protrusion there on your end. If one of us could just slide through and grab it from the top, we'll be in business. Dammit, I just lost an inch of skin. Do you have a good grip?"

"I have it, and I'm losing my own skin by the second. Move sideways, and maybe I can wiggle up and through," Quinn said, her breathing labored.

"I'm making a mental note that you girls will need tetanus shots when this is over," the first lady said, her voice ringing with elation.

"Don't forget the skin grafts," Sadie said. "Okay, Quinn is through. Hold it tight, Quinn, and ease it back. I'm telling you, it's heavy."

"I've got it. I've got it. Damn, my jacket's in shreds. My slacks are ripped right down the side."

"Don't worry, dear, I'll buy you a new suit. Goodness, I was starting to worry that we weren't going to get out of here. You girls are the marvel in marvelous. I just know Jimmy Jaye is going to give you both a citation of some kind. Won't that be nice? Remember now, whisper."

The first lady climbed through the opening, then helped to lower the heavy iron floor.

As one, the three women looked around. "Thank God for the shutters on the windows," Quinn said.

"Let's just stand still till our eyes adjust to the darkness. There is a little moonlight filtering through the narrow openings at the sides of the shutters. Ma'am, you know this house. What do we do now and where do we go? Or are we just going to hide out here forever?"

The first lady clucked her tongue. "No, of course not. We're going to . . . *split* as soon as we can. These old houses are full of hidey-holes and little door-ways. They were such treasures when we were youngsters. I'm sure the Secret Service knows about all of them, but they won't be coming back here since the place is empty. I'm thinking they won't be expecting anyone to come out of *this* building. In the real kitchen in this house is a step-down pantry. Four steps if I remember correctly. I haven't been in this house for years and years. We should sell it. Anyway, there's this little door at the end of the pantry. My mother used to call it the mousehole. It was big enough for Cassie and me to crawl through. You don't even know it's there from the outside because the shrubbery is so overgrown. We'll have to fight our way through it. It's not thorny or any-thing like that. Now listen to me. This is the plan. One of you has to leave here and find the nearest phone booth. You're going to call Cassie's nephew, who will tell you where he's going to pick us up. That's the plan."

"And you think no one is going to see us, is that it, ma'am?" Sadie said sourly. "Do you have any idea how we look? We've lost skin, and we're bleeding. Quinn looks like she was attacked by some slasher. Not to mention how filthy we are. People will see us and remember how we look. Ma'am, you are the first lady; people are going to recognize you even if it is dark outside. The town is well lit."

"Yes, you have a point." A second later the first lady ripped the sleeve off her smock and tied it around her head. "Now I look just like any other bag lady," she quipped.

She's having the time of her life, Quinn thought. "I'm freezing," she said.

"I'd toss you if I had a coin, but I don't. I'll go since you're half-naked. What's the number to call and where is the nearest pay phone. I'm going to need a quarter. Does anyone have one?" Sadie asked.

"I do!" the first lady chirped. "Cassie gave me change earlier, and I just stuffed it in my pocket. Here, take two quarters in case the first one doesn't work. I think there's a pay phone by the market. Just act nonchalant, and if you see a police officer, hide. They're all over the place in the evening. We do have some crime here at night."

"That's just great," Sadie muttered. She listened as the first lady rattled off the directions to Market Street. When she was satisfied that she had it down pat, she said, "Do I come back here or wait at the pickup point?"

"Too risky to come back," Quinn said. "Cassie's nephew will tell you where to wait. Then, you come and pick us up. Where should they meet us, ma'am?"

"Right around the corner on Atlantic. We'll be in

the shrubbery. I'll recognize Leander's truck, and as soon as you stop, we'll hop in. Tell him to bring us clothes and food. Money will be good, too," the first lady said helpfully. "Hurry, dear, and whatever you do, don't get caught, or the jig's up."

"Yeah, Sadie, don't get caught," Quinn said, echoing the first lady's words.

"All right, all right, open the door and let me out. Wait a minute. How do you know what time you should meet us in the bushes?"

"Thirty-five minutes. Leander lives two blocks from here. He's waiting for your call. It's only going to take you ten minutes, if that, to get to the market. Try to act natural," the first lady said soothingly.

Her heart hammering in her chest, Sadie wiggled through the dense oleander and wisteria bushes outside the little door. She stopped just long enough to get her breath and her bearings. She closed her eyes and listened to the night sounds, to the traffic, and to any alien sounds. Satisfied that there were no bullets about to zing by her head, she stayed in the shadows and bolted.

It was a cool evening and dark, with excellent cloud cover. Just minutes before there had been a three-quarter moon, but it was no longer visible. Nor were there any stars to light her way. She remembered her mother saying God always watched over drunks, fools, and babies. She almost laughed knowing which category she fit into.

Two young men, probably students at the College of Charleston, were ahead of her discussing a girl named Stephanie Williams and her ample endowments. She wished she knew the faceless Stephanie so she could give her a heads-up where the two creeps were concerned. She was almost sorry when they veered off down a dark side street.

She looked to the right and the left as she crossed the street to approach the market. The blue-and-white phone cone welcomed her like a beacon in the night. She crossed the street purposely. She waited patiently while a *skuzzy*-looking individual stuck his finger in the change slot to see if there was any change. He leered at Sadie, who boldly opened her jacket just wide enough for him to see her shoulder holster. He took off at a dead run, tripping over his own feet in the process.

It took her three tries before she could successfully drop in her quarter and dial the number she'd memorized. She was breathing like a racehorse as she struggled to speak clearly and distinctly.

The voice on the other end of the phone was brisk. Directions were given to the Custom House. "I'll be there in seven minutes."

The voice was as good as his word. Exactly seven minutes later a dark-colored sporty Dodge Durango whipped by her. The door opened, she jumped in.

He was as young as the two boys who'd been discussing Stephanie, possibly a little older. "Where to, ma'am?"

Ma'am. That's okay, I feel like a ma'am at the moment. "The corner of Atlantic and East Bay. Did you bring clothes, food, and money?"

"Everything is in the cargo hold."

"Where are you going to take us?" Sadie asked peering through the tinted glass windows.

"Summerville. I have a friend who is house and dog sitting for some lady who is away doing research for a book she's writing. It's a perfect place for Miss Lettie. Iron gates, lots of space, real private. I don't see anyone."

"Slow down, they'll see you. There they are!"

Ten minutes later they were headed for I-26 and the town of Summerville.

17

Ezra Lapufsky clicked on his cell phone before it stopped ringing. He barked a greeting, his eyes on the kitchen clock. It was eleven o'clock. "No, sir, we haven't found them. I'm sorry as all hell, Neville, but I can't conjure up bodies just because you say I should. They're gone, that's the bottom line. Did you speak with the president?"

"The president of the United States is mighty upset, Lapufsky. He said there are no secret rooms in that old house. He also said he isn't aware of any blueprints. I'm thinking National Registry here since the house and the two on the side are listed with them. Whatever is on record is going to be faxed to me. I guess you know your name is going off the short list, Lapufsky."

Puff's eyes narrowed at the chief of staff's words. "One more time, Neville, I did not lose the first lady or her agents. I wasn't even here. The Secret Service lost them. Why isn't Ballinger here?"

"Because this was your show all the way. The president signed off on it, and you loused it up. I want your ass back here right now."

"How do you suggest I do that, Neville? Do you want me to flap my wings and fly?"

"Remember who you're talking to, Lapufsky. You could be on the unemployment line tomorrow."

Puff lifted the dome off the chocolate cake and stuck his finger in the icing. He licked his finger. "If I'm on the unemployment line, you'll be right next to me." He sucked in his breath before he said, "Who's that guy you've got in the White House subbing for the real president? I know all about it, so don't think you're fooling me for one minute. You know what else, Neville. There's nothing wrong with the first lady. All she wants is the husband she went to Washington with. You know, the one with all the warts. The *real* one. She's gone, Neville. She fired the two special agents she and her husband hired, and she had every right to do that. Agents Star and Wilson are no longer Secret Service Agents, so you better advise Ballinger to tell his agents not to get trigger-happy. They went to ground, Neville, and the first lady isn't coming up for air until she gets her husband back."

"Get your ass back here immediately, Lapufsky. That's a goddamn order."

Puff shrugged. He looked around at the agents standing in the kitchen. "Cake anyone?"

"This is charming, absolutely charming," the first lady said as she stepped out of the Dodge Durango. "Thank you, Leander, for bringing us here. Now what are the rules?" she asked briskly as she looked around at her surroundings.

"Go into the cottage and get cleaned up, Miss Lettie. There's a phone inside that you can use if you need to make calls. No one knows you're here, so it's safe to use the phone. Clothes are in these shopping bags. I'm hoping they fit. I took three hundred dollars from my buddy's ATM, and it's in there, too. There's a ton of food inside. Keep the shutters closed. Don't go in or out. With all the shrubbery and trees no one will even know you're here. This little cottage can't be seen from the street or even the surrounding properties. There really isn't anyone around during the day because they all work. And everyone in town knows the author who lives here is reclusive and doesn't invite company. There's no way they can put you and the author together. I'm going to drive to Savannah now and stay with some friends. Aunt Cassie will say I left earlier in the day. We got you covered. If they catch up with me, I won't say a word. The guys will cover for me. I'll clue Dennis in before I leave. Dennis Schwartz is the house and dog sitter. Is there anything else you want me to do before I leave?"

"I don't think so, Leander. Thank you so much. Don't you believe any of that stuff you hear on the television, honey," the first lady whispered in his ear as she hugged him good-bye.

"Never in a million years." The youth grinned as he climbed into the Durango and turned it around.

Inside the little cottage, the women looked around. "It is so charming. It's like one of those Swiss chalets." The first lady beamed happily. "It has everything. Girls, make a note to remind me to buy the author's books. I'll have Jimmy Jaye write her a letter, too. I think she would like that. Oh, this is such an adventure. Who gets to take a shower first?" she asked brightly.

"You go first, ma'am," Sadie said. "I think I'd like one of your cigarettes if you don't mind sharing."

Quinn looked around at the well-built cottage with its exposed beams and heavy hardware bolted at the joints. "This place could probably withstand a class-five hurricane. I bet we could live here for quite a while if we had to. These chairs are like butter, so soft they just mold to your body. State-of-the-art kitchen, a powder room, two bedrooms, a small dining area, and this glorious living room. We could pitch a tent inside that fireplace and still have room left over. Definitely cozy. What's your opinion, Sadie?"

"Quinn, right this second, I don't have an opinion. I'm numb. I keep asking myself if we're crazy. Do you think it's possible both of us could go insane at the same time?" Sadie puffed furiously on one of the first lady's cigarettes.

"I'd feel better if we had a plan. We need a plan, Sadie." Quinn reached for a cigarette and fired it up. She blew a perfect smoke ring. "I'm almost certain we're still her agents. I don't ever remember reading anything like this in the manuals. If she wants to call us companions, I guess that's okay. She just did that firing thing to protect us. She watches a lot of those blood-and-guts movies and thinks she was doing the right thing."

"Are we just going to sit here and watch television or what?"

Quinn shrugged. "Sadie, how knowledgeable is your brother? I know you said he was a superduper, whiz-bang, high-tech wizard, but can he bounce phone calls off satellites?"

"I'm sure he can. Listen, Quinn, they've got him covered, trust me. My little high-tech firm is and has been under the microscope since day one. I'm thinking, I'm thinking. No matter what we do, we're involving other people. Leander is just a kid. He took risks by helping us. Well, not us but the first lady. All of us," she snorted. "The kid could be in big trouble. Hell, we could go to jail if they don't kill us first."

Quinn felt a lump rise in her throat at her partner's words. "Your brother could do it, though, right?"

Sadie nodded.

"Didn't you tell me once that he belongs to those *tekkie* clubs that meet all over the country and come up with all those way-out ways of doing things?"

"Yes. He lives and breathes that stuff. He's the one who should be working for the FBI, but he says they're so far behind the times it's pitiful. My brother has a really big ego."

"We need someone trustworthy to go to your firm to talk to Mickey. Someone who won't blow our cover. Someone like . . ."

Sadie leaned forward on her chair. "Someone like . . . Alex Duval. He should be pissed to the teeth about now because of the way the nomination went. If you could convince him to help us . . . we might stand a chance. Whom do we want to call? The president?"

"Get real, Sadie. They'd never put me through to

the *real* president. What would be the point in talking
to the bogus one? No, I want to talk to Puff. We have
to tell him the first lady is safe. We can even let her
talk to him. Alex might still be under scrutiny because
of me, so he may not be a logical choice. Who else do
we know that we trust and can pull this off?"

Sadie's face was glum as she shrugged her shoulders.

The first lady walked into the living room, her hair
wrapped in a towel. She pointed to her bib overalls
and tee shirt. "Cassie and I used to wear overalls like
this when we were youngsters. They had patches on
them, though. We always managed to wear the knees
and the seat out. You look . . . *desperate*, girls."

"We are desperate, ma'am," Sadie said. "Is it possible you have a plan? If you do, this is the time to
share it."

"Good heavens, no. I thought you girls would
come up with one. I'm going to make us some sandwiches. You go ahead and do whatever you were
doing while I fix us something to eat. Did anyone
knock on the door while I was in the shower? Probably not, it's too soon," she muttered, answering her
own question as she trotted off to the kitchen.

The two agents looked at one another, their eyes
full of questions. "What the hell is she talking about,
Quinn? Oh, jeez, I bet I know. It wouldn't surprise
me one little bit if she sent that kid to break into
those doctors' offices. He wouldn't know how to say
no to the president's wife. I think we need to ask her
about that right *now*."

Both agents marched into the kitchen. "Mrs. Jaye,

did you send Leander to break into those two doctors' offices? Please tell us the truth."

Lettie Jaye stopped spreading mayonnaise on a
slice of bread she'd taken from the freezer. "Cross my
heart and hope to die, I did not send Leander to bur-
glarize anyone's offices. Now, do you feel better?
You know a Southern belle never uses Miracle Whip.
We make our own mayonnaise for our chicken salad.
You might not know this, but if you put dark meat
in your chicken salad and use Miracle Whip, they'll
drum you right out of the Junior League. That would
be *tacky*. Jimmy Jaye loves dark meat, and he likes
Miracle Whip. Cassie always hid ours in the pantry,
so the girls would never know. It was like a secret if
you know what I mean. Now, tell me, do you want
lettuce on your sandwich? We're having baloney and
cheese. It's been years since I had a baloney and
cheese sandwich. It's Cassie's favorite."

"Lots of lettuce," Sadie said.

"One piece of lettuce and light on the mayo,"
Quinn said.

"Coming right up. Now, see if you can find us a
good movie to watch. One with lots of blood and
guts. Oh, I wish Jimmy Jaye was here. He would love
this little place. What do you want to drink, girls?"
she babbled.

"Whatever. She's lying," Sadie hissed as she
returned to the living room.

"Water's fine," Quinn said. "Yes, I know. She
probably doesn't think of it as lying, though.

Five minutes later the first lady entered the living
room carrying a loaded tray. "We're having beer. Oh,

a Steven Seagal movie. I've seen this one at least eight times. I can tell you what happens if you want to know. Help yourself, girls," the first lady said as she lowered herself to the floor in front of the television set and crossed her legs. She chomped down on her baloney sandwich, swigging from the Budweiser bottle from time to time. Both agents stared at her in awe.

Lettie Jaye stopped chewing long enough to ask, "What's wrong?"

"Well, ma'am, you are the first lady of the land. It just seems strange to see you sitting on the floor in your bare feet eating a baloney sandwich and swigging beer."

Lettie Jaye's eyes filled with tears. "I would really like it if you girls would call me Lettie. I thought we agreed on that. Yes, I am the first lady, but I'm Lettie Jaye, too. Like you're Quinn Star, and you're Sadie Wilson. I like sitting like this. My husband liked it, too. Sometimes he'd put his head in my lap, or I'd put mine in his. We often ate dinner sitting on the floor. Sometimes we'd even fool around after Cassie went home to her cottage. It just makes me feel better, even if I do sit by myself. I don't want to lose all my memories. Can't you understand that?"

Both agents nodded.

"Okay, now I feel awful," Sadie whispered in Quinn's ear.

It was two o'clock in the morning when the first lady got to her feet and announced that she was going to bed. "First one up makes breakfast," she chirped. "Oh, look, there's something stuck under the door."

"Stay where you are, ma'am. I'll get it," Quinn said.

Quinn scanned the single sheet of paper, Sadie peering over her shoulder. "Ma'am, you lied to us."

"I did no such thing. You asked me if I sent Leander to . . . you know. I told you the truth. It was Dennis, Leander's friend, who did the breaking and entering. I consider this war. What does it say?"

"It says, there are no records in either the dentist's or the doctors' offices that have your name or your husband's name on them."

"I thought Harvey Ladson would have kept a set of records. Those . . . those . . . *turds* took them so there would be no proof. I knew I was right; I just knew it. Right now I feel vindicated. Remember now, first one up makes breakfast. Good night, girls. Sleep tight."

"She made a mess in the kitchen. I'll clean it up," Sadie said, "and I'll take the first watch, three hours on, three off. I'll wake you when it's your turn."

Quinn nodded as she headed for the stairs, the paper that had been slipped under her door, still in her hand. She lay down on one of the twin beds in the sectioned-off loft, fully clothed. She needed to think, to plan. A moment later, her eyes closed, and she was asleep.

Quinn woke, almost to the minute of her allotted three-hour sleep to a strange, muffled noise coming from her left. She swung her legs over the bed and tiptoed to the section of the loft where the first lady was sleeping. She peered around an elaborate Chinese screen to see the first lady sitting in the corner crying, a pillow clutched against her chest. Sensing the agent's presence, she looked up.

Quinn walked over to where the first lady was sitting and dropped to her knees. She knew what she was doing wasn't in her job description, but she didn't care. She put her arms around the first lady and made soothing sounds. How vulnerable and frail she felt. How fearful she must be.

"He's sick, isn't he, Quinn? My Jimmy Jaye is sick, and they don't want anyone to know. That's what this is all about. I didn't want to believe it because I couldn't face it. I should be stronger, tougher than that. I think I knew a year ago, maybe longer, that Jimmy Jaye was different. Oh, he still wrote me little notes, still called me on the phone, and we did a lot of the things we'd always done, but it wasn't the same. Sometimes he'd look right through me as though he didn't even know me. Sometimes it was just a flash. He would forget what he was saying in midsentence. I'm starting to think . . . maybe Jimmy Jaye has Alzheimer's.

"My husband should not be running the country." Lettie Jaye slapped at her forehead. "You see, you see, I say stupid things. Jimmy Jaye isn't running the country. That other person is, or else it's all those new people. They don't want anyone to know.

"All those new people wanted to keep their powerful jobs. The old ones, our friends, would have noticed the change in Jimmy Jaye. Maybe they saw more than I did at the beginning. I'm even beginning to think that Jimmy Jaye's doctor, the one who is the Surgeon General, knew about it. That's why I wanted to see his records. There *is* a conspiracy going on in the White House. That's why my husband's security was so tight, and why they tried to keep him away from me as much as possible. I should have been smarter, wiser. How did I let this happen? It's all my fault. I'm just a foolish old lady who isn't fit to be the first lady. I don't know what to do. Tell me what I need to do, Quinn, and I'll do it." She blew her nose on a wad of toilet paper she had clutched in her hand.

Quinn looked up to see Sadie standing next to the Chinese screen. She nodded, indicating that she'd heard what the first lady said.

"We'll think of something . . . *Lettie*," Quinn said.

Lettie Jaye sniffed tearfully. "Does that mean I have to reinstate you as my agents? Would you rather be my agents or my companions?"

"I think they're one and the same," Quinn said soothingly. "You need to get some sleep now while Sadie and I put our heads together. Hopefully, things will look different in the morning, and we'll have a plan to put into action."

"I hope so," Lettie Jaye said wearily as she climbed into the single bed and pulled a colorful patchwork quilt up to her chin.

Downstairs in the living room, Quinn looked at Sadie before she threw her hands in the air. "I don't know what to do, Sadie. For the first time in my life, I honest to God don't know what to do. Do you have any ideas? Never mind. Go to sleep. I'm going to sit here and think. If I don't come up with a plan or an idea, we might get lucky and you'll dream of one."

Sadie rolled her eyes as she walked up the steps to the loft.

Quinn stopped what she was doing in the kitchen when she heard Sadie gallop down the circular staircase. "You sound like a herd of elephants. Eggs or pancakes?"

"I don't care. Listen, I just thought of a guy we can call. I remember Mickey talking about him. They hang together when they go to those tekkie shows. Mickey said there was nothing he couldn't do when it came to high-tech stuff. Mickey said he could hack into anything. He doesn't," she added hastily. "He just knows how. He's like a tekkie god or something. All those people look up to him. I think he lives in Pompano Beach, Florida. Do you want me to try and call him. It's early, so maybe we can still catch him. He could call Mickey at home and use that high-tech lingo they use. Mickey will get the drift. It's another person, though, Quinn, who will know what we're doing. I'll have to level with him. What do you think?"

"I think it's a very good idea. I'll take the blame for all of this, so I don't want you worrying," the first lady said entering the kitchen. "Write down what you want me to say, and I'll do the talking."

"Ma'am . . . that isn't a good idea," Sadie said.

"It's all we have going for us at the moment. I have to call Puff to let him know the first lady is alive and well. I'm sure he knows it, but we can't assume anything at this point. Go for it, Sadie." Sadie ran to the living room and dialed the long-distance infor-

mation operator. Her fist shot in the air when Bradford Hollister's telephone number was announced.
She copied it down and immediately dialed the
number.

"Eggs or pancakes, ma'am?"

"Both," the first lady said smartly.

"You got it." Quinn grinned.

As Quinn whisked the batter for the pancakes, she
could hear Sadie in the living room. She felt light-
headed when she listened to Sadie go into her spiel.
"I have someone here who wants to talk to you,
Bradford. It involves national security, and you have
to keep your lip zipped. You have to swear to me you
won't breathe a word of this to anyone. Okay, Bradford, hold for the first lady of the United States.
Ma'am, this is Bradford Hollister on the phone."

The first lady squared her shoulders. "Mr. Hollister, this is Letecia Jaye. My two agents and I need
your help. Please listen to me carefully and tell me if
you can do what we want as quickly as possible. No,
Mr. Hollister, I am not being held hostage. I can tell
you anything you want to know about Sadie and her
brother. A personally autographed picture of the
president will not be a problem. If you care to travel
to South Carolina, you can be in the picture. I'll take it
myself. Good. This is what we want you to do, so listen carefully. We'll wait for your call, Mr. Hollister."

In the kitchen, Quinn leaned against the refrigerator as she fought to stay calm. The only thing she
could think of to say was, "Sadie, set the table."

"One hour and you can make the call," the first
lady said, taking her place at the table. "Mr. Hollister

sounds like a lovely person. If he comes to Charleston when this is over, we'll invite him to dinner."

Ezra Lapufsky looked like he'd spent three days in Baghdad when he strode down the hall in the White House in search of Lawrence Neville, the president's chief of staff. Surprisingly, no one gave him more than a cursory glance.

Lawrence Neville, looking as dapper as a man seventy pounds overweight could, reared back at the sight of the acting associate director of the FBI. He correctly interpreted the murderous look in Lapufsky's eyes. He tried to stare him down, but in the end had to walk around to his desk, where he sat down, motioning for Puff to take a seat. Instead, Puff started to pace, his brain whirling and twirling.

"I want to know what's going on, Neville. This isn't going to go away, and, no, we still haven't found the first lady and her two agents. If you think for one minute you're going to be able to shut the first lady up, you're wrong. A doctor shooting her full of tranquilizers isn't going to work either. This would be a real good time to tell me what's going on here. In the interests of national security, of course."

"There's nothing going on here, Lapufsky. Your imagination is running wild in my opinion. It grieves me to say the first lady has some serious mental problems. We didn't want it to get out. Think about it. How's that going to look for the president and the country? She is wily, I'll give her that. Somehow she managed to bamboozle your two top-notch agents. The two agents you recommended so highly to the president. You just dug yourself a deep hole, Lapufsky, and there's no way out.

"The president is taking you off the case and reassigning you to the field office in England."

Puff ran his hands through his already disheveled hair. He stared at the chief of staff as though he had sprouted a second head. "I'm AAD until a replacement is found for my successor. Only the president can remove me. Why don't we call him in here and put this all to the test? The real guy, Neville, not the one with the heels on his shoes."

Lawrence Neville's voice turned conciliatory as he sat down and folded his hands across his broad chest. "This whole thing with the first lady has made us all a little touchy. It goes without saying the president is worried sick. He is trying to run the country, Lapufsky, and he trusts us to take care of his wife. Something we seem to have failed to do. I admit you weren't there when she took a powder, but you must know where she is or how to find her. I've had Ballinger on the carpet all night long. And, for God's sake, will you stop believing that crap the first lady keeps feeding you about *two* presidents. The last time I looked, there was only one. You won't like England at this time of year. It's cold, it's raw and damp, and it rains constantly. Their central heating is nothing like ours. You shiver night and day."

The fine hairs on the back of Puff's neck sprang to attention when the phone rang. He made no pretense of not listening, wondering at the same time why his cell phone hadn't rung in hours. *Stupid is as stupid does,* he thought. *Of course. The battery is dead.*

"It's your agent Star. A call is coming through from her. She wants to know if you're here. Find out where she is and bring her in with the first lady in tow." Puff watched as he pressed a series of buttons on the console, then barked, "Trace this call. All right, go ahead, you can talk now."

Puff walked around to the side of the desk and picked up the phone. "Where the hell are you, Agent Star? Is the first lady all right?"

"The first lady is fine. That's what I called to tell you. You don't really think I'm going to tell you where we are, do you? We went to ground. Remember how you always used to say that I was smarter than you on your best day? Well, it was true back then, and it's true today. The first lady wants her husband. The real one. I know what's wrong with him, Puff," she whispered. "It's what we talked about the last time," she continued to whisper. Didn't she know *they* were listening to the conversation. Perspiration beaded on his brow.

"Keep her on the phone, Lapufsky," the chief of staff ordered. Puff nodded.

"They're tracing this call, aren't they?" She laughed, a sound that sent shivers up Puff's spine. "I'm going to give you a few hours to think about all this. Then I'm going to call you back, and you damn well better have some answers for the first lady. She wants her husband. The one with the warts. I'll call you sometime tonight. If not tonight, tomorrow. Wait for my call. I'll only talk to you, so be ready to take my call." She laughed just as Lawrence Neville grabbed the phone from Puff's hand.

His eyes narrowed to mean little slits in his jowly face as he slammed the phone back into place, his eyes on the minute hand of his watch. "Three minutes, we should have her location in seconds," he said tightly. The phone rang almost immediately.

Puff watched as the chief of staff's face turned red, then purple, and then white. He turned away to hide his weary grin.

"What do you mean you couldn't trace the call?" Neville bellowed. "What in hell are you telling me? She's a woman, for Christ's sake. She doesn't have the capabilities to bounce calls off a satellite. Argentina, Greece, Costa Rica, back to Greece, Russia!"

Sputtering, Neville turned his rage on Puff. "Where the hell do you think you're going?"

"Home to take a shower and get a change of clothes and pack. You said you were sending me to England, didn't you?"

"I didn't say when. That dimwit said she would only talk to you. That means you have to be back here tonight, and that means through the night, into tomorrow if she doesn't call tonight. She's going to pull the same crap, but this time we'll be ready for her. You get your ass back here by six tonight."

"You might as well give it up, Neville. Haul out the real guy and send him home. Star said she *knows* what's wrong with the president. In order for her to know something like that, the first lady must have finally talked. I'm no shrink or medical doctor, but my guess would be that the real president has some kind of serious medical problem you guys in here are covering up. Like I said, that's a guess on my part. If

Star does call back tonight, you won't be able to track her. I told you she was smart, but you wouldn't listen to me. Your chickens are coming home to roost, and they're laying eggs. She'll call all the networks, so be prepared."

Neville's hand was on the phone the moment Puff closed the door behind him.

Puff skirted the gaggle of paparazzi vehicles outside the White House and made his way down Pennsylvania Avenue. His destination: Birdie Langley's yellow house on Connecticut Avenue.

His thoughts drifted as he drove along, his weary eyes on the traffic ahead of him. Where was Quinn? The main thing was that the first lady was safe. With that thought safely tucked away, he gave over to trying to figure out how Quinn could have bounced the phone call off a satellite. She had to know some pretty impressive people to do that successfully. His chest puffed out with pride knowing she'd pulled it off.

Damn, he was tired. He realized he wasn't as young as he used to be when he could pull all-nighters, take a shower, and put in a second shift. Life was passing him by, and he had nothing to show for it except a healthy pension fund, a nice savings account, and a sizable checking account. He didn't own a house or a dog. His loss. A wife would work into the mix very well.

Puff frowned when he saw the flurry of white flakes swirling about the car. Snow before Thanksgiving! Amazing. It was Arctic cold in Washington. It had been chilly in Charleston, but nothing like it

was here. He couldn't help but wonder if the three
women were dressed for the cool days and nights.
Where the hell were they? How far could they have
gone? Pretty damn far in seven hours was his best
guess. For all he knew, they could have left the state.
Among the three of them they probably had a mile-
long list of friends who would be willing and able to
help them out.

The big question still remained, how in the Sam
Hill had they gotten away?

It was snowing harder when Puff parked in Birdie's
driveway. He could hear Winnie barking inside. A
tired smile tugged at the corners of his mouth when he
climbed out of the car and made his way to Birdie's
back door. Within seconds he was covered with light
snow. He knocked sharply on the door and waited
until the sour-faced nurse opened the door and
marched back to the living room. Birdie was seated at
the table sipping coffee, Winnie at her feet.

The fat little dog waddled over to Puff and
whined to have her belly scratched. Puff obliged.
"Hi, Birdie. Do you mind if I take a quick shower
and shave? I'll fill you in when I'm finished."

"Of course you can take a shower. Would you like
some lunch? My new cook made some delicious vegetable soup and fresh bread this morning. Doesn't
the kitchen smell wonderful?" She tapped a yellow
envelope that said McNALLY'S FUNERAL HOME in the
upper left-hand corner. She mouthed the words, "the
flag report."

Puff felt his heartbeat accelerate. He nodded as he
headed for the steps, Winnie behind him. He watched

in amazement as Winnie hopped onto her side seat and pressed the button with her front paw. She barked as she rose quicker than he was walking and reached the top before Puff did. She barked again as she waddled down the hall to the room where he slept.

On top of his neatly made bed was a pile of Winnie's treasures. Six Hershey bar wrappers, two old socks, one of Birdie's combs, a bright red mitten, four rawhide bones with all the flavor licked off, her string of bells, and the cat with one eye and whiskers. She hopped on the bed, settling herself among her things before she closed her eyes. Puff smiled and scratched her behind the ears. "I wish you could talk, Winnie."

18

Cassie Franklin knew almost to the minute when the Secret Service found the trapdoor in the summer kitchen. She didn't know how she knew; she just knew. Maybe it was because her bedroom window was on the first floor, and she always cracked it open before she crawled into bed. Or maybe it was because she heard people walking around, or perhaps the bushes rustled or birds took flight. She felt naked fear for the first time in her life. She lay quietly listening to her husband snore lightly. Usually Jacob's lusty snores irritated her. That day, though, they were like music to her ears. She reached out to touch his shoulder.

Her husband Jacob knew about her part in Lettie's escape and hadn't batted an eye. Jacob was like that, always easygoing, always even-tempered, going with the flow of things as long as no one got hurt. The Jayes had given them both a good life, and they were grateful for that life. Jacob loved sitting with Jimmy Jaye on the verandah in the summer late at night, both of them smoking good cigars and talking about what was going on in the world. The Jayes never treated either of them like the hired help. They were simply friends.

Jacob Franklin was a big man with arms like tree trunks and hands as big as ham hocks. Jacob turned over, the bed groaning with his movement, and gathered Cassie close. "What's wrong?" he whispered. "What time is it?"

"It's eleven o'clock in the morning. Neither one of us has ever lain in bed past six o'clock. There didn't seem to be any reason to get up. They found the trapdoor. I'm thinking they discovered the little door in the summer kitchen where Lettie made her getaway. I've been listening to all the rustling out there for a good fifteen minutes. All they had to do was follow the footprints and those prints would take them to the fireplace in the Ashwood Jaye house. Took them long enough. They'll be here pretty soon, Jacob. Do you think we should get up and get dressed, or should we just stay here in bed?"

"Cassie, we didn't crawl into this bed until five-thirty, so it's okay for us to be sleeping this late. You didn't sleep, did you? Just how nervous are you?"

"Not as nervous as I thought I would be. Maybe I'm jittery. I wonder if that's the same thing as being nervous. I knew sooner or later they'd find it. I lied to that FBI person, but I wasn't under oath, Jacob. I'm going to keep on lying to those Secret Service Agents when they come over here. I'd do it all over again, too," she said staunchly.

"I know you would. If Lettie says evil is afoot, then evil is afoot. Lettie was never one to make something out of nothing. She's even more grounded since going to Washington. I'm sorry to hear that Jimmy might be ill. If he's sick, then he belongs here with us so we can take care of him. He doesn't belong back there in Washington, where they try to hide him from people and his wife. It's not fair to the country and the people who voted for him. If that's what they've been doing, then Lettie is right, it's evil."

Cassie squeezed her husband's hand. "They're coming now, I hear them walking up the path. You go to the door. Put your slippers on, Jacob, the floors are cold, and I don't want you getting sick on me. Lettie and Jimmy are going to need both of us. Try to look sleepy."

Jacob smiled as he dutifully wiggled his feet into his slippers the minute the doorbell rang. He was tying the belt to his old flannel robe when he opened the door. He yawned elaborately as he stared at the two agents in front of him, the same agents who stood guard over the Ashwood Jaye house. "What can I do for you young men?" he asked bluntly. He looked down at his watch to see the time.

"We would like you and your wife to come with us to the main house. We'll wait inside for you while you get dressed."

Jacob yawned again. "Did something happen? Did you find Mrs. Jaye? Is she all right?"

"Get dressed, Mr. Franklin. Leave your bedroom door open."

Cassie was already dressed when Jacob entered the bathroom. She handed him a pile of clothing.

"What's this all about?" Cassie asked coldly as she entered the cozy living room. "What right do you have to come to my house and wake me in the middle of the night . . . well it's not night now, and tell me what I have to do? This is a free country, and I resent this invasion into my home. I'm going to write a letter to the editor of the paper, and then I'm going to call the president. I know the president, and we're on a first-name basis. The only reason we're going to follow you is because we care about the first lady's safety and her husband's well-being. You don't scare me, so don't even think about threatening me or my husband." She huffed and puffed to make her point.

"Shush, Cassie. The men are just doing their jobs. We didn't do anything, and we don't have anything to hide. Let's just see what they want to talk to us about before we get excited," Jacob said, playing his part in the game.

There were at least a dozen Secret Service Agents in Lettie Jaye's kitchen. Cassie looked each one of them in the eye. She was reminded of a small army of dark-clad robots. "Who ate my cake?" she demanded furiously. When she didn't receive a response, she clamped her lips together.

"Where's the first lady, Mrs. Franklin?"

They all looked alike to her. Lettie always said they looked like a group of Stepford men.

"I must have told you a dozen times I don't know where Mrs. Jaye is. How could I possibly know something like that?"

"We know how the first lady and the agents got out of here. You helped them, didn't you, Mrs. Franklin?"

"I did no such thing. Don't you be spreading

rumors about me that will ruin my reputation. You lost my Lettie, and you're trying to blame me." *Don't let them intimidate you,* was what the first lady had said. "It isn't going to work. If you know how they got away, why aren't you out looking for them? Tell me that, young man."

"You lied to Acting Associate Director Lapufsky. This is your chance to make things right. Tell us where they are." He was so relentless, Cassie almost buckled. *Don't let them intimidate you.*

Cassie squared her shoulders. "I didn't lie. I don't know where they are. You can pull out my toenails, and it won't change a thing. I don't know. You should be out there scouring the streets looking for my Lettie. Instead you stand here in her kitchen and accuse me of lying. Not to mention eating a cake that didn't belong to you. That cake was made especially for the first lady. That tells me you aren't very interested in finding the first lady. I can't help you."

"How did you put the cobwebs back?" one of the agents asked. His question was more curious than demanding.

"What cobwebs? What are you talking about?"

"We found the trapdoor in the fireplace and the tunnel, and the root cellar," the agent said in a voice that was as cold and hard as his eyes.

"What trapdoor and what fireplace are you talking about? We don't have any trapdoors in this house, and if you are implying there are cobwebs here, there aren't. I know how to clean. We *do not* have cobwebs." *Don't let them intimidate you.*

"Mr. and Mrs. Franklin, follow me," the agent

said, moving toward the steps leading to the summer kitchen.

Cassie blinked at the array of floodlights hanging from the rafters. Dark brown extension cords coiled like snakes led up the steps to the kitchen and the outlets all along the countertops. It took only a glance to show her what the agents already knew; someone had carefully reattached the cobwebs. A sloppy job at best. So much for the Shoppers Channel crash course in Halloween decor. In the dim yellow light from the sixty-watt bulb, her handiwork had passed muster. Now with five thousand watts of brightness, it looked like she was dead in the water.

Don't let them intimidate you. Easier said than done. Jacob squeezed her hand. It was all she needed. Her thin shoulders squared again. "What is it I'm supposed to see other than a trapdoor that's open? A trapdoor that I didn't even know about. Jacob, did you know about this trapdoor?"

"No, honey, I sure didn't. I'm thinking we need to call a lawyer. I won't allow you to impugn my wife's honesty. We said we don't know anything about the trapdoor. I don't know how to attach cobwebs, and neither does my wife. I repeat, we want to call our lawyer."

"You can call your lawyer when we say you can call your lawyer. Where did they go? I suppose you're going to tell us you don't know about the little door in the house next door, too, right?"

Cassie let her eyes pop wide. "You mean the mousehole? Of course I know about the mousehole. There used to be one in this house, too, but the first lady had it closed up. Mr. Jaye's brother used to play hide-and-seek with the president, and they would use that little mousehole to hide from one another. I don't even know if a grown person can get through it. The oleanders and the wisteria are so thick on that side of the house, I doubt anyone could get through it."

"Someone got through them. The branches are beaten back and trampled on," the cold-voiced agent said.

"Imagine that. I guess the first lady just walked over to the house and went inside. She does have a key. She would never"—she shuddered to make her point—"go through a trapdoor and a tunnel. She's afraid of bugs and spiders. Plus, she's the first lady of the United States, and first ladies of the United States do not do things like that. Do they, Jacob?"

"No, Cassie, they don't. We want a lawyer. This is the third time I'm requesting one."

"Make that four times. I want a lawyer," Cassie said. "We both want a lawyer. We know our rights. Mr. Jaye was forever giving us lessons on the law and the rights of citizens. We listened to him. It's cold down here."

The cold-eyed agent jerked his head at his partner and motioned to the stairs. Cassie and her husband trooped up the steps to the kitchen.

"Where would they go, Mrs. Franklin?"

"They could have gone anywhere. I don't have the faintest idea of where they would go. Charleston is not a city that the agents knew. I heard them talking at lunch one day. All the first lady's friends are here in town. There are no relatives on either side of the family. I think there might be some very distant cousins in Raleigh, North Carolina. There might be one in Vermont, too, but I'm not sure. Maybe they just walked away like normal people. They just walked out of this house, didn't they. No, no, you'll never convince me that Mrs. Jaye did that trapdoor tunnel thing. Never, ever, in a million years. I think you're just making this all up to make yourselves look good and make Jacob and me look bad. We want a lawyer! I'm not saying another word. Don't say another word, Jacob, until we get a lawyer."

Jacob nodded as he clamped his lips tightly together. Cassie did the same thing.

"Molino! Carpenter! Get the maps and show me where the other house is. What's the name of that town again?"

"Summerville," one of the agents called from the dining room that was now the Secret Service's command center.

The cold-eyed agent stared at Cassie and Jacob to see what effect his last statement had on them. They remained blank-faced and stoic.

"You didn't tell us about the house in Summerville, Mrs. Franklin. Why is that?"

"You didn't ask me. It's twenty miles away." Too late she remembered her declaration not to say another word. "I want a lawyer!"

"Stay put, both of you," the cold-eyed agent ordered.

In the dining room with the door closed, he called Steven Ballinger and reported his conversation with the Franklins. "They want to lawyer up."

"You are not to let that happen. Send a detail to . . . what's the name of that town?"

"Summerville. They're on the way. It's about twenty miles away."

"Obviously, they didn't walk. Find out who might have helped them. The housekeeper would be my guess. Put the fear of God into them. Don't make me tell you how to do your job. Check out her friends and family. Get back to me."

"We're on it. There's a nephew that goes to college here in town who's old enough to drive. The housekeeper has a sister and a brother, but they're on a cruise. There's a niece that goes to Texas A&M. That's it."

"Where's the nephew?"

"I don't know. He owns a Dodge Durango, and he's a political science major. That's as much as we've gotten so far. Kids have millions of friends, and kids don't talk to the law."

"Your job is to make them talk. Find the goddamn first lady and don't give me any more excuses."

Cassie's heart thumped in her chest when the agent said, "Where's your nephew Leander?"

"I want a lawyer."

"I want a lawyer, too," Jacob said.

The agent smirked. "We'll find him with or without your help."

The knock on the cottage door brought Quinn and Sadie to their feet. "Who is it?" Quinn asked cautiously.

"Dennis. Open the door. Hurry."

"What's wrong?" the first lady asked, alarm spreading across her features.

"They're onto us. The cops, those Secret Service guys, whoever they are, were all over the campus this morning asking questions about Leander. Don't worry; no one will tell them anything. They didn't get to me. I finished my last class and took off. I don't have another one till six-thirty. I have to get you out of here. I loaded up my truck with camping gear. Ladies, you are going camping."

Quinn stared at the chubby young man with the owlish-looking glasses. She could feel her left eye start to twitch. They were closing in on her. She looked over at the first lady, who was listening intently.

"What do you want us to do, Dennis?" she asked.

"Clean the cottage. Wipe off anything you touched. Dry out the coffeepot. Give me the wet towels. Make the beds. Make it look like you were never there. For now, no one knows I'm house and dog sitting except Leander. Be quick, okay? I'll pack up some food for you and whatever else I think you might need. The lady I'm sitting for has a cell phone in her office. It's charged, so we'll just borrow it for a little while. You can make all your calls using it. Can you think of anything else you might need? Okay, then, clean up the cottage, and I'll pick you up in twenty minutes. You just step out the door and into my Bronco. I know a campground up near Beaufort. I'll set up the tent for you and then I have to leave to make my six-thirty class. I can't blow it off, or it might cause suspicion. Move, ladies."

"Is that kid FBI material or what?" Sadie said, heading into the cottage. "Okay, everyone think, what did you touch? Wipe everything clean as a whistle."

Twenty minutes later, Quinn closed the door of the cottage and wiped the knob clean. She stuck the Clorox wipe in the bag with the wet towels.

Dennis backed the Bronco up to the door, and the women climbed in. "Stay down until I tell you it's safe to get up. This is the plan. We pull out of this driveway and go around the corner and head for Beaufort. All the action is in town. This is the end of town. Cops are everywhere, and so are those Secret Service dudes. There's nothing on the radio or television. I think I got you out just in time. I need to stop at a phone booth soon, so I can call Leander and warn him."

"Young man, you are a treasure. Somehow, I'll make this all up to you when it's over."

"You don't have to do that. Someday, though, when you can talk about this, I'd like you to meet my mom. She thinks you're the best first lady ever in the White House. She said you were a real person and that you had grit."

"Did she now? I would love to meet your mom. I'll make sure that happens," the first lady said from her position on the floor of the Bronco.

"How far is the campground, Dennis?" Quinn asked.

"We should make it in about an hour. Maybe a little longer. I don't want to get a ticket and blow this deal."

"No sirree, you don't want to do that," Sadie chirped from the cargo hold.

"I'm going to roll my window down and blast a little Three Dog Night. People expect kids like me to do that, so plug up your ears."

They plugged up their ears.

Ezra Lapufsky stared at his reflection in the bathroom mirror. When did he get the bags under his eyes and when had the hair around his ears turned so gray? Overnight? He was FBI; he was supposed to be observant. He tied his tie, slicked back his hair, and shrugged into his jacket. He looked at Winnie sleeping on the bed. The minute he sat down to put on his shoes, the dog woke and pawed among her treasures until she found the string of bells. She bit down on the string and swung the bells from right to left.

Puff leaned over and hugged the fat dog. "If that's a wake-up call of some kind, I'm not getting it, Winnie. Come on, let's go downstairs and get some coffee."

Winnie leaped off the bed and landed with a thump, the bells still clutched in her teeth. At the top of the steps she hopped into her side seat and waited for Puff. She swung the bells again to make her point, which was, get in. Grinning, Puff sat down and waited for Winnie to press the button that would take them to the bottom of the steps. "This is for lazy people or people who can't manage stairs. You need the exercise, Winnie. Shame on you!" Winnie snorted her opinion of Puff's statement. At the bottom, she hopped off and waddled to the kitchen, where Birdie was waiting for them, fresh coffee perking.

In the center of the table was the manila envelope bearing McNally's address in the top left-hand corner. Birdie nodded. Puff opened it. His eyes raked the printed words before they questioned Birdie, who nodded again, indicating she, too, had read the report.

"I'm going to pass on the coffee, Birdie. Thanks for letting me clean up. I've got to get to headquarters. I'll be in touch. See ya, Winnie. What's with the bells, Birdie?"

"I think she's making a statement of some kind. If I ever find out, I'll let you know. Stop by anytime, Ezra."

Puff debated all of a second before he bent over and hugged the little woman. "I like your dress, Birdie," he said, referring to the sunflowers splashed all over her loose-fitting muumuu. "I didn't know they made yellow Birkenstocks. When did you know?" he whispered in her ear.

"When Lettie came to see me at the hospital. She told me what she suspected was going on with Jimmy Jaye at the White House," she whispered back. She smiled as she returned Puff's hug. "If you hear from my niece, let me know."

Winnie rang her bells for her own benefit before she closed her eyes and went to sleep, the string of bells clutched between her front paws.

Birdie sighed as she flipped the remote control for the television sitting on the counter.

Puff barked orders the minute he stepped off the elevator. "Conference room, five minutes, every section chief in the building. Order coffee. Get me a new cell phone. Stan, call in all your crew."

"We going to war, boss?"

"You could say that. Move!"

Twenty minutes later, Puff drained his third cup of coffee. "Listen up, everyone. Stan, turn off the lights. Put this picture up on the screen and blow it up to ten times the size.

"It's the president," one of the agents said. "Did something happen to him?"

"Yeah, something happened to him," Puff said quietly. "Stan, put this picture up and blow it up to the same size."

"Different pose, different clothes, no smile," an agent said. The others murmured agreement.

Puff pulled the report from the Beltway Labs, and said, "Put this up and blow it up, too. Now, tell me what you see."

"Who the hell is Duncan Mazer?" Stan asked.

"Well, his fingerprints match President Number One. Duncan Mazer is a retired Navy captain. I'm not sure about this, but I think he headed up a SEAL team. He's a widower with no children. I think he thought it was his duty to help out the administration when they told him President Number Two was suffering from the onset of Alzheimer's disease. The first lady is the one who put me wise to what was going on. They tried to shut her up, but she's not one to be quiet where her husband is concerned. The reason the nation hasn't seen much of the first lady these past months is because they, as in the administration, have kept her under wraps. We think she was sedated a lot. Mrs. Jaye is a sharp cookie. I can personally vouch for that. She took matters into her own hands, and we're looking at the consequences. She's missing. I use the term loosely. She's with Agents Quinn Star and Sadie Wilson. They're safe. For the moment.

"You'll appreciate this, Sandusky," Puff said, eyeballing one of Quinn's previous tormentors when she worked at the FBI. "Star managed to call the White House and have the call bounced off satellites around the world. They couldn't track her. Look ashamed, Sandusky. You might want to think about transferring out of here when this is over, because I'm going to marry Quinn Star. My memory is long, and I am not forgiving. That goes for any of you yahoos who even looked at her or Sadie Wilson crossways." Puff jammed his hands in his pockets and stared down his men. There was no need to tell them he might not have a job in a few hours if he was wrong.

"Now listen up. This is what we're going to do . . ."

Lettie Jaye looked around the makeshift campground, a look of curiosity on her face. "I've never been camping before. Nor have I ever slept in a bag. It's going to be an experience, peeing in the bushes, isn't it? I can't wait to tell Jimmy Jaye about this."

"Think of it as communing with nature," Sadie said sourly. "Quinn and I did our share of bivouacking when we were at the Academy. We had to crawl through mud up to our necks, march in pouring rain, climb ropes, slide down mountains, sleep in ditches, and still manage to come out looking pretty. It never happened. That we came out looking pretty, I mean."

"Mercy," the first lady said suitably impressed. "I really enjoyed our talk yesterday. You don't ever have to worry about me telling anyone any of the secrets you shared with me. I've grown so fond of you both. I prayed all night that those trigger-happy agents don't *plug* you. I'll run and stand in front of you. I can promise you that. They wouldn't dare shoot *me!* Now, what should we talk about today?"

Quinn hugged her knees, her back against a monster oak tree. "I think we covered just about everything yesterday, Lettie. Right now you probably know us better than we know ourselves."

"When this is all over, I'm going to invite Birdie and her dog to come for a very long visit. Maybe she'll think about moving south even if it's just for the winters. I'm sure our funeral homes would avail themselves of her . . . her . . . *special services.* None of us are getting any younger, you know. Just look at these wrinkles on my arms. Now if you hold them down, the wrinkles don't show. I always thought I would hate getting old. I do, but I don't. Jimmy Jaye always said with age comes wisdom. I wonder if he'll remember saying that. What's it going to be like when he doesn't remember who I am? Do you think Nancy Reagan will talk to me if I call her up or write her a letter?" the first lady asked, shredding a dry leaf into little bits. When she was finished, she picked up another leaf and proceeded to do the same thing.

"I'm sure she will be more than happy to talk to you. You know what I think, I think you're one tough cookie, Lettie, and I think you're going to be able to handle whatever comes your way," Sadie said.

Lettie Jaye smiled. "Thank you. You girls have made this whole sorry experience bearable. I know in my heart if it wasn't for you, I'd be languishing in some private hospital somewhere being pumped full of sedatives to keep me quiet. I know that as sure as I know I have to take another breath in order to stay alive."

"Lettie, Sadie and I were talking earlier today, and we both agreed we're giving back the money you and the president paid us. It wasn't right of either of us to take it. I think I was trying to get back at Puff, and Sadie went along with it. I wanted to bust his chops. I never thought you would agree to such outrageous demands. When you agreed, I had to go through with it. We aren't sorry we agreed, Lettie. It's been an experience I'll never forget. All we want to do is help you and the president."

"No, no, no. A deal is a deal. My husband was so impressed with your haggling, he said it was worth it just to meet you. It was a small price to pay for all this freedom and to spring Jimmy Jaye. We are going to spring him, aren't we? What time are you going to make your call?"

Quinn held out her hands, palms facing the first lady. "Whoa. Time-out. The money goes back, and that's the end of *that*. If and when I get married and that's a mighty big if, your husband can walk me down the aisle. Do you think he would do that?"

"My dear, he would love to give you away. Consider it a done deal. So, what time are you going to make the call. Oh, Lord, it's starting to rain. What should we do now?"

"I think what we should do now is go in the tent and sit down," Sadie said.

Inside the tent, with the flap zipped up, the first lady poked around in the bag of food. "We have crackers and cheese, crackers and peanut butter, crackers and jelly, crackers and onion dip, crackers and cheese dip. Then we have crackers and more crackers. Dennis forgot the utensils, so we'll have to use our fingers. Oh, if Mary Alice Prentice could only see me now! It's all so tacky it makes my heart swell. That wasn't very poetic, was it?"

Quinn laughed as she eyed the first lady in her bib overalls, flannel shirt, and fishing hat, with the fishing lures hanging down the side. "Tacky or not, she'd be jealous, Lettie. I'm going to call at six o'clock on the dot."

"That gives us a few hours to eat some of this fine food and take a nap," the first lady said as she opened a box of cheddar cheese crackers.

"It's really raining out there," Sadie volunteered.

"It certainly is," the first lady said happily.

"I'm going to call Bradford now and tell him we want to do the call at precisely six o'clock."

An hour later, the rain pelting the tent, the first lady curled into a ball and was asleep within seconds. Both agents watched her for a time, each busy with her own thoughts.

"What's going to happen, Quinn?"

"I don't have a clue. What I do know is we can't keep running like this. I keep thinking of those kids and how far out on a limb they went for us. I don't know if Puff believes us or not. If he does, will he act on it? We're talking about the president of the United States, for God's sake. The president's men could blow in here with their sweep team, make us disappear, and dump the first lady in some private place where no one ever hears from her again. The only thing we have going for us right this minute is this cell phone that no one knows about. If Puff doesn't act and bring it all to a head, we have one more shot with a call. I say we call Bradford and have him ready to bounce our second call to the *Washington Post*. Sadie, I really don't know what to do. I'm just talking to hear myself. If you have any ideas, I'd like to hear them."

Sadie shook her head. "If we get out of this, I'm going to marry John. I don't want to grow old and not have children. I'm not too old to have a baby. Women have babies when they're forty-five, even fifty. I want a house with a yard, a couple of dogs, and maybe a cat. I'd like one of those birds that sings in the morning when you take the cover off its cage. I want to make brownies and go to PTA meetings. I want to scrub the bathroom on Saturday morning, and I want a living room big enough for a Christmas tree that goes all the way to the ceiling. I want the American dream, Quinn. I don't want to be shot down by some trigger-happy Secret Service guy who won't bat an eye in the interest of protecting the rights of the president."

"You never told me any of that, Sadie," Quinn said quietly.

"I thought you'd laugh at me. I've always wanted

that. I knew I had to work, and owning my own business was always a dream, too. I did that. Now I want to take the next step. Do you have any idea how nice it must be to give a baby a bath, powder him up so he smells the way a baby is supposed to smell, then dress him up for the night and rock him to sleep? When you tiptoe out of the room, the dog lies across the doorsill to protect him through the night. I want that. I really want that."

"You are one good actress, Sadie. I had no idea you felt like that."

"Well, I do. What do you want, Quinn?"

Quinn stuck her finger in a jar of grape jam and licked it. "I just want to be happy. If I . . . I guess I'd like to be happy with Puff. That isn't going to happen, though. I'm not going to marry Alex. I think he already knows that. I lied to you when I said sex with him was spectacular. I lied to Birdie, too, but I think she already knew. It was, at best, routine. He liked to . . . *wash up* after and wanted the *sheets changed.*"

"No!" Sadie gasped.

"Yeah. I guess I never got over Puff. They say some people just love once in a lifetime. I guess I'm one of those people. Puff's a what-you-see-is-what-you-get kind of guy. Alex is . . . all facade. I'm not sure I'm the mother type. That may be because I never really had a mother. I am going to get a dog, though. Maybe someday, I'll find my prince. If it's too late to have a baby, then I can always adopt a child. Why are we talking about all this? Is it because you think we're going to die?"

Sadie waved her hand in front of Quinn's face. "Earth to Quinn. Hellloooo. The answer is yes."

"I bet you could choke someone to death if you stuffed their mouth with peanut butter," Quinn said as she screwed the lid back on the jar of Jiff.

"I guess that's our game plan, huh?"

"Yep."

It was 5:10 when Dennis Schwartz let the dogs out for the last time. He waited patiently for them to do their business and troop back inside, where he handed out rawhide bones. He turned on the light over the stove and the one in the hallway before he gathered up his backpack, a can of Pepsi Cola, a Nutri-Grain bar, and a handful of French Chew taffy that he stuffed in his pocket.

The front doorbell rang just as he was about to leave by the kitchen door. The dogs bolted as one, barking and howling, for the front door. He whistled sharply for the dogs to quiet down but they ignored him. He turned on the porch light to see three men. He cracked the door slightly so the dogs wouldn't bolt. "Yes."

"Are you Dennis Schwartz?"

"Yes, I'm Dennis Schwartz. Why?"

"We'd like to come in and talk to you."

"About what? I have six dogs here. I'm just dog sitting."

"We want to talk to you about your friend Leander." One of the men held up a badge and his credentials.

"Okay, but you have to wait till I can get the dogs

back to the kitchen. I can't risk their getting out. How long is this going to take? I have a six-thirty class, and I have to drive to Charleston."

"Depends on what you have to say," one of the agents said.

Dennis hitched up his baggy pants, whose crotch dangled at knee level, and marched the dogs back to the kitchen. He closed the door, knowing they would paw it and scrape the paint off it, and the owner was going to skin him alive.

Back in the foyer, he opened the door and stepped aside.

Dennis looked at his watch. "We really have to make this quick, sir."

"Do you know Leander Martin?"

"Yeah, I know him. We're friends. We study together sometimes. Why? Did something happen to him?"

"Do you know where he is?"

Dennis shook his head. "We don't have any of the same classes. Well, we do, but at different times of the day. If he isn't on campus, he's probably home. Did you try there?"

"He isn't at either place. Do you know any other place he might be?"

Dennis shook his head again. "I'm not his keeper. Did you ask any of his other friends?"

"No one has seen him," one of the agents said.

"Well, I haven't seen him either. If that's all, I really gotta leave now," he said, looking at his watch. "I can't leave the dogs in the kitchen or they'll wreck it. The owner will hold me responsible. Look, I really gotta go."

The agents ignored him. "We'll call your professor and tell him you'll be late. We'd like to look around."

Dennis hitched up his pants again. "Do you have a warrant? This isn't my house. How did you get through those security gates anyway?"

"We don't need a warrant." The agent held out a little gadget in his hand. "This opened the gates."

"I think you're trespassing," Dennis blustered. He could feel his glasses starting to fog up. He kept his cool, though.

"No, we're not," the agent said. "If you know anything, you better spit it out, kid. We're talking national security here."

"Look, you can threaten to cut off my dick, and I still won't be able to tell you what you want to know because I don't know anything. I thought you guys were *supposed* to be smart and here you are, trespassing, harassing me, and you can't find one kid. Just for the record, I had a perfect score on my SATs. Leander was one point below me. Now, that's smart! He's probably with some girl at her pad screwing his brains out because he's so smart he doesn't have to study. How much longer?"

"No one here," one of the agents said. "No one's been here either. There's a guesthouse out back. You can see it through the trees from the back bedroom window."

"Don't tell me about it, check it out. Is it open, kid?"

"How would I know? The guesthouse has nothing to do with my job description. I feed the dogs and let them out. I play with them. The rest of the time I study. I've never been near the building."

"Check it out, Scrofield."

"I think you're lying, kid."

"I think you're a prick," Dennis said. "I think your two buddies are pricks, too." He unrolled a stick of French taffy and stuffed it in his mouth. He was glad his interrogators couldn't see the way his heart was slamming against his rib cage.

The front door opened. The two agents stuck their heads in the door. "It's clean. No one's there, and it doesn't look like anyone's been there either. Shower's bone dry. No wet towels. Sheets are clean and unwrinkled. Kitchen is spotless."

"Okay, can I go now?"

"Yeah, you can go now," the agent said, backing out of the door. "We're going to be watching you, kid. If I find out you lied to me, we'll be back. Regret is a terrible thing."

"Gee, you're scaring the piss out of me, big guy. I have to close the door now so I can let the dogs out. Was that a threat?"

"It's whatever you want it to be, kid."

"Nuts to you!" Dennis said as he slammed the door shut.

In the kitchen, Dennis took a deep breath and almost choked on the taffy in his mouth. He felt like a deer caught in the headlights, his heart beating so fast he thought he was going to black out. He gripped the countertop for support. He forced himself to take another deep breath as he left the house. The minute he turned the ignition on in the Bronco, he rolled down the window and cranked the volume up on his CD player. Three Dog Night blasted the early-evening air. The minute he drove through the gates he spotted the dark sedan parked across the street. "Assholes!" he shouted as he pressed his foot down hard on the gas pedal and roared down the road.

19

"I never really liked the dark," Lettie Jaye said as she moved closer to the circle of light in the center of the tent. "What happens when the batteries give out?" she asked, pointing to the small flashlight Quinn had propped up between two rocks. "Oh, I forgot, I have my lighter. We did leave in a hurry. Normally, I like to prepare for expeditions or trips."

She's just talking to hear herself, Quinn thought. She squinted to see the hands on her watch. "Forty-five minutes and we can make the call. We need to make a decision here, Lettie. Once I make the call to the White House, we're only going to have a minute at best to state our position. We'll be really pushing our luck to try it again, so we have to decide now if they aren't going to meet your demands, do you want me to call the *Post?* The fallout will be absolutely horrendous. You need to know that. You have forty-five minutes to make a decision. Be sure it's the right one, Lettie."

"I don't need forty-five minutes. I trust you girls implicitly. That's what we said we were going to do, and we'll do it." The first lady was so adamant, Quinn smiled.

Quinn looked at Sadie, who nodded as she rubbed at her arms in an effort to keep warm. The first lady did the same thing. Quinn, on the other hand, was sweating profusely.

Dennis Schwartz fidgeted in his seat just long enough to satisfy himself that there was no one in the class who didn't belong there. He turned to a spit-and-polish Ivy League type sitting next to him, and hissed, "Jerome, I need you to make a phone call for me, okay? I'll take your notes, and I'll also make sure you ace this class. Just make sure no one sees you making the call and keep your yap shut even if you get your ass hauled off to jail. We on the same page here, Jerome?"

"Yeah, sure. Whom do you want me to call?"

Dennis scribbled a number on a piece of paper. "When they answer just say, Dennis said go to Plan B. That's it. Hang up, come back here, and take a different seat. Don't even look at me when class is over."

Dennis smirked as he congratulated himself. He was so smart sometimes it was sickening. He was so far ahead of his class and his teacher, he could have taken his final in the next ten minutes and racked up an A. He listened to his professor drone on and on with one ear while he doodled in his notebook. From time to time he looked up to see if anyone was watching through the window in the door.

He was shaken from his reverie when he heard an ominous roll of thunder followed by a streak of lightning ripping across the sky outside the classroom.

The women were going to be soaked to the skin, and the temperature was dropping. Hence Plan B.

Plan B. Calvin Rutledge, his equal when it came to brainpower, would be on his way to pick up the three women and bring them back to the cottage as soon as Jerome called him. His job when class ended was to go to the library and hang out for three hours. He could hack that as long as he had his CD player and earphones. Let the dudes with the credentials get pimples on their asses as they sat around and waited for him to do something stupid. Like he'd ever done a stupid thing in his life. He couldn't help but wonder if the guys who knocked on his door were exceptionally stupid or he was exceptionally smart. He snorted. It wasn't even a contest. Guns and mouthy brawn versus brains just weren't going to cut it. He felt so pleased with himself; he raised his hand to ask a question he knew the professor wouldn't know the answer to. That was okay, he knew the answer, and his response would take up the rest of the class period.

Seated in his car a block from the White House, Ezra Lapufsky dialed the vice president's phone number and waited while his secretary said she would see if the vice president could pencil in some time for him. "Tell him it's extremely urgent and a matter of national security," Puff said. "And that it is important that I see him in his White House office."

She came back on the line and said the vice president would see him at the White House in an hour. He thanked her and broke the connection.

He looked down at the manila envelope on the seat across from him. Were the president's men arrogant, ego-driven amateurs or were the people surrounding the president so power-hungry they thought they were above the law? Did they really think they could get away with having a stand-in for the president until sometime next year when there was no way the substitute could run for reelection? Obviously, that's exactly what they thought. All they had to do was incapacitate the first lady to make it all work. *I wonder who the man behind the scenes in this deal is, the one who thinks he's going to step in and run for the presidency in the next election once the president resigns. Thanks to Letecia Jaye's bulldog attitude, that isn't going to happen.*

He grimaced. If they had allowed the first lady to stay in South Carolina months ago instead of forcing her to return to Washington, they probably would have gotten away with their scheme for as long as necessary.

Puff could feel his stomach start to churn. What was the vice president going to say when he told him he was going to be the next president of the United States? The title going to him in just a matter of hours. Possibly a day. Puff knew how that all worked, but at the moment his brain was on overload.

It was snowing harder. It would be rush hour in another fifty minutes. People were going home to their families after a long day of work, none of them knowing there was an imposter in the White House. He couldn't help but wonder if they would care.

People as a rule never had a kind word to say about politicians or lawyers. President Jaye's approval rating was a nice 65 percent, so maybe they would care.

He thought about Quinn. Quinn would care. She cared about the damnedest things. She cared about people, the environment, animals, her aunt, Judge Duval, her friends. The truth was, Quinn cared about everything. Once she'd cared about him. Once. Maybe he could make her care again. Maybe.

He wondered if she ever compared him to Alexander Duval. *Don't go there, Lapufsky,* he cautioned himself.

No one paid much attention to the vice president, including Puff. Now, he tried to remember what he knew about the man. He'd just had a birthday. He recalled a picture of a cake with sixty candles in a political cartoon in *USA Today*. A nice man, a quiet man. He hadn't done anything outstanding or even faintly remarkable during his time in the administration. His wife hadn't either.

Was Adam Waverly presidential material? Probably not. He sure as hell was going to learn in a hurry. It might be possible for him to step up to the plate. He might hit a few foul balls, but then again, he might smack it right out of the park. You never knew what you were capable of until you were put to the test. Another of Quinn's little aphorisms. His best guess was the vice president would turn out to be another Gerald Ford, not Harry Truman.

He closed his eyes to try to conjure up the vice president's likeness. He was tall but not as tall as the president. He had all his hair and a very toothy smile. Chocolate brown eyes thanks to contact lenses because nobody had eyes the color of chocolate pudding. He dressed well, and his shoes were always shined. You could tell the mark of a man by his shoes. At least that's what Quinn had said once. He'd made sure after that remark always to have a shine on his Brooks Brothers loafers.

He wished he knew how much time Adam Waverly had actually spent with the president. Probably not much since he was a figurehead in the administration, standing in for the president when necessary, going to funerals, and trying to look and act busy. He played a lot of golf and tennis, as did his wife. If memory served him right, Waverly had been in the banking industry before the president convinced him to be his running mate. Sterling character with no hint of scandal anywhere in his background. No skeletons in his wife's closet either.

Puff settled deeper into the seat of his car and watched the snow swirling outside the window. It was almost dark, the end of the day fast approaching. *What are they doing in the White House? Are they planning strategy? Are they scurrying around in a panic? Do they know that within hours it will all be over? Where are Ballinger and his army of Secret Service Agents? There will be a stench attached to Ballinger by tomorrow, after which he'll be transferred to some far-off post. Or if I have anything to say about it, he'll be locked up in some maximum security facility under the provisions of the Patriot Act. Are they out scouring the state for the first lady? How strange that they haven't found them. Damn, Quinn is good.*

He continued to watch the falling snow and decided it was time to go through the East Gate and wait for the vice president to arrive. Two minutes later, after going through the formalities of showing his identification, he was still seated in his car, looking at a roadway that was covered in snow. *What the hell is it with this cockamamie weather anyway? It isn't supposed to snow till Christmas.*

He wondered what he would be doing tomorrow when the sun came up. Would he still be the acting associate director of his beloved FBI? Would he be promoted to acting director, awaiting confirmation? Would they strip everything away from him? He couldn't imagine life outside the FBI. Maybe Sadie Wilson would hire him to work in her security firm. The thought was so ridiculous he laughed out loud. Quinn would laugh her ass off if that happened.

Suddenly he felt a wild urge to call his mother and didn't know why. He didn't stop to question the thought but acted on it instead. The moment he heard his mother's voice he relaxed completely. "Mom, it's me."

"Ezra! How nice to hear from you. Are you all right? You aren't sick are you?"

"Nah. I'm fine, Mom. How's everything? How's Pop?"

"We're all fine, Ezra. Are you coming home for Thanksgiving?"

"I'm gonna try, Mom. Mom, tell me what to say to get Quinn back. We met up again and I . . . I think she hates me. Are there special words I should say?"

"Tell her what you feel. Apologize if you have to.

It was all your fault, Ezra. She never got married, so that means she still has feelings for you. She told me she would love you forever and ever."

"Did she really say that, Mom, or are you making that up to make me feel better?"

"I wouldn't do that to you, Ezra. Your dad was sitting right here when she said it. She told me about all the wonderful plans she had. She was going to be the best wife and mother in the whole world. It was terrible how you let her down, Ezra."

"I know, Mom. She's not like she used to be. She's lean and mean these days. She's like a machine. She hasn't said one nice word to me since we came in contact again. I was sick a while back, and she took care of me. She made me this horrendous drink that I thought would kill me, but I bounced back real quick. She said the only reason she took care of me was to get rid of me."

"Her heart is the same. Once you get hurt the way she was hurt, you don't wear your heart on your sleeve. You learn how to guard your feelings. You burrow in and hope for the best. I taught you how to be nice, Ezra. She has feelings. That's what you forgot. When a man makes a woman cry . . ."

Puff looked down at his watch. "Mom, remember what you were going to say. I gotta run. I have a meeting with the vice president in two minutes. Thanks for talking to me. I love you. Tell Pop I said hello and give Indy a kiss for me."

Puff bounded out of the car and galloped down the street and around the corner.

Five minutes later he was mopping at his wet hair

with a handkerchief. He straightened his overcoat with one hand, the other firmly gripping the manila envelope.

The men shook hands. The vice president's grip was hard and firm. Puff was impressed. He sat down across from the veep and held out the envelope. "Do you know this man, sir?"

The vice president stared down at the picture in front of him. "He looks vaguely familiar. Should I know him?"

"He's President Jaye's stand-in. Oh, they fix him up with putty and spirit gum when they have to. President Jaye, according to his wife, has Alzheimer's disease. I don't know where they have the real James Jaye stashed. I think they haul him out when he has good days."

"This is preposterous. Nothing like that could possibly go on in the White House," the vice president blustered. "Could it?"

"Yes. I have fifty agents surrounding the White House. An even dozen are inside waiting for you and me to go up to the chief of staff's office, where he's waiting for me. A call is expected from the first lady sometime around six. She's set to blow the whistle."

"Are you on some kind of drug, Lapufsky? What you're saying is impossible. You're talking about a giant conspiracy. That means half the staff, hell, the entire staff . . . would have to be in on it. No, no, it's simply too far-fetched."

Puff said nothing as he watched perspiration bead on the vice president's forehead.

"If what you're saying is true . . . that means I have to . . ."

"Yes, that's what it means, Mr. Vice President."

Clearly flustered, the vice president stuck his finger between his collar and his neck. "How . . . how did you . . . confirm all of this? Surely you aren't going just on what Lettie Jaye says, are you?"

Puff told him about the flag the imposter had handed him. "The report is in the envelope, sir. Read it."

The vice president's hands started to shake. Puff almost felt sorry for him. "We can control this, sir. If we're lucky, and everyone fesses up, Mrs. Jaye won't call the *Post*. The woman wants her husband back. It's that simple. They make an announcement and *voilà*, you take over. I'm not up on all that protocol, but I'm sure you can all make it work. No one ever needs to know. The president steps down for the good of the country. You step into his shoes, and life will go on for all of us. It's almost six, sir. We have to leave."

"What if they . . . dig in? What if they refuse . . ."

"Then, Mr. Vice President, the brown stuff hits the fan."

"Ah . . . yes, I see. It could get dicey is what you're saying."

"Yes, sir, that's what I'm saying."

"Lapufsky?"

"Yes, sir."

"If I'm going to be the next president of the United States, I'm nominating you to head up the FBI. I told Jim you were the logical choice the first time around, but he said Duval was the man. It was a payback of some kind."

"Let's not worry about that at present, sir. We have more pressing problems to attend to right now. Let's just wind this up so we can all get some sleep. I want tomorrow to be a good day for this country."

"I'm ready."

"Then let's do it," Puff said, leading the way out of the office.

Flanked by six of his best agents, Puff followed the vice president as he strode down the hall to the chief of staff's office. Seated in a wide circle in comfortable furniture was the communications director, the deputy communications director, the national security advisor, the head of the White House Secret Service detail, Steven Ballinger, and the chief of staff, Lawrence Neville.

"You weren't invited to this party, Mr. Vice President. This meeting is just another hornet's nest the first lady has stirred up as she's wont to do from time to time. Her antics are legion. If we need your services, Mr. Vice President, we'll call you," Neville sneered brazenly.

"I'm crashing this party, Neville, on the AAD's invitation. As a warning, don't ever use that tone of voice with me again. I'm here at the request of the AAD of the FBI. If you can't remember that, I suggest you write it down."

"It could turn out to be a long night if Agent Star doesn't call early. She said sometime after six. It's exactly six o'clock right now. If you don't haul out the real president, Mrs. Jaye is going to the *Post*. You know what those guys are like. Think Watergate," Puff said coolly.

"You're as deranged as the first lady. Do you have any idea what you've done? The president is going to be joining us shortly to tell you he's very displeased with the way you've handled things, Lapufsky. The man is trying to run the country, which is his top priority."

"Is the president the least bit upset that his wife is missing?" Puff asked.

"Of course he's upset. However, he knows his wife and the trouble she can cause when she doesn't get her way. We're looking for her, and we'll find her."

Puff looked down at his watch. Ten minutes past six.

The phone rang. Everyone looked at everyone else.

"Somebody should answer the phone," the vice president said."

"Use the speakerphone so we can all hear," Puff said.

"Don't tell me what to do, Lapufsky," Neville said, pressing the button that allowed Quinn's voice to circulate around the room.

"This is Quinn Star. The first lady wants to talk to whoever is listening. Are you there, Lapufsky?"

"I'm here, Ms. Star. Go ahead."

"Ezra, this is Lettie Jaye. My husband has Alzheimer's disease. There is a man who stands in for him, but I don't know his name. Check his dental records, his fingerprints. He's shorter than my husband and wears heels on his shoes. His hair is wiry, and they never get the color just right. If I don't see my husband on the eleven o'clock news saying he's resigning because of his condition, I'll do what I said.

My husband needs me now more than ever, and I need him. We can save each other a lot of trouble if you tell me now that you accept my terms. If it's no, then I'm calling the *Post* when I hang up on you. I have absolutely nothing to lose. I want my husband, and that's all I want. What's it going to be?"

"Mrs. Jaye, your husband wants to speak to you. It will just be a second. Fetch him," Neville said to Ballinger.

Puff stared at the man walking into the room. He looked every inch the president. Adam Waverly narrowed his eyes as he, too, stared at the man approaching the phone console.

"Lettie, is that you?"

"Of course it's me. Are you all right, Jimmy Jaye?"

"I'm fine, darlin'. I hear you're giving my people some trouble. You have to stop doing that, darlin'. I want you to come home now. Tell us where you are so I can send someone for you."

"Jimmy Jaye, listen to me. You're sick. You know it, and so do I and all those people in that room know it. We talked about this that day I went shopping. Don't you remember, Jimmy Jaye? There are people in the room with you, aren't there?"

"How do you know all that, darlin'?" The president looked around and seemed to be surprised to see so many people watching him. He offered up a vague smile for everyone's benefit.

"Jimmy Jaye, you have to step down. Tell all those people right now that you don't want to be president any longer. Adam Waverly will make a fine president. Will you trust me?"

"What will I do if I'm not president, Mama?"

Ballinger stepped forward and reached for the president's arm to draw him away from the phone.

"Don't do it, Ballinger." Puff stiff-armed him to make his point. "Leave the president alone. Mrs. Jaye, what are you going to do?" he barked.

"I'm going to call the *Washington Post* and tell them who they can contact to get the real story on my husband. Then I'm going to wait for the eleven o'clock news."

The sudden silence in the chief of staff's office after the phone call ended and the real president left the room was ominous.

"Well," Neville snarled when the connection ended.

"Sorry, Mr. Neville. She bounced it again, South Africa, Rhodesia, India, Russia, North Carolina, Australia, and Culpepper, Virginia."

"Are you telling me some stupid *female* agent outsmarted you wizards! Again! I don't want to hear that poppycock! This is the goddamn White House! Ballinger, I'm going to personally fry your ass if you don't find those agents and the first lady. Go bring them in here! What are you still doing here, Lapufsky?"

"I'm waiting for Duncan Mazer to make his appearance," Puff drawled. He tossed the manila envelope on the chief of staff's desk and watched the man's face turn paper white when he read the contents.

"We sealed all the exits. We can salvage this, and no one but the people in this room will have to know.

You and your cronies can be so attached to the president you can't bear to go on without him at the helm. Otherwise, it's a maximun security facility under the Patriot Act for you and all these other guys. And that means for the rest of your lives. Now, where's Mazer?"

"He's upstairs in the family quarters," the deputy director of communications said. "I never wanted to go along with this, but I was pressured into it, and I know that's no excuse. I have no desire to spend the rest of my life in jail. I'll get him for you. You're right about the president, too. All he wants to do is go home to his wife. Today was a good day for him. I've been babysitting him for a year now, and I've seen his deterioration on a daily basis."

"Shut up, Cummings," Neville shouted.

"I'm sick of listening to you, and I'm sick of lying and covering up for all of you. That man in there deserves whatever dignity he has left in his life. He doesn't deserve what you've done to him. I'll be right back," he said to Lapufsky.

"I'll be damned," Adam Waverly said.

Lapufsky signaled one of his agents, who had followed the president from the room and returned. The agent left again and brought Jimmy Jaye back to the office.

"Mr. President!"

"Yes."

"Would you like me to take you home, Mr. President?"

"Can you do that, son?"

"Yes, sir, I can." Puff grinned.

"Is Lettie waiting for me?"

"Yes, sir, she's waiting."

"Does she have the cat?"

"I'm not sure about the cat."

"That's all right, son, you can't be expected to remember everything. I'm the president, and I can't remember a lot of things."

Puff felt moisture gather in his eyes. "We can work on that, Mr. President." He jerked his head in the direction of the agents. He made a pretense of throwing an imaginary ball to the vice president, who made a pretense of catching it.

"I think you need to make some calls, Mr. Vice President. McCoy, when we're finished in here, take Ballinger and Neville to a secure location. What happens to them next will be Vice President . . . I mean President Waverly's call.

The soon-to-be president scuffed a spot on the carpet the way ballplayers do before they swing their bats. "I think an announcement at eleven saying the president will speak in the morning will satisfy Mrs. Jaye. If we do it late tonight, it might cause a panic. What do you think, Lapufsky?"

"It sounds like a plan to me. McCoy, make sure Ballinger calls off his agents. Leave the normal detail at the Southern White House. I'm thinking the first lady and her agents are going to return there. That's what I would do if I were Agent Star."

Puff homed in on Ballinger, and said, "Your last official act is to get Air Force One or Marine One ready. Take your pick. I don't think the president will care which one he goes home in." The hatred spewing from Ballinger's eyes triggered Puff's tongue. "And something you ought to know about us FBI guys. We may not have fancy earpieces while we're working, and we may not hobnob with politicians like your boys, but we always get our man. I'll be taking the president home as soon as I get the all clear. We'll make the announcement from the Southern White House, with Mrs. Jaye standing next to her husband as soon as we locate her."

The cell phone in Puff's hand rang. It was his highest-ranking subordinate. "Follow through. We're waiting. I'm in Neville's offices. Show the Secret Service some respect even though they don't deserve it at the moment."

Puff extended his hand to the vice president.

"You'll see that *he's* well taken care of, won't you, Lapufsky?"

"You can count on it, sir."

"You going to take the job when I nominate you?"

"Can I get back to you on that, Mr. Vice President?"

"Absolutely. It looks like I'm not going anywhere for a while."

Puff looked around, wondering if he would ever set foot in the White House again.

The three women huddled in the tent, rain dripping through the top. It puddled all around them. They shivered and clung to one another.

Both agents were on their feet a moment later, guns drawn, when they heard the sound of a car, then the flash of headlights.

"Oh, God, they found us," the first lady whimpered.

"Shhhh," Sadie cautioned. "It might be Dennis."

"Someone's whistling! Listen. It's 'Dixie.' I think this might be a friend," Quinn said, relief ringing in her voice.

"Yo, ladies, Dennis sent me!" a voice said outside the tent.

Quinn unzipped the flap of the tent and peered out into the pouring rain. "And you are . . .?"

"Calvin Rutledge, I'm Dennis's friend. He wants me to take you back to the starting point," he said dramatically. "Hop in. The heater's on."

"What about the tent and stuff?" Sadie asked.

The young man shrugged. "The wind is whipping up. It's little more than a pup tent. By morning it will have blown away. Animals will eat the food."

"What starting point?" the first lady asked.

"A house on the Battery. You're supposed to know where it is. I didn't have a whole lot of time to ask questions. I'm just following my orders. Dennis is a mastermind when it comes to details and planning."

The women huddled in the backseat, whispering among themselves.

Her teeth chattering, Sadie said, "I suppose it makes sense in a cockeyed kind of way. Criminals always return to the scene of the crime. I'm assuming we're to go in the way we went out."

"It's entirely possible Puff convinced them we meant business, and the whole thing is over. We'll know by the number of agents left behind. I can't wait to take a nice hot shower and get warm again," Quinn said.

"Do you think I helped or hindered our cause?" the first lady asked.

Quinn rubbed at her dirt-stained face. "I don't know. Some newspapers are known to run with things. Others take their time and try to get a couple of sources to back up things. All they have is your phone call with no backup. I'm thinking they'll wait. At least for the next edition. We can't unring any bells here. There's no point in trying to second-guess anyone right now. What's done is done."

The remainder of the ride to Charleston was made in silence.

"This is East Bay, ladies. Tell me what you want me to do," Calvin said.

"Let us off on Atlantic. There aren't many people out and about," the first lady said, peering through the window.

"It must be the weather. Go around the block twice so we can be sure there isn't anyone standing guard," Quinn said.

"What'd you guys do to warrant all this attention? This is like something out of a spy novel. You didn't kill anyone, did you?" The kid's voice was so excited and cheerful-sounding, Quinn wanted to slap him.

"We just pulled some guy's tongue out because he talked too much," Sadie snapped.

"Okayyy. I'm rounding the corner now and turning off my lights. Hit the ground running, girls, because I'm not coming to a full stop. That goes for you, too, grandma."

The first lady started to laugh and couldn't stop. Sadie clamped her hand over her mouth and dragged her from the car and into the bushes. Quinn bailed out a second later, leaving the door hanging wide open.

"That was the nicest thing anyone ever said to me," the first lady chirped.

"Lettie, shut up," Sadie muttered through clenched teeth as she dropped to her hands and knees.

Quinn didn't think she'd ever been more miserable in her life as she crawled behind the first lady and wiggled through the mousehole.

"Okay, we're in. Now what are we supposed to do?" Sadie asked.

"We're going back to my house via the tunnel and trapdoor. You have my permission to shoot anyone who tries to stop us," the first lady said, leading the way to the summer kitchen.

"Right now, right this minute, I feel like shooting someone. I have never been this cold, this wet, this miserable in my life," Sadie said, her gaze sweeping the empty rooms.

"Don't dawdle, girls. The sooner we get to my house, the sooner we can get warm. Do you know what time it is?"

"It must be around ten," Quinn said.

"They left the trapdoor open for us. How kind of them," the first lady said. "I hope the other one is open, too."

"I think you can count on it. I wonder how they figured it out," Quinn said.

"Don't blame Cassie. She would die before she told anyone about that trapdoor. It's possible Jimmy Jaye told them. Right now it doesn't matter. Oh, my goodness, look at all those agents standing in my kitchen."

"Welcome home, ma'am," one of the agents said quietly.

Quinn bit down on her lip, her gun held loosely at her side. She could see Sadie's shoulders slump.

"Relax, Agent Quinn and Agent Wilson. You can holster your guns now. Things have changed. We're preparing for the president's arrival."

Lettie would have fainted if Quinn and Sadie hadn't reached out to grasp her arms. "Is Jimmy Jaye really coming home?"

"I was told his ETA would be sometime around midnight. The house is secure, ma'am. We'll stay out of your way. We've sealed off the area on the outside."

"Go along, ma'am. You'll want to get cleaned up to greet your husband. Sadie and I will be up in a minute. Are there any agents on the third floor?"

"Outside on the verandah," the agent said.

Sadie eyed the slice of cake under the dome. "I'll fight you for this, Quinn."

"I'm too tired to fight. It's all yours. I would like some coffee, though."

"How'd you do it, Star?" the agent asked curiously.

"Do what?" Quinn said, rinsing out the coffeepot.

"Who helped you? C'mon, it's all over. I know what's going on."

"Brains, ingenuity, guts, and a little luck. I'm saving the details for my memoirs," she said, watching the water drip through the coffee grounds. She hoped the strong, black coffee would prop up her eyelids. She looked at Sadie and smiled.

"Sadie, you take your bath first. I'm going to sit

here and drink my coffee. Boy, I really could use a cigarette."

"Here you go, Star," the agent said, tossing her a pack of Marlboros. "For whatever it's worth, you gave us a run for our money. You did good, and I'm glad you're on our side."

Quinn blinked. Had the man just complimented her? Was she so tired her hearing was impaired? "Thanks," was all she could think of to say. "I'm going to quit tomorrow. I already quit but sometimes . . ."

"This is sometimes. Take it easy, Star. I'll be in the front room if you need me."

"Yeah. Okay."

Quinn carried her coffee cup over to the seat under the bow window and stared out into the courtyard. There were so many things she needed to do. She had to call Alex and Birdie, and not necessarily in that order. She had to return the monies the Jayes had paid her and Sadie, and she needed to make plans to go back to her old life. She could hardly wait to hug Winnie. She closed her eyes just to rest them. A second later, she was sound asleep.

Upstairs, Sadie Wilson was asleep in the bathtub.

The first lady of the land was tripping about her suite, humming under her breath as she pawed through her closet trying to select just the right outfit to greet her husband. It was, after all, midnight, so she chose a flowing satin dressing gown. She did love fashions that swished and trailed after her and feathers that tickled if one knew just the right places. She slipped into it and reached for her favorite bottle of perfume and sprayed herself from head to toe.

The minute she heard the sound of cars out front, she ran down the steps, shouting to Sadie and Quinn. Sadie bolted upright and barreled out of the tub and into her fuzzy robe. She reached for her gun and ran down the hall and down the back steps to the kitchen, where she saw Quinn asleep on the window seat. "Wake up, partner. The president is arriving."

"Oh my God! I didn't take a bath. How do I look? You aren't dressed!"

"Look, we both look like hell, so accept it. Our Lettie is full of piss and vinegar and dressed to the nines. Can't you smell her? I suppose we could hide out here."

The agents cracked the kitchen door and peeked into the dining room in time to see Lettie Jaye running to her husband, her arms outstretched. "Oh, Jimmy Jaye, I'm so happy to see you! Wait, wait, let me feel your hair. I need to look at your shoes, too. What's the name of the cat, Jimmy Jaye?"

"Kitty Cat. What's wrong with my shoes? I just had a haircut. You look beautiful, darlin'." He hugged her tightly. "I'm not going to be president anymore, Lettie. Do you mind?"

"Not one little bit. I have so many plans for us. Are you glad to be home, Jimmy Jaye?"

"There's no place like home, darlin'. I didn't like that room where they had me signing papers all day long. Being president is not enjoyable. I'd rather be here with you. Where are we again, darlin'?"

"Home, Jimmy Jaye, home. Come with me. I want you to thank two fine ladies for taking care of me and making sure you came home. Then we're going to go upstairs, and we're going to do what we do best."

"That sounds like a splendid plan, Mama. Where are the girls?"

Tears sparkled in Lettie Jaye's eyes when she led her husband into the kitchen. "Jimmy Jaye, I'd like you to meet my friends Quinn and Sadie. It's a long story, and I'll tell you all about it another time. Just say hello and give them each a hug."

Quinn looked down at her grimy hands. The first lady smiled indulgently and mouthed the words, "It doesn't matter."

"Thank you for taking care of Mama for me."

"It was our pleasure, Mr. President," both agents said in unison.

"I'm not going to be president anymore."

"You'll always be the president," Quinn said softly. "Always."

"Did you hear that, Mama?"

"I heard Jimmy Jaye. It's true. Good night, girls."

"It's sad, and yet it's beautiful," Quinn said, dabbing at her eyes when the door closed behind the president and first lady. "I feel . . . important for some reason. How about you, Sadie?"

"Me, too. All is well that ends well. You smell, Quinn. Even Lettie's perfume can't cover it up. I'm going to have some coffee."

"See you in the morning, partner."

"Yeah. Sleep tight, Quinn."

Ten minutes later, Quinn slid down into the silky wetness that smelled of mysterious things to enhance the moment. She heaved a mighty sigh of pure pleasure. Nothing in the world could compare to a scented bubble bath. Absolutely nothing. She leaned back and relaxed, her thoughts drifting in a million directions. Her eyes closed, she heard the door open. "Don't bother me, Sadie. I am going to stay in this tub until I shrivel up. Every bone in my body aches. I would kill for a body massage. The only thing missing right now is a nice bottle of wine and a cigarette. Sadie!"

"Wrong name! I do have the wine and the cigarettes, though."

"*YOU!* What are you doing here? No! No, no, no! I said no. Don't you dare take off your clothes. What's in that box? Out! I want you out of here right now! This is the president's house for God's sake. They're right overhead. I hate your guts. Leave! I'll . . . I'll . . ."

Quinn looked on in horror when Puff stripped down to his boxers. "Look . . . this . . . this is not . . ."

"Shut up and turn on the hot water. We've taken a bath together before. Or did you forget how nice that was?"

"Listen, I'm engaged. I'll scream. I mean it. The president and the first lady will boot your naked ass right out of here. You'll never make director. What part of 'I hate your guts' didn't you understand?" Quinn blustered.

"The whole part. You don't hate me, Star. You want to, but you don't. I told you I was sorry. How long do I have to keep saying that?"

"Forever and into eternity. Don't you dare take off your shorts. I mean it, don't you dare!"

Quinn squeezed her eyes shut when Puff's boxers sailed across the tub to land on top of a chest of drawers.

She promised herself not to open her eyes until he was gone. She opened one eye for a better look. "Oh God!"

"Ohhh, this is nice. Move your leg a little. You up for some tomfoolery, Agent Star?"

Quinn shoved her foot directly into his groin.

"*Ourf*," he grunted. A second later she was under the water. When she came up for air she was in Puff's lap. "Do you want to know how many times I dreamed about this, Quinn?"

"No! This isn't going to work. I'm never going to forgive you for what you did to me. If you insist on staying in this tub, stay at your end and don't touch me. What's in the box?"

"My mother said you would forgive me if I told you the truth. I love you. I always loved you. I never stopped loving you. I plan to love you forever and ever. That's the truth. My mother is never wrong. Well?"

"Well what? What's in the box?"

"Will you marry me?"

"You want me to marry *you!* When hell freezes over. When it rains in the desert. You're crazier than I thought. What's in the box?"

"That's the way it works. You, me. As in together. If you want me to say pretty words, I don't know how to do that. I thought saying I loved you was enough. I never asked anyone to marry me before. I'll do my best to make you happy, Quinn. I'm sure we'll fight and do all the things married couples do. My mom and dad fight, but they never go to bed mad at each other. My family loves you."

"Let me get this straight. You bounce in here like we've been seeing each other for the last eight years.

You say a lot of things, you quote your mother, you even apologize, and for all that you really think I'm going to marry you! That was a proposal, wasn't it?"

"Hell, yes, it was a proposal. So, you're saying no. You're turning me down! I'm going to be the next director of the FBI. That's nothing to sneeze at. I'm a stand-up guy. Ask my mother."

"Yes."

"Yes you're saying no, or yes as in yes?"

"Yes as in yes. Now what's in the box?"

"Did you just say yes you'll marry me?" Puff said, slapping at his forehead with a soapy hand.

"Yes. What's in the damn box?"

"Listen, I have to call my mother. Do you want me to call Birdie?"

"I thought we were taking a bath."

"We are. Do you want to do that thing we used to do where . . ."

"Yeah, yeah, let's do that," Quinn said, diving under the water.

Bubbles surfaced in the heart-shaped Jacuzzi tub. More bubbles surfaced. Quinn's head broke through the surface. "What was that noise?"

Puff came up for air and reached a long arm toward the box and pulled it closer to the tub. "Your premature wedding present. One for you and one for me."

"Ohhhh, they're golden retriever pups. Do they have names?" Quinn squealed in delight.

"Not yet. The president's dog is the mother. He wanted to bring them along. He thought . . . I think he had them confused with . . . the cat. Anyway, the dogs really belong to one of the Secret Service guys. Photo ops with the president, and a dog always look good. Don't worry, I paid for them. Do you like them? I thought we could start out sort of as a family if we had some dogs. I know how much you love animals."

"Oh, I love them. Thanks, Puff. This one is mine. It's a girl. Yours is the boy. Is that okay with you? A family, huh?"

"Yeah. A family is important. So, when can we get married?"

"How about when the lilacs bloom? The first lady wants to plan my wedding in her courtyard. She said the president will give me away. I have to find a dress."

"Yeah. Yeah, my mother said that was important. The dress I mean."

"I think we've bathed long enough, don't you?" Quinn said slyly. "What do you say we take these two little love balls to bed with us?"

"I think these two little love balls should learn to sleep by themselves. If you dry me, I'll dry you."

"That's about the best offer I've had in a long time, Lapufsky."

"I don't think it gets any better than this, do you?"

"Nope. Stand still so I can get the tricky parts. Stop jiggling. Oh, you're ticklish. Uh-huh. It would be nice if you kissed me the way you did at the White House."

He stopped jiggling long enough to do what she asked.

"I hear the bells." Quinn sighed

"I hear the whistles." Puff groaned.

The pups tumbled over one another as they struggled to get back into the box.

Epilogue

Charleston, South Carolina
April 2008

"Oh, Birdie, I can't tell you how happy I am that you're here. Everything is perfect. I can't tell you when I've been this happy. You were always such a good friend to me, unlike some people I won't bother to mention, so having you here at this special time is the icing on my cake. I really appreciate your input on this little wedding we're arranging for Quinn. We could have done it up really grand, but Quinn said no, this was what she wanted. I've been holding my breath thinking she might change her mind. Cassie was so touched when she asked her to bake the wedding cake," Lettie said breathlessly.

"Quinn fell in love with this place in the short time she was here, Lettie. All she did was talk about it and you when she got back. Are you sure it was all right to bring Winnie with me?"

"Of course. Jimmy Jaye adores her. Right now he's sitting in his favorite chair in the sunroom with her. He mutters and mumbles a lot these days, but that's all right. Then five minutes later, he's working on a speech he's never going to give. I'm getting him a cat after the wedding. He's as fine as he can be, Birdie. I'm okay with it all. I hired a companion for him because he tends to wander off sometimes. Especially at night. The Secret Service Agents understand and follow him. I just felt better with Jacob becoming his constant companion. They play chess together, take walks, smoke their pipes and cigars together. Jimmy Jaye and Jacob have always been close, so it's working out nicely. We have breakfast and dinner together, and, when the weather is nice, we sit in the courtyard and talk and talk. Sometimes I go off by myself and cry. Then I think how grateful I am to be home. I wipe my eyes, blow my nose, and get on with it. We take it one day at a time."

Birdie patted Lettie's hand. "The only thing that matters is that you and Jimmy are happy. I have to tell you, Lettie, I'm madder than a wet hen that I haven't heard from Quinn's parents. Ezra helped me as much as he could. We contacted all the embassies overseas and the Red Cross. I sent out a ton of mail. Quinn hasn't said a word about her parents, but I know it's bothering her."

Lettie reached across the table to take both of Birdie's hands in her own. "You're her mother. You raised her. You took care of her and did a magnificent job. Look at who she is today. We wouldn't be sitting here today planning her wedding if she hadn't come through for us. That's what counts, Birdie. She loves you. She told me so. As far as she's concerned, you are her mother."

"I know all that, Lettie. It still doesn't change the

fact that they should be here. Their only daughter is getting married. How can they do this to her? I know Margaret is my sister, but I disowned her for what she did. Quinn called just a little while ago and asked if any last-minute responses had come. That was her way of asking. I had to tell her no. Do you have any idea how bad that made me feel?"

"Of course I do. We aren't going to dwell on it, Birdie. Let's go over the details one more time. We have a hundred confirmed guests. The ceremony is to take place at four o'clock tomorrow. Quinn arrives this evening. Ezra arrives early tomorrow morning. His parents are staying at a hotel in town. They wanted it that way. The chairs arrived a little while ago. The lilacs are being flown in tomorrow morning. I ordered tons of them. We're having a champagne fountain. Our dresses are due to be delivered this afternoon, as we speak, as a matter of fact. Cassie has it all under control."

"What about the boys?"

"Those dear sweet boys, Leander, Dennis, and Calvin are going to be here, all three of them, and a few of their friends. Some of their friends are providing the music. I invited their entire families. I even invited that author whose cottage we stayed in. She didn't respond, though. I bought every single one of her books to show my thanks."

"Lettie, do you think Quinn will . . . you know, not forget me but not have time for me now that she's getting married?" Birdie fretted.

"Birdie Langley, bite your tongue. That will never happen. Quinn is your daughter no matter what you say. Ezra adores you, too. If anything, you're probably going to see more of them than you can handle. I bet you're going to do a lot of dog sitting, too. How is Winnie with their dogs?"

"Her nose is out of joint. She tried showing them how to use the chair rail, but pups that they are, they had no patience for the slow ride and raced up ahead of her. She was a little perturbed over that. She does that thing with her ears going horizontal, and it spooks them."

"You never did tell me how it went with Judge Duval. Quinn sent me a little note saying she returned the judge's ring, but she didn't elaborate. Did she say anything to you?"

"She didn't say much. She said Alex had moved his things out of the Georgetown house before she got back. I believe they had lunch at the Jockey Club, and she gave back the ring. She said the meeting was chillier than the borscht. There are no regrets there." Birdie summed it up by saying, "Judge Duval is not an animal person."

"That explains everything then. Since everything is under control, would you like to take a walk around the block, Birdie? We can take Winnie. I love being able to walk out the front door and down the steps. I'm just a citizen now. People say hello or wave. I say hello and wave back. Do you see yourself continuing with your . . . your *calling?*"

"As long as people keep dying, I guess so. Let's not take Winnie. She has to sniff every blade of grass and squat two hundred times although nothing comes out."

"I do admire your grit, Birdie. You didn't say where Quinn and Ezra were going to live. Are they going to stay in her little house?"

"No. Quinn's going to rent it to some diplomat. They bought a house on P Street. They bought it because it has a garage. Can you imagine! Quinn said it's lovely, and when they return from their honeymoon it will be ready for them to move into. She said there's plenty of room for the dogs to run all around. They're going to have a room for me, too. I felt better when she said that."

"Look, Birdie, the air is so clean and clear. If we were standing on the upstairs verandah we could see Fort Sumter. All the flowers are blooming. Spring is my favorite time of year. The scent of tea olive always reminds me of bubble gum. Do you see yourself coming south in the winter?" Lettie asked as she tripped along.

"I've thought about it. Maybe I'll call a Realtor before I head back home. This past winter was more than I bargained for. Would you like me to be here in the winter, Lettie?"

"I would absolutely love having you here, Birdie. Good friends are hard to come by these days."

Lettie walked along, her arms swinging and pumping the air as she smiled at the people she passed. "My wedding present to Quinn is my house. Jimmy Jaye and I are moving back to Summerville, to the old house, next week. It's being refurbished as we speak. It's a small town, and I think that's what Jimmy Jaye and I need right now. Cassie and Jacob are going to go with us. We're getting older, and we don't need that big house. We're giving Kincaid's house to Sadie. Believe it or not, it was all Jimmy Jaye's idea."

"But, Lettie, what about all your friends? How can you leave something you love so much? You fought like a tiger to get back here."

"What friends?" Lettie scoffed. "I'm doing it for Jimmy Jaye. You *can* go home again, Birdie. I wish you could have seen Jimmy Jaye's face the day we drove to Summerville and went to that old house. We hadn't been there in years and years. I almost sold it a couple of times, but something stopped me. Now I'm glad I didn't sell it. There was such a look of rapture on Jimmy Jaye's face, I knew it was the right decision. He walked all around that old house, remembering what piece of furniture was where. He showed me his room and told me about everything that used to be in it. I have a really good memory, and it's going to look just like that when we move in. I just want him to be happy. I'll be happy if he's happy. All the rest doesn't mean a thing to me. I can paint anywhere as long as the light is good. That old house has a lovely front porch that gets the early-morning sun. That's when I like to paint. I can set my easel up. Jimmy Jaye can rock in his rocker and watch me. It's a good thing, Birdie."

"You are a wonder, Lettie Jaye. You really are."

"Do you remember how to skip, Birdie? Remember, step on a crack, break your mother's back?"

"Just how old do you think I am, Lettie? Of course I remember. My hip is healed, so yes, I can skip. Aren't you afraid people will talk about us?"

"That's the good part, Birdie, no one cares. C'mon, let's skip. Hold my hand. Right foot first, then the left. Skip to my Lou, my darling!" she sang off-key, Birdie joining in.

Breathless, they arrived at the house on the Battery to see a taxi sitting in front. Two Secret Service Agents and Cassie were squabbling on the sidewalk. Jimmy Jaye was walking down the steps, his walking stick in his hand, Winnie at his side.

"For heaven's sake, what's going on?" Lettie said. "Cassie, what's going on?"

The taxi door opened. Winnie waddled over to where Birdie was standing, her ears going vertical as she threw back her head and let loose with a blood-curdling howl.

"Oh, myyyy Godddd," Birdie said.

Lettie Jaye's jaw dropped as a tall stately woman in a flowing white gown, her hair trailing down to her ankles stepped onto the sidewalk. A crown of wilted flowers graced the woman's head. She stepped aside to allow a man, who was her equal in height, to step out of the cab. He, too, was dressed in a flowing white gown with a knotted-cord belt around his waist. His hair was tied in knots and hung to below his buttocks.

"They're jabbering something. I don't think they have any money. The driver won't give them their bag until they pay him. Who are they, Lettie?" Cassie demanded.

"This is just a guess on my part, Cassie, but I think they're Quinn's parents. Pay the driver for me, will you?"

Birdie Langley's Birkenstocks slapped on the concrete as she made her way to the strange-looking couple. "It is you, isn't it, Margaret? You're six months early for Halloween. Get your asses in the house before someone sees you."

Cassie reached into the cab for a sack with a twine string. "Is this all there is?" she asked the cab driver.

"Yeah, and it smelled up the cab. You better air it out," the driver said, pulling away from the curb. Cassie held it gingerly as she followed the parade up the steps and into the house.

"When in Rome, Margaret! Couldn't you at least dress like everyone else? What's with that hair? What's his name, I can never remember?" Birdie asked, pointing to the man staring straight ahead.

"Omar. His name is Omar. This is all we have in the way of dress, Bernice. We have no money. We traveled on the generosity of others. You asked us to come here. Do you want us to leave?"

She wanted that more than anything in the world. "No, of course not, but I don't want you looking like this when Quinn gets here. You could have let me know you were coming. How hard would that have been? Does he talk?" Birdie said, pointing to Omar.

"He talks when he has something to say. Most of the time he prays. What would you like us to do?"

Birdie was at a loss for the first time in her life. She appealed to Lettie, who was sizing up the situation with narrowed eyes.

"Is it a funeral?" Jimmy Jaye asked.

"Not yet," Birdie snapped.

"Cassie, show our guests to their rooms on the second floor. Point out the bathroom and show them how everything works. Give them some of that very fragrant soap. I'll call Olga's dress shop and tell her to send one of everything, then I'll call Berlin's and have them send over a suit. Whatever . . ."

Birdie, Lettie, and Cassie stood at the bottom of the steps and watched the strange-looking duo walk to the top. Omar turned around and made the sign of the cross. "Bless you for all this decadence," he said.

Birdie sputtered on the saliva in her mouth.

Lettie waved her hand limply.

Cassie followed the duo upstairs and led them down the hall and out of sight.

"What time is the funeral, Mama?" Jimmy Jaye asked.

"Later. We aren't going to attend, Jimmy Jaye," Lettie said patiently as she stroked her husband's cheek. "We're going to have some coffee now. Would you like to join us?"

"Not now. I have to finish my speech. Save some for me, Mama."

"Yes. I will do that. Save you some, I mean."

"Coffee. Phone calls. We have time, Birdie, to have some coffee. Loaded. Really loaded. I'm almost sure we can get them fixed up before Quinn gets here. We can, can't we, Birdie? You're an expert at fixing up *dead* people. How hard can it be to fix live ones?" Lettie dithered.

"The hair is going to be the problem. Never mind the damn coffee, Lettie, just get the bottle out and pour."

"My thoughts exactly." Lettie marched into the kitchen, Birdie on her heels. Winnie stayed in the foyer, sniffing the carpets.

An hour later, Cassie, Birdie, and Lettie carried the last of their purchases to the second floor.

Birdie gaped at Quinn's parents, who were sitting in the middle of the floor staring into space. Neither had bathed. Birdie stomped her way over to where her sister sat, grabbed her long hair, and dragged her backward. "Cassie, fill that tub to the top. Dump everything you have in it. You're next, Omar, so get ready. Are you speaking another language or just jabbering?"

"It's Punjabi," Margaret said. "Omar is praying, not jabbering. This decadence you surround yourself with is disturbing us. You're hurting me, Bernice."

"You're going to do things my way while you're here, Margaret. When you leave you can go on a broomstick for all I care. You are going to look and act like a mother and a father if it kills you. That goes for that . . . person . . . out there. Do you understand me?"

"Why do you insist on trying to make me into something I'm not, Bernice? Good heavens, this is such a waste of water. Do you save it?"

"Shut up, Margaret, and take off your clothes. Stay in that tub till I tell you to get out. Cassie, you're in charge.

"Okay, Omar, you're next. Lettie, fill the tub. Same drill."

"You must have many sins on your soul to live like this. It all belongs to the devil you know."

"Get off it, you quack. You were born and raised in the Bronx. How you ever snookered my sister to go off with you is something I will never understand. Now move it and strip down."

"They . . . they don't wear underwear," Lettie hissed.

"So I see," Birdie snapped.

"I'll get some of Jimmy Jaye's. This is so . . . so . . . unusual."

"Scrub, Omar."

Birdie looked down at the grimy gown with the cord belt. Using her foot, she slid the garment across the bathroom and out into the hall. She closed the door behind her.

Lettie held out a pair of boxer shorts with the presidential seal on one of the legs. In spite of herself, Birdie laughed. "It's going to be all right, Lettie. It really is. Come, sit with me on top of the steps, and I'm going to tell you a little about those two."

Lettie sat down on the top step, Birdie beside her. "You're probably thinking those two are some kind of holy people. They aren't. They're con artists, quacks. We're seeing what they want us to see. They have a temple in some third-world country. They live like a queen and king. They have loyal subjects, for want of a better word, who donate money to their cause. Their cause is themselves. They have impressive bank accounts. They have royal robes. They go on what they call holy treks to preach and scam money. Omar used to be a plumber. My sister was always trying to figure out ways to get money without working. This is just a show on their part. For us. I don't want you to think I'm unfeeling or that I'm this ugly person. They're the ones who are ugly. That damn Omar is sitting in your tub lusting after every possession you have in this house. His middle name is decadence. I'd like nothing more than to kick both their asses to the curb, but I can't do that because of Quinn."

"Good grief. How did you find this all out, Birdie?"

"There are ways to find out anything as long as you know the right people." She lowered her voice to a hushed whisper. "I even have a picture of the two of them sitting on a . . . on a *throne* decked out in elaborate gold robes, and Margaret was wearing a crown. A crown full of jewels, Lettie. They live in a fancy-looking palace, not quite as impressive as Sadam's were, and have some fairly substantial bank accounts here in the States and in the Middle East. They claim to survive by begging. They claim to eat nuts and seeds to stay alive. They look pretty healthy to me. I keep the picture in my safe-deposit box. I've known for years but never told Quinn. I thought it was better if she just thought her parents were on the weird side. Was I wrong, Lettie?"

"No. No, Birdie, I wouldn't have told Quinn either if I were in your place. I'll keep your secret. Now, what are we going to do with their hair?"

"I'd like to snatch Margaret bald. The hair is going to go. I think old Omar will look good in a buzz cut. Let's get to it," Birdie said belligerently.

Margaret spit and snarled like a wildcat while Lettie and Birdie held her firmly in the chair so the beautician, who was clearly out of her depth, could slice off her locks. "This will be all over town by morning," Lettie hissed in Birdie's ear. "I'm so glad I'm moving to Summerville next week."

The moment the beautician scurried out of the room, Birdie grabbed her sister's arm and swung her around on the stool so that they were facing one another. "One more sound, one more *anything*, Margaret, and the world will know about you two scam artists. I have a picture of you and that jerk you're married to sitting on your thrones all *duded* up in your fancy robes and crown. I know about your bank accounts. In short, I know everything there is to know about you. You will make nice, do you understand. You will be sweet and gentle when your daughter gets here. You will tell her how happy you are for her. You will tell her how lovely she is and how you think of her every day. The minute the ceremony is over, I want you to leave. I'm ashamed to say you're my sister. If that nutcase in the other bathroom doesn't follow the rules, I'll wreck his plumbing for good. Now, go in there and powwow with him. We are going to go downstairs to the sunroom, where we're going to have a nice glass of wine. You're welcome to join us as we wait for your daughter. Don't screw up, Margaret, because you aren't going to get another chance."

"I want my hair."

Birdie's Birkenstock slid the pile of hair closer to her sister. "Take your Lady Clairol hair. I certainly don't want it. Make sure you take *his*, too."

Tears rolled down Birdie's cheeks as she made her way downstairs. Lettie placed a comforting arm around her shoulders. At the foot of the steps, Winnie whined at the strange sounds her mistress was making.

"Cassie!"

"What is it, Lettie?" the housekeeper asked, poking her head out of the kitchen.

"Will you please bring some glasses, a bottle, and a bucket of ice to the sunroom?"

"Yes, ma'am!" Cassie said smartly.

"Here they are now," Lettie Jaye said, rushing to the door to greet Quinn and Sadie. "It's so nice to see you girls again. Believe it or not, I've missed you. Come in, come in."

Quinn didn't see them at first, her gaze going to Birdie, in her eye-catching dress full of red-eyed poppies, then to Winnie. Sensing other people in the room, she turned slowly, seeing the president relaxing in his chair and two other people. She risked a glance at Birdie, who inclined her head slightly.

Quinn took a step backward and almost toppled Sadie, who was behind her. She stared at her parents, wishing she could feel something. How nice they looked. How normal.

"Mother. Father, how are you? It was nice of you to come."

"Your father and I couldn't stay away. We wanted to see you get married," Margaret said quietly. "We have to leave immediately after the wedding. That won't upset you, will it?"

"No. I didn't think you would come. Thank you. Where are my manners? Mother, Father, this is Sadie Wilson, my friend. Sadie, these are my parents. Would you all excuse us for a few minutes? I want to hang up my wedding gown and unpack."

"Run along, girls. We're just having a buffet this evening. You said you didn't want a rehearsal dinner, so it's buffet. All the things you girls like," Lettie chirped, hoping to cover the awkward meeting.

Upstairs in her room with the door closed, Quinn collapsed against Sadie. "Oh my God, they're here! They actually look like other people. You know, normal people. What did you think?"

Sadie shrugged.

"There's a lot of stuff I never told you about them. A child should never be ashamed of her parents. Birdie sent me to her safe-deposit box once a few years ago to get something for her, and there was this . . . picture of them. There was a whole stack of reports on the two of them. I read them. God, I bawled my eyes out for weeks over that, but I never let Birdie know I knew. Later on, when I had time to really think about it all, I realized it was Birdie's way of letting me know who and what they were without saying the words out loud. We never, ever, talked about it. I wish they hadn't come. You have no idea how much I wish that."

"They're here, so make the best of it. They did say they were leaving right after the ceremony. C'mon, girlfriend, you can handle this. I'm with you. Let's get that Vera Wang creation hung up and go downstairs so you can start to socialize. There's no written rule that you have to love them, Quinn. Just think of them as guests at your wedding. It's all right not to feel anything. It really is. Don't let it spoil your wedding. You can compartmentalize. That is such a beautiful gown! You are going to look stunning!"

"You're a good friend, Sadie. I know you're chomping at the bit to go to the hotel to see John. I'm fine. Compared to some of the stuff we've been through, this is a walk in the park. Be sure you're here for Lettie's champagne breakfast."

"Trust me. I'll be the first one here. If you need me, call."

"I will. I wish Puff was here."

"I bet he wishes he was, too. Just a few hours, then you get to spend the rest of your life with him. I'm jealous," Sadie said as she skipped out of the room. "See ya."

"Okay."

Quinn sat down on the bed. She didn't know if she should laugh or cry. Winnie solved the problem by waddling into the room and lying down by her feet. She slid off the bed and curled up next to the basset, rubbing her belly with one hand and stroking her silky ears with the other. Winnie literally purred her pleasure. "You know what, Winnie, I don't want to go back down there. Let's you and me curl up here and take a little nap."

"All right, all right, listen you two," Lettie trilled. "All the guests are seated. Ezra is waiting outside the gate and will enter when he's given his signal. The minister has everything under control. Quinn, Birdie and your parents are seated in the front row on the left. Ezra's parents across from them. Miss Indy is with her mother, just waiting to throw her flower petals. The best that we can hope for is that she really does it. Jimmy Jaye is waiting to give you away. I think he's more excited than I am. You look so beautiful, Quinn. Be happy, that's all I ask. I have to go now. Sadie, take over. You look just as beautiful. Your beau is seated in the second row. Make sure you wink at him. For good luck. It's a Southern thing, honey. Lord, Lord, Lord, where is my head. Jimmy wanted me to give you our wedding present before the wedding. You know I always do what he says. He was, after all, the president. There's a gift for you, too, Sadie. Now, I really am going."

"What is it?" Sadie asked as she ripped at her own envelope.

"It's a deed. A really old one. Oh my God, it's to this house! It's in my and Puff's names. I don't know what to say! This can't be real. It's real, isn't it?"

"I got one, too. The house next door. We're going to be neighbors, Quinn. I can't believe this! You aren't going to make me give it back like the money, are you?"

"No. No, this is a gift from two incredibly wonderful, generous people who love us. We would insult them if we did that. I can be gracious in my acceptance. We can open the gate so we can run back and forth. My cup runneth over."

"Mine, too. Wait till I tell John."

"I can't wait to tell Puff. He's going to go over the moon. He fell in love with this house and this city. Oh, oh, that's our signal to go downstairs. I'm ready to become Mrs. Ezra Lapufsky. Boy, am I ready."

The moment everyone stood in place, the minister said, "Will the mother of the bride take her place," Quinn whirled around. She saw it all in one brilliant flash, her mother moved, her right foot stepped out, and Birdie closed her eyes. She moved then, faster than she'd ever moved in her life, and reached for Birdie's hand to draw her forward.

"Who gives the bride away?"

Quinn whirled around again and stretched out her hand to President Jaye. "This man," she said softly, her gaze going to her biological father, who stared at her blankly.

"Now we're ready! You ready, Lapufsky?"

"I'm ready."

"Then let's do it!"